THE GRAND *Ruin*

Editing: Ellie McLove – My Brothers Editor

Proofing: Rosa Sharon – My brothers Editor

Proofing: Britt - Paperback Proof Reader

Cover: Murphy Rae

Photographer: Michelle Lancaster

THE GRAND RUIN

LANCE & SCARLET - PART ONE

JC HAWKE

IVY ROSE PUBLISHING LTD

AUTHORS NOTE

For any content warnings you may need, please head over to my website.

For anyone who's ever held a book in their hands and felt a little stronger

Playlist

Home - Whitney Hanson.

Stay - Rihanna & Mikky Ekko.

Kiss Me - Dermot Kennedy.

Those Eyes - New West.

Wildest Dreams (Taylor's Version) - Taylor Swift

Purple - Wunderhorse.

To Have You Today - Dean Lewis.

All For You - Dean Lewis.

Blossom - Dermot Kennedy.

Unsteady - X Ambassadors.

Maybe - Matthew Nolan.

Leave A Light On - Tom Walker.

All I Ask - Adele.

Happiest Year - Jaymes Young.

Save Tonight - Tom Speight & Lydia Clowes

Who Knew - P!nk

PROLOGUE

Scarlet

I saved a life once. A single gunshot wound to the abdomen, and I managed to keep her alive long enough for the paramedics to arrive and take her to the hospital. I don't remember it fully, only the bitter chaos that followed.

And it still sometimes follows me.

On days like today, when the deceiving January sun settles beyond the meadow and threatens to send the darkest of nights, it reminds me. Because on the very day I saved my first *patient*, I lost another. That life belonged to Joey Wilson, and not a day goes by where I don't think about the dull thump of his heart before everything stopped, the hopefulness that one beat brought me only to slip away in the next second.

I carry the dead flowers I've collected through the house, pausing when I reach the sitting room. I peer over at the wingback armchair positioned in the same spot it's gathered dust in for over thirty years, a small smile gently banishing the fine lines gathered between my brows.

"You've been out there for hours, Scarlet. Aren't you cold?"

My smile grows, and I pull my cardigan tighter around my shoulders. I continue through the silent house and into the kitchen.

The flowers I pick from the gardens have no hope of survival, and I think I like that. If we don't have expectations of a long life, we might just learn to live in the light, to be a little wilder. Or at least that's what I hope.

I place the flowers onto the worktop in the pantry and remove the excess leaves from the stems. I organise them into smaller arrangements, not considering the colours or aesthetics I'm creating. They always seem to turn out better this way.

Cutting three pieces of string, I take my time to tie the flowers carefully and hang them upside down on the hooks, replacing the ones from last month.

My eyes scan the shelves for an empty mason jar to fill.

"Dammit," I tut, looking up at the top shelf where the stacked trays sit haphazardly. "Mason Lowell, I'll kick your ass if you've been in here."

I go in search of the stepladder despite the fact that I only have an hour before everyone will be home for the day, and I haven't started dinner.

My brother and I share our childhood home. It's big enough to house a small army, so we don't have any issues sharing it… unless he moves my things. Thankfully, he works in the city along with his wife, who owns her own dance studio, so I get most of my days off from the hospital to myself, which is how I like it.

I set up the ladder beside the cabinets and climb four steps, reaching for the tray. My hand curls around the cool glass of a single jar. "Gotcha!"

But then the faint but familiar sound of a motorbike engine drifts through the house, and my smile drops.

I pause for a second, slightly turning my head, listening to be sure.

One split second.

One single heartbeat.

Everything slows.

And then the tray topples from the ledge. The jars clatter and smash against the black flagstone as the flowers fall from the counter, my uncoordinated dismount from the stepladder causing my feet to crush them, the glass crunching under my thick-rimmed boots. Still, they carry me—even as they shake, my thighs trembling as the roaring engine tears down the lane.

Closer and closer.

It can't be.

I'm on the terrace with no recollection of the seconds that passed moments before.

My heart pounds, and it's almost painful.

No—it is painful.

I place my hand on my chest, the tips of my fingers dragging across my skin as I apply pressure.

"When the sun sets, and you start to forget me, remember every moment you fell in love with me in this meadow. Please, baby."

My mouth parts, the memory as vivid as the day he left London.

"I could never… I could never forget you, Lance."

I lift my arm to shield my eyes from the shrinking sun,

finding goose bumps pebbling on my skin. His bike appears through the trees, and I watch with my heart in my mouth as he bypasses the circular drive and rolls to a stop on the gravel.

He watches me through his visor, and I watch him right back.

Seven years.

I wonder what my face portrays as I stand here because it feels like I'm giving him everything I shouldn't, and it's devastating. I want to be stronger than this, but there isn't anything in the world that could've prepared me for this moment.

I'm acting on autopilot, and I'm allowed to feel every second of whatever this is.

He unclips his helmet and my breath hitches.

And then there he is. Lance Sullivan in the flesh. Seven years older and everything that I remember him to be.

His throat works. "Scarlet."

My eyes snap closed, my face screwing up in anguish. The way his voice washes over me. I never thought about the way that would make me feel. I thought about the way our eyes might meet—penetrating the very parts of my soul he once taught me to love. I thought about everything—so I thought. But never the way my name would sound the first time it left his mouth. The way it would lose all identity and become something else entirely.

An apology.

A plea.

A huge slap to the face.

"Why are you here?" I ask, barely recognising my voice as I punctuate every word.

He takes a step forward, and although I try not to look at him fully, I still see the very parts I've spent years trying to forget. His hair is as dark as ever, almost black. His beard looks pristine, trimmed short and smooth against his angular jaw, and for some reason, it bothers me. It bothers me that he looks so well. So put together. So okay.

"I felt maybe we needed some closure."

My mouth opens, but I quickly close it, my eyes wild and filling with unshed tears. "Closure." My voice betrays me this time. "You think we need…" I can't take my eyes off him.

The balls this man has.

"I know I never called—"

"You should leave."

"Scar—"

"No!" I cover my mouth and step back before walking forward in a rush, taking the steps until I'm in front of him. "Nothing you say to me—" I pause, bile rising in my throat. "There is nothing you could say to me that will ever give me closure."

His eyes bounce around my face, absorbing me as if it's the first and last time he'll get the chance. "I'm sorry, Scarlet."

"Yeah." I nod, shaking my head as a tear slips free. "But I'm not the one you should be saying it to. Your apologies don't mean a thing to me anymore."

His green eyes get shadowed by his thick brow, his nostrils flaring in anger. "I didn't come here to hurt you, but it felt wrong not to. I don't expect anything from you—I don't want anything from you. I'm going to stay in the city, see mum—"

My brows pinch as my chest burns. "You'll come back tomorrow," I say, cutting him off. "No… Friday. You'll come back on Friday."

I'll need to schedule an appointment with Fran before seeing him again.

"I just told you I'm going to stay with my mum. I won't be around here."

I look at him. Really look at him. I could let him go, not tell anyone he was ever here, but that would be selfish of me.

"*You're* selfish. Did you know that?" I snap. "Probably the most selfish person I've ever known."

He slips his hands into his jeans pockets as his jaw flexes.

"You'll come back on Friday." I turn and start back up the steps.

"Scar," he calls out, taking another slash at my heart.

I don't stop.

If I stop, I'll break all over again.

We all will.

ONE

Scarlet

It's my birthday.

Today, I turn twenty-eight years old. I have the whole day planned, and as my bare feet hit the wooden floorboards in the west wing corridor of my family home, my eyes blaze through the window and out across the meadow.

I smile extra wide.

I'd like to think the day will go perfectly, but there's no guarantee it will. Like the rain that taints the air as it patters the still-warm pavements in the heat of a British summer, this day will be unpredictable—I can feel it in my gut.

Perhaps my optimism—or lack of it—could be down to the book I devoured yesterday. The final moments of a happily ever after forcing me to sacrifice more sleep than I'd normally allow. But there's something about a fiery woman taming the older Mafia don I can't seem to pass up. Throw in an arranged marriage and a little praise, and I'll take the book with a double shot of my favourite coffee.

Keep the change.

I bound down the staircase with a spring in my step, fastening one of the clasps on my faded denim-wash dungarees with my smile firmly intact. The prospect of a new day is nearly as exciting as the fact that I'll be seeing my brother today. It's been months since I last saw the business tycoon that is Mason Lowell, and I'd be lying if I said I wasn't shocked when he called to invite me out for lunch. The man is impossible to get hold of. So, lunch, a whole hour dedicated to me… I snapped it up. Truthfully, I'd take five minutes of my brother's time if he would give it to me.

"Is that the sound of my beautiful birthday girl arising?"

I smile as I land on the bottom step, my father's voice carrying from the sitting room. I follow it and round the doorway.

My head tilts when I see him shifting to the edge of his armchair to get up. "Good morning, Dad."

His neck twists, his face transforming when he spots me. He slowly stands, working harder than fair to keep his face placid.

I meet him halfway, catching my feet with a quick gaze to right the concern that pulls between my brows. He doesn't want my pity.

"Happy birthday, Scarlet."

"Thank you." My lips twitch, and I look up at him. "How are you feeling this morning?" I ask.

"Grand. I made you breakfast."

"You did?" I say, surprised, as I follow him out of the room.

Anthony Lowell has always been my hero. From the day he carried me away from my mother's grave as a baby to the nights we've walked away hand in hand. He's the best man I've ever known—a true gent, attentive father, hard worker, and retired businessman.

Some would add alcoholic to that list—my brother sure would—but I prefer to call it what it is or what I've witnessed firsthand for the last fifteen-plus years.

A broken man, doing his damn best to make it into tomorrow.

Nobody gets to judge my hero. Not until they learn to fill the shoes he's worn for this family.

"You dyed your hair?" he questions, eyeing the lavender strands over his shoulder as we near the kitchen.

"I did. You were sleeping, but I think I did an okay job."

He smiles, easing his way around to the oven. "Looks like you got it all this time."

"Hmm, that smells divine. What did you make me?"

"Sausages and bacon with tomato and eggs."

My favourite.

"Your favourite."

"Thank you," I mutter, pushing onto my toes to kiss his cheek. "Go and sit down. I'll dish it up."

"It's your birthday. I can dish—"

"Dad," I warn.

He looks down at me with a stern glare that quickly softens.

"Go and sit down. Please. I want to do it."

He sits at the kitchen counter, crossing his arms over his still-firm chest. A protest he'll never win. He knows he should be taking it easy, and the fact he cooked is more than I like to see him do.

I lay our plates and cutlery on the counter, pour fresh

lemon water from the fridge, and then take the tray of food from the oven. My eyes roll as I inhale the heavenly smell of pork and apple sausages. I place the food in the middle of the kitchen island and then open the middle drawer. "I'll be two minutes, don't wait for me."

My father tuts as I slip from the room, but my smirk only widens.

I walk to the entrance of the house and slide on my boots at the front door. I rush outside, my stomach churning as I make my way across the terrace and down to my mother's garden.

The grass is long and overdue a trim, and I consider doing it later this afternoon with the weather being so good.

"Hey, Mum." I kneel on the ground beside her grave and take out the scissors I slipped into my pocket before. Lifting the heads of the barely thriving periwinkle that sheaths her, I snip their stems close to the ground and lay them beside me. "It's getting warmer out. These should do better soon."

I look up as the sun passes through a cloud and then emerges again, a little stronger.

"Thank you," I whisper softly, standing and backing away and out of the garden.

When I enter the kitchen, I find Dad devouring the mouth-watering breakfast he's cooked for me.

"I waited… for about two minutes."

"I told you not to." I smile, fetching a small mason jar from the pantry and running it under the cold tap, filling it a quarter of the way. I drop the flowers into the water and place them on the island in front of us. I spot the present on the table and pick up my fork, looking across at my dad. "Taste good?"

"Delicious." He grins.

Every year, my dad will buy me a first-edition copy of one of my mother's favourite novels. Over ten years of filling our library with what are now my favourite books. (Dad doesn't know about the *other* love stories I read, and I plan to keep it that way—I can do both.)

"Do you have plans for the day?"

My eyes drop to my plate, and I swallow as I reach for my drink. "I'm going out for lunch with Mase."

"You are?" he says, surprised, his brows pulling together.

"He invited me into the city this afternoon."

His smile grows, but I know it's for me, not his soul. "Good. Good. That's wonderful, Scarlet." He points his fork at the gift, a way to change the direction of the conversation. "Open your present."

"Would you like to come?" I reach for the book-shaped gift as he bites off a piece of toast before looking back at me, his face sad despite all the effort he put into hiding it.

"Did Mason ask for me to come along?"

I roll my lips and wince internally as the brown paper tears. My father and brother have a very fragile relationship.

"Right." His head bobs as he continues to eat.

"You don't need an invitation to come to lunch, Dad. I'll call Mase—"

"Scarlet," he orders, his no-nonsense tone I rarely hear and miss so much, telling me to stop. "Do something for me today."

I lift my chin in question, but I already know.

"Don't worry about Mason or me or anyone else. Make today whatever you want it to be, and don't worry about what anyone else has to say about it."

I roll my eyes and nudge his shoulder. "That's easier said than done with two stubborn men at the centre of my world."

He hums to himself, kissing the top of my head as I look down at the three books on my lap. First editions of Thomas Hardy's *The Return of the Native.*

"Hey," he mutters, and I look up at him, tension clenching my throat as I survey his tired eyes. "It could be worse—"

"Could be better," I recite back, our age-old saying spreading warmth through my chest. "Thank you, Dad. I love them."

"Good. Now go out today and enjoy it. You deserve to let your hair down."

The Montwell. A magnificent skyscraper located slap bang in the middle of London's financial district. My brother's kingdom and home to Ellis and Frey Real Estate. A company founded by Anthony Lowell and Glen Montgomery and now run by their sons, Mason and Elliot.

By the time I finished college, Mason had already left university and was in the process of taking over my father's role in the company. Taking it on myself was never a dream I possessed, and with Mason being four years older than me, it fell in his hands first.

You could say I love to hate it.

It holds childhood memories if nothing else.

Standing here now in the grand entrance, I find it awe-inspiring, if not a little concerning, to watch men and women carry themselves through the foyer with such importance. You can see their minds ticking, but what are they thinking about? The meeting that just went wrong, the bitter words yelled at a loved one before leaving for work that morning, or the shitty sandwich they had to bin because it didn't state it came with mayo. They seem happily unhappy. Contented. Bored, with not one smile in sight.

"Excuse me." A suited man blusters toward the glass revolving doors, knocking me in the shoulder. "Sorry. So sorry," he says, not stopping to check on me but so very British enough to apologise.

I sometimes wonder what my life might have been like if I was the firstborn Lowell. Would this right here be my world?

"Can I help you?" I turn in time to catch the receptionist's eyes scanning the length of me, from the top of my twisted lavender bun to the tips of my pale-pink Converse. Something tells me my presence displeases her somewhat. "Are you lost or something?"

Just be polite, Scarlet. I smile with a sigh and walk to the desk. "No. I have lunch with Mr Lowell today—"

She suppresses her snicker, but I catch it, and so does the woman at her back. "Yeah, we all do, sweetie." She dips her head to the side and looks at me like I'm stupid. "Mr Lowell left around twenty minutes ago. Are you sure you're not supposed to meet him there?"

"No, I was supposed to meet him *here*. But it's fine—I'll wait upstairs."

"Not without my authorisation, unfortunately." She pops

a perfectly sculpted eyebrow and averts her eyes, moving a stapler around her desk with a piece of paper in her hand, not doing anything while trying to look busy. I frown at her, curious why Mason and Elliot struggle to staff their building with friendlier people. "You can wait over there." She nods toward the chairs at the left of the entrance. "Or outside in fantasyland." She looks up at me through her lashes, her lip twitching. "I like your dungarees. Did you borrow them from the sixties?"

Okay, this bitch is an asshole. "Yes, actually, I did. I borrowed them from my mother, Ellis Lowell. Although, her best friend, Freya Montgomery—" I twist my head and smile thoughtfully as I gesture toward her. "You've heard of them both, right? Well, these belonged to Frey, looked better on Mum, and now me." I step past the desk and drop my eyes down her frame. She's stunning. "I love your dress… but it would suit you better in red."

Satan's bitch.

I take off toward the bank of elevators, knowing she'll be begrudgingly calling up to let them know I'm here.

The Montwell isn't somewhere I visit often, and I wouldn't usually wave my name around like a weapon—it feels kinda gross. I tend to stay out at the estate with Dad as much as I can, and when I do venture into the city, it's never for long.

I've never felt like I fit in here. It's partly a "me" problem, but it's also people like the receptionist who feel the need to not only judge a person based on the way they look but voice it, to go out of their way to make someone feel different and small just to make themselves feel better. It's people like my lecturer at university who took one look at me and my name and told me I didn't fit the image of a doctor and that I should go live off my trust fund instead.

I've learnt that being unapologetically myself only offends the people who need self-acceptance the most in life. I can do the dresses, curl and pin my hair, and then throw my favourite Louis over my shoulder while I walk down Oxford Street. In fact, it's one of my favourite forms of self-care when Dad is feeling well enough for me to venture out. But am I going to dress or conform to please anyone other than me?

Hell no.

I'd rather stick pins in my eyes.

The security guards give me a nod as I walk by, and I smile coyly when one of them reaches out to call the lift, throwing me a wink. He's beyond cute. Blond hair, pretty eyes, and shoulders that spread wide enough to make me blush a little.

"Thank you," I say, tucking a strand of hair behind my ear as I step inside.

"You're welcome, darlin'."

My eyes close as the doors ease shut behind me, and I turn. "Are you kidding me? What even is that accent, and why is it doing all the things?" I fan my face, rolling my shoulders.

"Irish. Northern, I believe."

My eyes snap open as my stomach drops, and immediately, I realise I'm not alone in the elevator. I turn my upper body to find a man standing in the corner. He has a sheet of paper in his hand, and his head is drawn down, not looking at me. *Thank God.*

"It's sensational," I say, then cringe, turning back to the

doors before I can embarrass myself further. *Maybe just stop conversating today, Scarlet.*

"Sensational?" he remarks, and I know his eyes are now on me.

"Uh-huh," I mutter.

"Are you—"

"Ignore what just happened, okay?" I look back at him and swallow my words.

Holy hot balls.

He's looking up at me now, his forehead wrinkling and making me a little weaker at the knees. "Ignore *me*," I tell him in a rush.

I don't want to be *that* girl.

I'm not *that* girl.

But my *that girl* flag is on its way out, and I'm about to wave it loud and proud.

Green eyes penetrate me. Calm, collected, and so unbothered, they capture me. His face is strong, with chiselled cheekbones sitting prominent enough to make his jowls hollow and dark inky strands of hair that lie in a mess on his handsome "I shouldn't be allowed to be this hot" head.

Damn, he's good-looking.

"Ignore you?" he rasps. "I was only asking if you're going to pick a floor." He nods toward the control panel as he interrupts my thoughts, and I follow his gaze.

"Oh, right. Yeah." I reach out and hit number seventy-eight, Ellis and—

"Ellis and Frey?" he questions, and I turn again. His eyes are trained on my hair but quickly snap to my face, curious—*doubtful*. "You have an appointment, sunshine?"

I nod, my eyes tightening on him. "I do."

"You do?" he says, surprised.

That raised brow again. Why is it sexy?

And yet so arrogant.

"I know. I can hardly believe it myself." I sigh and face the doors.

I don't look *that* out of place here, and I feel pissed that I'm doubting my choice of outfit because of two people who don't even know me.

I hear him moving behind me, the piece of paper in his hands getting folded up. "What's your name?"

"*Sunshine*," I shoot back.

I smirk and look at my feet.

He lets a breath out through his nose, a light snigger that makes me pull my bottom lip between my teeth.

"All right. And you have an appointment to see who exactly?"

I frown and peer over my shoulder to look at him again, finding his full focus on me. "What's your name?"

He regards me for a solid five seconds, and I wonder if he figures it out. I don't look like Mason, not really. But my mother? It's uncanny.

"Lance. Lance Sullivan," he finally says.

"Strong name. And why is it so shocking to you that I have an appointment at Ellis and Frey today, Mr Sullivan? Do you work for the company?"

He frowns and rubs his hand across his full lips. I don't miss the tattoos peeking out of his shirtsleeve, but I can't make out what they are or might represent. "I do."

"Interesting."

He tips his chin. "Why's that interesting?"

"It just is. How long have you worked here exactly?"

"Long enough."

"Huh… and it's shocking to you that I have an appointment because?"

"You don't miss a trick, do you, sunshine?"

"It's Scarlet."

"It's sunshine."

"Why?" I challenge.

His eyes rake down my front in answer.

"You must have a very sad little life to be so shallow-minded, Lance."

His lip twitches, arrogant and cocky. "I don't."

"A sad little penis, then?"

The elevator pings and the doors slide open, revealing a guy standing on the other side waiting. He nods at me and then at Lance before stepping in next to me.

Sad little penis. I laugh under my breath and shake my head, keeping my attention on the doors in front of me.

The polished stainless steel makes the suit at my back just visible.

Lance Sullivan.

I wonder who he is. What he does in the company. How he would feel if he knew my name paid his wages. I'd be lying if I said that didn't give me a power trip.

He's tall and slender but with enough muscle to fill his light-grey, pin-striped suit. His face is harsh but in the best way.

He's devastatingly handsome.

And he's watching me.

His eyes don't leave me, and I cannot look away. I even try. I do. I lose his eyes and look to the floor. But then I look straight back up, the need unexplainable.

I swallow before my lips part.

And then everything goes black.

TWO

Scarlet

The three of us stand in silence as the lift stops with a jolt, the lights cutting out on the panel and sending us into pitch darkness. I roll my lips and close my eyes as every muscle in my body goes rigid.

"It's stopped." I hear the guy at my side shuffle on his feet, then hear the telling sound of him punching the buttons. "It's not working," he says.

I attempt to find focus on the slightest bit of light, but there's nothing, and I quickly shut my fluttering eyelids again, rapid breaths passing through my open mouth as I try to convince myself that this is okay.

I'm okay.

"Does anyone have a phone?" I frown at the sound of Lance's voice, only just penetrating past the ringing in my ears.

"I don't. I was between floors!" the guy at my side replies.

My phone.

My phone is in my bag. But I can't move. I can't open my eyes.

"I-I can't. I'm..."

"You have a phone?" the guy closest to me snaps.

I open my eyes, a cold sweat gathering on the nape of my neck as I pull my bag off my shoulder. My hands shake as I riffle through it. "I have—I mine... Somewhere in here." I keep looking, curling my hand around my phone moments later. I pull it out and expect light, but there's nothing. I click the button on the side, but nothing happens.

"The battery's dead." My scalp prickles, dread sitting like lead in my gut.

I hear Lance take a step back, the feel of the lift bouncing making me visualise him leaning against the wall.

"Stop moving. Stop moving now," the guy to my right retorts.

Lance tuts, his tone biting. "Someone will come by in a while. The power's gone; it's happened before."

I can't see. It's so dark, and I can't see a thing. My worst nightmare. I take a deep breath in and close my eyes again, picturing the sun, bright and beaming, lighting up the fields at Lowerwick.

"What if there's a fire or something? We should do something."

A fire?

"If it's electrical, it could take hours. I don't want to be stuck in here for hours."

My chest starts to work as I imagine the darkness lasting *hours*.

"Or what if it doesn't alert them? No one will know if we can't ring down."

I reach blindly, missing and whacking the steel walls before I begin hitting the buttons, anything to spark them to life.

"We need to get out," I sputter, panic engulfing me. "Help!" I bang on the steel doors. "Help us, please. We're… we're in here!"

I look around, but no matter how hard I try, I see nothing. It's equal parts infuriating as it is terrifying. Everyone's gone quiet, and I know I'm slipping, but I turn and continue to bang on the doors.

"Help us! Please!" My eyes prickle at the sheer silence from the men around me. "Please."

This is… this is terrifying.

"I'm—I have this… thing with the… I'm afraid… I'm afraid of the…" My voice cracks, and I claw at my throat, feeling my pulse racing under my ice-cold hand.

"Hey, it's okay." The guy to my right places an arm around my trembling shoulders, his voice oddly jarring as it settles around me. "I'm sorry. I didn't mean to panic you."

"We need to alert them," I rush out.

"They'll be coming to find us. The other guy is right," he soothes me. "And if it's a fire, then the emergency services will already be on their way."

Why does he keep saying that?

Can he smell smoke?

My belly churns, and I settle for my own darkness as I close my eyes.

"I can feel you shaking. Try and calm down."

I can't calm down.

"My name's Ben. Now tell me something about you. What do you do for a living?"

"Nothing," I say in haste. "I don't do anything."

"You're not in college? University?"

I frown and try to concentrate on his question. "Sorry?"

"Are you not at uni?"

"Not anymore. I left."

"What were you studying?" He turns me in his arms and tries to hug me to his chest.

"Doctor. I wanted to be a doctor."

"Wow. That's impressive."

"Yeah?"

"My brother was a doctor."

"He *was*?" I ask.

I feel him tense, and my body burns. "He passed away three years back. It was an accident at his work."

My heart starts to beat uncontrollably as my distressed gasp kills the silence.

"I'm sorry," I manage. "We need to get out of here." My voice shakes, making me sound like a child. I cover my mouth with my fingers to hold in the cry that threatens.

I shake out of Ben's hold and bang on the doors. "Help!"

"Calm down," he tells me again, stepping up beside me.

My breathing is uncontrolled, and it's all I can hear.

I'm certain it's all they can hear too.

"You need to calm down—your breathing is—"

I stumble back, but he quickly grasps my hand in his, linking his fingers with mine in a strong grip. "Hey! It's okay," Ben soothes.

I wrap my free arm around his back, the bizarre need to take anything this stranger will give me overwhelming.

"You're okay. What's your name?"

"It's Scarlet."

His thumb brushes my knuckles, and I let out an exhale, sinking into his chest further. The smell of his cologne is sweet and sickly, and I turn my head to the side, finding a heavier, heady scent instead.

"Scarlet is a lovely name. What brings you to the Montwell today?"

I think about the suit at my back. The attitude he gave me which I gave right back.

He doesn't seem to have anything smart to say now.

"It's my birthday… I was meeting my brother for lunch."

"Today's your birthday?" The soothing motion pauses on the back of my hand, his grip tightening slightly before he runs the tip of his thumb over the cuticle on my thumbnail.

I nod as shivers rush up my spine from the intimate motion.

"Well, happy birthday."

"Thank you, Ben."

I feel myself calm a little, my breathing settling back to normal as his warmth swaths me. I squeeze his hand in mine, latching on a little tighter, thankful.

I'm okay.

Everything is going to be okay.

The elevator jolts under our feet, and Ben's free hand grabs me at the waist. We set off in motion again, the panel flickering once before the lights blind me.

I look up at Ben as his hands slowly pull away from my body, his smile awkward and his forehead shining with a sheen of sweat.

I frown down at my side, my hand feeling painfully empty.

"Just a glitch," he says, shrugging it off with an embarrassed smile.

My heart feels like it's grown three times its size and sits heavy as it thuds, slowly working its way back to a normal rhythm.

I go to look over my shoulder, but the doors ping in the next second, and I watch as Ben steps forward, as if the last couple of minutes never happened.

"This is me," he mutters, not sparing me a second glance as he walks out of the elevator.

My mouth opens and closes as the doors slide shut behind him. The idea of taking the stairs seems like the right one, but not one I act on quickly enough. I blink twice and turn fully. My gaze locks with Lance's.

He tips his chin. "You okay?"

I nod and give my best fake smile.

His arms are spread wide on the steel rail at his back, his eyes tight and anchored on me. "Your brother?"

"Mase. Mason Lowell," I reply with a croak.

His brows lift, and then he cocks his head, dropping his eyes down my front again. It's not sleazy. It's questioning, respectful… yet carnal? "Strong name," he muses.

Whatever it is, it breaks me out of the twisted headspace I've backed myself into, and I blow out a whoosh of air, blotting under my eyes with the backs of my index fingers. "Did that even just happen?" I say, looking around the confined space. My body feels agitated and not like my own.

I feel weak.

"You said you're having lunch with Mason today?" he questions with a slight shake of the head. "He's not in."

The elevator pings and he breezes past me as he strides out and into the foyer of the finance department.

The receptionist wasn't lying?

"Wait!" I yell before the doors can close. I rush forward on shaky legs, putting my hand between the doors and reaching for his jacket. I don't grasp it, but he does turn when he hears me.

He comes to a stop on the marble tile and shifts so he's looking down at me. "What do you want?"

I swallow around the lump in my throat. "Mason isn't here? Are you messing with me?"

He watches me, his eyes flicking between my own before he looks to the ceiling and curses. Then he takes off toward the other end of the floor with long, purposeful strides.

Did Mason forget? Why wouldn't he tell me he was going to miss lunch? Why would he embarrass me like that?

"You," Lance calls, poking his head around the doorframe. "Come here."

My feet carry me in his direction, but I have no idea why. I'd rather go home, spend the day with Dad and cut the grass in Mum's garden.

I need to leave.

As I reach the room at the end of the corridor, I see that what was once an empty space on this floor is now an office. I remember playing in this room when I was a child. Years of Dad bringing us here after school when Frey couldn't pick us up or watch us.

"Here." Lance holds out a phone to me, his face as hard as stone despite the kind gesture. "Use the phone and call him."

I give him a sad smile, realising he doesn't know a single thing about my family. Stepping further into the room, I cast my eyes over the furniture. "My brother cut open his finger on that door." I point at the bathroom that sits in the back of the luxury office space. "We were playing hide-and-seek—they didn't use this floor for years when they first bought the building. Anyway, our friend Elliot was seeking, and Mason and I were in the bathroom. I hid in the shower, but Mase stood at the door watching, a shit-eating grin on his face because we'd been hidden for ages. Elliot came to the door, and Mase wouldn't let him in, so Elliot started to push against it. Just as Mase curled his hand around the latch, Elliot yanked it open. Our dads were so mad at us."

My gaze is fixed on the lock, the memory vivid.

When did we stop making those memories? Why can't I remember the last time we were brought here, instead taken by our driver to the estate to fend for ourselves? I was ten. Mason fourteen. He didn't want to play with me at that age, and I spent the majority of my time on the estate alone while he was in his room. I'd paint—not that I was any good—or read or keep up with the things Dad never got around to—Mum's garden.

Being an oblivious child is utterly underrated.

Lance moves in my peripheral, and I tear my eyes away, catching him laying the phone back in its cradle. "If there's nothing else, I have work to do."

I watch him as he gets comfortable at his desk, already focused on his screen.

He seems aloof. Cold and detached from the world around him. Although, he didn't have to offer up his work phone or invite me into the office. It's not his fault he doesn't know that my brother won't answer. He never does.

My eyes scan the office one more time, noting the size and decor, almost an exact replica of Mason's. I clear my throat. "Will you call him from your own phone?"

He looks up from his screen, a black curl slipping down to dust his thick brow. "Me?"

"He'll answer for you, right?"

"I'd fucking hope so."

"Why? Because you're his…" I search his desk for the standard, gold-plated name plaque.

Lance tips his chin, his pride clear. "His CFO."

I pop an eyebrow. "Chief financial officer—impressive."

"I'm more impressed you know what one of those is."

Please. Someone get this guy a chair. He's got to be tired from carrying this conversation. "So, I need to set my name to "Asshole CFO" in my brother's phone to get an instant response. Good to know."

When his face remains deadpan, I decide to leave.

Today I choose happiness, and with the lift fiasco and now this guy, I'm ready to get home.

"You don't get out much, do you?" He stops me halfway to the door, his question lacking curiosity and reeking of arrogance.

I stop walking and let my shoulders fall, staring at the door for a beat before I spin. "A backward compliment?" Does this man have zero tact? "I'd ask you to let Mason know I was here, but it's pointless. There'd be no business deal at the other end of it to benefit him."

"You think that's all he cares about?"

"Am I wrong?"

"Yes."

I stare him down, his dark brow low and making his green eyes hard to focus on. "Do you even know my brother?"

He reaches for his mobile phone and quickly swipes across the screen, holding it to his ear.

"Wait—" I instantly regret telling him to call Mason. There won't be an excuse good enough, no matter the circumstance. It'll still sting.

That's if he even answers the phone for Lance.

"Lowell, I have your sister in my office."

I look to the carpet and close my eyes, hoping I'll miss the moment he remembers he has a sister. It slapped hard enough that he answered immediately.

Lance holds out his hand, his phone pointed toward me. "Here."

I sigh and smooth back my hair, lifting the phone to my ear. "Mase."

"Scar, I'm so sorry. I had a meeting and then had to go on site. Are you still at the office? I can be back within the hour."

I bite the inside of my lip. I've had two text messages today. One from Charlie Aldridge, one of my brother's best friends. And one from Vinny, my brother's driver, both wishing me a happy birthday.

"It's fine, don't stress it, Mase."

"Don't be like that. Elliot's AWOL, and I'm swamped."

"I know you are. I'm not mad." Just don't ask me out for lunch. Simple.

"Let me make it up to you." There's a large crashing sound down the line, and I imagine him on the building site. "The Hamilton Gala is tomorrow night. Come with me and the guys."

Wait, what? "You'd take me to a business event?"

He chuckles down the line, and I close my eyes and smile at the sound. "You could go without me. You have no idea the pull your last name has. They're bored of me, and you're the secret Lowell lovechild we locked away in our ivory tower for years. They're desperate to have you in attendance."

The idea of going to the gala is kind of exciting. I've seen pictures of Mason at the event, but also of Mum. Frey never let us miss a second of the short life she lived. The idea I could go and live it for myself, to be in the moment like she was. "Mase, I'd love to come."

"That's settled then, and Scar?"

"Yeah?" My eyes lock with Lance's, and the way his eyes hold on me, waiting, makes my skin burn.

"Happy birthday. I'm sorry I missed lunch, I completely forgot, and it's not fair."

"It's okay, Mase—"

"It's not." He pauses for a second, and it feels awkward. Like he wants to say more about it but doesn't, and Lance has the most beautiful green eyes I think I've ever seen. "I'll send Vinny for you tomorrow night, six o'clock."

I turn away from the desk, breaking my trance. "I'll need to come in earlier than that. I need everything. Hair, nails, and I don't think I have a dress I'd want to wear—"

"I'll sort all of that, don't worry, okay?"

I bite my lip and smile. "Okay."

"See you tomorrow."

He hangs up, and I pass the phone back to Lance. "Thank you."

He places the phone on his desk and shakes his head. "If that's everything?" he repeats.

My stomach drops, and I right myself at the same time his phone chimes on the desk.

How can he be so moody and thoughtful in one whole moment?

He lifts the phone and reads the message. I stand, for no logical reason, and watch him, catching the moment his face transforms into disbelief.

"What the fuck!" He looks up from his phone. "What did he say to you?"

"He invited me to a gala tomorrow night," I say, not helping my smile.

"And said I would take you to get all this… crap?"

I frown and step forward an inch, trying to get a glimpse at his phone as he waves it in front of my face.

"No." Mason asked *him*? "He said he would sort it. He never said—"

"Does your brother think I have time to go shopping, that this falls under my job title?"

Watching him lose his cool over this is oddly satisfying, and I give him a listening ear as I stand and soak it up.

"Can you not shop for yourself? I wouldn't even know how to dress a hippy. If he's that worried about how you'll look, why doesn't he take you himself?"

"You're right, Lance. I doubt you could dress a circus

clown." I drop my eyes down his torso. Although I doubt it bruises his ego. "I'll be just fine sorting it myself."

"Good." He stands and walks to a cupboard in the corner of the room. It's located beside the minibar, and I quickly hear the telling sound of a safe dial being tuned. When he returns to the desk and holds out the black bank card, I narrow my eyes on him.

"Knock yourself out, eight-two-six-five." And I get the sense he means it in more ways than shopping myself silly.

"Thank you, Lance, but keep the card. You can use it to buy some class—"

"Class—"

"You're without a doubt the most perfected definition of cockalorum I've ever come across. I get it now."

"Cock-a-what?"

"Goodbye, asshole."

"Yeah," he yells, clutching at straws. "Don't let the door hit you on the way out."

I turn and look over my shoulder, shaking my head at his terrible insult.

As I make my way toward the stairwell, I notice a guy sitting at the reception desk. A thought comes to me, and I make my way over.

"Hello. Scarlet Lowell." I present my hand to him, and he takes it with wide eyes.

"Of course! Hi. Can I help you?" He looks past me and down the hall.

"Yes, an appointment with Mr Sullivan tomorrow, please. He asked that I have you pencil me into his day."

"Uh…" He frowns and looks down at his screen,

clicking a couple of times. "What time did he suggest? He has a full schedule."

Hmm. What would piss him off the most? I get the feeling the man doesn't like people messing with his food, like a lion. Or maybe I'm naive to think he wouldn't have been such an asshole if I arrived after lunch today. "Eleven thirty." I try to remember the name of the shop the girls took me to when I was at uni. "At Nellie's. It's down on Finch Street." Far enough away with cobbles so uneven he'll have to walk the lane. Perfect.

"He wants to move the Jefferys meeting?"

The way he says it, his brows jumping to his hairline and his voice raising a little too loud for my liking, makes it sound super important.

"He sure does."

"Right." He blinks twice and starts to type. "Nellies. I'm not familiar with the name." He looks up at me once he's done typing. "Is that an office space? It would be more convenient for Mr Sullivan to meet here with his schedule being so full."

"You can ask him if you want? I'm just relaying the boss's orders." I smile and shrug, innocently checking my watch.

The poor guy is trying to figure out who I'm referring to, and it makes me feel like a horrible witch. It's not my fault his boss is an intolerable fool, though.

"No, that's okay. I'll go ahead and schedule it now."

"You're a star! Thank you…"

He looks up at me. "Harry."

"Harry." I lean in a little closer. "Could you put that in under Lowell, please, Harry?"

"Just Lowell?"

"Yes, please."

More clicking. "Okay, all booked."

"Wonderful!" I step back from the desk. "Enjoy your day."

"It was good to meet you, Miss Lowell."

"Please, call me Scar." I wink and carry on toward the elevators.

Or Satan—on my way to do the devil's work.

THREE

Lance

Vanessa: Rents due. Call me.

Thank fuck it's Friday.

I'm sliding my phone into the drawer of my desk when my assistant, Harry, walks in.

"Morning." He doesn't pause on the threshold or waste any time getting through his morning briefing, which I appreciate. "Copperfield emailed late last night. Did you see? Something was wrong with the payment. Tactical, I'd say, considering it's now the weekend and we won't get to it until Monday. I have a car ready for your eleven thirty, and your mother has already called this morning, asked if I'd pass on a message." He places the sticky note on my desk along with a coffee. "You're in office all afternoon, would you like that to be known?"

Call ASAP. Molly's broken down.

"Never, Harry. And thank you."

"Sure thing."

He backs out of my office, leaving me in peace. Or as much peace as I can get when my mother is on the warpath. I lift the note again and roll my eyes.

When Harry first started working here, he called an ambulance on my mother's behalf when she told him my sister Nessa Anne had fallen down the stairs. She had, in fact, fallen down the stairs, but not in the dramatised way my mother described. And when the ambulance arrived at the house, Nessa Anne was sitting on the sofa with a joint.

"I'm done with you all wasting my time! I have a job. Staff you're fucking with because you're all too selfish to do a single thing for yourselves."

"I fell down the stairs, Lance!"

"You look like you did."

"God, you're so uptight these days. So righteous. Here…"

"Fuck you, Nessa Anne."

I remember my mother telling me she would send me the invoice for a replacement carpet after knocking the joint from Nessa Anne's hand.

I laughed in her face and left.

My sisters (all three of them) and my mother are lazy. It's not even the girls' fault. My parents did a great job of giving them everything they ever wanted when they were growing up. They loved us. So much so, they fucked up the lot of us.

My phone starts to ring from inside my desk drawer, and I sigh before pulling it open. *Vanessa.* I decline the call and put it on silent.

Not today, Mum.

. . .

At ten past eleven, I leave my office and head toward the elevators, and as I step inside the steel container, I can't help my thoughts from wandering to the day before. Or more specifically, the purple-haired spitfire that came out of nowhere. I knew Mason had a sister, but the way he talked about her made me think that she was much younger than she clearly is. Maybe because the tolerance I have for my own sisters is so thin, it made me write her off as unimportant whenever she was talked about.

Not that she holds any importance now.

While the lift descends, I pull up Molly's number and call her.

"Hey, brother."

"Hey, Mol. Everything okay?"

Molly is the youngest of my three sisters at twenty. She's never been a part of the trouble my mother put on us, but she also never spoke up when she should have. If I had known sooner what my mother and sisters were doing—the mess they were in—I might have been able to help sooner.

"Yeah, fine. I'm on my way to my next lecture."

As I thought. "Mum messaged; said you'd broken down."

"Eh? I told her my fuel's low. I might leave the car on campus and get the bus home."

"Why haven't you put fuel in your car?"

"I can't afford it."

I scrub my hands over my face and try to control the bite in my tone. "Molly, you have an allowance—"

She tuts. "And I spent it. It's not like it's wasted money—"

"Well, I can't help you. I'm sorry, Mols, but—"

She sniggers, cutting me off and reminding me she's just like the rest of them. "You have to help me," she snaps.

"No. Sort yourself out. I can't deal with you all today. I'm busy." I hang up and slide my phone back into my slacks just as the elevator doors slide open. My driver is waiting for me when I walk through the doors of the Montwell, the blisteringly hot sun beating down and making my suit feel like a furnace. I unbutton and remove my jacket as I slide into the back of the car.

"Lance," Joe greets as he quickly pulls out into the constant stream of cars. "Beautiful day, isn't it?"

"Sure is," I mutter back, pulling up my schedule to double-check where I'm headed. My eyes pinch together when I spot Mason scheduled in. "Lowell?"

Where's that fucker got us going now?

I dial his number.

"Yeah?"

"Why are you in my diary?" I read further. "Nellies. What the fuck is Nellies?"

"What the hell are you talking about, Sullivan?"

"Pull up my schedule," I tell him.

"I'll call you back, mate. Not a good time." He hangs up, and I frown down at the appointment. I don't like being unprepared. In fact, it fucks me off that my schedule has been messed with to fit his day. He might be one of my best friends, but he's an inconsiderate prick at times.

"Joe, do you know what Nellies is?"

"I don't. I only took the address last minute this morning."

I try to call Harry to no avail, and by the time I arrive at the location, I'm still none the wiser about who I'm meeting with and what files to take from the briefcase Harry had ready for me this morning.

"I'm not able to get thc car down there, boss. You'll have to walk the last half mile."

"It's fucking boiling out, for Christ's sake." I pull open the door and take the whole case with me. The walkway tails off down a cobbled street, and who knows what's at the other end. Five-hundred fucking yards to the other end.

Lance: You can suck a dick today.

Mase: I'm picking up my tux. The fuck is your problem?

I stuff my phone in my pocket and walk the five hundred yards down the street. When I reach *Nells*, I look up at the double-fronted windows and come face-to-face with a sex shop.

"He cancelled fucking Jefferys for this?"

Lance: Are you okay in the head? That or you have far too much money.

I curse my best friend as I push on the door to Nells. Thankfully it's not busy, but I still get eyed by the three women shopping in the store and the two assistants at the front desk. They get straight to work.

"Hello! Can we help at all?"

"I can help," I hear one of the customers mutter.

"I'm here on business," I confirm. "I was sent by Mr Lowell."

"Oh! Oh, of course. Just a moment." The dark-haired shop assistant goes around the desk and bends behind the counter. "Please, follow me!" She pulls out a bag and then walks off toward the back of the shop and into a separate room. "Sorry, did you say Mr Lowell?"

"Yes." I take the bag even though she doesn't fully extend it to me. "Has this been paid for? Is there anything to settle?"

Get me the fuck out of here.

"It was your wife, Mrs Lowell, who left the package, sir. She requested you open it in-store in case you want to pick something different. For your benefit, we thought you'd prefer to open it out here."

Did I just hear that right? "My wife. Mrs Lowell?"

"Yes, and nothing to pay. A treat for the husband, she said, and asked that we put it on her account."

My jaw flexes. "She did, did she."

"We hope you enjoy your new purchase. If there's anything else you need at all today, just let me or Georgia know. I'll leave you to it!"

She backs away, and my blood starts to boil.

She's wasting my damn time.

I open the bag and peer inside, finding the contents gift wrapped. What is she playing at?

Lowell.

Jesus, why didn't I catch on to that?

I should leave the shop and the package but fuck if I'm not too pissed at her. There's a card attached to the box, and I rip that off first, chucking it onto the chaise lounge.

The box isn't small, and it's weighty. I sit down and pull off the black bow. As I lift the lid, I catch a glimpse of what's inside and close my eyes. A growl reverberates through my chest.

I secure the lid again and reach for the card.

Asshole CFO,

After realising just how busy you are, I'd hate to see you miss out on basic human needs. Especially with all the long hours and important business meetings you can't miss. It must be a hard little life you live. Painfully hard. Anyway, the penis extender isn't as brutal as it sounds. I thought so at first, too. The trick is lube (I got you plenty). The booty cruiser eXXXtreme anal massager is a gift to hopefully dislodge the stick you have wedged.

I hope this helps with your iddy-biddy problem.

Always a pleasure,

Lowell.

The little shit.

I drop the note and pull out the first box: the penis extender. She's right; it's not as brutal as it sounds. It's a transparent silicone penis that you slide your dick into and hook onto your balls. A fucking strap-on cock. The booty cruiser ass plunger looks terrifying, and I toss it back into the box.

I pull out my phone and call Mason.

"Sullivan."

"Your sister—"

"What about her?"

"I'm meant to be sorting appointments for her today, right? I lost her number. Send it over, will you."

"Fuck, I forgot. Is that what you were moaning about earlier?"

"Yeah, didn't have the time."

"Yeah, well you're doing me a solid. She'll only ask

about Dad, and at least tonight I can use the gala to steer the conversation into safer territory."

"Right, yeah."

"I'll send it over now. I have a meeting with Clements in five."

I wait for the number to come through, then call her, collecting up the box and leaving the shop while it rings.

I'm pissed at her.

She cancelled the fucking Jefferys meeting.

"Hello," her sweet-as-sin voice floats down the line, and I snigger, running my tongue over my teeth.

"Lowell." It comes out deep, like a reprimand.

"Oh.... Oh my god! Crap!" She laughs and splutters before hanging up.

Scarlet

I slam down my phone and put my hand over my mouth.

Izzy looks at me in the mirror as she starts to finish off with hairspray. "What's wrong?"

"Nothing."

"It didn't sound like nothing," she says, smiling as she adds a different spray.

I've had my hair done this morning, and I still have appointments booked throughout the rest of the day to get my dress, nails and makeup sorted.

I feel good. Or felt good until Lance Sullivan called me and reminded me of the gifts I left for him at Nells.

"I sent a guy to a sex shop and bought him toys as a gift, pretending to be his wife. He just called me."

"You did what?" she questions, clearly not expecting it. Izzy has been doing my hair since I started dying it, and although I now touch it up myself, there's no one else I trust. She whacks my arm. "Scarlet! Spill it."

"He's so arrogant. A complete jackass. I just wanted to give him a little reality check."

"By buying him sex toys! Have you ever even been in a sex shop?"

I blush, fanning myself as I laugh. "Once when I was in university."

"You shock me! You seem like such a good girl. So innocent. I can't believe this!"

"Shh!" I laugh. "I *am* innocent."

But shit, the way he said my name. It created an instant image. His green eyes, thick dark hair and sculpted face. His full lips.

I'm suddenly feeling all hot.

My phone starts to ring again, and I look down at my lap. Izzy must notice because she mouths "answer it" as if he can hear her.

"No," I whisper back.

"Is he hot?"

"Annoyingly so."

"Answer. Now!"

I pick up the phone and answer, the sound of cars in the background greeting me before he does.

"I'm on my way. Stay there."

"You're on your way where?"

I look at my phone to find it back on my home screen.

"I have to go!"

Izzy laughs as I shoot out of the chair. "I'm done anyway. Are you happy?"

Using the mirror, I turn to the side and admire the pretty plait she's woven into a bun that sits to the side of my neck.

It's simple, a little messy and purple; Me.

"I love it. Thank you so much! How much do I owe you?" I rush out, moving toward the front of the shop to pay.

"It's been months since I've seen you, and I'm sure you'll bag me some clients tonight looking so suave. No charge."

"Izzy, no!" I take out the cash in my purse and hand it over. "Here."

"It's not *that* much," she snaps.

"You look after me, and I appreciate it. Take Len out for dinner."

She shakes her head at me as I rush out of the shop, and I smile back at her.

I have half an hour before my appointment at Louise's Boutique, and although I don't believe Lance knows where I am, I'm also not an idiot. Because he sounded like he knew exactly where I was.

With time to kill, I hotfoot it to the cocktail bar across the street and snag a seat at the bar. I have a view of Izzy's shop, but I'm also far enough back not to get spotted.

"What can I get for you?" the barman asks.

I order an espresso martini and watch as it's made, occasionally glancing out of the window to check the street for Mr Asshole CFO.

The first cocktail gets drained within minutes, but it goes

down well and is clearly needed. I feel on edge, with a little adrenaline rush, like a child hiding out.

When I left the Montwell yesterday, a couple of silly toys seemed like a great idea. It definitely made me feel better. Sat here now thinking about it, I'm not sure I've done anything so childish in years, and the only excuse I have is the fact it's been nearly twelve weeks since I've been in the city.

Dad sleeps much of the day away now, which leaves me alone. So to hell with Lance's opinion of me. It was fun to mess with the grumpy beast sitting in his big, serious executive chair while being all arrogant and hot.

The bartender places another espresso down, and I nod in thanks.

As I turn my head to look out into the street for the hundredth time in twenty minutes, I spot him at the entrance of Izzy's shop.

"Crap," I mutter to myself.

He pulls out his phone—his Nells bag thrown over his shoulder as if he has no concerns with anyone seeing—and then plasters it to his ear.

My phone starts to ring in my bag, and I shake my head, feeling dumb. I should've expected that.

I let it ring out and pick up my drink as I slide from the stool. As I inch toward the window, I use a huge succulent to hide behind. My phone starts to ring again, and I laugh into my drink, taking a sip as I watch him.

"Catch me if you can, motherfucker."

. . .

After two cocktails, I'm feeling a little buzz. I want to think it's because of the alcohol, but sneaking out of shops and running away from a guy I just purchased a penis enlarger for seems to have given me a huge rush of endorphins.

I slip inside Louise's Boutique and breathe out a sigh of relief as I close the door behind me. The boutique is large, with three floors, each one getting a little fancier on each level. Casual, formal, best. For me, I'll be between levels two and three today.

The shop assistants greet me with champagne which I decline, knowing it's not a smart move on top of the espressos martinis I just drained.

We spend time searching for a dress or two-piece that will suit me and works for the gala. With over eight dresses to try on, I make my way to the private changing rooms and start to undress.

My phone starts to ring as I'm removing my bra, and I tut as I check the screen, expecting it to be him again.

"Izzy?" I bring the phone to my ear and answer. "What did I forget?"

"Don't be mad at me."

"Why would I be mad at you?"

"I gave him Louise's address."

I frown at myself in the mirrored wall. "You gave who Louise's address?"

"The angry hot god! He totally talked me into it—or his eyes did, or that suit. I wasn't going to tell him, and then he—"

"Izzy, you did not give that man the address."

"I definitely did."

I hear someone walking into my private room, and I move toward the divide.

"Scarlet, I have your husband here. Would you like me to send him through?"

"My husband?" I ask, peeking around the divide.

"Hello, *wife*." Lance greets me as we lock eyes. I gape at the assistant by his side, then swallow around the dryness in my throat.

Sure, just send him on in here! *Why did you even ask?* Her cheeks are pink, and she watches Lance as he places his Nells bag on the chaise lounge along with his grey suit jacket. He starts to roll up his shirtsleeves, and I roll my eyes. *Oh, please.*

"Oh my god, did she say husband? He did not?" Izzy is hysterical on the other end of the phone.

I roll my lips, goose bumps skittering up my arms and across my chest, setting my nipples into pointed peaks.

"Izzy, shh," I whisper, palming my forehead. "I'm so annoyed at you right now. I have a nipple-on from pure stress." I cover them with my palms and pull back on my T-shirt.

One appointment in eight months with my hairdresser, and I'm telling her about my tits.

You don't get out much, do you?

Asshole.

I hear wheezing on the other end of the line and shake my head. Useless.

"Let him in!" Izzy begs. "Mess with him. Do not send him away."

"No!"

"Scarlet, he thinks he can walk into your dressing room,

call you his wife—the real reason for the nipple-on—and that he's going to do it with all that arrogance and anger?"

"Can we get some more dresses? I'd like to see her in green."

The cockiness in his tone makes me groan in annoyance.

"Go get him, girl."

I hang up as the shop assistant leaves the room. Stepping out from behind the divide, I look across at him. He's standing, giving me a heavy stare, but I give my own right back.

"Do you think it's acceptable to come in here *lying*?"

"Do you think it's acceptable to cancel my meetings and send me on your little fetish runs around London? Did it scratch the itch?" He looks between my legs, and my jaw drops.

"You're a pig!"

"And you're a presumptuous witch."

"Get out."

"Absolutely not."

"Why are you here?"

"I told Mase I'd help. Besides, if you are arriving with us tonight, I at least want you to look semi-decent."

"You're going! To the gala?"

"Sure am, sunshine." He looks down his nose at me, his inked forearms flexing and telling me he's fisting his hands in his pockets. "Go get dressed."

I snigger and cross my arms over my chest, unmoving.

His eyes hold mine, and all I can think about is my nail appointment at three o'clock.

"Now, Scarlet."

"Pompous ass." I walk around the divide and start to change.

"Moany bitch."

My eyes tighten. "Egotistic fool."

"Cock clown. Hey, ever thought maybe the reason men need penis enlargers is that their cocks shrivel up the second you look at them."

My jaw drops for the second time in a matter of minutes.

"Yeah, well… you look like something I'd draw with my left hand."

The deep, rumbling laugh he gives me seems genuine, and it vibrates right through me. "Wounded, sunshine. If you need to give that left hand some practice, though, you just let me know—"

"I wouldn't eat your dick if I were starving, and it was the last on earth!" I pause and blink twice, one foot stilled in the opening of the beaded grey gown I have gathered in my hands. "I—"

"You make dick-eating sound like a sport. I'm impressed."

I pull the dress up my body and huff out a sigh. Why did I say that? It's like my current insult mixed with his last and my next. Walking around the divide, I pin him down with a glare. "Just go."

His lip twitches, clearly contemplating it. "I would, but I told Mason I'd see that you have a good day to make up for yesterday. And since you were so incessant in cancelling my meeting—"

"I'd have a great day if you left."

"I plan to spend the entire day making sure you're well and truly smothered in my happiness."

"I can hardly wait."

His smirk is damn right dirty. Knowing. Cheeky. Devilish.

"Do me up." I turn away from him, holding the gown against my chest and fighting the urge to add a please.

"It would be my honour."

My lip twitches, but I don't answer. I'll only go and say something ridiculous.

His hands grip either side of the open back, and he pulls it tight together, so tight it restricts my air supply and makes me gasp. "You okay?" he whispers, his breath dusting my ear.

A shiver ghosts down my spine, and as he loosens his grip to do the zipper, I pray he misses my body's traitorous reaction to him.

What is it about this guy?

"Does my brother know you're here?" I question.

"He asked me to be."

"I'm pretty sure he asked you to book the appointments, which I did on my way home yesterday. You don't need to be here."

"Scarlet," he says, and I glance over my shoulder, my gaze lifting to meet his eyes when I find his chest. His eyes crease in at the corners, but it's not enough to hide the spark in them. "That'll do."

I swallow any words that try to slip free and face the other way. Once the dress is zipped, I step out of his reach and toward the mirror. "I don't like it."

"Me neither." I turn to look at him, and he shrugs with a smirk. "I won't lie to you."

I make quick work of snagging the zipper down my back—it's not easy—and disappearing behind the divide again.

"I never asked for your opinion. Don't you have better things to do today?"

"Like the Jefferys meeting you cancelled?"

Crap. I roll my lips as I pull on a different dress. A Valentino gown with beautiful beading. "How important was it?" I ask, stepping back out into the room. The zip is low on the dress, so I don't ask him for any help. Instead, I go and stand in front of the mirrors, admiring the beautiful yet lightweight train that trails behind me.

"Important."

I cut my eyes to him, finding his attention and gaze firmly locked on me. Something fizzles in the air between us, and I do my best not to look away. The last thing I want him to think is that he has an effect on me. "Do you have an opinion on this one?" I ask, knowing I'm opening myself up to more trouble.

His tongue swipes through his cheek before his chin lifts. "I don't hate it."

My lip curls and I hide that too, this time turning. "I'm sorry that I cancelled your meeting. I was being childish."

"Don't try redeeming yourself. It won't work on me, and you're far too deep in the hole. It's your brother you should be apologising to. I was closing on a thirty-six-million-pound contract with Malcolm Jefferys this morning. Mase will be pissed at you."

Fuck.

Mason *will* be livid.

The idea of pissing him off or disappointing him is harder to think about than it should be. My brother's no angel.

"He missed your birthday, though. So maybe you'll get

away with it?" He gives me a pointed look as if his logic makes sense and belongs in a history book.

That, or he's laughing at me.

Mason works hard to keep the business at the professional level it's at. Lance has to be a huge part of that to be closing contracts with the big guys. Mason trusts this guy. "How come I've never heard of you before?" I ask, my brows drawing together.

Lance takes a couple of steps forward. My focus is glued to him in the mirror. "I guess it's the same reason I didn't know about you…."

Mason doesn't talk about me. He probably doesn't talk to anyone about Dad or me—the house. It sends a pang of sadness through my chest, and I have to look away to stop my eyes from misting.

Finding some composure, I turn to face Lance, feeling the need to explain the dysfunction that comes with the Lowell name. "Mason doesn't come out to the house—like ever. It's so far away, and with Dad… Truthfully, I don't visit him much either." I swallow around the lump in my throat as my eyes dart around Lance's handsome face. "It just gets hard when you feel like you don't know anything about your family. What they're doing in life or what they're feeling. The half-ass conversations are great, but what's hurting you, you know? What's making you happy? Or heavy. Or even a little richer? It's those kinds of things you should help and support them with in life, right? The things you should want to carry for them, so they don't have to do it all alone."

Lance's phone rings in his pocket, but he doesn't reach for it. He just stares at me, a slight nod moving his head as if in understanding, yet it's so slight, I could be imagining it.

When the phone starts to ring out for a second time, he pulls it from his pocket and brings it to his ear. "Mum?"

Those eyes. It's as if they're telling me everything and yet nothing at all.

He turns, and I sag in relief, not realising how intense the energy in the room has grown.

I hear him clear his throat. "No, I can't tonight. I'm out… A work thing… No, Mum…" His back goes rigid, and I roll my lips, slipping past him and behind the divide.

My hands shake slightly as I unzip the dress and pull it down my body. Why did I ramble on? I just made it painfully obvious that I'm an absolute loner. Not that I care. I love my little life. The estate and the grounds. I wouldn't trade it for the world.

"You're delusional, Mum, you know that? Fucking delusional."

I frown and look over my bare shoulder, finding Lance now pacing the room. When his eyes lock with mine, he stops. He sees the gown at my waist, my breasts exposed and barely concealed by my arm, but enough that I don't hide from him.

Goose bumps sheath me.

His jaw clenches, and he carries on forward. "Enough…. Enough, Mum. I'll come out," he says, a little raspier than before.

Does that mean he's leaving?

The silence stretches in the room for the longest time, and I think about the conversation he must be having as I slide my summer dress back on and then my sandals.

When I emerge from behind the divider moments later, he's gone.

Three knocks sound on the door, and I wait as the assistant walks in. "Scarlet. The green dress, as requested by your husband." She adds it to the rail and smiles. "Anything else you think you might like to try today?"

I walk to where the dresses hang and run my fingers over the deep-green silk gown. It's cute.

"No, I think I'll take the Valentino. I can bring it out with me when I'm done. Thank you, though."

"Of course."

FOUR

Lance

I don't remove my shoes as I enter my childhood home. There's a level of nostalgia that hits me whenever I come here, although with that comes rage.

"Who's pissed you off this time?" Chloe snorts as she passes me in the hall. She doesn't stop to say hello, regardless of the fact it's been two months since I've been here.

"Rent's due," I tell her. She doesn't reply and snakes off into the lounge.

My childhood home is nice. In a decent neighbourhood which is safe and mostly quiet. The only drama to have rocked Saints Lane in the last two decades was the death and then collapse of the Sullivan name—courtesy of the four selfish, money-hungry women who live in number sixteen.

"Lance, honey, is that you?"

I make my way into the kitchen and find my mother

standing at the breakfast bar, trying to decanter some kind of pinkish liquid into a clear bottle. "What are you doing?"

"I smashed the bottle. Did you bring the rent?"

I eye the mess she's making and shake my head, the fire I felt ignite in Scarlet's dressing room roaring to life again. I get to the point. "You need to get a job, Mum. You all do. I worked when I was at uni, and there's no reason the girls can't as well."

My mother chuckles, not pausing her task. "Now, those weren't the rules we agreed on. Quit being the big I am. It doesn't work with us. There's leftover pizza in the oven if you want it."

"Rules? I'm not twenty years old anymore, Vanessa!"

She puts down the plastic bottle and eyes me. "Vanessa? Really. Fuck you, Lance."

"I'll support you. I'll stick to every stipulation and rule, but you'll get a job. You all will."

"No." She picks back up the bottle and continues.

My blood boils. "Then I'm done. I won't help you if you can't help yourself."

Her eyes snap up. "Help me? Help me! You think you're helping me? You're nothing but a self-centred cold man who I barely recognise anymore. You think you would be where you are now if I hadn't let you leave? Let you sell your father's bike? If I didn't let you bugger off to university and abandon us all here?"

"It beat not having a roof over your head, surely? None of us would be where we are now if you hadn't lost every penny Dad ever made!" I spit the words and mean every single one of them.

"How dare you!"

"Get a job." I slam the rent down on the table, the thud making my chest ache. "Get a fucking job, Mum." I step back as her face grows guilty. She knows what she's done. "At least try."

I back out of the kitchen and walk into the lounge, finding both Nessa Anne and Chloe on the sofa watching TV. "It's three thirty on a Friday in the peak of summer. Why are you sitting indoors?"

"To piss you off, Lance," Nessa Anne retorts. "We live for it. You're the centre of our world. The core of this perfect little family."

I roll my eyes at her and look at Chloe. She doesn't even acknowledge me.

"Have you been out with any of your friends recently?" I ask Nessa Anne.

She shakes her head, not bothering to cut her eyes away from the TV.

When I left for university, I also left behind my sisters. They won't ever forgive me for that, not when Mum was at the peak of her depression. The alternative was too messed up for me to comprehend at the time, and I knew if I could get myself through uni, securing the house with the little money we had left before losing it, I could make everything okay. I'd put them through college, uni—buy them their first homes. I never considered them not wanting those things, and when I came home from my first year to silence, I knew having to do this for them would come at a cost. I didn't just lose my Dad; I lost everyone and everything that mattered.

Molly was the only one I could convince to study, but I

know she isn't interested in continuing next year and skips classes.

"You could just wire the money like you normally do, you know. You don't have to save face by showing up here. Or just have me do it like that time you had a 'cold' and couldn't crawl out of your penthouse apartment and to your one-thousand-pound laptop to pay us the pittance you toss us."

"To pay you for what, Nessa Anne? Existing?" I throw my hands out to my sides, looking around the darkened room. "Look at the state of it."

"You're boring me," Nessa Anne snaps. "Please go back to the hole you crawled out of, brother."

I leave the room and jog up the stairs, looking around the landing. I quickly cross to Molly's room. Pulling out my wallet, I slip five hundred pounds into her textbook, knowing out of everyone, she will be the most responsible with it.

Then I leave.

Scarlet

At five p.m., I arrive at the penthouse. With time to kill before Mason arrives home—Mason who, as always, seems to be missing my every call—I make use of myself and wash the three dishes he'd placed in the dishwasher, put on a load of washing, and then dust the few pictures I know he keeps in his home office.

It's where I find the image of Lance Sullivan.

I never knew how close he was with my brother, but the fact I'm holding an image of himself, Mason, Charlie and Elliot as they sit on the back of our boat in the lagoon in Bora Bora, tells me that he's someone that's *very* close to him. My brother and Elliot wouldn't take anyone they didn't consider family to the lodges. They're sacred and one of the few places we have to visit that doesn't hold painful memories.

I replace the image on the shelf and walk back out into the living area. The penthouse is nothing that I'd ever desire for myself, yet the fact my brother lives here, and the love he has for this city, it makes a part of me love it just as much.

"Christ, Scarlet. I could smell you from the elevator. Is that lemon?" I watch as he rounds the entry foyer and strolls into the open-plan room, a silly smile on his face.

"Mase!" I beam, concealing my toothy grin behind my closed mouth.

When he drops what I presume is a suit bag on the floor and opens his arms for me, I rush and hug him.

As he envelops me in his arms, my throat grows tight. "It's been so long."

"Yeah," he says, all gruff, his head resting on top of mine. "Happy birthday, Scar."

"What's the plan? What time is the car getting here? I called you, by the way. Why don't you ever answer?"

He chuckles at my fifty questions and pulls back. "I left my phone in the office this afternoon." He looks down at me, a guilty look masking his handsome face. "I tend to leave it in the office in the evenings and over the weekend."

"You don't have a separate phone for work?"

He looks between us, and I catch him working on a swallow.

"Oh. Right." I have my brother's work number.

Shit, I'm going to cry.

"Get your phone. I'll give you the number—"

"I need to get dressed. Just call up when the car's here, yeah?" I need to be on my own. I don't cry very often, and after my lapse in the elevator just yesterday, I want to be out of this situation immediately.

"Scar, the car isn't arriving until seven thirty. Have a drink with me."

I'm already turned and making my way toward the staircase when he calls out to me again, and I expect it. "I'm sorry. I don't…."

Knowing he won't finish, I ease around and face him, looking down from the middle of the stairs at my brother, who for all his flaws, I adore more than anyone on earth. Small lines crease the corner of his eyes—he's thirty-one—and I know it isn't from that winning smile. Life can be cruel sometimes. "I'll never be mad at you for how you choose to handle your pain, Mase. You have nothing to apologise for, and I'll love you regardless."

Then I run up the stairs and into the spare room, where I sit on the bed for an hour, staring at the horribly stark white wall in front of me.

I hear a knock as I'm fastening the clasp on my bracelet and poke my head around the walk-in wardrobe door. "Come in."

Mason enters the room, and I go back to my task.

"Looking very dapper," I call out as I hear the door click shut.

"Dapper," he murmurs, and I know one of his thick brows will be raised. "I suppose I do." He rounds the door and stops short on the threshold. "Wow."

"Shut up." I punch his arm, knocking him back a step as I pass him. I walk to where my shopping bags are laid out on the bed and pull out the matching necklace. "Will you help me?"

He nods with a warm, cheeky smile, and I can tell he wants to say something. "You look incredible, Scar. So grown up."

"I'm twenty-eight years old. When will you and Dad stop treating me like a kid?"

"You'll always be the baby. This dress is very… hmm…"

"I'm twenty-eight years old, Mason."

He lifts the necklace over my head and works at fastening the clasp. "The slit is a bit high, and the bust is busty. I once read something about women showing ass or tits but never both."

"Likely written by a penis-wielding, sexist pig. But I am proud you're able to read full sentences now. Also, what part of my ass is out?"

"It's not, but that slit is very high."

I turn and give him a look.

"You look beautiful, Scarlet."

"Thank you, Mason." I smile sweetly, happy that the look conveyed what I intended.

Who are you to tell me what to do, brother?

"The guys are here; thought you might want a drink before we leave. If you're not still mad at me."

"I'm not mad at you, Mase."

He nods and lifts his hand. "Shall we?"

I grab my bag and slide my hand into his. We leave the room and take the stairs to the ground floor. As I reach the bottom step, Elliot's voice floats from the entertainment room.

"There she is!"

I smile as I duck down to look through the double doors which are pulled wide open. Charlie is standing at the bar with a drink in his hand, and Elliot is leaning against the pool table, the look on his face one of knowing yet proud. It makes me feel good.

"Fuck, Scar," Charlie says, much to my surprise. He's the politest of my brother's friends and probably the one I trust most to look after me tonight.

"Right," Elliot agrees, still watching me. "If you weren't like a little sister to me, I'd totally admit to looking at your tits right now."

I chuckle and go to him, pulling him in for a hug which he welcomes. "Hey, stranger."

"Hey." I pull back and look at him. His blond hair, blue eyes and wicked smile that I've missed. It reminds me. "Your mum misses you."

"Don't I fucking know it."

He lets me go, and I turn to say hello to Charlie. But then I catch something shifting out of the corner of my eye, and I spin around again to see Lance sitting in the corner of the room.

Everything becomes a little bit more. My heart rate, the sharpness in my spine, the quietness in the room, the music —as if it's a part of me and this moment and not just a speaker fixed into the ceiling above me. His eyes dance over me, unforgiving and unafraid.

I swallow. "Hi."

Lance dips his head as if it's greeting enough before lifting his drink and taking a sip. His eyes remain on me.

It's a hungry "I want to rip that dress off you" look.

Conflicted between turning away from the green-eyed gaze in the corner of the room and potentially revealing the scarlet flush that's burning its way up my chest, or staying facing the green-eyed gaze, revealing to him the power he seems to possess, I choose to do neither. I beeline for the small bar and lean over to kiss Charlie's cheek. "Charles. Wanna make me a drink?"

I hear Mason and Elliot talking at my back and breathe a sigh of relief, my eyes moving back to Charlie. He's smiling as he reaches for a glass. "Sure. But I'm privy to the knowledge that Sullivan makes a killer cocktail."

I swallow as if I've done something naughty and am getting caught. Truth is, I'm just a horny twenty-eight-year-old woman who can't make eye contact with a man without blushing.

"You're not good at it?" I ask, trying to keep the conversation alive before I melt on the spot. I'm pretty sure there're eyes burning a hole in the back of my dress.

"Not *as* good. I mean, anything else, I'm better. Girly cocktails? He can have it."

My nerves seem to ease as I sit at the bar and watch Charlie make my drink.

"How's Anthony?" he asks.

"He's okay. The same."

Charlie nods. Mason doesn't talk to me about our Dad

—ever, but I know that he's extremely close with Charlie and Elliot, and they will know everything there is to know and would never let him struggle with the weight of it.

"I'll pop out sometime. Maybe we could go down to Rosestone, see Glen and Frey."

Rosestone. Elliot's parents' estate and the neighbouring estate to Lowerwick. The only reason Charlie would suggest that is because Mason would never contemplate coming home. "I'd love that," I tell him, knowing he's being genuine and will want to come out and see us.

"Scar, I want a picture of you, please."

Spinning around in my seat, I eye my brother as if he's grown three heads. "You want a picture of me?"

"Is that okay?"

I frown, sliding off the stool. "I guess so."

Elliot grins at me as I follow Mason out of the room and over to the entrance, where the matte-black tile wall works as the perfect backdrop.

My heels tap against the floor as I approach the wall, and as I turn, I hear my brother's camera clicking off. "I'm not ready. Wait!"

"I'm trying to get some candid shots."

"Bullshit, they're blurry as shit, aren't they?"

He chuckles, and I roll my eyes. The shutter goes off again. "Mase!"

"Here." Charlie takes the phone from Mase and pushes him toward me. "Go stand with your sister."

Mason joins me by the wall and wraps an arm proudly around my waist. We smile and laugh, and something special seems to happen in the brief moment. One of those memories so small and unplanned that I'll remember it forever.

"Thank you for this evening," I say, looking up at him.

He glances down at me. "Thank you for coming." Leaning in, he kisses my forehead. "I'll do better, yeah?"

I smile, not trusting a nod.

"Aldridge, get in here," Mason tells him.

Charlie swaps with Mason, and we have a picture. Then Elliot insists he can't be left out. And then Lance strolls around the corner, his black tux, with a crisp white shirt and braces stretching over his strong chest, making me want to run a mile.

"Lance," Charlie says. "You'd better get over there too."

God, no. *Charlie Aldridge, I will murder you!*

At first, I don't think he'll do it—he's not even spoken to me yet—but then something sparks in his eyes as he watches me.

His feet set off toward me.

I swallow, my body burning as his arm brushes my shoulder. I probably look stiff and uncomfortable, but I can't even think straight to correct the expression on my face. I glance up at him, catching a glare directed at me. A hard, pained look marring his already harsh face. But still, he slips his arm behind my back, his fingers splaying across my dress and flexing into my hip as we both turn toward Charlie.

His touch so soft compared to the story his face tells.

The shutter goes off, and my eyes widen. I didn't smile.

"You miserable fuckers," Elliot quips, walking from the entrance and back into the entertainment room.

"Smile, sunshine. You can't hate me that much…" Lance leans in a little closer, his lips dusting my ear and making my head curl in toward him. "Considering you wore the dress I picked out for my bitching *wife*."

I suck in a rush of air.

I'm mortified. This is mortifying. I knew he'd be at the gala. Not at my brother's now, but I was well aware he would be at the event and would see me in the dress.

"I wore it for myself, not you," I confirm.

"That's exactly what I told myself this afternoon as I lubed up my cock and tried to attach the fake dick you bought for me—we'll both pretend it's the truth."

I snap my head up to look at him. "You tried it?" I shake my head. "Wait, it didn't work?"

His lip twitches, but it doesn't transform into anything more. A painful mask slips back into place as our eyes lock. "Something like that."

I want to peel the mask off and see what's underneath. See the smile that lurks—

"Think I got the shot… among other things." Charlie's voice pulls me out of the moment, and I step away, noticing it's only the three of us in the foyer. "He's getting a drink."

The fact Charlie feels the need to reassure me that my brother didn't witness whatever that was, sets alarm bells ringing in my mind.

My face burns and I open my mouth to explain, but explain what?

"Scar, it's good. You're all good," Charlie tells me, stepping forward and passing Lance Mason's phone.

I frown and stand like a lemon as Charlie leaves the room. Lance starts doing something on Mason's phone, and curiosity gets the better of me. "What are you doing?"

I peer over his arm and watch as he goes to the deleted

images and erases the first picture, a picture of us that I can barely make out.

Good. I don't ever need to see that scene played out again.

He locks the phone and hands it to me, walking off in the direction of the kitchen. "You look good, wife."

FIVE

Scarlet

Mason took my hand and guided me quickly into the gala when we arrived, not stopping to speak to anyone and refusing to stop for pictures. I'm sure it's because he wants to protect me in some kind of big brother way, but I can't help but feel a pang of sadness as we pass the long lenses of cameras and step into the event. All of the photos of Mum and Dad at the Hamilton Gala were taken by the photographers outside, and I won't get one like that for myself tonight. Maybe it's why Mason had us take photos at home.

"Stay close tonight," he says, leaning down and muttering into my ear.

I squeeze his hand and give him a pointed look.

"Behave, and I'll let you go." He smiles.

I'd never admit it to him, but having Mason by my side and not wanting to let me go makes something deep inside of me soar. It makes me believe he cares about me.

"Piss off, Mase—"

I get a nudge in the back from Charlie, cutting off what I was about to say. "Scarlet Lowell? Are my eyes deceiving me?"

I plaster on a smile as I turn to face the gentleman nearing, who quite clearly knows who I am.

Mason leans in again before he can reach us. "Old man Hemmings and his son Cooper. Both cunts."

"Mase! You can't—"

"I can." He looks down at me, his face stony compared to the softer guy I had by my side moments ago. "Trust me. I can."

"Mr Hemmings, a pleasure to meet you… again." I look at Mason, hoping I've run into the older man in the past and I'm not talking completely out of my ass.

"Please, call me Rupert. And what a treat to have you in attendance this evening. You're well?"

"Very."

"And your father? How is Anthony Lowell these days? He didn't feel like showing his face tonight, no?"

"No, he isn't a hundred per cent at the moment." Mason's hand grows tighter in mine. "But you already knew that, right?"

"I… uh… well, yes, but—"

"I appreciate your concern, Mr Hummings. I'll send your regards."

"Ouch." I eye the tall man standing beside Mr Hemmings. Cooper, I believe Mason said his name is. He's currently smiling at me as if he knows my dirtiest fantasies, his eyes roaming me.

Elliot leans in, his shoulder blocking my body from view. "You'll be smiling with a giant black hole if you even look at her again tonight. Fuck off."

Cooper scoffs at Elliot, his lip curling. "So polite. Seriously, how do you get invited with such professionalism?"

"The fact you need to ask that question shows just how clueless you really are, *Coop*," Elliot snarls.

"Rupert." Mason nods farewell as he leads me away and through a door to our left.

"Hummings." Elliot chuckles at my back. He leans in and kisses my cheek. "Fuck, I've missed you, Scar."

We're greeted at the door with glasses of champagne, and as we make our way through the room, we're approached by more servers carrying canapés. Mason refuses to let go of my hand even when we're inside the event and only releases me when we're seated at our table for the meal.

I'm sat between Mason and Charlie, then Elliot is to Charlie's left and Lance beside him. There are four other seats at our table, but they've yet to be occupied.

"Malcolm, how are you?" Mason stands and puts his hand out to the gentleman approaching the table. "Mrs Jefferys."

Malcolm and Mrs Jefferys? I snap my eyes to Lance, but he doesn't meet my gaze, his face as stern as it was in the penthouse. What's his problem tonight?

"I wasn't sure you'd show, Mason," the gentleman says, making Mason's brows meet in the middle.

"Sorry?"

Lance clears his throat and places his tumbler on the table. "I can assure you, Malcolm, what happened today is a rarity at Ellis and Frey. You'll accept my deepest apologies for the miscommunication, and rest assured it won't happen again. The meeting has been rescheduled."

"Why was it cancelled?" Mason questions, his voicc as firm as Lance's.

I watch on as Lance works his jaw, and I know my name is right there, sliding across his tongue. "Something came up."

"Something more important than the meeting?"

My brother's pissed, and I know I have to say something.

"Mase, I—"

"Yes. It was more important."

It was? Why does that make my stomach flip?

Reiterating my earlier thoughts that Mason trusts Lance, he nods, losing all annoyance from his features. "Right, then. I'm sorry, Malcolm. Like Lance said, it won't happen again."

"Let's hope it doesn't. Shall we sit?"

I blow out a harsh breath and relax back into the seat as Mason, Malcolm, and Mrs Jefferys take their places at the table. Charlie leans into my space and whispers into my ear, "Scarlet Lowell, I can smell a rat from a mile away."

I suck my lips into my mouth and turn toward him. "I don't know what you're talking about."

We're both wearing knowing smiles, and it's impossible to hide.

"Be fucking careful, you little shit. You'll send your brother bald."

I glance around the ballroom, hating how he can see through me so easily. "For a smart man, you sure like talking in riddles, Charles."

"Lance didn't cancel that meeting. Want to know how I know that?"

"Nope. Couldn't care less."

"I was scheduled in."

I turn to look at him again as I butter my bread roll.

"You think Mason would sign anything without having me check over it first? Harry called me to cancel, said you'd been in."

"I—"

"Be. Fucking. Careful."

"I—"

"I trust him. I trust you—"

"Nothing has—"

"And I'm here. Always."

"Charlie, whatever you think you know, you're wrong."

"Okay, but hear me. You know we're all here, yes?"

I nod my head and take a sip of my drink, feeling guilty when I know I have nothing to feel guilty about. Lance did exactly what Mason asked him to do today. Remove the conversation at the penthouse about penis extenders and wife duties, and there's nothing I wouldn't share with my brother about the day.

I lift my eyes, and they lock on Lance's.

Deep, dark, needy and on me.

Needy for what? I don't know. But they call to me. They make me doubt everything in my head. Because there's not a soul on earth that I'd want to let see the inner reaction I get whenever those eyes catch me.

I lean into Charlie. "Why is he always so angry?"

"Who?" he asks, baiting me.

"Mason's friend. Lance, isn't it?"

He chuckles under his breath and peers across at his friend. Lance glares hard back at him before looking toward the bar.

"It's none of my business."

"But you trust him."

"I do."

"And you know why he's always angry? Even if you won't tell me."

"Lance isn't angry. He's careful. Calculated. Maybe more than any of us. He has good reason to be wary and doesn't want the fake that's thrown around the room at events like this. And what's a smile if it isn't real?" He shrugs.

"Umm, manners?"

"Scarlet, if it's manners you're looking for, you've been cancelling the wrong business meetings."

"Charles." I slap his arm.

He laughs and bumps his knee against mine. "I'm messing with you. He took the fall for you just now. I don't think you realise what it would have taken out of his ego to do that. That's about all the manners you'll get from the guy, and it would've been out of respect to your brother, no doubt."

"I didn't ask him to lie."

"Exactly. Reiterates the kind of man he is, wouldn't you say?"

Lance didn't have to take the fall for me cancelling the meeting, and I don't know why he did, but I am thankful.

I also don't fully believe he did it for my brother.

Our food is served, and I sit quietly for the remainder of the meal, only speaking when someone asks me a question.

When I see Mason locked in a conversation with Malcolm, I take it as my chance to slip away from him and our group, needing a minute alone. As I pull my chair back, all four sets of eyes land on me.

This is ridiculous. "I'm going to the toilet."

Mason looks back to Malcolm and then goes to stand.

"I'll go," Lance speaks up, placing down his tumbler as he leisurely rises from his chair. "I need to speak with Jake."

"I can take myself to the toilet, thank you."

Charlie lets out a "hmm" at my side, and I give him a death stare in return.

"Go with her," Mason says to Lance.

I roll my eyes and walk away, but I'm pulled back by my hand. Mase looks up at me as he leans back in his chair. "You told me to *deal* however I need to. Well, this is part of it. I want someone with you tonight."

My face softens, and I nod in understanding. My brother hasn't ever been this protective of me, but I guess I've never been anywhere like this with him before either. I'm not in anyone's way out at the estate.

I link my arm in Lance's when he holds it out to me, and we walk through the ballroom.

"Do you go to all work events with my brother?" I ask, sighing as the smell of him washes over me. It's all man, but it's not natural. Soap maybe? I need to know what he uses.

"The ones I want to go to."

"You're close with him."

"I am." He side-eyes me. "But that wasn't a question."

"He took you to the lodge. Our place in Bora Bora."

"And that's monumental because?"

"It just is." I look up at him and find his eyes scanning

the bar area. I'm not tall enough to see what has his attention, but a part of me wants it to be me. "You're in a mood tonight. What's wrong?"

"Nothing that concerns you," he murmurs nonchalantly as if this is the most uninteresting conversation he's ever had.

"But there's something?"

He releases my arm and points to a corridor that leads off to the side of the room. "Toilets are down there. I'll wait here."

When he looks down at me, his face hard and tense, I frown.

"Down there," he repeats.

Our gazes are tied, but I choose to step back.

I use the bathroom and top up my lips in the mirror, taking a little longer than Lance will likely appreciate.

He's barely said a word throughout dinner, and I found myself constantly watching him as the conversation got lost to business. He didn't look at me once, and he didn't smile. Not at anyone. He came into the boutique mad and frustrated today, but he still had something about him. A genuine amusement lurking below all that *man*. It made me feel like I could go right back at him. Toe to toe. But not right now. Right now, he's caught up in something else, pissed off at the world.

I can't help but care.

When I leave the restroom, I find him leaning against the wall on his phone. His brow is pulled low, and his eyes are closed as he listens.

"Lance," I say, and he lifts his head up, opening his eyes to look at me. "I want to dance."

He drops the phone from his ear, not hanging up. "Then go dance."

"I need someone." I give him a coy smile. "Will you be my guy tonight? My wingman?"

"*Wingman?*" He lifts the phone again. "I'll call you back." Once the phone is nestled in his trouser pocket, he steps toward me, the air getting thinner the closer he gets. "You're on the prowl tonight? Does Mason know that?"

"On the prowl?" I question with a snigger. "No. Definitely not on the prowl. There isn't a man in this room who interests me enough to engage."

"Then why do you need a wingman?"

"Okay, fine. Lance, will you come dance with me so that I don't look lame dancing on my own?"

"Mason will dance with you."

"I want you." *To smile. To tell me I'm being a raving bitch or look at me as if you want to eat me alive like you did in the changing room today.*

"Don't say that." His jaw flexes as his nostrils flare.

"What?"

"You're far from innocent, Lowell, so don't try fucking with me. I heard that filthy mouth at work this afternoon."

"You don't want to dance with me?"

His face is like stone, a waging war he's fighting with himself.

"I'll dance with you, darling." My neck twists, angling up to see the guy at my back.

Cooper Hemmings.

"Uh—"

"Go for it," Lance says, cutting me off, and I whip around to face him. "I've got to get out of here anyway."

He throws me a look full of pity, and I get a sad sinking feeling in my gut. A stupid, childish disappointment.

"Shall we?" Cooper asks, holding out his hand.

Lance doesn't break our trance, and I don't want to either. It's as if he's challenging me, but I don't understand what he wants.

"I'll see you, then," I tell him, leaning in and pretending to kiss his cheek. Instead, I whisper in his ear. "Your anger's wasted," I say quickly. "Whoever hurt you—made you feel this way tonight, can they feel it right now? Are they here in this room, or are they just in here?" I tap his temple. "Don't lose today to pissed-off yesterdays."

His eyes narrow, but I'm already standing back beside Cooper. I place my arm in his and head toward the dance floor, walking around the outside of the crowd to avoid my brother.

Maybe my opinion is unwelcome, probably irrelevant even, and I can understand if it is. It's not like I've faced hardship in life or know what Lance is dealing with. Other than losing my mother before I could learn what her face truly looked like when she laughed, I've lived a sheltered life.

I've been lucky.

"You've never been to one of these events. Why?" Cooper asks, taking my hand as his arm bands around my back. I slip my hand over his shoulder and move with him.

"I like to be at home with my dad. He doesn't need a carer or anything, but I don't like to leave him."

Cooper nods. "So, this is a one-off? A special occasion."

"It was my birthday yesterday. Mason wanted to bring me. My parents used to attend the gala together."

"Ah, of course. We're cut from the same cloth, me and

you, Scarlet. My parents own Foundation Works Limited. Your father's company is one of my biggest competitors."

"My brother's company," I correct him.

"Of course. *Mase.*"

The way he says his name makes the hairs at the base of my neck stand on end.

"FWL is a sinking ship. Stay the hell away from it, Anthony. Corrupt—the lot of them."

"Come on, Glen. He has kids."

"You'll never see a penny of it back. I don't believe a word out of his mouth after the Track Moore fiasco. He isn't being honest with you."

I remember the conversation between Dad and Glen. Glen was so mad at Dad but stood by him when he'd decided to help the family. I wonder if Glen was right. Mason and Elliot definitely don't hold any respect for the family.

"The hell do you think you're doing?" Mason's voice is a gravelly growl at my back, and I drop my shoulders as he pulls me away and behind him. A human shield I never asked for. "You stay the hell away from my sister."

"She wanted to dance, and besides, you seemed too busy selling the unsellable."

"You sound like a dumb fuck. Do you even look at the market, or do you just take the money Daddy gives you and skip off into dreamland?"

Cooper's chest grows as he steps up to Mason, but Mason just shakes his head, laughing at him. "Fucking clown." He looks over his shoulder at me and then beyond, his eyes catching on to something or someone before he nods his head once. He shifts to look down at me. "Don't get into any more trouble, or I'll be taking you home." He says it with a smile, but I know he means it. It was probably a bad idea to accept a dance with Cooper, but it beat the hell out of asking the three men everyone knows are like brothers to me.

I turn to go back to our table but get caught on the spot.

Lance's eyes roam me so leisurely it makes my pulse jump beneath my heated skin. He saunters the last three steps to me, placing a strong hand around my waist without permission, that core-melting scent making my body loosen as he pulls me close to his. His mouth dusts my neck, and I close my eyes, unsure how I should take him and his forwardness.

"I thought you were leaving?" I ask.

"I was."

My lip curls and I let my arms glide up to his shoulders, bringing us closer than we probably should be.

When he speaks again, it's quieter, less him and a little vulnerable. "Sometimes the anger tastes so bitter, it feels impossible to let go of."

My eyes drift closed, and a soft smile eases across my lips. "That's because we're not supposed to let it go." He pulls back a little, his green eyes homing in on mine, desperate for something… more? I go a little deeper. "We learn to accept that people make shitty decisions, Lance, and that they're not ours."

His face turns stony, anger pulling him back into whatever headspace he's trying to escape. "What if it's not something you can just accept and drop? What if it's family?"

"You're delusional, Mum, you know that? Fucking delusional."

I look across the dance floor to where Mason is sitting at

the table. "Then we carry as much as our hands can hold. And we don't feel guilty about anything that spills over."

"Mason loves you," he reassures me, and my eyes pull back to him.

"I know that. It doesn't make it any easier to accept the fact that I remind him and hold an attachment to some of his most painful memories. When he doesn't show up, when he doesn't call or answer my texts, I choose to remind myself that it's his decision. That's not on me, it's not because of me, and there's nothing I can do to change his mind—not in the moment, at least."

"You don't get angry?"

I smile up at him and shake my head. "No, I don't. I let that sad, sinking feeling settle, just long enough to appreciate that I still love him enough to allow him to hurt me, and then I carry on. Just with a heavier handful."

"You're not wired up right, Lowell. A little anger is good—necessary."

"Maybe I'm just lucky. Maybe I've never truly experienced *this*." I gesture toward him as if he's a big angry hulk of a man. "I've happily flown under the radar in my little bubble."

"You think you're flying under the radar." He sniggers. "Everyone took notice when you walked in here tonight. They're taking notice now, too."

I shrug, my cheeks flaming a little beneath my makeup. "Is that why you came and danced with me, wanted to be seen with the *it girl* of the party?"

"It girl?" He laughs freely, throwing his head back, and I inhale it, focusing on him intently in the hope I'll remember the moment.

"You're a terrible wingman. Everyone's staring now because you're making a scene."

His laughing smile eases but remains full, as if he can't control it. "Nah, I told you." He flexes his fingers against the dip in my back, and I suck in a breath that he without doubt catches. "They were already staring."

I try to hide my grin and look at his chest. "What happened between 'I've got to get out of here' and *this*, anyway? What brought you back in here?"

"Why is '*this*' getting deeper and deeper every time you say it?" He smirks down at me, and I loosen my hold on his shoulders.

"Are you going to answer all my questions with one of your own?"

"Will you answer my question?"

I think about it. "I don't know why." I shrug. "I like it deep."

My eyes shoot wide, and I freeze. "Oh, fucknuts, I didn't mean deep, like fully penetrated depth. I meant deep, like getting a feel of those inside inner bits that people don't tend to share with strangers."

My brows pull in, and I shake my head as I backtrack. "But not sexually. Like sharing emotions and shit."

"Emotions and shit?"

"Yeah." Goddammit.

"All right. I think I understand."

I need a drink.

The strongest shot they have.

"Scarlet?" he whispers, his lips ghosting my ear, the smooth pouty skin stretching as he smiles. "I like it deep, too. Really fucking deep."

I nod, completely rattled. "Deep is good—important."

"Agreed. I'm glad I found a wife who isn't afraid to demand a little more…."

"Depth?"

"I was going to say emotion."

Crap.

"I'm curious, how much depth my wife can take, though?" *Did he just?* "Is she going to stop me when I make her cry? Will she take more when it's been a long hard day and I need to off-load?"

He spins us and pulls me back against him. I swear I feel something harden.

I will myself to regain some of the composure I lost down the metaphoric rabbit hole and go for my own strike while he's least expecting it. "If she does start to cry, she'd probably like it if you covered her mouth and went a little harder. She'd want you to off-load everything you have."

He eases back and drops his gaze.

I shocked him.

"I mean, I can't know for sure," I clarify.

One dark brow lifts, and I relax a little. "You can't?"

"I'm not your wife."

"Right," he tuts. "I forget."

Who knew I'd be quoting the smut I read in private tonight? I knew those books would end up good for something.

"But if you were…."

"Your wife?" I frown, coming back to the now.

He nods.

"Hmm… I don't know, Lance. I'm *very* deep."

"Like… balls deep?" He bites his lip around a full smile,

and I throw my head back as we both burst out laughing. I don't try to savour this one. Something in my gut tells me it won't be the last I get from him.

"This is the most ridiculous conversation I've ever had," I tell him, feeling a little more at ease with him than I have all day.

"I'll admit that you're not a complete drag, Lowell. You've surprised me."

"It was my only mission," I say sarcastically.

"Yeah? My *it* girl," he says, looking down his nose at me with pursed lips, a cheeky look on his face.

"Now that's *deep*."

"Scarlet." Charlie slips up behind me and hands me my phone. I step away from Lance's embrace, pulling up the missed calls and messages right away. "Sorry, I knew you'd want to take it."

They're from our private doctor.

> Dr Sarnmer: Hello, Scarlet. Your father called me out to the estate tonight. He refused to have you contacted, but I'm unable to secure a nurse for the night. It's best he isn't alone. Please call if you have any concerns.

"Crap, I have to go."

"Where?" Lance asks.

"Home."

"Is Anthony okay?"

I look at Charlie and smile, not bothering with the lie.

"Scarlet—" Lance tries.

"I'll get Vin to bring the car around," Charlie says.

"Scarlet," Lance repeats, picking up my hand. He wets

his bottom lip and looks from the exit and back to me. "Don't leave yet."

Something warms in my chest. "I have to."

He fiddles with my rings, his hand heavy in mine. Then, as if it's a habit, his fingers twist, and he slowly traces his thumb around the cuticle on my thumbnail.

My breath hitches as shivers snake down my spine.

I look up at him as realisation hits.

It was him.

In the lift.

Lance held my hand?

"You can't stay?" His brows drag together, and I swallow, a little overwhelmed by the memory of darkness.

Twenty-eight years old, and I'm terrified of the dark. I smile at the beautiful, chequered tiles beneath our feet, knowing it's time to leave and go home. "Be happy, Lance," I tell him, finally finding a smile. "It's what your *wife* wants for you." I go up on my tippy-toes and whisper in his ear, "She'll find great pleasure in *that*."

I leave the gala alone. Because home isn't a place my brother can face right now, and Lance Sullivan isn't someone I can hold in my hands.

Not when everything else feels like it's spilling over.

SIX

Scarlet

One Year Later

"Mason will be here for your dinner this evening." My dad's voice floats into the spare room as he walks past the door. I quickly rise from my spot on the ground and rush after him. He's slow, likely in pain, so I catch him as he approaches the landing.

"Dad, wait! Did you say Mase is coming over?" Something deep inside of me baulks at my wishful thinking. I frown, dropping the paintbrush I'm holding up to my side. "I misheard you, sorry. What did you say?"

His lip curls as he braces his thinning frame on the banister. "I can't tell if you're being sarcastic, but no, you didn't mishear me. Your brother will be joining us for dinner, along with the Montgomerys and Charlie."

"Shit," I say in disbelief. "Is he feeling okay?"

Dad chuckles, shaking his head and then cringing as he

turns and walks further down the hall toward the east wing. "In all fairness, I thought the same."

I quickly catch up with him, linking our arms to give him a subtle aid. "So you didn't have to beg him?"

"I didn't. I told him you were cooking and asked if he wanted to invite anyone other than the boys."

"You didn't give him the option." Sneaky, I like it. "So he only went along with it because it's my birthday tomorrow, and he didn't want to feel guilty."

"He's coming. Let's make the most of it, hmm?"

I smile up at him, grateful that he's bothered to invite the family over when he's likely feeling rotten. "I'm going to drive down to the village. Get some more bits for dinner. Are you okay here while I'm out?"

"I'm fine. I have a headache and will likely take a nap."

He eases into the chair beside his bed as I watch on from the doorway, my heart hurting to see him fading away from what he once was. "And Scarlet, I'll be down to help you cook. Or you can call in someone to help you. Robert and —"

"I'll be fine, Dad. You know I love it."

He nods. Just nods as if he doesn't have the energy to argue with me.

The past year has been hard—maybe the hardest yet. He's had constant appointments at the hospital while doctors and specialists try to figure out what can be done to make him better, but every option so far has had side effects that seem to trigger something new—occasionally worse. His body's failing him; it's heartbreakingly obvious. It's not just his organs giving up. It's his spirit. That shine for life that keeps us on this side of the track, it's fading.

And I'm terrified that soon it'll fade to complete darkness.

"Get some rest, Dad. I'll be back soon."

I spent the entire afternoon in the kitchen preparing my brother's favourite food. I've made side dishes and dessert and took nearly an hour in the wine cellar, picking out some of our favourite labels for the evening. Everything will be perfect when Mason arrives.

Charlie arrived before anyone else and tried to meddle in my kitchen, but I quickly sent him on his way and out onto the terrace with Dad.

Cooking is therapeutic for me, but I rarely get the opportunity to entertain. I would like to think I'm good at it, considering I cooked for my brother and dad from the age of fourteen, and neither has ever complained. Or died.

I'm taking the roasted potatoes out of the oven when I hear the front door ease open at the entrance of the house. Freya's voice, like a song, drifts through the house a moment later. I place the tray on the kitchen island and follow the sound.

"Scarlet, darling, you look beautiful. Look at you!"

I rush forward and hug her, smiling over her shoulder at Glen. "I'm covered in flour, and God knows what else. What are you seeing?"

"I know what I'm seeing, young lady."

When Frey eventually lets go of me, Glen leans in and kisses my cheek, handing me a bottle of wine as he steps back. "I presume he's outside."

I nod. "With Charles. Is Elliot on his way?" I ask,

looking behind them. I wondered if he'd walk over with his parents, but I'm sure, like Mason, he had work today and will hopefully be here soon.

"He's on his way. Got caught up at the office, I believe."

"Did you know Mason is coming tonight?" I tell Frey, pulling on her arm so that she follows me into the kitchen.

"No?" she snaps, wide eyes as her smile spreads. "Well, knock me over with a feather."

I chuckle and start to flip the potatoes in the tray. "You're not alone. I was sure he'd stand us up, but when I texted him the details and told him he had to be here for seven, he texted back and said he'd be here."

"That's wonderful, Scar. How perfect for your birthday. I'm happy for you." She leans in, a nostalgic glee on her face as she lifts my chin so that I'm looking at her. "I've missed that smile these past few months. I worry, but you prove me wrong time and time again. You're an incredible young lady. So strong. Your mother would be unbelievably proud of the woman you're becoming."

"Frey." I gently twist my head to the side and out of her grasp, my eyes glazing.

"What can I do to help?" she says, knowing I will appreciate the change of direction.

I hand her the bottle Glen passed to me when he walked in and give her a soft smile as I blink away the mist in my eyes. "Open this."

I'm running behind. Everyone's here bar my brother—no surprise, and I'm not ready. Rushing down the stairs in my pale-blue midi dress, I contemplate for the third time if it's a little risqué for dinner on the terrace. With not enough time to worry, I pull on my black boots one by one and hop across to the kitchen. I pick up a tray of canapés and make my way out onto the terrace.

Just as I breach the threshold to the back doors, I walk into a solid wall of muscle, and the tray goes flying.

"Fucking great shitballs!" I shriek as the canapés fall to the floor with a clatter. I look up at my brother, and my shoulders drop. "Mase! Why are you storming through the door like that? Look what you've done!"

His head rears back defensively. "Me? It's not my fault; you had the damn thing in front of your face."

I tut and shake my head, my lip twisting up at the side. "Always my fault." I pull him in for a hug. "It's good to see you, big brother."

Bar the two times I've had to call him out in the night to help me, it's been months since I've seen him. And even then, it was nothing more than him standing on the front terrace, telling me it was not fair to me and that I shouldn't have to babysit our father through his addiction. Sometimes I feel like punching him in the face and reminding him that he could help me. He could make it easier for me.

"Hello."

I snap out of my head and pull back, turning toward the female voice. I blink twice, finding the most beautiful brunette staring back at me. "Hello." I shake my head, realising I'm staring. "I'm sorry, who are you?"

"This is Nina," Mason replies with a broad smile.

"This is Nina," I recite, still smiling as I look between them. "And Nina is…"

"My girlfriend."

"The what the what? Girlfriend?" I laugh weirdly. "That's a first." Another gargled laugh awkwardly falls from my mouth, and I pray someone takes me out. Assassinate me, please. "Well, it's lovely to meet you. I'm sorry my brother caught me off guard. He didn't tell me you were coming."

"It's fine!" Nina waves me off, bending to pick up the canapés. "Do you need a hand? I can help you with these."

I drop to my knees with her and start to scrape up the mess on the tiles.

"You don't have to do that, Nina," Mason tells her.

She shrugs him off, and I hide my smirk. "It's fine. Two sets of hands will get it done twice as fast."

Never in a million years did I expect Mason to bring a woman to the house.

"My name's Scarlet, but you can call me Scar." I extend my hand to her but quickly realise that it's covered in the mini crab cakes I was carrying.

"It's lovely to meet you," she says, laughing with me when I retract my dirty hand.

"My brother hasn't told you anything about me, though, I presume." I look up at Mason, and he gives me a guilty look.

"I brought her to meet *you*, Scar."

To meet me. The way he emphasises the word—and for whose benefit? Does he think it will make me happy to hear he comes here for me and not our dad? He has no idea how much he hurts the people closest to him sometimes. "Dad's been struggling," I tell him, going back on my word to get him in the door before I go in on him with the family crap.

And I'm met with silence. Awkward, sad silence.

I lower my eyes to the ground and sigh. "I'm going to get some more champagne," I say without thought.

We don't even have champagne.

Mason gestures for Nina to walk in front of him, but she doesn't budge. She looks up at Mason with a thoughtful look. "It's okay, you go. I'm going to help your sister."

I watch as he whispers into her ear, "You don't need to."

Nina turns, kissing the side of his mouth. "I want to."

He watches us go, not moving from the doorway as we wander off down the hall.

"I think we just removed his shield," I whisper, quiet enough for him not to hear.

Nina gives me a subtle nod as she looks over her shoulder one last time before entering the kitchen.

"Would you like a drink?"

"I'd love one, thank you," she says, sliding onto a stool at the island as she surveys the kitchen. "Your home is beautiful."

I turn, wine bottle grasped in my hand. "Thanks. As you can see, it needs some TLC. I've barely managed to scratch the surface over the years, but I'm getting there."

She looks at me, slightly confused, and I wonder how much my brother has told her about us. "You wouldn't get someone in to do the work for you? I'm sure Mase would know someone. It's real estate your family is in, right?"

"My dad and Mase, not me. I wouldn't know where to start with the '*family*' business, and have you seen Mason's place? I'd never let his minions loose in here." I grin at her, hoping she doesn't think I'm horrible. "And I kind of love doing it myself; it's rewarding to finish one room and then pick the next."

I ease around the kitchen, collecting a second wineglass and opening a bottle of wine.

"I love that. I'm completely awful at all things DIY." Nina laughs, and it makes me smile. "Would Mase not come and help you at least?"

So he's told her nothing. "Oh boy, you're in for a ride. He doesn't come here. Not unless he *has* to."

"Like when your dad is having a bad day?" She gives me a tight smile, and I tilt my head, wondering if maybe she does know and was being polite before.

"Exactly." I slump down into the chair next to her, filling both glasses with wine. I think back to the last time Mase came out here just weeks ago when Dad was sick. "He told you about that?" I ask, my eyebrows dipping into a frown.

"Yeah, I mean, not all that willingly"—she takes a small sip—"but it came up."

It's hard to think about Mason being able to talk openly with someone so new in his life when it's all I've ever asked for. But I also know that this is good. The fact he is here, with Nina, and she knows things. It's a step. "Mason had our parents for three years more than me, and I think he remembers a lot about Mum, whereas I only have the pictures."

"I'm so sorry, Scarlet."

"Please, call me Scar." I clink our glasses together, taking a large gulp from my glass. "How did you meet my brother?" I ask, hoping to lighten the mood.

"Ah, through Elliot and Charlie." Her lips pull up in a smile, cheeks reddening as she asks her next question. "Hey, do you know why Elliot would call me Pixie?"

I snort, choking on my wine as I seem to inhale instead

of exhaling at the wrong time. Wine starts to drip from my nose.

"Oh god, are you okay?" Nina grabs a napkin and hands it to me.

Did she say… "Sorry, did you say *Pixie?*"

"Yeah, since the first night I met Elliot, he's called me Pixie."

I hesitate, smiling beneath the napkin. God, those boys. You'd think they were five years old. "No, I'm afraid I don't know, Nina." I wipe the remnants from my chin as I shake my head.

"Wow, *Scar*. Are we really starting this friendship off on a lie?" Nina teases, reaching over to top up my glass with wine.

"Not my story." I shrug with a smile before changing the subject to anything else. "You know, it's nice to have a female around here. Some days I feel like saying screw it and finding myself a job." I pause as guilt catches me off guard. Such a throwaway comment. And yet the truth in it… "I just can't leave Dad right now."

"Have you ever worked?" she asks, her face pinched as if she feels guilty for asking, but it doesn't offend me.

"Nope, I feel like it's too late now. I'm twenty-nine tomorrow, and I feel like my time to study has run out."

Nina rears back. "Your birthday is tomorrow? And it's not too late to study! This is the prime of your life."

I chuckle at her enthusiasm and nod. "I wanted to be a doctor. Started studying medicine after college but dropped out when Dad got sick. I never really thought about going back," I say, my chest aching with the lie.

"You should absolutely go back. Surely Mason could

help you with your dad?" She pops her brows at me over the rim of her glass, but as if she thinks better of it, she drops the conversation. "What are your birthday plans?"

"Nothing really. Dad has an appointment at two, and I will need to drive him to that."

"What about tomorrow evening? Will you be out with your girlfriends?"

"You mean the snooty girls who haven't reached out since I left college?"

"Did you reach out?" she questions.

Crap. I shake my head sarcastically. "Just when I was starting to like you."

Nina's face lights up. "We are sooo going out!"

"Out? Out where?" My eyes bug out, but I wiggle on the chair, an excited ball of energy forming in my gut.

"Wherever you want. I have a morning class, but I could be here by twelve thirty. We could go anywhere."

Dad's appointment is at two, so I couldn't leave until at least five once we're home, and I'd have to get someone to be here for the night. Maybe Vinny. "What do you do?" I ask, feeling rude that I never asked.

"I have a dance studio in London."

My eyes widen a fraction. "That's amazing." I smile in awe before my shoulders drop. I can't imagine what it's like to be so independent. To have something of my own. Something *I* worked hard for.

"Scarlet, I don't want to impose."

I catch her intuitive, assessing gaze. "But you're about to anyway." I nudge her with my elbow, my lips twisting in a knowing smile.

"If there was a way to go back to med school, would you go?"

I snigger, my heart somersaulting. "I couldn't. My father doesn't have his health anymore. Mase doesn't get it."

"And neither do I, so ignore me. But you shouldn't put your life on hold for anybody else. Even if that person is your family."

She isn't wrong, and I've told myself the same thing over and over. I've just never felt ready to act on it. I eye Nina behind my wineglass, a slight smirk pulling at my lips. "Okay, it's official. I like you."

At first, I felt a little jealous that this woman came home with my brother tonight. As if bringing her here to meet us was the only reason he came at all. But now that I've met her, sat here and devoured half a bottle of wine with her, I'd be lying if I said she wasn't super cool. It's like catching up with an old friend. And the fact she's invited me out for my birthday tomorrow. I don't understand why she would want to. Why she'd even offer?

It isn't until Mason comes looking for her a little while later, the way he looks at her—at me, that I see how much Nina already means to him. How maybe he did only come to the house tonight because of her, but only because she made him believe he could.

SEVEN

Scarlet

"Happy birthday, Scarlet!"

I tear open the brown paper and smile down at the books in my lap. "Thank you, Dad."

"What time are you off today?" he asks, looking at me with the widest smile I've seen on his face in maybe years.

My brother came to dinner last night. Not only did he show up at the estate and stay for longer than five minutes, but he actually sat at our dinner table and ate with us.

He also brought home a woman.

It's groundbreaking.

"Vinny's picking me up at twelve, and I think Nina finishes at one."

"And you have no idea where you're going?"

I shake my head and place the books on the worktop. "Not a clue. I guess we'll go out?"

"No plan. I like it." He grins, giving me a glimpse of a youthful man I know isn't truly there anymore.

I chuckle to myself as he walks slowly to the sink. "Could be worse."

"Could be better," he replies, and I know he's smiling too.

"Mason will be here to pick you up for the hospital when I leave, and then Vinny will be here later this evening. I won't be out late."

"Don't rush back for me. It's your—"

"*Birthday, Scarlet. Go out and let your hair down.*"

He gives me a look over his shoulder, his eyes narrowing on me. "Have fun, okay."

"I will. I promise. And make sure you listen to what Dr Sarnmer says, please. I know what you're like, and Mason will likely zone out the second you get in the car."

"Why, thank you, sweet child. Kick a man while he's down."

"I'm kidding, Dad. Mason came to dinner, brought a woman home, and *then* offered to take you to your appointment. The Iceman is clearly melting."

"Iceman, I like it."

"Suits him, right?" I slip into the pantry and grab my gardening gloves. "Just make sure you take notes or have Dr Sarnmer email me the info after. I don't want to be left in the dark about anything, and if you need any prescriptions picked up—"

"I could ask the Iceman to get them?"

I step out of the pantry, a smirk lifting the corner of my mouth as I pull on my gloves. "Could be pushing it." I lean in and kiss his cheek. "Thanks for the books, Dad. Are you coming outside this morning? It's glorious."

"Maybe in a little while." He smiles.

"I'll hold you to it," I tell him, walking out of the kitchen and through the entrance to the front door.

Lance

"Sullivan, where the fuck are you?"

Sweat runs between the crease of my lips, and I swipe at it as I reach with my other hand to put my phone on loudspeaker. I have a meeting in a little under an hour, and I'm currently going hell for leather on my treadmill. It usually doesn't take me more than a five-minute shower and cup of coffee to get me out of the door in the mornings, but today, I have all the motivation to die on my gym floor.

"I'll be there," I tell Charles Aldridge, my best friend and lawyer.

"Now. I need you here now. Did you even read over the documents I sent last night? It's airtight, but the way you trust me to the point of signing shit you don't read disgusts me."

My meeting is with my mother, and I'm almost certain I know how it will go.

"I read it. I'll see you soon." I hang up and increase my speed, knowing I sound like a prick, but I also know I need to get rid of this shitty energy that's been hanging over my head since yesterday.

My entire life, I've only ever wanted to see my mum happy. Before Dad, after Dad, and even up until yesterday when she called me and told me she'd spent the entire month's rent on a puppy and that she needed more to cover the bills because they'd overspent.

I up my speed, gritting my teeth as I ignore the burn spreading through my hamstrings.

Vanessa Sullivan dreamt of having a daughter, so when I came along and crushed that dream, she very quickly conceived again and had Nessa Anne. Chloe came two years later and Molly eighteen months after that, and if my dad hadn't put his foot down and said no more, I'm certain she would never have stopped. For years I watched her eyes light up. Their first steps, words, ballet and swim classes, they had it all. Didn't want for anything.

Those girls were everything to her.

So, I took everything I could from our dad… until I lost that to them too.

To this day, they still don't want for anything. I made sure of it. I did everything I could for them. For her, for him.

My fist snaps out and connects with the emergency stop on the treadmill. I kick my feet out, standing on the edge as my forehead meets the screen. "I tried. I *fucking* tried."

But something's got to give.

"You greedy shit! You can't do this. You shouldn't even have control of my money!" My mother's eyes are filled with unshed tears, and I stare fixated at her, too afraid to blink. "Who do you think you are, Lance? Tell me because I'm at a loss for words standing here looking at you now."

"Mum. I only ever—"

She throws her arms out at her sides. "Do I not deserve any grace? After everything I went through."

"Mrs Sullivan, please sit down," Charlie tries.

"Oh, fuck off, you fancy-ass prick. You don't think I can

see through your expensive suit and flashy office? You forget this was my life once." She turns her eyes on me once again. "You forget that I'm the foundation of the very money you think you can monopolise."

Charlie clears his throat and stands from his chair. "The money he *can* monopolise. You signed a document that made it possible."

"Whilst grieving my dead husband!"

I shake my head and swallow in an attempt to douse the anger growing in my gut. "Mum, please. Listen to me—"

"No. You're not doing this. I'll take you to court."

"Vanessa," Charlie snaps. His voice holds a sharp edge that whips, a tail end rasping around to soothe before it can fully sting.

My mother's shoulders straighten.

"You're being unintentionally rude, and I ask that you take a second to calm down and listen to what *I* have to say, considering you cannot afford the same respect to your son. I understand this is difficult for you." She doesn't bother to look at me. Charlie walks to his desk and picks up the file, opening it and handing it to my mother. "This is your expenditure from the last twelve months. Every transaction in and out of the account—not counting the rent or bills Lance already pays for."

Her chin lifts. "And?"

Charlie's eyes drift to me as he fixes the knot in his tie. "You're out of touch. It takes a lot to shock me, Mrs Sullivan, but that number right there, considering your son is a very good friend of mine, and I happen to know how hard he works, is inexplicable and quite frankly disgraceful. Why don't you take a look at it yourself."

After a couple of seconds of staring Charlie down, she dips her head to read the numbers.

"We had an agreement," she defends.

"And now we'll make a new one," Charlie tells her.

"No... no, we agreed." She looks at me, panicked, a tear sliding down her cheek.

"The girls need this, Mum. You need it. A job will be good for you."

"Don't you dare tell me what's good for me," she spits, deep-rooted anger lacing her voice.

My nostrils flare. I push my hands into the pockets of my slacks and lift my chin. "I'll pay the mortgage and all the bills, but you'll pay for everything else. I'll give you six weeks to find a job. We'll help you look."

"What? I haven't worked since I had you, Lance. I can't—I can't do that. Please, Lance." She walks to me and places her warm hand on my face, smoothing her thumb over my cheekbone. "Please, son. Don't do this."

My heart thrashes, her gentle touch throwing me off. It would be so easy to wrap my arms around her and tell her I can do it; *I can make you happy. I can do what Dad would've wanted me to do and take care of you.*

I pull back from her reach, masking my contorted face with a hard frown. "I'm sorry, but I've made up my mind."

I watch as her lips bunch together, her eyes livid—no light in them. And then she slaps me.

"You're an embarrassment to this family. Your father would be appalled if he could see how you're behaving."

"Leave my office immediately before I call the police, Mrs Sullivan."

I hold my hand up to Charlie. "It's fine, Aldridge—"

"I'm leaving," my mother interjects. "We'll discuss this later. When you've calmed down and can see some sense."

My mother makes a brisk walk to the doors where Charlie is standing with her coat held out. "I'll have the new terms of agreement sent to your home to be looked over." She swipes the coat from his hands and quickly slips from the room.

I make my way to the sofa and sit down on the arm, running my hand through my hair for the hundredth time this morning.

"You're a saint, Sullivan, my friend. I don't know how you've just kept your mouth shut."

A bitter laugh slips past my lips as I look up. "It's been a long time coming."

"Agreed." He sighs. "Stick to your guns on this. They're rinsing you and don't give a shit about how it affects you."

I nod, knowing it's true. It just leaves a really bad fucking taste in my mouth.

"It was the right thing to do," he reiterates.

I stand, the need to bury myself in work fast becoming tunnel vision. I collect my jacket from the back of the visitor chair and stroll toward the door. "I won't make it out tonight. I've got some things to sort."

"Don't be a killjoy, it's Scar's birthday. You should be there with us. It's been a long time since she's been into the city."

A year. It's been a whole-ass year since I saw the little spitfire.

"I'm certain I won't be missed."

He watches me from his desk. "The two of you seemed

to enjoy each other's company the last time you ran into one another."

"It was the first time, and she proceeded to call me a pompous, egotistical fool among a string of other insults. Trust me, there's no love lost."

"You'll get your ass there, Sullivan. Those girls are another level when they get together, and Elliot will be… Elliot. Add Scarlet into the mix, and it's going to be a night. *And* we can celebrate the—" He lifts the sheet of paper from his desk and whistles. "Three-quarters of a million you'll save over the next year."

How did they blow through seven hundred and fifty grand in the last year? I give them enough for the bills and to keep the house. They have cars and their individual allowance, which is more than a fair amount. After seeing their bank accounts—which isn't something I ever believed I'd need to check—it makes my blood boil to think I fed into their bullshit pleas month after month.

"I'll see what I can do," I tell him, needing to get out of the office. "Thank you, Charles. I appreciate your time today."

I don't bother to look at my friend before leaving because I know his assessing eyes are already trying to read me. And I sure as shit don't want to be read.

Once out on the street, I contemplate the work I can get done when I get back to the office. I have a mountain of emails to get back to and a meeting with Ben to hopefully put to bed the unidentified payments that have been leaving the company's account. All perfect distractions from my mother.

Thinking of distractions, Scarlet Lowell quickly stomps

her way into my mind—and not for the first time this year either. Three times I almost reached out to her in weeks following the gala, and at Christmas, I went as far as looking up her address, thinking I could take a trip out to their home. To do what? Who fucking knows. I never went. But it's safe to say that my mother isn't the only one who's been living rent-fucking-free.

I pull out my phone and find the reel of images I have favourited on my camera roll, my feet coming to a stop on the pavement.

My teeth pull in my bottom lip, and I glance up and down the street, contemplating another option.

No, you dumb shit.

Work.

I need to work.

Scarlet

My stomach churns as we pull up to Nina's dance studio, but the nerves are short-lived as she eases over and pulls open the back door to the Audi.

"Hey, you!"

"Hey!" I say, reaching for the bouquet of flowers that are lying in the crevice of her arm.

"Thank you." She slides in next to me as Vinny shuts the door behind her, placing her bag on the floor at her feet. When she looks up at me, smoothing out her dark-brown ponytail, it's with the most perfect smile. "Happy birthday, Scarlet!"

"Thank you. And I told you it's Scar."

"Right, of course!"

Vinny leans into the back seat with a bottle of champagne and two flutes. "From your brother." He smiles, handing me a gift-wrapped box.

I look at Nina in shock. "Okay, you've taken my actual brother and replaced him with an impostor. Mason does not do gifts."

"He sent me those flowers this morning." She laughs, arching a brow at me as if she's challenging my words.

"Well, maybe there's hope for him yet. How do you do it? He just came to the house and took Dad to his appointment. That's twice in one week he's voluntarily come to Lowerwick."

Her face grows sly. "I may have used some really hot lingerie to persuade him last night."

"Oh, wow, too much information." I chuckle.

Her eyes widen a little. "Shit, sorry. I tend to have zero filter."

I nod, laughing as I say, "I gathered that when you told the entire dinner table that I wanted to go back to uni last night. You really threw me under the bus with that one."

The wine we'd consumed had made me a little loose-lipped during our conversation in the kitchen. I'd told Nina I wanted to go back to study medicine, and she seemed to see straight through my excuses when I told her I was happy waiting for Dad to get better.

She cringes, grasping my arm, her eyes genuine. "No, because I thought about that all night when we got home and into bed. I overstepped. It's not my place, and I'm so sorry for doing that, but Mason needs to help you. You should be able to study, Scar. I told him of it too."

I look into the rearview mirror and catch Vinny's eye.

He likes her too.

"I know, and I want to. I just don't know if now's the time." Which is the truth. If anything, it's harder now to find spare time than ever before. With Dad's appointments and health being that much worse.

"That's fair enough, but definitely don't write it off." She side-eyes me, her smile sly.

It's always been my dream to be a doctor. When Dad got sick, I had to leave university. It gutted me to quit. I lost my friends and my dream job. But being away sent Dad into one of the worst relapses I've ever witnessed.

Being alone is a trigger for him, and we're fortunate enough that he doesn't have to be alone. He has me.

"I won't," I promise.

She hands me the champagne flutes and starts to fill them. "Good! Now… are you excited to meet the girls?"

I don't know what I was expecting with "the girls," but it definitely wasn't Lucy and Megan.

The two girls live together. Lucy works in a dress shop designing custom-made outfits for some of London's richest socialites. And Megan is a columnist for a women's magazine.

"This. Is. Heaven," Lucy mutters, her words slightly muffled from her head being face down on the massage table.

"I've not had a massage in years," I tell her, my eyes glued to the paintbrush as it glides across my big toe. The therapist smiles at our bliss-filled conversation.

I was nervous about what we'd be doing when we arrived at my brother's penthouse to a sea of balloons—and what looked like an entire spa set up in the sitting room—but after a full-body massage and a couple of glasses of champagne, I couldn't have planned a better day for myself.

"Thank you, Mason Lowell," Megan hums in appreciation. "Nina, does being a stubborn fool and paying for your own treatments get you out of sexual favours? Or..."

"Piss off, bitch!" Nina tosses a discarded gel eye mask at her friend. It lands on the underside of her arm before dropping to the hardwood floor.

"Eww! Nina, no."

"Leave me alone then."

"You paid? I thought Mason was—"

"He is." Nina nods, rolling her lips as if she's embarrassed or uncomfortable. Both make me want to drop it. "I like to pay for things like this myself. He paid for everything else today. The food and decorations."

"Oh." I've never had to worry about money. I don't work, and yet I have thousands of pounds transferred into my bank monthly. The idea that Nina's financially independent seems like such a monumental thing to me. I nudge her arm. "There's something to be said for a woman who can do it alone."

"Exactly, and it feels more rewarding this way. I work hard to have days like this," she says as if trying to reassure herself.

"I work hard," Megan pipes up. Nina rolls her eyes. "I also have nice things *and* snap gazillionaires' hands off when they offer up spa days and all-you-can-eat catering. I don't even have to put a penis in my mouth. Work smart, not hard, girls."

"Megan," Nina warns.

I chuckle as Megan sits up from her massage bed. "You know I'm messing with you."

"Yeah, well, pick on someone a little less sensitive."

They all laugh between themselves, and I sit and watch them with a smile on my face.

"How was dinner last night?" Lucy asks Nina. "I mean, I know it was to meet the family and Scarlet is here, but any details we should know?"

"It was incredible. The house—" Nina turns to look at me. "Is it even a house? What do you call it?"

"I normally just say the estate, but I guess it's a manor house."

"You live on an estate?" Lucy rises from the bed, wrapping a towel around her chest. She thanks the masseuse and then hops down to grab one of the platters of food before getting back up to sit on the massage table.

"I do. You girls will have to come out and see it with Nina at some point. It could do with some new faces."

"It's out of this world, girls. Peaceful and full of life."

I huff out a laugh under my breath, knowing the girls won't catch it. It's not funny, not really. But it's a little ironic to me that Nina can spend a couple of hours at the estate and see everything I do, yet my brother, who was born and raised there, can't stand the thought of the place. He certainly wouldn't say that it was *full of life*.

"Do you have a title, Scar?" Lucy asks, her brows pulling together as she thinks on it.

"She's not a fucking royal, Luce." Megan snorts, shaking her head at her friend. "Lady Scarlet of Lowerwick."

"You're both idiots," Nina tells them, standing from the pedicure chair. She slips off into my brother's kitchen, returning moments later with a gift box. "Shall we open presents?"

I sit up a little straighter in the seat. "You didn't buy me a gift?"

"It's small. Much too small for the Lady of Lowerwick." She throws me a wink. "But we all pitched in, and we think you'll like what we got you."

I take the box as she hands it to me, my fingers running over the giant red bow. My throat catches. "You guys barely know me."

"How all the best friendships tend to start out," Megan tells me with a wink. "Open it already."

I pull off the bow and lift the lid.

"Oh my god!"

It's filled with gifts. Gift vouchers, lipsticks and glosses in various shades, face creams, miniature vodka bottles, textbooks—university textbooks.

"How did that get in there?" Nina proclaims, frowning over my shoulder. "Does it have a name? Who does it belong to?"

I open it up and chuckle when I see my name on the "this book belongs to" line. "Nina," I say in wonder, flicking over the next page. An envelope drops out into my lap. I pick it up and flip it over, pulling out the papers inside. "An application."

"Bachelor of medicine, bachelor of surgery MBBS."

Nina leans in closer. "I'm well and truly over the line. But this is just a little nudge. You don't have to fill it in."

"I want to." I look up at her with shining eyes, my mouth pulling up into a sad smile. "I want to go back to university so bad."

Nina looks at me with pity in her eyes. They all do.

"Enough of this, sorry," I tell them, placing the forms to my side and digging in the gift box for the vodka shots. There are at least ten. I throw one to each of the girls, and they catch them. "We go on three."

"Three is for the weak—and men. We go on one," Megan states.

"One…"

We went on one.

We were drunk by three.

And Lance Sullivan showed up at six.

EIGHT

Scarlet

I have no idea who is walking into my brother's penthouse when I run for the entrance, and the second my eyes land on Lance Sullivan, my heart plummets to my ass.

"Did someone say stripper?" Elliot Montgomery, Mason's best friend, business partner, and our nonbiological brother saunters around the entrance of the penthouse, pulling his shirt from his slacks as if he's about to put on a show.

"Me, I did," Lucy shrieks, jumping down from the sofa and throwing her hands in the air.

We've danced, sang, and drank for the past hour. I'm well and truly tipsy. It's not often that I drink, let alone with these girls. And now I'm standing here, not feeling myself fully as Elliot, Charlie, and Lance step into the living area… I regret nothing.

"Put your damn clothes on. I do not want to see that." I

go to slap Elliot's arm, but he pulls me to him, tucking me into his side.

"Happy birthday, Scar." He kisses my head.

"Thanks, Ell."

Charlie greets me next, giving me a tight hug. "Happy birthday."

"Hey." I close my eyes and squeeze him back.

Out of everyone, Charlie makes the most effort to stay in contact. I could count on my fingers the number of times I've heard from Mason in the last year. Elliot's always there for me but isn't the best suited of the group when it comes to needing someone to talk to. Charlie will call me every couple of weeks to make sure Dad and I don't need anything, and it keeps me in the loop with Mason.

He lets me go and gives me a wink before moving into the room to say hello to the girls.

As I turn my head back to the entrance, I lock eyes with the man I've not seen in an entire year. And he looks as devastating as he did that first day I met him in the elevator. His eyes are unforgiving, haunting me like they sometimes do in my sleep.

"Hi," I say, not knowing if I should lean in and hug him. "I wasn't expecting *you*."

He raises a thick, dark brow. "No?"

"It's been a whole year since I saw you last… I was considering getting us a marriage counsellor." I look to my feet and then back up at him, the slight twitch at the corner of his lips telling me he remembers that night.

Our stare-off continues for what seems like forever, and I wonder if I've actually spoken or if I imagined the whole interaction. But then my heart thrashes with a violent jolt as Lance removes his hands from his pockets, casually stepping toward me. His hair's cut shorter, but it's hot. *Too damn hot.* And I'm flustered, caught off guard by all the things I'd forgotten about him.

The firm grip of his hands coils around my waist as he leans in to kiss my cheek. My eyes drift closed as the smell of him takes me right back.

He smells like sin.

He smells like… fun.

"Baby Lowell," he drawls out, his lips ghosting my ear before he steps around me and into the living area.

I'd be lying if I said I hadn't thought about Lance over the past year. Just last night, I wondered if he would make an appearance at my home for dinner, but I guess my dad wouldn't know to invite him, and Mason isn't about to pull anyone else into that situation unnecessarily. To ask would've only made my brother and likely Charlie question me. I always wondered what it would be like if I saw him again. Would he be like he was when I first met him—cold and detached, or would he be like the man I had a glimpse of at the gala?

We end up migrating to my brother's entertainment room while we wait for him to get back from Dad's appointment, and the later it gets, the more my stomach starts to twist. I know Dad will be offered a transplant. It's been the talk of his last four appointments, and it's our only other option at this point—unless there's been some kind of miraculous improvement since last week.

I just hope he and Mason can talk. They'll never truly fix what's been broken, but I need them to at least try.

"Cocktails, girls! Scar, do you want one? Lance is our designated shaker," Megan tells me.

Elliot swipes his tongue through his cheek and laughs, clasping Lance on the shoulder. "I didn't know you could make them shake, mate?"

Lucy rolls her eyes and throws Lance the shaker. "She meant Chief Tosser."

Lance catches it, throwing a glare at Lucy. He's been in and out of the room all evening on his phone, and each time he comes back inside, he seems to get more and more miserable. Charlie said his sisters are usually the thorns in his side and to ignore him. Pretty easy when he refuses to even look at me.

He steps behind my brother's bar and starts to pick out multiple spirits and mixers.

I slide up onto the barstool and watch him. "You were a barman before you were an *asshole CFO*?" I say with a smile, curious if I can entice more than three words out of him.

His eyes lift to mine before they drop back to his task. "Something like that."

Tough crowd.

"You know, if you let me assume, I might end up making bogus assumptions that you might not like. Like, maybe you did work in a bar. Or maybe you were a butler to a woman who loves a good cosmo. Maybe cocktails are a metaphor for something else, and you're into some weird fantasy—"

He places the bottle in his hand down and leans on the counter, finally looking at me, that pissed-off look he wore at the gala a year ago to the day firmly in place. "Maybe I don't care what you think."

My face must flash with emotion because he frowns as I

ease back. I don't care what it is souring his mood, being a dick is unnecessary. "You know what I think? I think you're not the vibe I'm looking for tonight, and you can go choke on your own saliva."

I give him a forced "fuck you" smile and slide off the stool, picking up a small bottle of vodka as I back away.

Asshole.

I'm standing with Charlie, unscrewing the cap, when the bottle is taken from my hand and replaced with a cocktail glass—a cosmo. "Don't ruin your birthday on my account, sunshine."

I turn my head to eye him over my shoulder, his tall frame towering over me, maybe a hint of a smile ghosting his lips. "I'm adding pretentious to the list—you couldn't make my tears wet, pretty boy."

He sniggers, leaning in closer. "I could make your tears wet."

"Yeah?" I pop a brow, challenging him.

His eyes roam my face, wanting to say something. I'd give anything to know what he's thinking. He knew he was rude before. The cosmo and pet name are damage control because he likely doesn't want to upset my brother by upsetting me. Not that Mason cares.

Something flashes in his eyes, and then the elevator pings. Mason strolls out, his head down as he walks toward the entertainment room. Lance leans back an inch, casting another fleeting glance at me before shaking his head and stepping away.

If I had to guess, I'd say that Lance Sullivan *is* a dick, and the guy I met at the gala was on something.

. . .

When Mason arrived home and told us he didn't want to drink, I knew my dad's appointment hadn't gone as he'd have liked. Instead of asking questions—something I was desperate to do, I didn't say anything, taking a leaf out of his book and pretending our dad wasn't sick.

I texted Dad and then Vinny to check what Mason had told me was true—that he wanted to have an early night and was headed to bed. I decided to make the most of my evening after that. If I could remember the last time I went out drinking with friends, it would be a miracle.

Dinner last night, having the guys all here now, and also having the opportunity to meet Nina, Lucy, and Megan makes today feel special.

It feels like an actual birthday for once.

My brother is sitting on the opposite side of the firepit to me, his arms wrapped around Nina as she lies between his legs. "He's different with her," I say to Elliot, my eyes not leaving the loved-up couple.

"He is," Elliot agrees. "We have wagers on how long it will take him to propose."

I snap my head toward him. "He's *that* serious?"

"I don't know a woman he's ever been like this with. He's obsessed."

Nina's a dream. Yeah, I've only known her for two days, but I can already see that she's a good person. The idea that my brother might be serious about her after so many years of giving us nothing but rumoured flings and a reputation that's nothing to be proud of shocks me as much as it makes me happy.

"How long?"

"You want in?" Elliot asks me.

I shake my head. "No. I won't bet on them, but I want to know what you idiots predicted."

Elliot takes a swig of his beer. "I gave them six months. Charles said two months—not sure if there's something I don't know going on with that, and Sullivan doesn't think it will happen."

I frown, then look at where Lance is sitting next to Charlie.

"You don't think he'll propose?" I ask him.

Lance eyes me for a moment before he looks at Lucy and Megan, who seem to be waiting eagerly on the next word out of his mouth. "Who fucking knows. Maybe I'm wrong."

Lucy huffs, and everyone's eyes draw to her instead. "I give them a year. I don't think Mason will rush into it. He's starting to see what Nina's like—what she needs."

"I don't know. He bulldozed her lunch with Joey the other week. He seems like the type to act first, think later." Megan shrugs, putting her two cents in.

I look to Lucy on my right. "Who's Joey?"

"He's Nina's friend. He tries hitting on her every time we go out, and the last time it happened, the night we met these heroes"—Lucy looks between Charlie and Elliot sarcastically—"they scared the poor boy away."

"Nina wasn't interested. It was obvious. If she was, I would have helped him with his chat."

"He didn't have the best chat," Charlie confirms.

"Nina said you called him soft cock," Lucy accuses Elliot.

I fight to hide my smile as Elliot shrugs and changes the subject back to my brother's impending nuptials. "What are you saying then, Megs?"

"Two weeks."

Everyone sniggers, but Megan sits with a smile, confident.

"What about you?" Lance asks, directing the question at me.

What about me…

I want to join in. I want to play along and feel a part of their group, but the truth is, I don't have a clue how long it will take Mason to propose because I don't know who they truly are. As a couple, nor as people. I might have the same blood as my brother, but a last name is about all he's willing to share with me anymore. "I said I wouldn't bet on them."

The group falls silent, and I focus my gaze on the drink in my hand, knowing I've created an awkward void.

"I'll give them a year," Lance announces.

"Why the change of heart?" Charlie asks as I lift my head.

Lance shrugs, his eyes locking with mine as he knocks back the rest of his drink. "Caught me on a good day, I guess."

I can't look away as he stands and moves past Elliot, Lucy and me. He disappears inside the house.

"I'm freezing my tits off out here. That fire couldn't burn even Lance's icy ass."

I smile at that and stand. "I'll grab you a throw, Megan."

NINE

Scarlet

We end up moving inside to the lounge instead, the British summer not quite warm enough this late into the night. Lucy was the first to disappear to bed. Elliot followed not long after, and then when Nina fell asleep in Mason's arms, he told us to carry on while he carried her upstairs.

Megan, Charlie and Lance are the only ones still awake, and although the alcohol I'd drank earlier in the evening has worn off, I have a buzz about me I know won't wear off for a while. When I'm at home, I rarely drink unless we're entertaining. Dad insists it doesn't bother him, and I believe it. He has control when the house is full. It's when he's alone that things get bad.

The idea of this day ending and routine resuming tomorrow makes my stomach churn, which gives me terrible guilt.

It makes me want to disappear for a little while.

"I can feel your mind working."

I look up at Charlie next to me on the sofa and swallow before giving him a soft smile. "I'm fine."

"Yeah, you're always fine."

My eyes seek out Megan and Lance, but both are focused on the movie we put on nearly an hour ago. Although Megan talked through the first thirty minutes, everyone seems to be pretty invested now.

"Do you ever wish you could be invisible? Not forever, but just long enough to become a thought in someone's mind."

Charlie frowns but then looks up and over my shoulder. I turn my head and find Lance staring at me.

"What do you mean?" Charlie asks, drawing my gaze back to him.

I chance a look back at Lance, but he's on his phone and not focused on us. He's not spoken to me since the terrace. He's barely spoken to anyone all night, his face like stone. "No responsibility, complete freedom with no judgement, and the validation that you're still needed in the world."

"You could never be invisible, Scar." He pulls on a loose strand of my lavender hair. "But, yeah. It sounds pretty fucking epic."

"What would you do?" I ask him.

"How long do we get?"

I purse my lips as I think. "A day."

"Hmm. I'd probably fuck with some people." I smile, knowing he's doing everything he can to lighten my mood.

"The guys," I confirm.

"I'd definitely use it on a case."

"Sounds illegal."

"Very." He chuckles. "And I'd likely do it all naked."

"I mean, why not?"

I get a rare wide smile from my lifelong friend, and it warms me to the soul.

"I'd be robbing a bank…" Megan looks at Charlie thoughtfully. "Naked."

The three of us laugh, and then I look to Lance and decide to extend the olive branch. "Lance?"

He looks up from his phone, bored. When I don't speak right away, he pops an eyebrow as if to prompt me.

"You're invisible for one day. No responsibility and complete freedom. What would you do?"

His face seems to harden further until his jaw tics, and then his eyes pin me.

"Oh," Megan mutters, and the air in the room becomes thicker.

"Tell me what you'd do?" Charlie asks after a beat, cutting the tension.

I go to say all that was in my head moments before but sat here now, I can't think of anything other than green eyes.

I have nothing.

"I don't know yet."

Charlie nods, accepting the answer.

"Yet," Megan says. "We love an optimistic queen."

Charlie nudges my knee with his. "You can think about it while you make me a drink."

I snatch his tumbler and pull the blankets off my legs, throwing him a silent thank-you with my eyes as I make my way to the entertainment room.

When I reach into the icebox, I stand for a moment and allow the chill to calm me.

I'm not sure why Lance Sullivan affects me the way he does, but when he looks at me like he'd take great pleasure in causing my demise, at the same time his eyes burn through something deep at the base of my stomach, it annoys the shit out of me.

"What are you thinking?"

My eyes shutter closed, and I roll my lips as his deep voice washes over me. "Do you really want to know the answer to that?"

Something passes over his face, his own mind reeling, and then he shrugs as if the answer doesn't matter to him.

"Why did you do that before, on the terrace?"

"Do what?" He leans against the doorway watching me, his ankles crossed.

I tilt my head, knowing he knows exactly what I'm talking about. "You changed your mind about the bet between the others to take away from me not having a clue."

"And you're pissed off at me for that?"

"I'm not pissed off at all." I place Charlie's glass on the countertop, the ice making it rattle on the wood.

"Right, the girl who can't get angry, if I remember correctly."

"I'd rather that than the man who lets a phone call derail his entire mood. What a pair." I smile sarcastically.

"You're as sharp as ever, I see. So perceptive… for a recluse who's seen me once in an entire year, it's impressive you know so much about me."

And for that year, I wondered what Lance might've been doing. If he thought about me, too.

"If that's me being perceptive, what does it make you? You happen to have me all figured out in that handsome head of yours."

He takes a step toward me, his face growing impossibly harder as he rounds the bar and stands at my back. I swallow and look out into the lounge. "You were at that gala for no more than an hour when you ran out on me, and then I don't see you for a year. Tell me, have you been living outside of that prison you willingly put yourself in, or am I wrong?"

I lean back, looking up at him. "Maybe I am a recluse, Lance, but at least I'm happy. And just so you know, I'm one more asshole comment away from throwing this drink in your face."

He frowns, clenching his jaw, but says nothing. No smart-ass replies or snappy banter. Something builds inside of me. "What is up with you tonight?" I ask as if I know him at all.

He just stares down at me, his eyes eating at me and driving me to continue.

"It bothered you that I left the gala?" I say, slightly quieter as I take the parts I shouldn't.

Annoyance spreads over his face as if he's slipped up, and then he quirks a brow. "You think I'm handsome?"

"Are you going to answer all my questions with one of your own?"

"Will you answer my question?"

I snigger and pick out a bottle at random to fill Charlie's glass. Lance's presence at my back makes my stomach flutter like a complete traitor. "You've looked miserable and bored all night. You're probably the hardest person I've ever tried to read."

His hand reaches forward, his chest brushing my shoulder as he swaps out the bottle in my hand. Strong fingers smooth over my waist as he reaches across the length of the bar and grabs a different bottle, and then he's pouring the drink for me. "Maybe I am bored."

I try to steady my voice, annoyed his touch alone has me so flustered. "If you were bored, you wouldn't be here."

"So you think I'm here for you?"

My skin burns under his touch. Why is he still touching me? Why does it feel so good? "No," I say, shaking my head.

He tilts his neck back, looking down his nose at me with a smirk. "I am."

He's laughing at me.

And he's enjoying it. "You're toying with me."

He sniggers. "You have no idea."

I drop my head, eyeing the amber liquid in the glass. "Why are you acting like you hate me?" I ask, confused.

"Hate you?" he snaps back, fingers flexing before they disappear. I instantly miss their warmth. He shakes his head. "Is that what you think?"

"You've barely said a word to me all night. Then you look at me like you want to kill me. Then you're nice to me on the terrace. Then you come in here being a complete jackass—"

"Come with me."

"Come with you?" Is this man deluded?

"Move. Your. Ass." He walks from the room, hitting the button for the elevator.

My nerves spark in my gut like firecrackers.

"Where are you going?" I hiss, looking across at the lounge where everyone is sitting.

I cannot read this man.

He's maddening.

The doors slide open as I approach, and I swallow down the uneasiness in my throat as Lance shakes his head. "*Hate you*," I hear him mutter under his breath.

My nerves come back full force, but this time, they feel warmer. A little tighter.

I step into the lift after Lance and take another glance back out into the foyer, wondering if the others will notice us gone.

The doors start to close. "I don't think—"

"I want to fuck you." He leans back against the railing, looking me dead in the eye. "Every time I look at you."

I blink once, the air becoming stifling in the confined space. "I—"

"I can't fuck you, Scarlet."

"You can't?" I sound disappointed even to my own ears.

He shakes his head, his jaw ticcing as his eyes roam my face. "Your brother would fucking kill me."

"But you want to?" Something inside of me soars, and I know he sees it. My stomach flips.

"I spent a year with you out of sight yet could never get you out of my mind. You're like poison."

"That's probably the nicest thing anyone's ever said to me."

He doesn't laugh with me. He doesn't do anything. He just stares me down like he wants to rip my clothes off me here and now.

So, he doesn't hate me… he wants me…

It feels too powerful. Too fucking euphoric to be wanted by a man as formidable as Lance Sullivan.

Boldly, I walk toward him, pushing my chin up and feigning a confidence I don't fully grasp. "I think—when I look at you, I think—"

"I know," he mutters, his voice thick as his eyes devour me. It's electric. It's dangerous. He shakes his head. "Fuck, I know." He reaches for me, pulling me to him by my nape.

Our mouths meet, desperate.

His large hands are on my face. Demanding, strong and controlled. He moves me to where he wants me. Only I'm as frantic as him, unable to just stand still and kiss this man. My body rolls into his, my hands on his strong forearms. Then his hair. His stubble. His neck.

Deep wet licks.

Painfully tender bites.

Long, needy kisses.

And I'm lost to every single one of them.

I slide my hands between us and start on his shirt buttons, but a growl reverberates through his chest, and he gives me one more deep sucking kiss before pulling back. His heavy gaze shifts from my eyes to my lips and back again. "Scarlet."

"We're in my brother's elevator." With my head tilted back, my eyes widen as the realisation sinks in. I remove my hands from his chest and step back. "Sorry. I'm so sorry, I—"

His body blankets mine again, only this time, he has me against the wall. His strong thigh is positioned between my legs, and he pushes into me, just enough to make my body lean into his as it craves a little more pressure.

"You don't apologise for kissing me, ever. Do you understand me?"

When I don't speak, too lost to the crazy sensation pulsing between my legs, he takes my mouth in another kiss. Only this time, it's all him. Lance kisses my lips, licks through my mouth, nibbles at my jaw. He gives to me, and I give nothing back.

Our faces are barely apart when he looks into my eyes, yet I can see his beautiful green ones vividly. "I don't hate you, sunshine." A smile. "You made me wait a year for that one, but I won't wait a year for the next."

The doors ping and slide open. Before I can even think to say anything, to call him back or fix his unbuttoned shirt, he's gone, striding out into the living room and joining the others on the sofa.

I take off up the stairs to my bedroom, quickly going to the en suite.

Lance

I thought I'd be fine. Until she fucking smiled at me.

Scarlet

We kissed.

I run my fingers over my lips as I stare at myself in the bathroom mirror. My cheeks are flushed, and I fan my face, not wanting to mess up my makeup by dampening my cheeks with cold water. But I need it. I need a cold shower at this point.

My phone pings in my cardigan pocket, and I pull it out.

Asshole CFO: Do I need to come and find you, or are you going to be a big girl and come back downstairs?

Crap. I'm acting like a teenager that's never been kissed.

Scarlet: I'm coming

It's gone midnight when we eventually go to bed. I walk arm in arm with Megan down my brother's landing, trying not to make a sound as we search for Lucy. "She's with Elliot!" Megan hisses.

"No, she isn't." I chuckle. "Elliot's in the room next to Nina and Mase." I push on one of the eight bedroom doors and smile. "See. There she is." Lucy is curled up in the middle of the large bed. "There's another spare room if you want it?"

"I promised her before we came that we'd share," Megan tells me, stepping into me and giving me a hug. "I hope you had the best day, Scar. Welcome to our chaos."

"I have my own kind of chaos, so…."

"It's why we like you."

She says good night and closes the door, and then I make my way to my room, a heavy feeling weighing on me.

Tomorrow's so close, and I don't feel ready for the day to end.

"Lowell." I turn at the sound of his voice. "Keep the noise down, yeah?"

I shake my head and dip it, smiling. When I look back up, Lance has already slipped inside his room.

Inside my own room, I take a shower, slide into the T-shirt Mason left out for me, and plait my hair in two French braids. It isn't until I'm climbing into bed that I notice the box placed on my nightstand. It's gift-wrapped but has no tag.

I open it, finding a card inside.

Lowell,

I wasn't sure what to get you, but I'm certain you haven't attracted any cock in the last twelve months.

Enjoy.

Lance x

I pull out my phone and text him before unwrapping the box.

Scarlet: You got me a present?

What the hell?

I wait as three dots bounce.

Asshole CFO: It's your birthday?

Scarlet: Charlie and Elliot didn't get me anything

Scarlet: You haven't even said happy birthday to me

The three dots bounce again, over and over, before they stop. I find myself waiting, hanging on for the next text to ping.

Then there's a soft knock.

I place the box on the bed and rush to the door. When I pull it open, I find Lance leaning in the doorway, hands on either side of the threshold, his bare chest taut and his abs viciously flexing.

"Did you like your gift?" he asks with a slight smile.

Fuck. Me.

My eyes dance up to his face, not being able to focus on one part of him. Some men are men. Some are boys. Some are men who are pretty and know it. And then some… some are all man.

Six-foot-something, two-hundred-and-who-cares pounds. Complete. Rugged. MAN. Lance is Man. "It's lovely."

"*Lovely*?"

I snap out of my fuzzy head and concentrate on him—or his words. "Oh. Yeah. It really was, thank you."

"You haven't opened it, have you?" He pushes past me and into the room.

I scan the landing before shutting the door. "I was about to open it."

"Go for it. I want to see what you think."

My gaze is assessing as I walk toward the gift box.

He's stretched himself out on the chair at the end of the

bed, his arm thrown over his head to prop it up. "Am I putting you off?" he asks when I make no move to open the present.

My mind goes back to the card.

I wasn't sure what to get you, but I'm certain you haven't attracted any cock in the last twelve months.

"Oh, god. What is it?"

"It's lovely." He grins.

I sit on the bed and tear into the wrapping paper, only now realising it has Nells written on the packaging. When I see the box, my face heats.

"Lance."

"Yes, my darling."

"You bought me a vibrator. What if my dad finds it?"

He shrugs. "Where do you normally hide your toys?"

"I don't! I live with my dad."

He sits up a little. "Wait—"

"What if Mason sees it? I didn't bring an overnight bag because I didn't expect to stay. How do I sneak it out of here?"

"You don't have toys at home?"

"No!"

"So where do you keep them?"

I look at him, wondering what else, other than pure stupidity, is rattling around in his brain. "There's no them. This is it." I hold up the box, shaking it, and the weight of the vibrator has it falling from the cardboard. It slips through my grasp and lands on the comforter.

He grins again. "I'm your first?"

"Shut it." My eyes can't help but roam his chest, the muscled arm thrown over his head, the veins dancing along his golden skin. The deep vee at the base of his chiselled abs that leads to—

"Have you ever got yourself off with one? I mean, I'm guessing not." He bites his lip, smiling, looking like pure sin.

"Why would I tell you?" I stare down at the obnoxiously large purple vibrator instead.

"Why do you have an account at Nells if you don't own any toys?" he asks, ignoring my reply, his face screwing up as he looks utterly confused. I pinch the bridge of my nose when he points at himself as if it's all making sense. "Not for me?"

When I don't say anything, he throws his head back and laughs.

"You're an asshole." My lip twitches before a full smile breaks free, and then I'm laughing along with him. I pick up a cushion off the bed and throw it at him as he stands, still laughing. "An absolute…" I throw another. "Asshole."

I reach for a third but get taken out when he throws one back.

"Hey!" I yell.

"Shh," he tells me, hurling another at my head. "You'll wake everyone up."

I rush him and swing for his head.

"Jesus Christ." He grabs my arms and turns me to the side, our bodies flush. "Why are you so wound up?"

"You bought me a vibrator."

"Yeah, and maybe it's exactly what you needed."

"You don't even know me. I don't know you."

He throws me to the bed and starts to crawl over me, pinning me to the mattress as his knees hug my ribs. He tips his chin at me, daring. "Then get to know me."

My heart thrashes behind my rib cage, and I swallow, trying to get a handle on my erratic pulse. "Has anyone ever told you you're a lot?"

"I'm no more than you, sunshine." He gives me a panty-melting smile, and I feel him relax a little.

I quickly flip us, putting him on the bottom and me straddling his hips—he definitely let me do that.

"You're right. I've never..."

"You've never what?" He smiles, cocky.

My lip twitches and I'm pretty sure my body is on fire as I reach for the vibrator. His smile drops. "I've never used one." I lick my lips, flipping it over in my hand. "I'm not stupid, and I know how to use it... but you're kinda doing things for me right now." I rock forward, and Lance groans. "And maybe you want to help me on my first try?"

His mouth opens and closes, and then his eyes darken.

I don't wait, and I make it clear who's in control by telling him softly, "Open your legs a little for me."

"Scarlet—"

My head dips to the side, and I stare down at him.

His head hits the mattress before he snaps it straight back up. He creates a gap between his thighs when I stretch my knees further over him. I slide the vibrator between us, pushing his legs together after. The fake penis is long and wide, terrifying really. My face is on fire, and I'm clean of my makeup, but I've never felt more powerful as I straddle his waist.

I look at the purple head and then his face. "Is this okay?" I ask, my voice sultry and nothing like my own.

He nods, a breathless chuckle on his lips as if he can't believe I've just done what I have. *I can't believe I've just done what I have.* "Yeah—" He clears his throat, and I shimmy forward, noticing my nipples are taut and showing through the white T-shirt. "I—uh—I actually got you lube." He reaches for the box, and I smile, sitting back on his lap. I can feel how wet I am already.

"I don't think I need it."

His eyes spark, and he visibly swallows. "No?"

I shake my head, readjusting myself over him as I lift my T-shirt and slip my lace underwear to the side. "But if you want, we can use it. I like the idea of you putting it on."

"Putting it on?"

"On the vibrator," I confirm, knowing his mind has drifted someplace else.

Lance pops the lid off the lube and squeezes it onto the head of the vibrator. We look up at one another when it melts down and coats his groin. It's no secret that Lance is enjoying this as much as I'm about to. His erection is rock hard inside his boxer briefs. I eye it, slowly licking my lips.

"I feel like I drew the short straw with this." I wrap my hand around the silicone, coating it with lube. My knuckles graze the base of his own cock as I twist my wrist.

"Sunshine, you can't…" He drops his head back to the bed, his hands covering his face. "Don't put those thoughts in my head."

"*Please.* What else are you thinking?" I smirk, rocking forward so that the head of the vibrator slides through my pussy. My breath hitches when I realise how sensitive I am.

"Jesus Christ." He leans up on his elbows to watch.

My eyes roll and then close at the feeling of my clit already pulsing. "This will be the biggest thing I've ever had inside of me."

He groans.

"I'm nervous it might hurt."

"Go slow," he snaps as if the idea I might hurt myself makes him feral. He sits, fixated on my pussy, as I glide the tip over me again. One of his hands reaches out, smoothing up my thigh, but he quickly drops it to the bed, as if touching me is too much. "You're killing me."

My thighs shake as I rock forward, lifting myself on my knees slightly and then positioning the thick head at my entrance.

I lean forward so our chests touch and whisper into his ear, "Thank you, Lance." I sink down, my eyes closing as I'm slowly filled. When I meet Lance's thighs, I whimper and his body tenses.

Needing more, I roll my hips forward once, twice, thr—

"Scarlet."

The need to work my body over him, over the fullness between my legs, it's indescribable, and I have no shame for the way I fight against the hold he puts on me. The panic in his voice.

"You're going to fucking ruin me."

"Please," I moan. "Let me."

Lance grasps the back of my neck, his other hand at my hip, pinning me to his groin. He rolls his hips, forcing the vibrator deeper. I arch back, my body seeking the deeper changed angle, but Lance holds me firm, keeping us close. I feel myself getting hotter, my skin prickling, and not just mine, but his breathing becomes heavier. Louder.

Lance reaches between us, and I whimper again, ready to beg him not to stop this. *It feels too good.* But then the vibrator starts to pulse, vibrations shaking against my core that make my toes curl against the sheets. My mouth falls open, and I rock harder as Lance moves the rabbit ears to hug my clit, the feeling of his thumb brushing my sensitive flesh sending me free-falling. He holds my hip firm as I grind down, his other hand fisting in my hair as I ride his lap.

"Fuck. Bring your knees up."

I do with his help and instantly start to buck, my movements sharp and messy as everything inside of me burns. It's deep. So deep I come in seconds. My body releases, clenching and squeezing as Lance closes his eyes and rocks me harder on his lap. I feel him losing control beneath me, and I realise that he can come like this too. He's just as into it as I am.

"Scarlet, shit."

Our mouths meet, teeth clashing, breaths ragged, but we don't kiss. It's impossible when our bodies are rippling uncontrolled. Our foreheads together and my arm around his back, we hold each other up, riding out the remnants of our orgasms as one.

Lance shakes his head, panting. His hooded eyes are fixed on me, as if I might disappear if he looks away. He takes hold of my face with one hand, keeping me right there against his heaving chest. "Happy… birthday… Scarlet."

We both smile through breathless chuckles, and then he urges me forward to kiss him.

It's deep, slow, longing. More. So much more than anything I've ever experienced before.

When everything eases enough for me to lean back a little, I do, and the heavy-lidded look on Lance's face makes me feel even better.

"The fuck did you do to me, sunshine?" He looks down at the wetness coating his boxers.

Me and him.

And as if it's his only salvation, his mouth takes mine in another searing kiss.

TEN

Lance

“Everyone thinks you’re sweet, Baby Lowell. It’s all a ruse.”

Her smile could light a village, and I’m entranced by it. I’ve seen a thousand smiles in my thirty years, so why is hers always slapping me so damn hard?

“I can be sweet,” she says, locking her legs tighter around my waist. “When I want to be.”

I have no idea what time it is, but we’ve yet to go to sleep. After she obliterated my boxers, we kissed like teenagers for long enough that my lips ached. I made her leave the room with me so I could go and get my trousers from my own room and food from the kitchen. Neither one of us brought a change of clothes with us, and I wasn’t ready to leave her right away. Not when she looked at me as if being alone terrified her. Now we’re tangled in the sheets after another painstaking kiss. I’m not sure my cock has ever been so hard, and my ability to not fuck her senseless is dwindling with every smile she gives me.

"You really set up an account at Nells so you could buy me those toys last year?"

She nods. "I went with my friends when I was at uni. I couldn't even remember the name of the shop."

"It was in my diary as Nellies." I remember, smiling down at her.

"That's it!" She chuckles, running her nose and lips up my chest. *Lowell will fucking kill me.* "I can't believe you went back. They must have had a field day with you."

"They loved every second of it."

"It's got to be at the top of women's 'things I want my husband to do' list."

"What? Go and buy them a vibrator?"

"Uh-huh. It's hot."

"Noted." I chuckle.

"Thank you," she says after a beat of silence.

"For what?" I frown, sensing she meant it in more ways than me buying her a vibrator.

"For making me feel something today." She contorts her lips into a pout. "Something a little… more."

I stare at the bedside light, wondering what *more* is for her and why I feel like she's exactly the distraction I needed tonight. The minute I saw her in Mason's lounge, I was fighting against the anger I carried with me from my meeting with my mum and then Ben. Half a million pounds is currently missing from Ellis and Frey's bank account, and I have no fucking clue where it is. I swallow and pull her closer to my chest. "You really don't have any toys at home? Isn't the house huge?"

"It is, and I could, but I rarely get the chance to go into

the city, and can you imagine my dad taking in a parcel for me? I'd be mortified."

"Have you ever thought about moving out? To be closer to the city?"

I feel the sadness wash over her, like a wall being forged between us. "I couldn't move out, not while Dad's sick. I love it at the estate. It's like a different world compared to the city."

"What about when he's better?"

She looks up at me, her smile sad. "Maybe." It feels like a lie. "It's going to take time. He's been poorly for over ten years now; the idea of that changing seems impossible."

"Would you go back to uni?"

"If you'd asked me that last week, I'd have said no." She chuckles. "Nina actually gave me forms today to sign up for the same degree I was studying."

"She did?" I say, frowning.

"That surprises you?"

"A little." A lot, actually. "I'm not sure about her yet."

Nina has problems. Money and family. I've seen too many women manipulate Mason to let her worm her way in so easily. If he won't be careful, I will.

"But you're sure about me. After what? One night…"

"Two nights and two days, technically. But maybe the verdict's still out on you."

I feel her smile against my skin. "Whatever. Nina's lovely. Don't be so hard on her."

"Hmm, we'll see." I smooth my hand down her back, enjoying the way she fits against me a little more than I should. "So you do want to go back to uni?"

She nods. "It's my dream, but honestly, I can't see it ever being possible."

"Surely there are people you could pay to stay with your dad while you study?"

"Nina said the same thing." She chuckles sadly. "He's a proud man. I could never have someone else care for him. Not when I'm able."

"What does he think about that?"

"He stopped asking when I told him my decision was final. I needed him to accept that it was my choice and what I wanted."

Something tells me it wasn't what she wanted.

Something tells me I shouldn't care so much.

But knowing shutting her down and ignoring the fact my cock twitched whenever she fucked with me left her thinking I fucking hated her before makes me throw caution to the wind. Consequences be damned. "Do you ever feel like you're missing out on…"

"Life?" she fills in when I trail off, shaking her head. "No. I honestly couldn't be happier. The idea of working an actual job is a goal, and I know I will have that one day, but when the time's right. When I'm ready to. For now, I feel like I'm exactly where I should be."

"Which is?"

"On the estate. Doing up the house room by room. It will be mine and Mason's one day, and if he doesn't want to live there, I'll keep it for myself."

She's telling the truth, I don't know why I can tell, but I can. "You'd live there alone?"

"I'll never leave…." She looks up at me. "Did you know my mother's buried there?"

I shake my head, and she hides her face in my chest again. "I don't remember her, but from what I do know, the videos and photos and her diaries my dad kept, she loved it as much as I do. I guess I've lived out a very different, unconventional relationship with her by falling in love with what she once did. Her garden is beautiful. Maybe one day Mason will invite you out, and I can show you."

"She has a garden?"

Scarlet beams. "Filled with her favourite flowers."

I smooth my hand down her side and let the silence settle until something foreign and unstoppable happens. "My dad died when I was sixteen." She doesn't say a word, just silently rests her lips against my left pec. "He used to ride, had this Harley Davidson that was his pride and joy. He stopped when we were small, wanting to be around, and I guess work got in the way of time. When he was forty, he was invited to go on a ride through America, but he got into an accident, and he was killed."

"I'm so sorry, Lance."

My jaw clenches, not wanting or needing to tell Scarlet the rest.

"Are you close with your mum? I remember Charlie telling me you have sisters."

Of course that's what she'd ask. "I have three sisters. Molly, Chloe, and Nessa Anne."

"Were you close growing up?" she asks, tracing my ribs. "I'd have done anything to have more siblings. I have Mase and, by default, Elliot." I can hear the smile in her voice. "But a sister would've been super helpful in my teens."

"We were close before. Everything changed when Dad died."

She stops her hand on my side and shifts her gaze up to my face. "The same thing happened when Dad got sick. I felt like I had Mason for a time, and then he grew up, and everything kinda went to shit. I rarely see him now."

"Mase has had… a weird couple of years. He's—"

"Lance," she says, cutting me off. "I appreciate it, and I get what you're trying to do, but I don't want excuses from anyone but him, and even then, I don't believe he has anything to explain. I have no idea what he's feeling or what he's been through, and my mental well-being isn't his responsibility."

"I'm sorry."

"What for?" she asks, and I can tell she's frowning.

I have no idea. "I don't know exactly. Everything."

"I can assure you, Mr Sullivan, you have absolutely nothing to apologise for." She bites my nipple, and I pull back.

"That hurt," I say, deadpan, rolling us so I'm hovering over her. Her hand lies between our bodies, rubbing over my pec as her thumb soothes my nipple.

"You don't like it?"

My brows lift. "Do you?"

She shrugs and bows her back. "I'm not sure. Check for me."

A wicked smile dances across her lips, and I lean down, sliding my hand around her waist to hold her back at an angle. Her pinkish nipples are peeking through the cotton T-shirt, driving me crazy. I dip my head and bite on the pointed end, and she hisses.

"Well?" I ask, nose nuzzling her breasts as she snakes her body under my hold. She's fucking perfect.

"Is that all I get?" she asks, and my cock twitches.

I lift my gaze to look at her and swallow when I see the need in her eyes.

A split second and somehow, everything I've fucked up in my life unravels. My dad, the business, my relationship with my mum and the girls—Chloe, Molly and Nessa Anne, the bike. I've never held anything in my hands that has felt as important as Scarlet Lowell does, and the fact she's Mason's sister is enough for me to stop. After everything he's done for me, everything that's happened. He's about all the family I've got left.

My thumb brushes her ribs beneath her shirt as I say, "For now."

"For now?" And the disappointment on her face jabs me right in the gut.

I snigger, fucking lost in uncharted territory. "How about a date?"

She sits up, forcing me back and putting us nose to nose. "A date?" She grins, but a slight frown mars her brow.

I shrug, resisting the urge to kiss her. "If you want to."

"When?"

I kiss her. "Whenever."

We stare at one another, and I can see her mind running a million miles an hour. I look away as my stomach twists into knots. "You don't have to."

"It's not that I don't want to."

She doesn't want to.

Fuck.

"I want to." She pushes me back until I'm on my ass, and she's straddling my lap. The way she takes control, unlike I'd let anyone, is fucking crazy. I grasp her waist, keeping her there. "Let me see, okay? I just don't know if I can right now, with everything Dad's going through."

I stare up at her, our gazes transfixed.

Lowell will fucking kill me.

"Don't be all grumpy again." She smiles.

"I'm not grumpy." She pushes her hand through my hair, and I lean into the touch, my eyes closing.

No, not grumpy. Just utterly fucked.

I fall back to the bed, taking her with me. She lies across my chest, her body wrapped around me as we settle into the quiet of the night. "Can I tell you a secret?" she whispers after a while, sounding not far from sleep.

"You can tell me anything."

I feel her smile on my skin, and then she snuggles in closer. "This has been the best birthday I've ever had."

I feel her drift off to sleep moments later, and I know that I won't be getting any sleep for a while, not with the bedside light still on.

I don't turn it off, worried she might wake up to darkness.

When I wake up the next morning, she's gone.

"Do I want to know what's crawled up your ass, Sullivan?"

I don't reply to Charlie. I don't need to. I just continue to stare at the elevator doors as we're carried to the seventy-eight floor.

"If it's Vanessa, then you've done the right thing. They don't have a leg to stand on, and it's not like you've played your worst card. They needed a good reality check."

I turn to look at him standing in the back of the elevator,

realising he hasn't a clue what's wrong with me. "I couldn't give a fuck about my mum right now."

His face narrows in, his chin lifting as he tries to figure it out. I don't know anyone who can do what he does with such little effort. "Then it's Scarlet," he says as if it's something he didn't consider, but it doesn't shock him.

He nods and rights himself, not asking me anything else.

I straighten my tie, squaring my shoulders. She's not replied to the text I sent yesterday morning. "Do you know where she is?"

"She'll be on the estate," he says, ignoring my agitation with a steely expression of his own.

"Have you spoken to her since Wednesday night?" I ask.

"I haven't."

My frustration rises. "Has Mason?"

"I wouldn't know."

"Will you ask me something back and not be such an annoying prick for two minutes?"

His head shifts to me, a warning look in his eye. "No. Scarlet isn't some girl you pick up on the weekend, Lance. She's important to too many people who will come for your head—including me. I ask you questions and leave myself open to answers I don't want to hear. It's better for your pretty face this way."

"You wouldn't hit me." I snigger, knowing he's a changed man from the one he once was. "So because Scarlet's Mason's sister, I can't talk about her?"

"Depends," he mutters, striding out onto Mason and Elliot's office floor where he turns. "Do you have that same faith in Mason's fist as you do mine?"

No. Mason really would come for my head if he knew

what I'd bought for his sister's birthday. What she did to me on the bed. What her body felt like riding my lap.

Fucking hell.

"You want a question, Lance?" Charlie asks, looking around the reception area.

I tip my chin in answer, not sure I'll like what he has to say.

"Why?"

"Why?" I frown.

"Why Scarlet?"

What sort of question is that? "I've met her a handful of times. It's not a thing."

Fuck if I don't want it to be, though.

To know a little more.

One more night.

"It's not serious?"

I keep my face neutral. "No."

"Then why are you checking your phone in meetings and huffing like a child when your notifications are empty? —don't answer that," he snaps, impatient. "Sullivan, you can stick your dick in whoever you want. You're a big boy. I happen to trust your stupid ass not to fuck this up. Just pull your shit together and spare me the details."

I follow him out of the lift and catch up with him in the corridor. Once a week, we meet for lunch in Mason's office. Charlie's firm is in a building only a short walk away from the Montwell, so if he isn't knee-deep in a case, he makes the walk over.

I look up at the hard-faced lawyer many fear—he's a teddy bear really. Soft prick. My lip curls as I ask, "So, should I call her?"

He shakes his head and pushes into Mason's office.

He's on the phone when we enter, and we make ourselves comfortable on the sofas while we wait. And like they have for the past two days, my thoughts quickly drift to Scarlet. I pull up the messages I sent.

Asshole CFO: Cinderella forgot her knickers

I attached a picture of her lace underwear. They're now washed and lying in my nightstand.

When she didn't reply all day yesterday, my message not even being read, I texted her again early this morning.

Asshole CFO: I'm adding rude to your list.
Don't make me add stalker to mine.

I opted to run the five miles to work after that, desperate to shake off the thoughts and feeling that I had so much more to say to her.

I asked her so many questions.

I lay with her without needing to fuck her.

I told her about my dad.

"Sullivan, what are you eating?"

I swipe out of my messages and look up at my friends' eyes, all now focused on me.

"Hurry up, asswipe. I've got a meeting in half an hour," Mason snaps.

"I'll have whatever the special is." I wonder what her favourite food is…

Asshole CFO: What's your favourite food?

I've got to get a hold of myself.

I knew she'd be poison.

> Asshole CFO: Leave me alone now, sunshine. I'm trying to have lunch with your brother, and you're distracting me.

She doesn't reply, and it's not until an hour later, when Mason is already long gone to his meeting and we're getting up to leave the office, that George, their receptionist, walks into the room.

"Am I able to interrupt Mason this afternoon? I have an urgent call from his sister."

Charlie side-eyes me when I flinch, likely catching my frown at the same time.

My messages are still unread, which means she's ignoring them.

"What's up with Scarlet?" Elliot asks.

"I'm not sure exactly. It's a woman from the local pharmacy that called."

Elliot stands along with me. "Put the call through," he tells George, walking to Mason's desk.

He picks up the phone a couple of seconds later. "Hello?" I wait, leaning against the solid wood desk as I try to catch what's being said. "No, it's Elliot Montgomery… Yes… Is she okay?" Charlie stands. "I can be there within the hour… No, nothing that I'm aware of… She's away with my dad for a long weekend and won't get back until Monday… Thank you." Elliot puts the phone down and turns toward Charlie.

"Scar's just fainted in the pharmacy."

Something cracks in my jaw.

"Is she okay?" Charlie asks.

"She's come around and seems fine. She wants to go home, but they ask that someone goes and picks her up. I'm not pulling Mason out of Austin's meeting; he'll just worry about Scar the whole way there…" Elliot runs a hand through his hair, concern drawing in his brow. "He's away tonight. Tell him what's up when he comes out and to call me. Can you cancel my two o'clock, George? I won't be back in today."

I ignore everyone in the room, thinking about how I've been texting her bullshit messages while she's passed out somewhere.

Fuck.

"I hate to be the bearer of bad news," George announces from the doorway. "But you moved Mrs Langley up to one thirty so you could get out a little earlier. She's waiting in reception for you."

"Good god." Elliot tips his head back. "The woman's a witch."

"I'll go," Charlie tells him. "You see to Langley."

"You can blow off the afternoon?" Elliot asks him, sceptical.

"With ease." Charlie sniggers. "I'll call you once I get there."

Elliot nods and reaches for his jacket that's lying across the back of the sofa. "She's at the village pharmacy." He buttons it up and strolls out. "Wish me luck, fuckers."

Charlie turns to me when it's just us. "Did you drive in?"

Why didn't *she* make the call? Why was it someone else? Could she not speak?

Charlie reaches into his pocket and takes out the keys to his Jag, throwing them at me.

"She's fine, Sullivan. See that she gets home safe."

He starts to leave. "Aldridge?"

"What?" He turns at the threshold.

"You think *I* should go?"

He shakes his head and smiles, then carries on out the door.

ELEVEN

Scarlet

It's been nearly an hour since I fainted on the floor of the pharmacy, and they won't let me leave. Lifting my floppy hat, I continue to fan my face.

"Can I get you another glass of water, Scarlet?"

Smiling politely, I shake my head no at Jack, the pharmacist, praying Elliot arrives soon so I can go home and live out my embarrassment in peace.

I knew it was hot out today, but running on an empty stomach, rushing from Dad's appointment at the hospital, then dropping him home and hotfooting it down to the pharmacy to get the prescription filled was apparently too much.

I've never fainted in my life, and it's not on my list of things to ever do again. One minute I was bent over looking at makeup remover wipes, and the next, I was lying on my back with three women around me and my head held in

Jack's lap—Jack's gorgeous, of course. Dark curls, tanned skin, and freckles I chose to count while he checked me over.

Thankfully, they set up a chair for me around the back of the shop. I'm in the shade and have a half-eaten banana in my hand that they practically forced down my throat when I told them I hadn't eaten yet today—it's nearly three p.m., so I understand their concern.

After getting home on Thursday morning to the news I was expecting—Dad needs a liver transplant—I managed to shock even myself with the way I reacted. The guilt I felt consumed me. The fact I stayed out all night, that I wasn't there at the appointment even though I knew it was a huge step to have Mason go with him, the way I laughed all night and didn't even think to check my phone once I was in my room, it made me feel like the most selfish, horrible person on earth.

I look up when Charlie's black Jag SUV rolls around the side of the building and breathe a sigh of relief.

I go to stand, but Jack must have been lingering again because he appears out of nowhere, sliding an arm around my back and taking a supportive grasp on my forearm.

I give him a tight smile, thankful and still mortified. When I look up from his hold, I find none other than Lance climbing from Charlie's car.

And damn it, I stagger.

"Whoa, easy. Sit back down," Jack tells me.

"No, no, I'm fine… I just want to get home now."

I blink, and Lance is in front of me, little white dots making my eyes widen at him.

Why is he here?

"I want to check your blood pressure once more before you leave. Please, sit down," Jack reaffirms.

"I'm fine," I snap, brushing him off.

I feel terrible.

"Sit down, Scarlet." My eyes shift to Lance, and I swallow around the dryness in my throat. I lower to the chair and let Jack wrap the Velcro strip around my arm. Lance's eyes stay glued to Jack's busy hands.

"Where's Elliot?" I ask.

"He had a meeting. Your brother too."

"Why do you have Charlie's car?"

"I didn't drive into the office today."

Jack looks between the two of us and then pops his brows, standing from one knee and folding up the machine. "You need to take it easy for the rest of the day. And eat. You need to make sure you're not skipping meals, Scarlet."

I nod, ready to go but knowing I need to get up slower this time.

"We offer a delivery service for prescriptions. You should make the most of it when necessary."

"Thank you, Jack, and I'm sorry."

"Don't be sorry. I'm just glad you were in the shop with us and not out on the road."

He steps into me when I go to stand.

"I've got her," Lance tells him, sliding between us. The smell of him makes my body instantly warm all over. He's so close, his mouth right by the side of my face. "Put your arms around me."

"What?" I stare at him nose to nose and wide-eyed, telling him with a look not to do anything that will embarrass me further. "I can walk."

One of his arms slides under my legs, and I slap his hand away. "Scarlet," he grounds out, annoyed, ignoring me as he lifts me into his arms.

"I can walk."

"You can walk after I've fed you," he tells me, striding toward the car. Jack moves in front of us and opens the door. I'm placed in the front seat, and then the door gets shut with a thud.

I try to listen while Lance and Jack talk, but I can't make out a thing they're saying. When they shake hands and part ways, I look to my lap and pray the ground will swallow me up.

The back door opens, and I do anything but turn around.

"Do you need anything from your bag?"

Frowning, I reluctantly glance back, finding my bag, hat, and Dad's prescriptions on the seat. I shake my head. When Lance gets in the car, I close my eyes and rest my head back against the seat. My head is starting to pound. The last thing I need is Lance being in an arrogant, I-know-best mood.

I just want to be alone.

The car falls quiet, and I exhale. After the emotional barrage that hit me yesterday and now this today—

The warmth of soft fingers gently flutter across my chin, and then they direct my face to the side.

I peel my eyes open to look at him, the concern on his face making my heart beat out of rhythm.

His brows crease as he stares at me, and I wait, unsure of what it is he sees. "Are you okay?"

I don't like how much I like the way Lance is looking at me.

It's as if he cares.

Seconds must pass, and he eventually sighs, leaning across my body and pulling my seat belt into place.

"I'm taking you to dinner. Is there anywhere you'd like to eat?"

Dinner sounds incredible, but so does my bed. And then there's Dad, who will be wondering where I am.

"I need to go home. My dad will be worried and needs his prescription before bed."

"I'll stop there first."

"I need to cook him something for dinner. I—"

"He can come with us."

I frown. "What? No. He won't want to."

His grip tightens a little on the steering wheel, and he chances a glance at me, his face still full of worry. "Then I'll order him something to the house."

"Lance, I can cook dinner. I just need to eat something. I already feel better."

He glares at me, not believing a word of it. As he puts the car into gear and pulls out onto the main road, the satnav starts.

"I can give you the directions."

He ignores me, and I sigh, choosing to stare straight ahead.

We drive for a few minutes before he eventually speaks again.

"Why aren't you eating, Scarlet?" he questions. "And what if you were out on the road like Jeff said? I texted you. I had no idea. Do you not have a car?"

When he's done, I roll my head toward him. "Firstly, I do eat. I eat a lot and never skip meals, which is why it hit me so hard today. Secondly, I wasn't out on the road, so you can lose your dad tone when speaking to me. Thirdly, I have a car, but I also have legs. And lastly, his name was Jack, not Jeff."

I expect something smart from him, but instead, he throws me a full smile.

It's so unexpected my face burns. "What?"

"Nothing."

I glare at him, and his grin gets bigger. "It's definitely something."

"I'm just glad you're okay. Is that okay?"

I look out the window, hiding my own smile as I shrug. "I guess."

Trees flash by as we head toward the estate, and despite the short drive, my eyes start to drift closed, my stomach lightly churning.

When I open my eyes again, Lance is opening my door. I feel him gently reach over and unfasten my seat belt.

Everything feels heavy, and I fight to keep my eyes open as he lifts me from the passenger seat.

"Sleep. Just sleep for a while," he whispers.

"Lance?" I mutter.

I feel his eyes on me, but he doesn't respond.

"Don't let Elliot tell Mase. Please."

I feel weightless as I'm placed on something soft, and I sense a presence at my side as I drift back into a deep sleep.

Something pings in the room, waking me.

My eyes peel open, taking in the bedside light and

drawn curtains. I frown, sitting up quickly. I regret it immediately when my head spins.

I'm in the east wing.

This isn't my room.

Another ping and my eyes shift toward the sound, finding Lance sitting in the armchair on the other side of the room. He's sleeping, making me wonder what the time is. I can't see any sign of light through the drapes.

I slide my legs from the bed and make my way around the room, picking up Lance's phone from the arm of the chair.

It's eight p.m.

No wonder I'm starving. I've been asleep for hours.

Lance has two new texts from someone called Vanessa, and my eyes read the first line before I can consider how wrong it is.

Vanessa: Make all the demands you want

Vanessa: You can't cut us off

I place the phone down where I found it and observe his resting form. He looks so much softer like this, but also really uncomfortable. His brow is relaxed, his legs spread wide with one arm hanging between them as he rests his head on the other. His suit still looks immaculate, and I take my time, admiring just how well he fills it. His body is visibly defined. Strong and masculine in ways that make me want to spend time tangled in the sheets with it.

My thoughts go to Wednesday night. The way he lay on top of me, his cock hard against me.

I wanted him so badly.

I still want him now.

And he's here.

It surprises me he stayed.

Leaving him sleeping, I slip out of the room and quickly head down the corridor to my dad's room. I knock on the door, concerned it's been hours past when he should've taken his pills.

When he calls out for me to come in, I push on the door.

"Scarlet. You were home? I didn't see you this afternoon and presumed you were out this evening." My dad is sitting up in his armchair. Much like the one Lance is currently sprawled in.

"Uh, yeah. Sorry. I crashed pretty hard when I got back from getting your prescriptions. Have you eaten? I'll go get your pills."

"I've eaten. I had the pasta you left in the oven. It was lovely, thank you. And my pills were on the kitchen island." His head tilts. "I can take care of myself, you know."

I frown. *Pasta?*

"Are you okay, Scarlet? You look pale this evening."

I nod. "Yeah, I'm fine. Just hungry."

"You didn't eat this morning. Did you get something from Frank's bakery?"

I was going to, but then I passed out and had to be collected by the man whose lap I rode Wednesday night and who's now asleep down the hall…

"No, but I did have a banana." Not an outright lie. "I'll leave you to sleep, Dad. Good night."

"Good night, Scarlet."

I leave his room and head down to the kitchen, wearing

a confused frown. The smell of carbonara makes my mouth water the closer I get.

As I round the kitchen doorway, I find it immaculate. The dishes I'd left on the drainer this morning cleared, and the worktops wiped clean. I open the oven door and find a saucepan. Removing the lid, I take a deep inhale of the creamy pasta and groan. It smells delicious.

I grab a fork from the drawer and take a greedy mouthful.

Did Lance do all of this?

It's not Frey's recipe. I know Frey's cooking. But surely Lance didn't make this. Dad would have said if he'd seen him.

Unless he didn't see him?

Why would Lance do that?

Why did he stay?

Taking another mouthful, I leave the pasta and grab my keys to the wine cellar. I find a bottle of my favourite red and make sure I lock the door behind me.

Once I'm back in the kitchen, I fill a bowl with pasta, grab two wine glasses and my phone charger, and then disappear back up the stairs.

Lance

"Cinderella forgot her glass slipper; she wasn't the type to leave her panties lying around. My favourite food is pasta—but that could change depending on what you feed me next. And you'd make an oddly good stalker considering the nature of these texts."

My eyes drift open, revealing Scarlet standing at my side. She's pouring wine into one of two glasses on the dresser. She looks divine in her pale-pink sundress that hugs her every curve.

"Do you want to stay the night?" she asks, looking down at the other glass.

I shouldn't want to stay the night. I should say no and leave. I should, but… "Do I have to sleep in this chair?"

"No, you can take the bed." She fills the empty glass and hands it to me with a smile on her face. "I'll sleep in mine in the west wing."

I shake my head, sitting up straight in the seat. Everything's gone stiff, and the way my back aches has me questioning how long I've been sleeping. "Someone needs to keep an eye on you tonight."

"And you think you're the man for the job?" I don't miss the hint of playfulness in her tone.

"I don't know." I reach for her dress and pull her toward me until she falls into my lap. "The way you were making eyes at Jeff earlier…"

She tips her head back and laughs. "It's Jack."

Fuck, I want to kiss her neck. Explore that skin at her throat. Taste it. Feel it heat under my touch. But I can't. "He gave me his card. Said I could call if you needed anything. I can call him."

"Give it up already," she says, elbowing me in the ribs as she settles on my lap. She shakes her hair off her shoulders and looks up at me. "You made me pasta?"

"It's about all I know how to cook."

"I don't believe that. And it's delicious."

"Well then," I tell her, my eyes dropping to her full lips. "I'm glad I could satisfy your appetite."

Her lips twist together, knowing. As if she knows exactly what she does to me. "I'm sorry I didn't reply to your texts yesterday. My phone died."

"Do you ever charge it?" I ask, raising a brow as I think back to the day we got stuck in the elevator.

"*Yes*, but it's rarely with me when I'm here. I tend to leave it in a room and forget until the end of the day." She drops her eyes and shrugs. "When I got home on Thursday morning, I ended up out on the meadow. I didn't think you'd message, and I needed to switch off for a while."

I reach up and push the hair that's moved forward back from her shoulder again. I don't know if she prefers it off her face, but it's a good excuse to touch her. "Because of what happened on Wednesday night?"

I asked her to go on a date with me. I spent all day yesterday in my own head, wondering if it was too much. The present and everything that followed.

She shakes her head, and I focus back on her. "I don't really want to talk about it. But I can promise you, Wednesday night was everything I needed and more."

Relief spreads.

But if not me, then what?

She reaches across us and picks up the bowl of pasta from the sideboard. "Did you eat without me?" she asks.

"No, I was waiting for you to wake up." No matter how hungry I was, the thought of eating when she hadn't in over twelve hours made my stomach ache for a completely different reason.

"Are you hungry now?"

"I'm starving," I tell her, my mouth twitching when she happily stabs into the pasta and holds it up to me.

"Here."

I hesitate, inching back. "Have you had enough?"

She nods. "I had to fill a second bowl. You fed me, and now I need to feed you."

My eyes hold hers as I lean in and eat from the fork. I chew and swallow as she watches me. "It's good. Might be my best yet."

She laughs, shifting on my lap.

My cock twitches.

She's wearing the sundress she had on earlier, her hair down and curled with two pins pulling back the strands on the left side of her face.

She's so fucking beautiful I have to look away.

"It's so good," she tells me, taking a bite herself. I focus on the bowl between us instead of her. "You really can't cook anything else?"

I shrug, my heart beating a little too quickly. "My nan bought me a cookbook before I left for uni."

Can she tell?

Can she hear my fucking heart right now?

"What was it? A thousand ways to cook pasta?"

I look up as she quirks a mocking brow, taking another mouthful.

"One hundred, you smart-ass." I laugh, shaking my head. *Snap out of it, Sullivan.* "I became a pasta king in halls."

She chuckles and reaches for her wine. "I love that. So you're close with your nan?"

"No," I say, my chest growing a little tighter. "She passed away."

"Shit, Lance, I'm sorry. I didn't—"

"It's fine," I shake my head, reassuring her. "It's fine."

"I don't have any living grandparents. I don't remember them either. Dad's parents both died young, in their late sixties and seventies. And my mum's parents didn't like my dad." She sips her wine and looks up at me. "At all. Dad was five years older than Mum, and they thought he was manipulating her. They lived in the north and never reached out after she moved away."

"So, it's just you, Mase and your dad?"

She nods, her eyes sparkling as she stares through me. "You told me everything changed when your dad passed away, are you not close with your family?"

I look down at her, brown eyes big and waiting. Sharing this kind of thing with her feels easier than I ever expected. "Not as close as I'd like."

With a sad smile, she picks up more pasta and holds it up to me. "Functional families are entirely overrated, in my opinion."

I smile at that. Then I take the wine from her hand and take a sip, changing the subject. "How are you feeling now?"

"I feel fine. Just a little mortified that I made such a show of myself in the pharmacy." She dips her head, and I hate that I can't see her face fully. "Did Elliot tell Mason?"

My jaw clenches, but I shake my head. "No. He didn't think it was necessary. Said you need to call him when you wake up, though."

"Why does that piss you off?"

"If I were Mason, I'd want to know. Wouldn't you?" If Mason wasn't so wrapped up in Nina and whisking her away for the weekend, he'd be more aware that his sister needs him here.

Her features are soft as she turns in my lap, her knee bending to lie across my groin as her other leg hangs. "I don't know. Mase hasn't felt the need to tell me a thing in almost fifteen years." She sighs. "Dad had an appointment at the hospital on Wednesday afternoon. They were told he needs a liver transplant. I guess Mase is pretty twisted up over it."

Is that why she needed to switch off?

"And you? How do *you* feel about it?"

She toys with a button on my shirt, then visibly relaxes, taking the wineglass back and placing it with the bowl on the dresser. "Maybe a little numb. I feel like I've not let my feet touch the ground since I got home yesterday morning. I'm scared that if I do, I might… I don't know… break."

"I'm sorry, Scarlet."

"Don't be. You're actually the first person who's bothered to ask how I'm doing." She leans into me a little closer. "I appreciate that."

Our gazes are fixed, the air around us charged. It's as if, in this moment, we're both the ink and the paper, so close to something unwritten we're tainted by the unknown, yet it's clear as fucking day that I should kiss her.

"I don't tend to kiss on first dates," she tells me, confirming my thoughts.

"I don't normally offer up dates." I give her the little snippet too easily. If I hold any cards, then she's quickly stealing them one by one.

Closer. "Should I be grateful you asked then?"

Her nose brushes mine as I speak. "No. You should put your lips on mine and be quiet for a little while."

Her voice is a soft whisper. "Just a little while?"

She rocks forward, sliding her lips over mine. My hands immediately slide around her hips and over her ass, squeezing. I groan. Her tongue explores my mouth, a little more confident than the last time we kissed, and the way she licks at my lips, the corner of my mouth and then through it, searching, greedy. It makes my dick ache. It makes my dick ache so fucking bad. I can't even imagine what she would be like beneath me. The way her body would feel bare against my skin.

My hands glide from her ass to her waist and back again, my head dipping to catch another exploring kiss. "I want to feel your skin against mine," I rasp. "Every inch. Your body… it's nearly as perfect as your mind."

She pulls back, her face flushed. "What?" She smiles.

I kiss her jaw, shaking my head in disbelief at what I've just said. "See. Poison. That's what you are."

"You think my mind is perfect?"

"I said shut up and kiss me."

She laughs, leaning back to stop my assault. I just dive for her tits instead, her cleavage looking like the perfect place to busy my mouth.

"Wanna know what turned me on the most when we first met, Lance?" she says, a little breathless as I drag my tongue across the swell of her breast.

My eyes snap up.

Desperate prick.

"What?"

"The security guard's voice… it was Irish, northern, I

believe… and the way it made my—"

She squeals as I bite down on her pointed nipple. Her laugh is loud, filling not only the room but parts of me I never knew existed. She takes my head in her hands, pulling it up so she can look at me. "You're not jealous, are you?"

"I shouldn't be, should I?"

Her leg slides across my lap fully, straddling me as her dress rises to her hips. Without much thought, and with the way she's looking at me, my hands disappear beneath it. With her knees tucked at my sides, I smooth my palms from her spread thighs to her hips and then up to her waist. Goose bumps scatter the path beneath my fingers. Our eyes meet.

"That depends if you want to be honest with yourself."

"Honest about what?" I rasp.

"That you want me."

The tips of my fingers dig into the skin on her thighs too damn hard. But Scarlet reacts by snaking her body closer, grinding herself over my cock. "Will bruising me make you feel better, Lance? Will it make you feel less jealous when I'm walking around with marks on my body that you put there?"

Her lips nip at mine, teasing.

"You're pushing it, Lowell."

"Imagine when we met. Imagine I had bruises here." She gathers her dress, revealing my hands gripping the tops of her thighs, my thumbs spread wide and dangerously close to her pussy.

She rolls her hips again, and bears down, the lips of her sex parting despite the lace concealing it. I groan as she teases over the length of my dick through my slacks.

"What if *he* put them there?"

I grip her harder, keeping her close when she eases back. And I know my hold on her will bruise, but my control is out the fucking window already.

"Carry on, sunshine. The only thing you'll get yourself is fucked."

"Maybe that's exactly what I want."

"You don't know what you're asking for."

"Sex?" She smirks, leaning back.

It can't just be sex with her. This is Mason's sister. There's a line, and I'm riding it as flush as her pussy is with my cock.

"Unless you don't want me." She looks down at my lap, my cock solid and aching for her. "Maybe I've read the situation all wrong."

I move us fast, lifting her and walking to the bed, where I drop her down. My body blankets hers as I kiss her long and hard before pulling back. I grasp her behind the knees and drag her to the bed's edge, dropping to my knees as I ease one of her legs over my shoulder.

"Doubt my motives." I hook a finger into the saturated lace between her legs, my knuckle grazing the silky flesh beneath. "Doubt my every word." I gently tease a kiss over the red marks on her inner thigh. "But do not ever doubt my want for you." I lick up the centre of her pussy, and she moans, arching her back.

I close my eyes as I swallow, fucked.

Fuck.

"Lance."

I indulge in another taste, licking my lips as I pull away. "Get up. I'm taking you out."

"Lance," she begs, and I have to stand and turn away from her pleas.

"The quicker I take you out, the quicker I can do everything I want to do."

"You said you never date—"

"This is different," I snap a little too harshly. "Mason is my best friend."

"And I'm just another woman. Mason sure as shit doesn't care what I do, and I don't want or need to be… courted."

"We're doing this my way or not at all."

She watches me from the bed, her eyes hard and assessing. I stand with my hands on the back of my neck, desperate to fuck the look right off her face.

"Who's Vanessa?"

Who's Vanessa? Two words, and my dick's halfway to soft.

I pinch the bridge of my nose. "Fucking hell."

"Is she the reason you won't sleep with me?"

I look at her and frown. "She's my mother."

Her features relax. "Oh."

"You're jealous?"

Her lip twitches and I look away again.

"Get dressed, Scarlet. I want to feed you and then fuck you, and my patience to do the latter is running thin."

"This is ridiculous." She huffs, pulling down her dress as she stands and works her underwear down her legs. I step out of the room, catching her as she mumbles, "It's not a date."

My back hits the closed door as I scrub my hands over my face, willing myself to calm the fuck down.

TWELVE

Scarlet

When I leave my bedroom, Lance is nowhere in sight. The man must have run from the house for him to be out of sight in the time it took me to pull off my ruined underwear and put my dress straight.

I head for my bedroom in the west wing and pull on some fresh underwear, and then I change into a pair of light wash, loose jeans and a thin white T-shirt, forgoing a bra.

If he's going to try and take me on a date, I'll make it impossible for him to take me anywhere swanky.

The idea of this being anything more than fun isn't something I want to think about. Lance is fun to mess with. I can imagine he will be even more fun locked between my thighs. I just need to convince him to drop the "your brother will kill me if I touch you" act, especially when his mouth has already touched the parts of me that matter.

I find Lance in the car waiting for me when I leave the

house, and he barely glances at me before looking through the windscreen and driving down the lane to the main road.

I'll make the bastard crack.

And I'll enjoy every second of it.

Lance

We don't speak in the car, and the only time I dare look at her is when I'm certain she won't notice. She's wearing a sly smile I can barely make out in the dim lighting.

When we pull up to the restaurant half an hour later, I jump out and walk around to her door.

She steps past me and looks down at her T-shirt, then up at the restaurant again. "Can we go to a drive-through?"

I shake my head, my lips twitching.

Her eyes narrow, and she turns, walking off in front of me. I quickly catch up and lace our fingers, putting her slightly behind me and keeping her close at my side as we cross the car park.

I don't know if she wants to hold my hand, but I don't care. It feels too good having her at my side.

Once inside, we're seated quickly and shown to a round booth on the far right of the restaurant.

"Can I get you guys some drinks?" the waitress asks us.

"A water for me, please. With lemon, if you have it and no ice," Scarlet answers.

"Can we get a jug?" I say, sliding in next to Scarlet.

I can feel her eyes on me as the waitress backs away, and I turn to look at her, finding her staring at me unbashful.

My eyes narrow at the same time her lips twist up. She drops her gaze to my mouth. "How'd I taste?"

This fucking woman.

My head tilts, more in warning than anything else. But the way she only smiles back, not giving a shit, has my head leaning in, my hand grasping either side of her mouth. I pull her face to mine so I can kiss her hard and fast.

"You tasted like I knew you would," I groan, pulling back an inch.

"Which was?"

Sweet. Addictive. "Trouble," I tell her. "But I knew that from the moment I met you."

"In the elevator with the hot accent guy?"

"Are you baiting me, Scarlet?"

"I'd never. But an FYI…" She leans in, her body brushing mine as she whispers in my ear. "When you say my name like that… a little pissed off, and fully, it makes me—"

"Two glasses of lemon water. Are you ready to order?"

I can't take my eyes off her despite the waitress standing over us. I lift a brow and ask, "What would you like to eat, Scarlet?"

Her eyes say *me*. Thankfully her lips say, "I'll have a sundae, please. The triple chocolate."

"I'll get the steak and chips, thank you."

Once we're alone again, I pour the water and place it in front of her. "You don't want anything else to eat?"

She shakes her head. "You made me pasta. And ordered chips…"

"I don't share my food." I pause and lift my gaze to hers. "I don't share *ever*. You want chips, you order your own."

She places a hand over her chest and leans back in the

seat. "How romantic."

"You said yourself this isn't a date."

"It's not."

"Why fucking not?" I challenge.

She sighs and looks at the table. "Does there have to be a reason? Why can't this just be fun?"

"It can be fun. But I also won't treat you like it's all I want from you."

She bites her lip, her doubtful gaze shifting back to me. "Is it not all you want from me?"

My jaw tics. "No."

She goes quiet for a beat. Just looking around the restaurant as she thinks. "Well, call it whatever you want. Just please don't expect more than what I give you. It's all I have right now."

My eyes linger on her before I snigger, leaning back in the seat, baffled. I'm pretty sure I'll be begging on my knees for whatever scraps she'll give me by the end of the night.

What the fuck is wrong with me?

I'm needy.

Desperate.

But so is she. She wants more than a quick fuck. I can see it in the tortured gold flecks that make her eyes shine.

That, or I've got this all wrong.

"If this were a date," she says a little quieter, her thumbs swiping through the water droplets on the outside of her glass. "Then you should know it's my first."

I shake my head. "What?"

"You're my first date."

My brain all but evaporates. "Scarlet, you're twenty-nine years old."

"It's not *that* shocking." She looks at me as if my reaction is over the top. "You said you don't date," she defends.

"I've still dated. Back in college, when I was a boy trying to be a man—"

"Right. And that's when I was experimenting myself. None of them ever wanted to take me out after. It was a 'fuck 'em and chuck 'em' mentality. The slogan was even written in the guys' toilets on campus. Vile."

"And since uni?"

"I left in the middle of my first year to be with my dad."

"You've not been on a date in… ten years?"

"Tell the whole restaurant, Lance," she snaps.

"Have you been with anyone?"

"Yes." She straightens herself in the seat and then starts rearranging the knife and fork on the table.

"When?"

She tuts, rolling her eyes. "I don't keep a diary, asshole."

She's so defensive it makes my cock twitch with the possibilities. No wonder she's been dry-humping my lap whenever she gets the chance. "When, Scarlet?"

Her eyes flick to me, her name on my tongue making her putty in my hands. "When was the last time for *you*?"

I don't hesitate. "Last month. Tell me when?"

"Not last month… or last year."

Shit. How can someone who's as smart as she is, as beautiful, with a mouth filthy enough to make a grown man fall to his knees, not have slept with anyone for over a year?

"It was the night of Elliot's parents' wedding anniversary. We were at Rosestone Estate, celebrating, and the barman caught my eye." She shrugs. "That was four years ago."

My face drops. I scrub a hand over my mouth and drag it down the length of my neck, looking to the ceiling.

Four years.

I look back at her, still caught off guard by her revelation. Small white spots invade my vision, and I reach for my water.

"Lance." She grins, sliding closer and reaching for my tie when I place the glass down. She's more in control than me. When the fuck did that happen? "You look too dressed."

I stare at her, lost for words as my tie slips from my neck and she unfastens two buttons. Gaining some composure, I reach up with my hand and dust my thumb gently over her nipple. It pebbles under my light touch, and she shivers. "At least one of us is."

Her face is coy. Perfect. "I was trying to make you crack."

"Don't worry, sunshine. You've fucking broken me."

The drive back to Lowerwick Estate is mostly made in silence, giving me entirely too much time to think.

And with Scarlet at my side, her presence commanding and addictive, my thoughts easily get lost in her.

"You've really never been on a date?" I ask, chancing a look at her.

"Never." She shakes her head and smiles. "I liked my first, though."

"There's no way that was a date. I'm going to have to take you out again."

"No can do. You had your shot."

"You wouldn't give me a second date if I asked?"

"I'd give you a free pass to take me to bed."

I narrow my eyes at her, but my cock twitches—fucker.

She's giving me everything I'd normally want, and yet it doesn't feel anywhere near enough this time.

"What if I want more?"

"Lance—"

"What if I need another date?" I stare through the windscreen, wondering what the fuck I've just said.

"I can't give you that," she says with a gentle sadness, but when I flick my eyes to her, I find her smiling still.

We pull up to the estate, and I turn off the engine. "I only want to know who you are, Scarlet. I want to know more before I take you to bed—and don't ask me why. I tried to figure it out all afternoon while you slept."

"You don't know why? I'm wounded."

If I could return her smile, I would. But I'm hanging on by a thread, not knowing if I should walk away and leave her alone or pull her over my lap and fuck her senseless.

She sighs, mistaking my silence for something else. "I guess the men in my life haven't always been the most reliable. I know it might seem unfair, but right now, while Dad is so sick and with what's to come when he eventually gets his transplant, I can't commit to something more. Even a date. We barely know each other, and I don't have the time to get to know you. It seems like messy territory, throwing feelings around."

Her dad drank from when she was just a kid, and then Mase left her to deal with everything that followed alone. That shit's bound to change you. She's hurting, even now.

And fuck if that doesn't make my head spin.

My nostrils flare as I look back at her.

Reaching out, I cup her face, lifting her chin up so she can see my eyes fully when I say, "What if I said I won't let you down? What if I swear it? One date. If I lose interest, I'll be honest with you. I'll fuck off and leave you alone. But I won't disappear before you give me a chance."

The need to have this woman in my bed, locked in my penthouse barefoot and in my arms long after dark, it's toxic. Because there's nothing, not a damn fucking thing I wouldn't do to get her there.

Her eyes dart between my own, the hopefulness on her face making my heart pound. I wet my bottom lip. "I won't disappear on you, Scar."

Her head tilts as her eyes narrow, but then she leans in, shocking me as she softly and quickly kisses me. "You get one more date," she whispers.

I can't help my grin.

She rolls her eyes, turning to sit square in her seat.

One more date.

I don't know what I'm playing at, but as I reach out and grasp the back of her neck, pulling her to me so I can kiss her properly, nothing has felt so good in a long time.

"I'm going to date the fuck out of you, Scarlet Lowell."

She smiles against my mouth, but I don't let her go, needing more.

When I ease back, dipping to her neck, kissing the length of her throat, she buries her fingers in my hair and forces my head up.

"Can I show you something?"

I nod. "Show me everything."

THIRTEEN

Scarlet

I won't disappear on you, Scar.

And my needy little heart beat for it. Begged me, even, to open up a little and let him fill the cracks.

I'm not sure how he knew, but with one dinner and a car ride home, Lance found a way to call out the darkest parts of me, smothering my biggest fears with promises he shouldn't be making.

I can't even imagine having someone I trust wholeheartedly to be there for me, and I'd be a fool to assign that task to a man I barely know—a man like Lance Sullivan. But maybe having someone to get lost in right now *is* what I need.

After today, a date doesn't feel as impossible as it did when I left him in bed yesterday morning.

"You're not leading me to my death, are you, Lowell?"

I chuckle and pull on our joined hands, shifting under his

arm and into his side when he steps closer. We're walking toward the meadow, the moonlight our only guide, and I have to admit, if this wasn't my home, I'd be thinking the same thing.

"So, I should trust you, but you don't trust me?" I tut and smile at the ground, the grass dry underfoot thanks to another beautiful summer's day.

"I've not given you a reason to doubt me yet. But here you are, leading me through a dark field in the middle of nowhere."

I look up at his six-foot-three frame. "You scared, big man?"

"No," he baulks.

"Good." I smile before ducking out from under his arm and running for the top of the hill. The moon's full, waiting for me on the other side of the lake.

"Scarlet."

I chuckle, wondering if he can see me fully. "Don't get lost out here… the bears will get you."

He's walking at a normal pace, hands in his pockets, unfazed, while I'm running backward, a smile spread wide as a fresh night's breeze sets me free.

"Don't dirty that pretty suit, princess," I taunt, reaching the brow of the hill.

I rush down the bank, ducking behind the large aspen tree at the bottom. The lake is beautifully still tonight despite the light wind. It's like this most nights, but there's not a time it doesn't enrapture me.

It embodies everything that the estate is for me.

I see Lance meet the water's edge, and if he was searching for me before, he's been distracted. The moon reflects off the water, glowing across his face as he gazes past the boat and beyond the wide expanse.

I follow his gaze and then wait as the view ebbs away the adrenaline coursing through me.

"Without the moon, I'd be nothing at night."

He shifts his head toward the tree I'm holding on to. I smooth my hand down the bark and step out from the shadows.

"You don't come out here alone, do you?" he asks, concerned.

I nod, standing beside him. "It's safe. It's only me out here. And you, tonight." I smile, looking up at him.

He frowns. "I thought you… in the elevator that day, you said you were afraid of the dark."

"I'm terrified of the dark."

He looks down at me as if I've lost all sanity.

"This isn't darkness, Lance."

He turns to look up at the hill, then back at me. "Mase doesn't come out here?"

I shake my head and say, "Never."

He sets his jaw, eyes troubled as he stares back out over the lake. "Will you tell me why?"

"Why Mason doesn't come out here?" I ponder the question as I take a relaxed breath.

"No," Lance says guiltily, forcing my eyes up to his. "Why are you afraid of the dark?"

Oh. I swallow and shrug. "Honestly, I don't really know. When I was a baby, I slept fine. When my mum died, Dad co-slept, but then when I turned three, he moved me into my own room. It was right next to his, but the second he shut the light out and left the room, I screamed the house down." I roll my lips, feeling so stupid. "It went on for years. I didn't know it then, but he was drinking at the time, which is why he couldn't co-sleep anymore."

"Did anyone know he was drinking?"

I shake my head no, a sad smile thinning my lips. "I was too young, and eventually, I felt like I was causing his sadness and change in moods. I started to pretend to read. I'd hold a book in front of my face for hours to give myself, and anyone who cared, a reason not to switch out the lamp… I guess old habits die hard."

Lance's eyes are shadowed by darkness, but the green flecks that are visible enthral me.

"We've had power cuts throughout the years," I tell him, knowing I've left a lot out. "I'm not afraid of a lot, but the depth of nothingness that darkness brings terrifies me."

Lance doesn't say anything. He smooths his hand across the nape of my neck and pulls me closer.

Should that feel as natural, as good as it just did?

I didn't tell him to be comforted, but having him hold me right now, after the week we've had as a family… I slip my arms around him, looking out at the lake. "Can I ask you a question?"

I feel him nod.

"Why is your mum's name saved under Vanessa on your phone and not Mum?"

I feel it leave him. The lightness. And in its place forms something I can't place.

I'm thankful when he doesn't let go of me, instead leaning back. "Things got really sour after my dad died. I thought my mum and sisters were struggling because he'd died so suddenly. But I wasn't there to see what was happening. I went away to university. Knew I had to finish my degree and take over the company like he wanted me to."

"What was happening?"

He stares through me, that same look in his eye that he had on the night of the gala. Anger, I had told him, and maybe there is anger there deep within, but the look in his eyes right now is the harsh reality of a betrayal. Someone hurt him.

"They destroyed everything we ever worked for."

I wince, heat spreading through my chest like fire. "What's everything?"

"My dad's company, the house, any money to our name and then that too… everything that held value was lost. And then, when our nan got sick, and I asked them to take care of her, to take turns each day because they weren't working, they told me they couldn't and said they'd put her in a home. She died a week after being admitted."

"Lance—"

He shakes his head, realising how far he's gone and turns away from me to look back out across the lake. "You don't…" I see his jaw clench. "Your brother saved my ass. Don't apologise."

"Mason helped you?"

"He gave me a job. I mean, I'm the shit when it comes to numbers." My lips twitch when he shifts his face back to me, his voice thick with emotion as his eyes shine. "My dad's bike was all we had left when I found out what was happening. It was a wreck from the crash and worthless to my mum and sisters. I could've got it fixed and sold it on, but I didn't have a penny to my name. I tried. I worked in a bar on campus for a bit. Learnt how to make a pretty good cocktail." He gives me a killer smile, lighting me up from the inside out. "But that was never enough. And then Mase told me he'd cover the arrears on the mortgage, said to come in and play with some figures for your dad until we were square. He bought the bike from me, paying me what it was purchased for. Said I could buy it back when I was straight. Things got back on track after a while, but my dad's company had already been in liquidation and sold off by that point, and there wasn't a single client in the country that wanted to work with me."

"You lost the company completely?" I know how much blood and sweat my father put into Ellis and Frey. I know how much it means to him. To lose that…

"We lost everything but the house… thanks to your brother."

"And the bike."

He flexes his jaw, a slight shake to his head. "No. Mase still has it."

I frown. "Why?"

"It's a wreck. I don't want it."

Mason has the bike? I had no idea. "I'm sorry you went through what you did, Lance. That your mum and sisters did that."

He eyes me, arching a thick brow. "It's not all bad, Lowell. You pay me well."

I push him back a step, breaking the mood that's been cast over us. "I'm kinda your boss, right?"

"Absolutely not."

"It's my name on the door." I shrug, stepping back when he steps forward. "I could get a position tomorrow and be set up on your floor by the end of the day." Another step.

This time I remove my phone from my pocket and throw it to the sandy area between the grass and water. "I could have your fancy office for myself. I could fire your ass."

His eyes follow my phone, then come back to me.

"You can try. I don't know how easy it will be with my cock in your mouth."

I roll my eyes, fighting my smile. "Overconfident, audacious man."

"I'm not overconfident. I'm certain of it. I'd have you on your knees by lunchtime, begging to take my cock down your throat." He kicks off his shoes, and I grin, unbuttoning my jeans.

"Ironic, really, considering it was you on your knees just hours ago."

He waits with a face that could have been carved with stone as I pull my jeans down my legs and throw them at him. He catches them as my feet hit the water's edge. I step backward into the water, our eyes locked. He makes me feel so sexy and seen. He makes me feel… alive.

"Are you coming in, or do I have to *beg* you?"

When the water reaches my waist, he lowers the zipper on his suit pants and removes his shirt. Muttering something under his breath.

I chuckle and dip under the water, surfacing moments later. As I clear the water from my face, I find Lance stalking toward me, his body everything my greedy little eyes crave.

"It's fucking freezing."

"You'll warm up," I tell him, swimming further back.

He shakes his head as if he's annoyed when I know he isn't, and then he dips under the water, disappearing. I smile and start to swim away.

When he surfaces, he glares at me. "Come here, Scarlet."

"Come and get me," I taunt.

He does, lunging through the water and grabbing my ankle before I can pull away. He drags me to him, and I go willing, wrapping myself around him when he's close enough.

"See. Not so bad, is it?"

His arms band around my back, making me feel tiny in his hold. "Tell me you don't swim out here alone."

He has an intense look in his eyes. A protective fierceness I've not seen before. "I don't swim out here alone."

His eyes narrow. "You're being smart."

"I'm doing as I'm told."

His face turns harder. "So, you do? You swim out here alone?"

I shrug. "What do you want me to say?"

"I want you to call me the next time you think it's a good idea."

I can't hide my amusement. "You're being irrational right now."

"Does Mason know?"

I chuckle, shaking my head. "Mason doesn't know what colour my car is." I run my hand through the hair at the nape of his neck. "Can you stop caring so much? You're making it impossible for me not to fancy the pants off you."

I agreed I'd date the man, and now he's looking at me as if he'll have me pregnant before we get to first base.

"What if I already care too much?" He swallows, sobering my features as he looks between my eyes as if he's worried his honesty might scare me away. "When the phone rang today, and it was you… I didn't know up from down or left from right. Not until I pulled up to the pharmacy and saw you sitting on that chair. I was fucking wild. Out of my mind with worry. I've never felt that way over anyone, and especially not…"

My heart thumps so hard, so steadily, it sparks a memory. I smile as warmth spreads through my chest.

"I have my mother's diaries," I tell him, not making him finish. "Dad had them reprinted after they were damaged and gave them to me when I was twelve." Lance moves so that I ease back slightly, our faces only inches apart as he holds us in the water. "There's this one entry, it's from the week after she met him, and it's always been so confusing to me because she barely even knew him, and yet it's my dad in every way that matters. It says… *That man has a wild heart. One he'd give too easily and never ask to be returned. One he'd take from his chest and place into my own if asked. He's a good man. Mother would hate him.*" I smile, knowing I've likely terrified Lance. I grasp his hand and pull it to rest on my chest, above my wild heartbeat. "You did that. It happened in the dress shop that first day. At the gala when you came back to dance with me. On my birthday when I found your gift. Today… when I woke up and found you asleep at my bedside." I think about how hard my heart had raced when he threw me to the bed and licked me. How whenever he looks at me, my stomach flutters like a million butterflies taking flight. "You showed up for me today, Lance. Thank you for that."

We get lost in a trance, his hand still lying on my chest. "Would she hate me?" he mutters.

My throat aches, the realisation that maybe this is different, that he's different somehow. "I wish I knew the answer to that… But, Lance, if my mother's diaries have taught me anything, it's to chase today like tomorrow doesn't exist. Stop thinking about what has or might happen and let be what's happening right now. I want you. I want you so bad it makes me ache."

His jaw clenches, his forehead meeting mine. "There's so much I want to know, Scarlet," he mutters, guilty. "So much I should give before I take."

"Lance—"

"Don't let me take too much," he rasps out. "I already know it's going to be impossible to stop."

I frown, reaching up to smooth out his furrowed brow. He leans into my touch, turning his face to rest his lips against my palm, kissing it.

Something inside of me sparks, the gesture unexpected and tender.

His loyalties lie with my brother. I can see it holding him back even now. And after everything he's told me tonight, it's obvious that Mason was all he had after his dad and nan died.

Who else does Lance have outside of my brother, Elliot and Charlie?

"Scarlet—" He groans.

Our noses brush, lips grazing. Desperate but afraid. "It's impossible to take too much when it's given to you freely, Lance. Let me drown in you."

I'm not sure what I'm saying because this isn't how it's supposed to go. This wasn't the plan. It wasn't what I was saying in the car an hour ago. But I've not told one lie. Not fumbled one word.

"Jesus Christ."

His mouth crashes to mine, my eyes closing as I kiss him back. I move my legs higher up his waist, locking them tighter.

I feel the water moving around us, and then he's reaching behind me. I'm lifted from the water and settled onto the dock. The wood is cool against my back, but Lance quickly pulls himself up and is on me before a shiver can pass through me, his hands going straight for the T-shirt that's stuck to me like a second skin. He throws it to the dock once it's clear of my head.

My breasts are wet, nipples firm and when Lance groans, reaching out to fill his hands with them, I give in to him completely.

"Lance, please." I arch my back, needing more.

He kisses the space between my breasts, then my throat, and then my mouth. "When you're under me, you're mine to do with as I please. Don't tell me how to fuck you, Scarlet."

I moan.

I can feel his cock through his briefs, the thick head heavy against my groin. Everything aches. "I need you inside of me. Don't make me wait. Please."

His eyes close, and when they open, I know the reluctance he had before is held together by a thread.

"Are you wet for me?"

I nod, my cheeks flaming. I drop my knees to the dock.

His cheek tics, a silent approval. And then he hooks a finger under either side of my underwear, pulling them down my legs.

"Keep talking to me," I rasp. "Please."

His palm dusts south over my stomach, and when his thumb brushes through my centre, pausing at my throbbing clit, I moan entirely too loudly. "Look at you. Dripping for me. Do you have any idea how perfect you are like this?"

I feel a rush of heat at my core, the stickiness between my legs getting worse.

"Lance—"

"You like it when I talk to you?" His brow quirks. "You want me to talk to you while I finger you, sunshine?"

I nod, trembling when he smiles down at me, brushing his thumb over my clit again. "Don't stop."

"Can you give me a couple of minutes?" He eases back, his head dipping between my thighs. "I need to indulge a little first."

His mouth slides over me, and my head falls back. The need I've felt since I rode his lap days ago still burns deep within me.

His tongue glides over my slick skin. Lips dragging, sucking, teasing me with soft nips. I whither under his assault, unable to utter words.

As if he can't get enough, he slides his hands under my ass, forcing me harder against his mouth, burying his tongue deep.

"Work your hips. Fuck my face like you did my lap."

I whimper, losing all my inhibitions and pretending I won't have to look him in the eye after. I start to work my hips under his hold as he urges me on, letting me know I can go harder as he sucks and licks. I watch his throat working, swallowing, his tongue plunging into me.

I'm on fire.

My hands reach for his head, fisting in his hair.

"Good girl. Show me exactly what you like."

I buck, and tears prickle in my eyes as my mouth hangs open. My orgasm rips through me, and I work myself on Lance's mouth and chin with no thought for him, only the pleasure erupting at my core.

When it starts to subside, I look down the length of my body, finding him cleaning up my orgasm with his mouth, an accomplished look on his face as he kisses my sensitive skin.

"Ruined," he mutters, pulling his top lip into his mouth as if to savour the taste. "You've ruined me for any other woman."

I sit forward and demand his lips with my own, loving the way he groans into my mouth when I pull him over me.

He rocks into me, his cock hard and punishing against my too-sensitive clit. I reach between us and pull at his briefs.

"Scar—" He kisses me, cutting himself off. "Fuck!" He kisses me again, my hand wrapping around his thick length in the next second. He breaks the kiss, closing his eyes. "Scarlet."

"I want you to ruin me for any other man."

His eyes snap open, and he instantly shakes his head, pulling back. "You don't mean that—"

I nod quickly, whispering against his lips. "I do."

We kiss. And I know he's tethered on the edge. I pump his cock with leisurely strokes until his hand wraps around mine. "Later." Another kiss. "I'm about to embarrass myself with three pumps."

I smile and lift my hips, making the head of his cock glide through my pussy. I turn my head and lick up the column of his neck, the skin salty. And then I push the tip of him into me right as my teeth pull on the lobe of his ear.

"Scar, stop. Fuck! I don't have a condom."

"I don't care." I push him a little deeper, frowning when I realise how big he feels with just the tip inside.

I move my hips, trying to ease the pinching sensation.

"Scarlet, we can't—"

"I'll go to the pharmacy in the morning. Jack will help—"

His chest vibrates between us as he sinks all the way into me, a groan tearing free from somewhere deep in his throat.

"Taunt me, sunshine," he rasps against my ear. "I'll fuck his name right out of your mouth."

"You promise?" I force from my lips, my voice breathless as I try to accommodate the size of him.

He's big, far bigger than I thought, and he doesn't promise me with words, he demonstrates his promise with a thrust so deep, I cry out.

"Lance," I panic.

"Tomorrow, when you walk into that pharmacy, you'll stand there with a throb that starts right here." He flattens his hand on my pelvis, pushing down and making my eyes roll. He grinds his hips deep, and I reach for him, a distorted moan passing my open lips as I come around him. "And you'll think of *me*. You'll feel *me*. You'll ache. For. *Me*."

He's everywhere.

Undoing everything.

"Lance—"

"Tell me who you ache for?"

I meet his next thrust, frantic for more and wince, the

pleasure and pain hard to distinguish but the perfect mix. I chase it.

"You. I ache for you."

"Fuck yes, you do."

He snaps, grabbing my damp skin and pounding into me until the slapping of wet skin is all that can be heard across the water. My body moulds to him, the feeling of a body so close, so fully given, more than I've had in maybe ever. The second his hand lifts my leg and places it over his arm, I wrap my own hand around his neck and pull him flush to me, needing a little more than I thought I would from him.

Our lips meet, his frenzy halted with the changed angle. And yet the feel of his cock as it slows, the ridged, veiny lines that I can feel more than I thought was possible as he's sucked into my heat, it's the most erotic thing I've ever experienced.

And he knows it, making enough space to look between us.

"Listen—listen to how wet you are for me."

The slickened sound of my arousal is all I can hear as he grinds deep against me.

His hips shift, and I gasp, my nails dragging through his hair and down his back as my insides clench around him.

"Fuck," he groans, his arms giving out as his body betrays him. He thrusts deep and then releases inside of me, jolting above my body as his cock twitches.

I swallow, letting my head hit the deck. His head meets my chest, his ragged breath panting over the taut skin between my breasts.

"Baby Lowell—"

"Shh," I hush breathlessly, running my hand through his hair and over his strong back. "I need a second."

He chuckles and pushes up onto his strong arms. "Next time, I'm going to enjoy you properly. I shouldn't have rushed that."

I lift my head up, looking at him incredulously. "You're joking."

I'm completely ruined right now.

He smirks, sucking my left nipple into his mouth and nipping it with his teeth. "I hardly appreciated these babies. You've got perfect tits." I feel him continue to twitch and harden inside of me, but he quickly pulls out, kneeling between my thighs.

I go to close my legs, but he lifts a hand and touches the back of it to my knee, halting me as his eyes glaze, hungry and on my aching pussy.

I feel the trickle of his cum as it leaks from me, know it's what he's fixated on.

I've never felt so exposed.

I've never felt more turned on.

Two of his fingers brush low, and I gasp as he gathers what's leaked out and pushes it back inside of me. His fingers sink in to his knuckles.

"You're full of me," he marvels.

"Lance, I can't." My hips roll, contradicting my words.

"You will," he tells me. "I'm going to fuck you just like this, watching my cum spill out of you over and over again while my cock fills you. Tell me you'll love every second of it."

His fingers curl, my body arching as my mouth opens

and closes. “Speak, sunshine, or I’ll give you something more than words to choke on.”

When I don’t, only whimpering, he sniggers.

Cocky bastard.

His fingers leave me, but then he attentively lifts my knees from the dock, my legs bent but in line with his body. He pushes down on the back of my thighs, my feet meeting his chest. And then he feeds his cock into me slowly, looking down between my shins as his cum is forced in and then out.

“Lance,” I moan.

He flicks his eyes up as he smiles down at me. “Yes, darling?”

FOURTEEN

Lance

"Are you cold?"

Scarlet smooths the back of her finger up my side, shaking her head slightly at my question. "Are you?"

I shake my head, working my hand into her hair. We're lying on the wooden dock—or I am. Scarlet's naked body is draped over me, just as spent as my own.

"Do you ever masturbate and it's like the best of the best and then after, feel like utter trash? Like completely drained and not entirely with it."

I smile, and then a deep chuckle vibrates from my throat, echoing across the lake and surrounding trees. "Don't tell me you feel like utter trash right now, sunshine. You'll bruise my ego."

She sits up, resting her forearms on my ribs as she laughs with me. "Utter trash in the best possible way, I promise. I've never felt like this after sex."

I tuck a piece of loose hair behind her ear, the damp

strands a darker lavender than before. "Tell me about all the times you've masturbated."

She relaxes again, her hair spreading across my chest. I can feel her smile on my skin. "Well, I don't keep count, but I guess if we said once a week at most since I was in my teens, so that's…"

"That's seven hundred and thirty weeks from your sixteenth birthday."

"Really," she says, surprised. "Why does that sound painful? My poor vagina."

I can't help but laugh with her again, our bodies shaking.

"I don't remember all seven hundred and thirty of them but pick one, and I'll tell you everything I remember about it."

I stare up at the clear sky, the stars brighter than I've ever seen them. "The one when you got home from the Hamilton Gala and couldn't think of anything but my face."

She chuckles some more. "You wish. I slept on the chair in my dad's room for the night. He had an infection and was sick."

My smile drops, brows drawing in. The idea of her here alone, curled up at his bedside while we were at the gala, carrying on as if everything were normal. It pisses me off. "Mason and the guys are like family to me, but I can't help but feel pissed when you tell me that Mason straight-up refuses to help you with this."

"He doesn't do it selfishly."

"No?"

She shakes her head. "He's afraid."

"Afraid of what?"

"Losing any more than he's already lost. I think it's why he's grown so close to Nina so quickly. I'm not sure there's an in-between with him. You said yourself he pulled you in when he met you, gave you a job."

I think about what she's said. Outside of the guys and me, he doesn't let anyone get close. "He's been with loads of women. Why would Nina be any different?"

I feel her mouth twitch against my skin. "There's this thing with a pixie. Long story, but when Elliot met Nina, he unknowingly made her something Mason could never forget. He'll likely make many decisions because of it."

"What?"

She laughs and says, "He's hopelessly in love, basically."

"Did you know he took her to Paris this weekend?"

"He did?"

"Flew her out tonight—just to show her the ballet."

She moves her body over me, quirking a brow when we're nose to nose, my cock trapped and twitching between us. "See. Hopelessly in love."

"I just fucked you under the stars. What does that make us?" I ask, rubbing my hands down the length of her naked back.

"Exhibitionists, Satan's spawns, or just really horny fuckers?"

"I'd say one and three are the same."

"And you'd agree?"

"No—" Her lips steal mine, and I frown because I know it's fucked up. But as my heart pounds out of rhythm against hers, I only kiss her harder and say, "We're hopelessly." Kiss. "Fucking." Kiss. "*Wild.*"

Her eyes spark, and she pulls back, looking down at me. "You're smooth, Sullivan. I'll give you that."

And you're like nothing I saw coming.

"You're beautiful. I'm not sure I've ever told you that."

"You haven't." She smiles, biting her full bottom lip.

"Well, you know now. Don't forget."

Our kiss is slow. Dangerously so. A kiss that's gentle enough not to leave a mark but one that could bring a man like me to his knees. I reach up and take hold of her face, tilting her chin as our tongues intertwine.

And then I roll her over and fuck her wild.

Scarlet

What has he done to me?

Lance is laughing. Bastard. And I'm on my hands and knees trying to stand.

"It's like Bambi on ice."

"Lance!"

I want to scold him, but for the millionth time in the last couple of hours, I can't help but gawk at him as his laugh lights up his whole face.

"Let me carry you."

"I think you've done enough," I tell him. Finally rising to my feet, my knees shake, and I fight the urge to step forward, knowing I'll hit the deck. "This isn't normal."

"I'm carrying you," he tells me, not caring to listen to my demands as he finishes buttoning his suit pants and walks toward me. He's already put his shirt on me, my T-shirt ending up in the lake somehow.

When he reaches me, he looks down and grins. "Your knees are quivering like the oak trees, sunshine."

I look out at the trees hugging the boundary of the meadow, bristling as a slight breeze moves over the hillside.

"They're aspens, asshole, not oak."

He only laughs harder. "Sorry. I made you quiver like an *aspen*."

"You're not funny."

He picks me up, clearly proud of himself, as he walks up the wooden walkway and toward the hill.

My eyes close, giving in as I rest my head against his shoulder. "I think I need to eat something."

I feel his hold tighten. "You're feeling faint?"

"No," I murmur, the warmth of his body making my eyes heavy. "Just hungry."

Lance carries me back across the fields, his stride not easing until we reach the house. He slides me down his body once we're on the terrace, guilt marring his brow as he watches me.

"Why are you looking at me like that?"

"I told Jack I'd look after you and then took you home and fucked you."

I purse my lips and then run my hand down his bare chest, pushing him back a step. "You excelled yourself."

"Can I stay?" he asks, cocking his head toward the house. "I'd feel better if you'd let me. We can eat, and I'll sleep in the chair. No more sex."

"You can stay on one condition."

He tips his chin, taking a step toward me again and eating up the space I created.

"You let me do whatever I want to you."

His step falters. "Scarlet—"

"The choice is yours, Lance." I turn and walk inside the house, making my way to the kitchen so I can make myself something to eat.

There's cheese in the fridge, a selection of my favourites, and I place them on the island along with crackers and fresh butter. As I go to close the fridge, I spot the cold beef that I cut into slices yesterday and reach for a piece.

"You're nothing like I expected you'd be, you know."

I slide up onto the worktop, making sure his shirt covers my bare ass. "What were you expecting?"

"A child. Mason never told me you were… I guess I pictured a spoiled little sister who likely knew nothing about life."

I smile. "And what about now?"

He steps into the room, rounds the island and eases himself between my legs. I bite into the beef, my eyes closing with how good it tastes. "Hmm."

"I think you're too smart for the likes of me."

"You're smart, Lance," I tell him, patting the scruff on the side of his face playfully.

"If I were smart, I'd have left just now."

"I already told you what a horny bastard you are." I reach for the cheese board, my attention slightly wandering. "Want some?" I ask, holding out a piece.

He leans in and eats it from between my two fingers.

"So, you like cheese?" he asks, eyeing the giant board as he swallows.

"I love cheese," I correct. "In fact, I'm known for my love of it."

"Known for your love of fermented dairy?"

I nod, a slight smile tugging up my mouth. "I once cried on a flight home from our lodges in Bora Bora because they didn't have any more cheese toasties. Glen and Freya vowed we'd never fly commercial again after that and invested in the jet." Judgement passes his features, and I chuckle. "I know how it sounds, but I was starving and irrational. I hadn't eaten, and as you learnt today, I don't do well without my food. Mason was mortified, and I was embarrassed for myself."

"You cried over a cheese toasty?"

"I cried over the woman behind me ordering the last one and then not eating the whole thing. I resorted to pasta and then made Mason stop off on the way home so we could get all the cheese I could get my hands on."

He shakes his head and leans his hands on the counter on either side of me, inching closer. "Do you have a favourite?"

I lick my lips and smile. "Raclette."

He simply nods, and I can tell he's stored the information away.

I think about the text he'd sent me earlier that day. "What's your favourite food?"

He doesn't hesitate. "Steak."

"Movie?"

"*Shawshank Redemption*." He smiles. "Yours?"

"*Pretty Woman*." I smile back as he lingers close to me. "Colour?"

"Lavender." Our noses brush as he adds, "And sunshine."

"That's not a colour," I whisper, grinning against his lips.

"It isn't? I could have sworn—" His lips curve against

my still swollen mouth, and I arch my back, pulling him in closer when his tongue lashes against my own, demanding and untamed. "You're unravelling me," he moans between kisses. "Ruining." I pull on his bottom lip. "Me."

Whatever game I'm playing with Lance feels dangerous with an inevitable end. He's got me right where he wants me, and I've let him do it with ease. There's no doubt that I wanted this. The penthouse, the dock tonight, him showing up at the pharmacy. I've had more fun in the last two days than I've had in over a year. But there's still a rational part of my mind screaming at me to shut him down.

Dad's sick, and he needs me more than ever.

I don't have time for more of anything.

"Thank you, Scarlet."

I frown as I pull back, but he leans in and takes my lips in another quick kiss before answering, "For showing me."

The idea of more of this man terrifies me because he's saying all the right things.

He's proving me wrong.

"You're welcome."

But there's not a single person on earth I've ever loved that hasn't let me down.

And that's terrifying.

Terrifying enough that I pull back slightly.

"What's got your head in a spin?" he asks, tightening his eyes on me. He reaches out with his hand and lifts my chin up to his face when I don't reply. "You can talk to me."

I look at him and frown before I tell him honestly, "I'm not sure I trust you."

His face transforms in an instant, a hint of amusement flaring in his eyes as he picks up my hand and settles it over his bare chest, right above his racing heart. "I know. I'm not sure I trust you either."

He readjusts himself, resting his arms on either side of me again. I leave my hand resting over his inked skin. "I know it's only our first date," he says with a smirk, leaning in to gently kiss my cheek. "But I've never in my life wanted to prove myself to anyone as much as I do you, Scarlet Lowell."

I sigh, reaching up and running my hand through his damp hair. "Well, I guess that seems like a pretty good place to start."

Maybe I need to take my own advice and stop fretting about what could be tomorrow.

Lance shakes his head no, lifting me from the counter in one swift movement. "Me buried deep inside of you is where we'll start. The rest will come."

I smile against his neck as he carries me through the silent house and up the stairs. When we reach the top, he looks down at me in question.

My head flicks to the right. "West wing."

He walks us down the long corridor. "Why the west?"

"If you put me down, I'll show you."

I pad barefoot to my room, pushing open the door and flicking on the light. I pull Lance inside and watch him as he walks further into the room.

It's one of the smaller bedrooms in the wing, but it's mine and decorated exactly how I want it in soft beiges and blacks. My king-size bed sits in the middle of the room against the wall, my scattered pillows making me want to evaporate when I see that I left them on the floor this morning.

To the left of the room, there's an en suite with a walk-in shower and a large bathtub.

And although it's likely nothing Lance is used to, his eyes seem to scan around every inch of it as if he is committing the smallest details to memory.

His head trails back as he follows the fairy lights that twist up and around the exposed wooden beams already lit up from the solar charge outside.

Stepping closer, I pull on his bicep and lead him to the curtains, drawing them back to reveal the balcony.

I feel him stiffen under my touch.

"Lance, meet my mum."

The wildflowers sway gently under the moonlit sky we had lain beneath only moments ago. Only it's my mother's garden that seems to have Lance's full attention now.

He reaches for the handle and slides the door back, lacing our fingers and stepping out onto the stone balcony. He stops once he reaches the wall, and I brace myself for what he might say. What he might think of the view I wake up to every morning.

"Shit, Scar." He pulls his eyes away from my mother's headstone, his eyes zoning in on me. "It's incredible. You're incredible."

I wave him off. "It was her idea. I barely even know the woman." An awkward chuckle slips out as I say it, but it's true. I only know what's written in her diaries and what Freya has told me.

"I don't think we have to know everything to see that someone is good. Sometimes we're allowed to presume."

"Maybe." I rock forward as I look up at him.

"You're incredible," he repeats.

I smile. "You said that already."

"I'm just making sure you believe it."

My face heats, and I dip my head before looking straight back up, not wanting to hide. "You said that sometimes we're allowed to presume."

He nods, smoothing a frizzy curl back behind my ear.

"I think she would have liked you. I think she'd have smiled her big smile and told me to enjoy this while it lasts."

His lip curls up, a dark brow quirking as he shifts his body to face me. "Me and your mum, we're like this." He crosses his fingers together and holds them up.

I laugh and step into him, not giving him a choice but to wrap his arms around me.

His lips touch my head, and I sink deeper into him. As my hand flattens on his bare back, I feel goose bumps spread. "You're cold."

"I'm fine."

Pulling back, I glance down at the garden once more, then take Lance's hand and lead him into my room. As my eyes land on my bed, my bed that I've never shared with anyone before… "I have a spare toothbrush," I say, disappearing into my bathroom.

Why do I feel like a naughty teen having a boy over for the first time? Because it's my first time? I'm twenty-nine years old, for goodness' sake.

Lance follows me into the bathroom, his movements relaxed compared to my own.

Do I have a side I sleep on? I think I sleep in the middle… or slightly to the right with my knee bent up.

"Scarlet." My name on his tongue, the way he says it…

"Yes," I answer, turning with mine and the new toothbrush packet in my hands.

He pushes off from where he's sitting on the bathtub and stands behind me in the mirror. I look up at him in the glass, swallowing as his warmth surrounds me.

He lifts his chin in question, asking me what's wrong. As if he somehow knows my mind is running a million miles a minute.

"I've never had a man sleep in my bed before."

He tenses momentarily but then catches himself. Gently, he wraps an arm around my waist, tucking me into the safety of his chest as he takes the toothbrushes from my hand and places them down. "Do you want me to sleep in the chair?"

The chair. Not leave.

I shake my head.

"I'm not used to having company, but the thought of having you in my bed for the night makes me feel… some kind of way."

He leans down and kisses the bare skin between my shoulder and neck. "It makes me feel some kind of way as well, sunshine."

Sensing his smile, I turn in his arms to catch it. My hands run down his chest, rippling over his abs. "I have some of Mason's old clothes… if you want something to put on."

What? God, no. *Please say no.*

His eyes darken, and he must understand the panic on my face because in the next second he pushes his boxers down his legs, completely baring himself to me. His thick cock bobs between us, brushing against my stomach.

I swallow and bite my lip as my legs brush together, trying to ease the ache growing there.

"I don't want anything to put on, Scarlet." He fists his cock, closing his eyes as he squeezes tight. When they open again, they pin me, and I feel the stickiness of my arousal between my legs. "I want to take you right here, messy and hard against the sink. And then I want to fuck you slow and deep in the shower while I wash every inch of you. And then, once you're utterly fucked and can't take any more of me, you'll climb into bed and let me soothe all the parts that ache while you lie in my arms and sleep. Does that sound okay?"

Instead of answering him—because I'm unsure anything would come out coherent—I simply lift his shirt from over my head and drop it to the tiles. My breasts sit full and heavy, nipples hard and begging for the warmth of his large hands, but his eyes don't leave my face.

He reaches up and dusts his thumb across my bottom lip, his gaze following the motion as he rasps, "Turn around and spread your legs, Scarlet. Make sure you hold on to the sink."

FIFTEEN

Lance

The warmth of her body is absent when I wake up on Saturday morning, but the need to go and find her like I did at Mason's place on Wednesday isn't there either.

I can tell she's somewhere close.

We haven't long been to sleep. The sun was slowly rising as I wrapped her in a towel and carried her to the bed. She bound her arms and legs around me and was asleep before any doubt could settle in her mind.

And then I spent entirely too long just watching her.

She's under my skin, and I don't know how to stop. I don't want to stop. I don't know how I tell Mason that I've spent the weekend lost inside of his sister. Because I am. I'm completely lost in the feel. The sounds she makes. The way she touches my skin and it soothes something deep inside of me. The way she smiles at me like I can fix all the shit that's broken.

I should start by getting up out of bed and putting some clothes on. But I don't do that either.

"Hey, asshole."

I sit up in the bed, grinning when she walks into the room with a tray. "What's this?"

She's wearing a fluffy white dressing gown, wrapped up as if it's not summer outside. "I cooked you breakfast."

I need to stop fucking smiling.

"Come here," I tell her.

My eyes lock on her as she steps up to the bed. I remove the tray from her hands and place it on the bedside table. Then I grab her by the waist and pull her onto the mattress, putting her under me. I have her robe undone and my mouth on her skin within a second.

"You're hungry?" I can hear the smile in her voice.

I bite down on her nipple, and she cries out, wiggling to get away from me. "Starving." I work up her body, kissing her neck. "I missed you."

She chuckles, running her hand through my hair. "You were sleeping."

"Stop leaving me in beds alone."

Her phone starts to ring, and I groan.

"It could be the hospital."

I quickly fish it out of her pocket and pass it to her.

"It's an unknown number."

"Answer it." I frown.

It rings out, and she curses. "I have our doctor's number saved. If it's him, it would've come up with his name." She looks to me for reassurance. "If it's important, they'll leave a message."

Her phone pings a second later.

She presses play and puts it on loudspeaker.

"Scarlet, it's me, Lucy! Your brother booked a table at Groulx for Megs and me tonight to say thank you for getting Nina packed for Paris without her knowing. You're coming with us. Please come!" I shake my head at Megan's voice screeching in the background. "We really want you to come with us, Scar," Lucy adds, and I watch as Scarlet's whole face lights up. "I can come out and get you, or maybe you can get a lift. Let us know!"

She sits in silence once the voice mail ends. I fill the void by leaning down and kissing her stomach. "Are you going to go?"

She chews on her bottom lip. "I can't. Groulx is on the other side of London. I'd be gone for hours, and I was out for most of the day yesterday. I don't want to leave my dad again."

"Is Vinny not around this weekend?"

I can practically hear her thoughts running. "Maybe," she says.

She wants to go out with them. As much as I want to lie here all day and get lost in her, I want to see her eyes as bright as they were when Lucy invited her out more.

"You should go out. Why don't you text Vin."

Her face transforms again, and then she drops her phone to the mattress and pulls me over her, putting us nose to nose. "What are you going to do tonight?"

I kiss her long and deep. "Catch up on some sleep."

"Hmm… I'm sorry."

"Don't be." Our tongues meet, and I have to pull back, knowing she's still sore from last night. "I can take you into the city if you want. I need to drop the car back to Aldridge anyway."

She shakes her head, her chest working from our kiss. "I have things to catch up on from yesterday, but thank you. I'll get a taxi into the city this afternoon."

I nod. "So I only have a couple more hours."

She smiles, her nails dusting across my shoulder blade. "Why don't you eat breakfast so I can say goodbye to you properly."

"Are you kicking me out early, Baby Lowell?"

She shakes her head, catching on and then sucking my bottom lip as she kisses me. "I want to savour the taste of you," she whispers. "If you'll let me."

I close my eyes and groan. "Don't tease me."

She gives me a smile that's supposed to be coy. "You know, I thought about how you might feel against my tongue whilst making your breakfast. I wondered if it would be soft and velvety or hard. Or maybe it would be hard, velvety *and* soft? Will it taste salty or sweet when you—"

"Bitter. It's a bitter taste." My eyes widen when I say it, and she bursts out laughing. "Don't ask me why I know that."

"Lance!"

"Scarlet," I warn.

"Was it your own or someone else's?"

My face drops, and I look down at her in mortification.

She continues to laugh.

"Get on your hands and knees."

"What?"

"Hands and knees."

"Lance!" she proclaims, seriousness taking over but a hint of a smile still pulling at her lips.

I take her by the waist and flip her, discarding her robe in the process.

She cries out when my hand connects with her ass cheek.

"You're going to have to be quieter than that, sunshine."

"I can't," she moans.

My hand comes down again, the print of it turning her skin pink.

"Lance—"

I glide my palms over her ass cheeks, spreading them so I can look at her pussy. My cock is rock hard, precum beading at the tip. Lining myself up, I slowly slide into her, my eyes closing with the way she takes every inch.

The way she feels in this position.

Fuck.

I pull out, and she whimpers, but I'm quickly in front of her, standing at the side of the bed. "Me *and* you." I grasp her chin and push the head of my glistening cock past her lips. "It's how I learnt what I taste like, sunshine. Just last night, actually… while you were sitting on my face."

I hit the back of her throat and hiss, the resistance torture. She pulls back, mumbling something, but I roll my hips forward, gliding back in.

"Lesson one: When my cock's in your mouth, you suck it until I tell you to stop. You get one free pass since it's your first time. Now, what is it?"

I pull back to give her a chance to speak, but her teeth catch me, gently—too fucking slowly—trailing to the swollen head. Reflexes have my hand snapping out to grip her throat.

She flutters her tongue across the tip. "You couldn't make my tears wet, pretty boy."

Her cheeks hollow, and then she's sucking me so hard and slow I see stars. Her fingers wrap around the base of my cock, twisting as her tongue licks and rolls. This time when I hit the back of her throat, she lifts her eyes, locking onto my own. Her chin tilts, and then she swallows hard against my hand at her neck.

A challenge.

I tilt it further, inching my hips forward to sink a little deeper. I drop another inch, and her eyes widen a fraction.

"Don't panic, pretty girl. You're doing so good," I soothe, my thumb dusting the column of her throat. "A little more."

She gags as I roll my hips, and I groan, pulling back before easing in deeper. "Again."

My chest starts to work as she swallows around me, her head bobbing as she pulls back and sucks on the tip, only to draw me right back in again, her throat tilting so she can take me even deeper than before. And fuck if my entire cock isn't nearly there.

I thrust forward, back, forward, and slide all the way in. Her nails rip into my thighs.

I groan and move my hands to her hair, pulling back the strands that have fallen around her face in two fistfuls. Her nostrils flare. "Look at you. Fucking look at you, Scar."

A tear leaks from the corner of her eye, and I flinch. I fucking flinch, my jaw clenching.

I drop my head back and look at the ceiling, blinking

away the image of her that's likely seared into my memory for eternity. When I glance back down, I see her hand between her legs, her fingers working in circles.

Fuck.

She's fucking me up.

I'm so fucking fucked up over her.

"Scarlet—" I catch a tear with the pad of my thumb, rubbing it along her lip line. My blood pumps faster. My hips work harder. "I'm going to come."

I pull back an inch, but she holds me close, her eyes demanding my own and holding. A groan rips from my chest as I still, releasing down her throat.

She swallows everything I give her, teasing me with her tongue when she eases my cock from her mouth.

My chest works, the sound of my rapid breathing all I can hear.

What the fuck was that?

Goose bumps cover my skin as I stare down at this woman knelt on the bed. Her big brown eyes sparkling from the tears that streak her face. And suddenly, I don't quite know what to say. Because the way my body relaxes. The calmness that comes over me. The way I fucking feel in this moment.

She's Mason's little sister.

She's Mason's little sister.

Jesus…

"Scarlet… I—"

"Shower with me," she interrupts. "Shower with me before you leave me."

I frown and nod, taking her hand and helping her from the bed.

I need to get out of here.

Scarlet

"What do you know about Lance Sullivan, Dad?" I tighten my hold on his arm as we walk through the grass and toward the bench in my mother's garden. It's midafternoon, and the sun is high in the sky, creating a golden veil over the grounds.

"Other than him not being as stealth as he thinks he is?"

I chuckle. "I wasn't trying to hide him, so you know. But, yeah, what else?"

My dad shakes his head with a small smile. "He was always a good lad. A grafter."

"Did you work closely with him?"

"No. But I know your brother does now." He lifts a thick bushy brow, and I roll my eyes, looking away. "I like him enough. Will he be coming around here again?"

"Not likely."

"No?"

My teeth pinch together. "He's Mason 2.0. Probably worse." And he practically ran from the house after our shower this morning.

He looked down at me while I was on my knees as if he'd seen a ghost and then completely shut off.

"You know what they say about people who assume, Scarlet. Do you know him well enough to form that opinion?"

No… "I know enough."

He looks down at me sceptically.

I sigh. "Be on my side for once. I'm moping."

"I am on your side." He bumps my shoulder. "No more Lance. Got it."

"Thank you."

"So, why do you want to know what I know of the boy?"

Crap. For a second I forgot that I started this conversation. "I'm just curious. He kind of bolted this morning."

He stays quiet for a moment, peacefully gazing around the garden. "Does your brother know he spent the night here?"

I side-eye him. "No. Mason's busy in Paris with Nina."

"Really…? Good. That's good." He rubs his hand over his face, and I look up to see a spot of blood on his knuckle.

"Dad, your nose. It's bleeding again."

"It's fine." He brushes it off. "It's been like it all week."

"I'll call Dr Sarnmer back when we get in. We can get an appointment for today." I already called our doctor once today to ask to have the morning-after pill sent to the pharmacy.

"Not necessary." He shakes his head, clutching my hand. "It's fine. I promise. Just the side effects from the tablets."

I nod my head, knowing he's right, but worry still echoes in my gut. "You'll tell me if you don't feel right?"

He nods, squeezing my hand and pulling me to his side for a hug. I close my eyes and breathe him in, the smell of my mother's wildflowers and his natural scent making my body slacken. "And Scarlet, I'm sorry if Lance upset you."

"He didn't upset me."

He really didn't. But I feel annoyed that I care so much about the way he left. I spent all morning going over everything we said last night. Everything he told me about his life.

And honestly, it made me look at Lance completely differently than I did just a few days ago. I don't want to think about the fact that he sees my brother like family or that maybe Mason and the guys are the only family he has to truly rely on. I don't want to care that he shut down on me. But I do.

"Well, that's good. I didn't want to have to beat the poor boy."

My face transforms, and I laugh. "Hmm. You'd do some damage with these chicken legs, Dad." I grin as I grip his thigh right above his knee. He's skinnier than he once was, the muscle that once lined his body seemingly weakening by the day. But with the hold he has on me, the way his arm wraps around my back and his wide chest that expands with each breath beneath my cheek, I know he'd give it his best shot.

"Less of the cheek, thank you."

I chuckle, feeling his smile on the top of my head.

"Vinny called me before. Asked if I wanted to watch the rugby with him this afternoon."

I'd contemplated going out with the girls this morning and texted Vinny, but the idea of leaving Dad now feels rotten. I was up until the early hours of the morning with Lance. I feel stripped, drained and in desperate need of a long soak in the bath.

"Is his nephew playing?"

"No, Miles is out for the season. Which makes me think he was asking for another reason."

The last thing I want to do is offend my dad, and I know having Vinny here, essentially babysitting him, probably frustrates him.

"Nina's friends, Lucy and Megan, invited me out to dinner tonight. I'm not going to go, but Lance nearly talked me into it. I'm sorry I called Vinny. I should've asked you about it first."

"I've told you before that I don't need anyone out here watching me. I have the best doctors money can buy. I'm more upset at the fact you think you have to stay here and look after me all the time. You can't keep putting your life on hold, Scarlet."

"I'm not."

His jaw locks against my scalp, but I stare ahead at my mother's headstone. I don't know what he expects me to say sometimes. Who wouldn't care for their dad if they were sick?

"When you came home from university, I told myself I'd never let my health interfere with your life again. I've failed on that promise, and I'm sorry—"

"Don't be ridiculous, Dad—"

"—you don't have any friends, Scarlet. You don't go out. And I can already see you putting blocks in front of yourself with Lance. Likely because you're too worried about me, and I don't care if it was just one night. I know you. I've seen it time and time again with people coming and going from your life."

I swallow, gritting my teeth. My eyes burn, and I know it's because I'm overtired.

I need sleep.

My dad continues, and I contemplate blocking him out, but it's impossible when his voice reverberates around his chest, settling in my ear. "I'm here, and that's about all I am. Anything else is because of you. I love you for it, sweetheart,

I do. But *you* can't just be here. You're more than this estate. Go out with those girls tonight, okay? Tomorrow we can sit here, and you can tell me all about it."

My stomach twists into knots just thinking about going into the city, leaving him here again for another night.

"I don't know…"

"I already told Vin to come by at four when the game starts. Did you plan to drive in?"

I look up at him and shrug.

He just smiles back at me. "Figure it out and let me know. I can arrange a driver for the night."

My eyes well up, and I nod. "I love you, Dad. I'm sorry."

He wipes my cheek, catching my tears with the back of his finger as he has for the past twenty-nine years. "You never apologise for being you. Ever. You're Scarlet Lowell, and you'll let the whole world know it."

SIXTEEN

Scarlet

I should have known going out for a meal with Lucy and Megan would lead to drinks at a bar. I guess my friend etiquette is nonexistent after years of not having a social life. After a meal at Groulx, we moved on to The Pearl, one of the girls' favourite spots to drink at. It took me five drinks before my body grew loose and my ass was on the dance floor with them. We danced for hours, laughing like schoolgirls over stupid, meaningless stuff.

The night hasn't been about hookups or impressing anyone, and I think it's made me fall in love with these girls even more.

"Luce…" Megan stumbles on air as she approaches where Lucy and I are standing. "Luce, that man is doing damn well fine over there by the quirky lantern lightsabre thing. If you don't ask him if he needs his balls holding tonight, I just might."

I pull Megan under my arm and laugh. "Water. You need water."

"Make it holy. The other stuff won't fix that monstrosity." Lucy dips two fingers into her drink and flicks them at Megan's face. Megan sticks out her tongue to catch the splashes.

My stomach aches from laughing so much. I feel like we haven't stopped all night.

"I might actually ask him," Lucy eventually says, and I frown as I watch more alcohol get sucked up her straw.

"I'll believe it when I see it. But you've got this girl." Megan holds her fist out to bump, and Lucy cups it.

I've learnt tonight that Lucy is the romantic of the group. She's never had a one-night stand in her life, which is why I'm so surprised by her enthusiasm for the hunky guy.

"I take him home, tell him my rules, and just have sex." She exudes so much confidence that, for a second, even I believe her.

"Rules?" I question, lowering my drink as my voice slurs. I don't need any more alcohol tonight.

"No names. No eye contact."

Megan nods, too convincing. "She even has a 'Cocktact Only' sign on her bedroom door."

I flick my eyes to Lucy to find her head thrown back, laughing. "I don't, but I'm getting one."

"Me too." I grin.

"I feel like it's time. And Nina isn't here to talk me out of it. I have my bad influence—the devil on my shoulder," Lucy says, cocking her head toward Megan.

"I'll take the flack," she confirms with a nod.

"Wait. Should I be talking you out of this?" I question,

placing my hand on my chest. "Because I don't want to. That man is fine, and he's been watching you all night."

"Right. He screams clit man," Megan adds.

"Clit man?"

"The man doesn't need any training. He's driving home without Google Maps turned on."

I laugh, but my thoughts instantly go to Lance and how I came so many times at his skilled hands. How he touched me as if he already knew exactly what I liked.

"Does that come with practice for a guy?" I ask.

Lucy shakes her head. "I believe it's about the connection. A man caring enough to make a woman feel something. Which is where I lose all faith in this plan. You bitches better not have me faking it tonight."

Lucy stands, straightening her stark white dress. "Someone stop me."

Megan reaches into her purse and then dangles a set of keys from her pointer finger.

I roll my lips, excitement fluttering in my stomach as Lucy finishes her drink, taking the keys.

Megan latches on to her hand as she eases by us. I see them lock eyes, something passing between the two friends. "Stick to the rules."

"Promise."

"Are we really letting her go with him?" I lean into Megan as we watch Lucy walk to where the guy is standing.

"*If* she goes home with him, then it's a one-night thing to Lucy… but I already know the guy's name's Nick. He's a paramedic who lives with his parents and has a dog named Elvis. I had Mason's stalker guy Scott look him up while you guys were in the restrooms."

I frown. "Mason has a stalker guy?"

"You don't know Scott?"

I shake my head no.

"I'm pretty sure Scott is Vinny's right-hand man."

Another thing I didn't know. "So, she's safe?"

"I wouldn't let her leave if she wasn't."

My eyes stay on Lucy as she talks to the tall, dark-haired man, her hands working as she explains something. He's fixated on her. Giving her his full attention.

"You're a good friend, Megan."

"I'm a fucking great friend," she corrects. "But I'm drunk, and that's not helpful. I'm getting myself water. I need to stay up until she checks in and will need about fifty coffees to stay awake. Do you want one?"

"Yes, please."

Megan slips into a gap at the bar while I find a table nearby to sit at. I pull out my phone and, with little thought, decide to text Lance.

> Scarlet: Are you a clit man through practice or because of our connection?

I stare at the words after I send the message. "That sounded better in my head."

> Asshole CFO: Am I a what?

> Scarlet: Do you use google maps when you drive?

I think back to the day before when he picked me up from the pharmacy.

Scarlet: Oh shit, you do!

Scarlet: Was it all a fluke?

Asshole CFO: Where are you?

Scarlet: We're at The Pearl.

I've had entirely too much to drink, but I know what I want right now, and I don't think past that need—or the fact he bolted on me this morning—when I type my next message.

Scarlet: Come and get me.

Scarlet: I want you.

How did the tables turn so quickly from last night? I went from not wanting anything more than a night with him to craving everything he'll give me. The thought of his body warming mine. His heady scent wrapped around me. His deep voice, a steady hum as he held me close and answered every question I asked him.

I wait for what feels like forever for his message to come through, and when it eventually does, my heart sinks.

Asshole CFO: I'm a little tied up right now.
Get a lift home.

Tied up. Where? With who? It's one a.m.

I sit and stare at the message for a couple of minutes, annoyed that I've even put myself in a position to be shut down after the way he left this morning.

Asshole CFO: Home. Now, Scarlet.

Is he with someone else? The guys? I kind of hope it's them. Or maybe it's another woman. Would he be with someone so soon after being with me? Disappointed, I slip my phone into my bag and wait for Megan to come back to the table with our water. I down my whole glass, and then I tell her I'm ready to leave. My dad had someone drive me into the city this afternoon, and I text the number I was given to ask them to come and pick me up.

They arrive within three minutes of me sending the message.

"Do you want a lift back?" I ask Megan.

She waves me off. "I'll wait and see what Luce is doing. Don't worry about me. I can see myself home."

I pull the business card out of my bag and hand it to her. "My dad trusts these guys. Call them when you're ready. I'll let them know, so they'll be expecting you."

She takes the card and flips it over in her hand. "This is next-level rich people shit."

"It's a taxi," I tell her, laughing. I pull her in for a hug. "Thank you for tonight. You'll never know how badly I needed it."

"You thank me now, but you're stuck with us for life. We'll probably meet next week when Nina's back from Paris. We'll let you know when."

A smile forms on my lips. "Okay."

I say goodbye to Lucy and then meet my car at the front of the building. Once we're out of the city and deep into the long drive home, I pull out my phone and call Vinny.

"Scarlet."

"Hi, Vin."

"Everything okay?" he asks, genuine concern lacing his voice. He's been my brother's driver for over fifteen years and is more like family than a staff member.

"Yeah, I'm okay. On my way home now."

"I see."

I hear cars in the background and frown. "Is Dad okay?"

"Yes, he's fine. I never made it over this afternoon. Something came up that I couldn't put off for the night. I sent Charlie instead."

Charlie's with Dad? And Mason's in Paris, which only leaves Elliot, who Lance might be out with. And Elliot Montgomery is the biggest playboy known to man.

Let it go.

I sigh and focus back on the call. "Is everything okay?"

"It is now. Who's driving you home, Scarlet?"

"Preston."

"Good. I'll let Charlie know you're on your way."

"He's deep in that case, right?" I know he is, and guilt eats at me to think he was cooped up at the estate over an hour's drive away from home on a Saturday night when he's so busy with important work.

"He's always deep in a case. Don't worry about it."

"Tell him to head out now. I'm about half an hour away."

"I will. Can you text me when you get in?"

"Yeah."

"Good night, love."

"Good night, Vinny."

I hang up the phone and let my head hit the rest, my

eyes closing as a small smile turns up my lips. Today's been long, and I'm drained, but I can't help feeling a sense of contentment. The girls are beyond any friendship I've ever had. Dad is okay and wants to watch his rugby. And well, Lance. If nothing else, he made me feel insanely good last night.

I just hate that there's a pang of disappointment lingering now that I think of him.

He said he would tell me if he wasn't feeling it between us. Then, said he was going to date the fuck out of me.

My stomach flips at the thought of how he kissed me in the car afterward.

I look down at my phone and reread his message.

> Asshole CFO: I'm a little tied up right now.
> Get a lift home.

How embarrassing.

I want you.

What was I thinking?

I sound desperate.

I'm asleep when we pull up to the estate. The driver wakes me up with a light tap on the shoulder. "Miss Lowell, we're home."

Looking past him, I see that the house is mostly in darkness. "Thank you," I tell him, taking his hand when he offers it.

My body feels heavy, and I'm beyond tired as I trudge up the steps in my heels. I need to strip out of this dress and go to sleep immediately.

I push on the door and see the lamp in the hallway is switched on. My stomach unknots, and I walk further into the house.

Charlie must have left it on.

I slip off my shoes and check everything is off in the kitchen and main sitting room, and then I use my flashlight to run as fast as my tipsy self can carry me to the main landing.

I need to check on Dad, but the hallway is barely alight, with a small lamp at the other end of the corridor.

It's gone two a.m., and I should just go to bed, but I won't sleep unless I see for myself that he's okay.

I'm halfway down the east wing when I see jean-covered legs spread out on the wooden floor. I pause on the spot, unsure if my eyes are deceiving me or if Lance Sullivan really is sitting outside of my dad's bedroom door.

I swallow and move closer, reaching for the main light switch when I'm close enough, just to be sure it's him.

Lance is asleep. His arms folded and his face as hard as always. His hair looks mussed, like he's been running his hands through it.

I'm a little tied up right now. Get a lift home.

He came here to look after my dad?

I squat at his side, placing a hand on his arm. His black sweater is soft under my fingertips, and I yearn to be wrapped in the warm fabric.

"Lance," I whisper.

He startles awake as I squeeze his arm, green eyes widening when he finally focuses on me. "Scarlet." He looks at his watch, but not long enough to catch the time. He's disorientated and jumpy. "Shit, I'm sorry. I fell asleep."

"Hey," I say, reaching out and smoothing his brow. He goes still under my touch. "It's fine. Everything is fine."

He blinks once. Twice. And then he relaxes, his hand reaching up and latching on to my own that's twisted in his hair.

"Where's Charlie?"

His brows lift, eyes flashing with amusement. "You don't want to know."

I frown and smile simultaneously.

"You stayed with my dad tonight?"

He nods. "Is that okay?"

"It's more than okay, Lance." It's a Saturday night, and he already did the drive home after driving out yesterday. "You didn't have to do that."

"I wanted to."

I pull my bottom lip into my mouth. All I can think about is how it shouldn't be this easy to stare into his eyes. The way his gaze holds. So demanding. Yet I can see a softness there too. And he lets me see it.

"Thank you."

"You don't have to thank me."

I nod, looking at the floor between us. The intensity of the situation, of the way it feels, it's all a little too much. But in the best way imaginable.

My eyes shift back up, and still, he's watching me.

I smile, then lean in and kiss him, my lips coaxing his through the groan that leaves him.

"Take me to bed," I tell him, sliding my hands across his short beard as I pull his mouth closer.

He works his face free from my clutches, his eyes dark

and filled with the same hunger I feel. "Not tonight. You've been drinking."

I edge him back to me, shaking my head. "I'm fine."

A sigh escapes him as he kisses me, and I can feel him caving. "Not tonight."

"Lance."

He smiles against my mouth, enjoying my pleas. "Yes, my sunshine."

I pull back, our mouths only a breath apart. "*Your* sunshine?"

His eyes close in reverence as his head knocks back against the wall in defeat. "Make it make sense."

My lip twitches, but I suppress it. He doesn't know what to feel, and I'm not about to make it any harder on him. "You'll figure it out."

I smooth my thumb over his cheek, and his eyes open as he leans into the touch.

"You like it when women do that. Little"—I smooth my thumb around his jaw and over his lips—"intimate"—his eyes close again. "Touches."

Is physical touch Lance Sullivan's love language? I'd never have thought.

"Woman. Only you. I don't want anyone else's hands on my body but yours, Scarlet."

My belly bottoms out, and a flush of heat warms me to my fingertips. "Then let me put my hands on your body."

I slide across his lap, seating myself forward until I'm flush with his chest. I work my fingers up the back of his neck and into his hair.

He groans in appreciation, his palms snaking under my dress to rest on my spread thighs. "I should leave."

I can't help my smile.

"Don't do that," he warns.

I roll my lips and keep quiet.

"Are you tired?" he asks, eyes dropping to my mouth.

I shake my head. "I was… but then I found you."

A light chuckle vibrates off his chest, and then he lifts me. I wrap my legs around his waist as I cling to his neck. I don't have to tell him where to take me. The second he took off toward the west wing, I knew he was taking me to my bedroom.

My eyes roam his handsome face as we walk, the moonlight flooding in through the glass panes, the only sliver of light on this side of the house.

But I don't feel as afraid in his arms.

He makes me feel like maybe I could survive in the dark.

"Are you hungry?" he asks, pushing open my bedroom door. "What did you eat today?"

I keep my eyes on him, taking him in as he carries me with ease into my room. I could easily slip my feet to the ground and stand on my own, but the way his hands grip me at the tops of my thighs tells me that I wouldn't be allowed down even if I tried. "I ate when I went out with the girls. Three courses."

I hold up three fingers.

"And this morning? You didn't eat the breakfast you made for me. What did you have?"

I didn't think he'd noticed that I didn't eat. His mood had shifted so fast it was as if the guy I'd spent the night before with, the guy who just sat outside my dad's bedroom door for hours while I went out with my friends, hadn't existed at all.

"I ate after you left. I tend to sort Dad out first in the morning, then me. I had an extra stomach to fill today."

"You're not hungry now?"

I shake my head. "I'm all good. I promise."

He takes my word for it and lets me down. "It's late. You should get some sleep."

Leaving me at the end of the bed, he walks to my bedside and flicks on my lamp, then locks my double doors, pulling the curtains closed to cover them.

"Are you going to sleep, too?"

He looks over at me briefly, pulling the pillows from my bed. "Do you want me to stay?"

"Yes."

Shit, I said that fast.

Too fast.

He gives a firm nod. "Then I'll stay."

Relief bleeds through my body, relaxing me to the point I yawn.

"I thought you said you weren't tired?" I catch his smirk as he takes my shoulders and turns me. "Teeth."

"I lied. I'm so tired. Some sex-crazed man snuck into my house last night and kept me going until sunrise."

Lance follows me into the bathroom, picking up the spare toothbrush he used last night and this morning. I pick up mine. "Sounds like a good time."

"Hmm. Mediocre at best."

He slaps my ass as I reach for the toothpaste, and I whimper. "Need a reminder of how mediocre it was, sunshine?"

Silly man.

Silly, silly man.

"You already told me you won't fuck me, Lance, so tell me… are you trying to give yourself blue balls, or are you actually going to follow through and try harder to impress me?" I pop a brow at him in the mirror.

His eyes crease at the corners, hard and frustrated. He lifts his toothbrush when I lift mine and begins brushing his teeth.

"I've cracked you once, Sullivan. I'll crack you again."

"Sullivan?" he snaps around his toothbrush.

My lip curls at the corner. "It's your name, isn't it?"

I bend, spitting in the sink. My ass accidentally grinds suspiciously hard over his dick.

"I'm more of a tit man, baby."

I can hear the smile in his voice but choose to ignore him, finishing off my teeth and leaving him at the sink.

Fucker.

Lance

A part of me wants to slip that dress over her hips and fuck her into tomorrow, but that wouldn't be very smart of me. She's been out drinking, and the way her eyes are glossed over, shimmering with every tempting gaze, I know she isn't fully in control of herself tonight.

Denying her, though, goes against everything my body wants and needs. I just need to make it through the night.

I rinse my mouth and wash my face, hoping the couple extra minutes settle the erection that's bulging against my zipper.

When I step into the bedroom again, I find Scarlet

with her dress gliding up her waist. Her eyes lock on me as if she was waiting before, and then she pulls the tight material over her chest, her breasts heavy and bared to me.

"Scarlet," I warn.

The material bunches at her neck. "Help me, please."

I look to the ceiling, the fairy lights sparkling above. *Give me fucking strength.* I take long strides toward her, stopping when I'm a foot away. She closes the distance with one step, her nipples brushing my chest.

I shouldn't want to be naked.

Her tits are fucking perfect.

I gently lift the fabric from over her head, helping her pull it up her arms. She takes it from me and drops it to the floor.

My eyes blaze over her face. "I'm trying so fucking hard here," I say in disbelief.

She reaches for my hands that hang at my sides, then drags them up her ribs and higher to cup her full breasts.

"Scar…" I squeeze them, teasing my thumbs over her nipples, desperate to lean down and ravish the rose-pink buds with my mouth. "The things I want to do to you. You'd think I'd be satisfied after last night."

Her head tilts. "If you thought you could fuck me out of your system, Mr Sullivan, you were sorely mistaken."

No, I knew that would never be possible again when you looked up at me on your knees this morning.

God, I'm too fucking far gone.

I move my hands around to her sides and lift her body in my arms. "Bed." I drop her to the mattress and try not to look at her as I pull back the covers.

She slips under the sheets, and I have to tamp down my disappointment when she covers her chest.

I begin to strip, leaving only my boxer briefs on.

"Are we just going to cuddle?" she asks sarcastically.

"That's exactly what we're going to do."

She grins, rolling to her side as I climb in. I face her, lifting my arm and nodding for her to slip into the gap, but she's already there, filling it. Her body is cold compared to mine, and she plasters herself against me, searching for more warmth. I wrap her in my arms, my eyes closing once her shoulders relax.

"You're really hard, Lance."

"Go to sleep, Scarlet."

After a few moments of silence, her breathing evens out, and I'm certain she's asleep. I smooth my hand down her spine, pulling back to see her eyes are closed. My lips meet her forehead, and I pause there, appreciating the feeling of having her so close to me. I've not held someone like this in so long. And when she was out tonight, I couldn't stop thinking about where she might be. Who she was with, and if she was safe.

"I shouldn't want to keep you." My jaw flexes, and I shut my eyes, shaking my head.

She makes me softer somehow. I've never been able to talk to a woman like I do Scarlet. I'd never tell the guys half the things I've said to her.

I'd never hear the end of it.

"But I'm your sunshine when all you can see is the moon and stars." I snap my eyes down, finding her awake and peering up at me. "It could be worse."

Fuck.

Fuck. Fuck. Fuck.

My knee parts her legs, and I roll us, stretching out over her. Our mouths meet, and I kiss her so damn hard, but she puts up resistance, locking her hands around my neck, fingers running through my scalp.

"You make me a bad man, Scarlet Lowell."

She pulls back, panting as she halts me with a fistful of my hair. Her eyes jump around my face as if my words annoy her. "It doesn't feel that way. Not even a little bit."

I groan, raining kisses down her neck.

Her breasts.

Her stomach.

I am a bad man.

SEVENTEEN

Scarlet

"Do the two of you have any plans for the day?"

My eyes lift to my dad, and I give him a warning gaze. I know when he's in a playful mood, and today, he seems to be in top form.

We're sitting around the twelve-seater table in the dining room, eating the breakfast I've cooked.

"I was going to ask if Scarlet wanted to come to my mum's for dinner, actually."

I pause with my fork halfway to my mouth. "You were?"

What the hell?

I've only heard terrible things about his mum. Why would he want to take me to meet her?

"I have some documents for her to sign," he says, as if sensing my thoughts. "It won't be an all-day thing."

"Well, that will be lovely, right, Scar?" My dad prompts me, brows rising as if to tell me not to be so rude.

I watch Lance, waiting for him to look at me, but he doesn't.

I really don't want to go. I have a feeling my dad can sense that. His gaze keeps coming back to me as if he can see my internal struggle.

Lance accidentally met my dad. It's not like I wanted them to meet. This isn't supposed to be anything serious.

And I definitely can't do this long term. He knows that.

My stare shifts to my dad. His skin is sallow and drained of its usual brightness. He's sick, and I'm "meeting the family"?

"Scarlet." The panic inside of me sparks as I look up at Lance sitting to my right. His face is softer now, his gaze reassuring. I have a feeling if my dad wasn't at the table, he'd kiss me. Instead, he finds a slight smile for me. "You don't have to come."

You don't have to come. *But I want you to.* I can see the unspoken words lurking like the pain in his eyes. He doesn't want to go to his mum's on his own.

So, he asked me to go with him.

Me.

"I'll come with you," I decide. "I want to come with you, Lance."

"I didn't take you for a car man, Sullivan." I give Lance a cheeky smile as I slide into the sleek black McLaren that was tucked away in my garage for the night. "It's nice." I glance up at him, my hands running over the interior.

"It's my baby." He reaches for his seat belt, and I follow his lead.

"Your baby?" I fight my smile because he's too damn serious.

He sits for a second, staring out of the garage door, hands resting atop the steering wheel. I wonder if he's in his head about going to his mum's. He's been quiet all morning.

His eyes eventually slide over me, and with the car, the way his muscular arm grips the wheel so tight I—

"Why did you ask me if I was a clit man last night?"

My smile must light up my entire face because Lance's lip twitches just the slightest bit. He looks away, rubbing his fingers across his mouth before looking back.

I shrug. "Just something the girls said."

"Those girls are trouble."

"I know."

He licks his lips, and I know he's desperate to reach for me. "You had a good night with them?"

I nod, sliding my hand into his lap, resting on his thigh. The man definitely likes physical contact. "Do you want to talk about why we're going to your mum's?"

He starts the engine, and my body comes alive with it. "Oh my god."

"I have some documents to pick up. She told me she would only agree and sign the terms of the new contract if I came for lunch." I watch him, the tic in his cheek, the sadness in his eyes.

"Okay." I don't want to push him on it. When he's ready, he'll tell me.

His eyes fall to me as we gently roll forward and out onto the drive. "I'll make it quick, and then I'm going to need to get lost inside of you for as long as you'll let me."

I smooth my hand up his thigh, but he stops me, linking our hands.

I smile. "Can you not control yourself, Lance?"

He side-eyes me with a sinful smirk on his mouth, making my stomach flip. "Not where you're concerned."

"Insatiable man."

His phone starts to ring a moment later, and I look down at where it lies in the centre console.

My brother's name lights up the screen.

Lance's thumb trails from the bottom of my right thumb to the top, then curves down around, smoothing over my cuticle.

He doesn't answer the phone.

Vanessa Sullivan's home is beautiful, and as we pull up to the gated, detached family home, I have to take a second to remember everything Lance told me about his life. Because although I knew he had money, I didn't realise quite how much until today, and it only makes me wonder what they once lost.

"It's incredible, Lance."

He sighs in frustration, his body already visibly tense now we're here. "Out here it is. Just don't look too closely." He's around the car and opening my door before I can think of anything to say.

I place my hand in his as he helps me from the car, and when he tries to let go, I lace our fingers tighter together, refusing to let him disappear inside his own head.

We approach the front door, and Lance knocks. *Knocks.*

On his mother's front door? I swallow down all the reasons that make it so wrong.

The door swings open moments later. "Lance," the woman says sweetly, her eyes widening. "Oh. Is this another lawyer, or have you actually brought a girl home?"

It takes him a second, but Lance eventually looks at me. And it's years of hurt, pain and maybe even need that I find in his eyes. As if he's just a little boy not knowing how to take the woman before him.

I shrug, telling him I can be either.

I'm here for you.

Use me.

"Mum, this is Scarlet."

"Scarlet." She smiles. "What a lovely name. I'm Vanessa."

I step forward when she steps to the side, inviting me into her home. "It's nice to meet you, Mrs Sullivan. Thank you for having us to dinner."

"I recognise you," she says, her weary eyes locked on me when I look up. "Your face, it's so familiar."

I turn to Lance, unsure and then back toward her. "Do you know my brother Mason?"

"Mason." One of her perfectly sculpted brows twitches. "You're a Lowell." She nods, staring at me. "Of course you are. You look just like your mother."

I've heard that my whole life, and yet it still makes my heart sink whenever someone tells me. "Thank you," I say, handing her my coat when she reaches for it.

She seems… nice.

"Chloe's in the lounge. Nessa Anne is out with Ben but is due back any minute now."

"She's with Ben?" Lance asks, his mood shifting. "And where's Mols?"

"She's at a friend's. And you know what they're like." She waves him off, disappearing down the hall. "On, off and on again."

I follow Lance into the kitchen, where his mum starts to pull food from the fridge. It all looks fresh and unbranded, as if she took a trip to a butcher this morning.

"Can I help at all?" I ask, finding my manners.

"No, no. I have it covered." She peers up at Lance as if expecting him to disagree with her.

I wait for Lance to do something, to say something, but he just watches his mother as if she's a movie he bought a ticket for.

Waiting.

Waiting.

I wonder if maybe he only came here to have the documents signed, but I can't help thinking he wouldn't have invited me if he didn't want me to meet his mum and sisters. And the look on his face, the hopeful sadness he's doing nothing to hide, tells me he came here for more than just the documents.

There's a scuffling noise at the door, and I frown, peeking around Lance's tall frame and toward the double doors.

There's a cream Labrador puppy scratching at the glass. My eyes widen, along with my smile. "Oh my goodness, is this your puppy? It's adorable."

Silence. Loud enough to steal my attention away from the pining animal outside and to them.

Vanessa drags her unapologetic gaze from her son to me.

"It is. His name's Bear. He's five months old." She swallows as if the words somehow fester there even after they're out of her mouth. "But I wouldn't let him in for a minute, not while the food's out. He'll just whine."

Oh.

Lance pockets his hands, his jaw rigid beneath his short beard. Feeling awkward and not knowing what to say, afraid of saying the wrong thing, I focus my attention on the kitchen island in front of me, pretending I can't hear the little scraping of claws.

After a couple of seconds pass, I rearrange the bag strap on my shoulder, chewing the inside of my lip as I side-eye the puppy.

"You can go outside with him if you want to, Scarlet."

I cut my gaze to Lance, slowly smiling up at him when I find the softness in his features. "I'll be five minutes tops."

I make my way to the door, my feet moving as my mind trails a few steps behind, lingering with the man and his mother at my back. I'm not sure leaving them alone is the right thing to do, but the awkwardness between the two of them is bad enough to steer me out the door.

Bear jumps at my legs the second I'm outside, and I bend down, letting his paws rest on my knees. "Hello." The second I drop my head close enough, his tongue lashes at my face. I laugh and turn my head, but he goes for my ear instead.

I stand, and he bounces at my feet, ready. "Show me your garden, then," I tell him, and he just sits, staring up at me.

The second I take a step forward, he takes off across the

patio and toward the steps that lead down to the large open garden. I follow him.

He runs around and around me, his ears flapping around his face as he zooms past. "Bear!" I call.

He doesn't acknowledge his name, and I bend, picking up a beat-up tennis ball from the long grass. "What's this? Go get it!" I throw it, and he's gone in a flash, searching for the ball and then bringing it back to me. I throw it over and over, smiling as he bounds around the garden.

"You're a good boy! Yes, you are, Bear." I rub his head and around his neck, patting his chest as his tail wags. "Such a good boy." He jumps at me, and I lose my footing, falling back into the grass.

"Bear!"

He's on me and licking my face before I can blink. "Oh my god." I laugh, my eyes closing as I try to dodge his tongue and move him off me. "Bear, stop," I try to catch my breath, unable to stop laughing.

"I thought he was your good boy?"

I twist my neck to find Lance standing with his arms crossed over his chest above me. He's upside down and looks ready to fight the dog.

"Help…me…" I chuckle as Bear steps on my shoulder, my hair flying across my face.

"Bear," Lance commands and whistles.

The dog flies off me, standing at my side as he looks up at Lance. Waiting. I wait too, but Lance doesn't give any orders. He just stares back at Bear.

I pull myself up, and it snaps Lance back into the now. He pulls me to him when I'm halfway off the floor and starts to check me over.

"Are you okay?"

"I'm fine. I love him." I grin.

"Seems he likes you too."

"You two don't get along?"

He shakes his head and sniggers, looking back down at the dog. "Today's the first time meeting him. Come on, dinner's ready."

He laces our hands as we walk back to the house, and I can't help the disappointment that starts swirling in my gut.

Is it going to be as awkward as before?

Did Lance and his mum talk while I was outside?

As we reach the patio steps, I pull him to a stop, silently commanding his attention as I stare up at him.

"Are you okay?" I ask, squeezing his hand in mine.

He brushes his lips across my knuckles as if he's done it a million times before and then tips his head toward the double doors. "Ask me that in an hour, sunshine."

Lance

We sat down for dinner fifteen minutes ago, and already I'd rather be outside with the dog.

I still can't believe she got a fucking dog.

I'm wasting my breath even being here, thinking it could ever be any different. My mother's silence when we walked in here was proof enough that if she didn't get what she wanted from me, I'd get nothing back.

"So Scarlet, what is it you do?" Nessa Anne asks, not looking up from her plate of food. She arrived as we were sitting down to eat, and like my mum and Chloe, I've not even had a smile.

I wish it didn't set the sinking ache sailing down my chest, but it does.

It fucking hurts.

It's been years since we've sat around this table as a family, and it's clear the only reason we are today is because my mum will do anything to put off getting a job.

She doesn't want to sign the contract.

That's the reason for this facade.

Not me.

"I don't work, actually. I dropped out of university when I was twenty and haven't been back."

My sister's head lifts in interest, a wicked, sarcastic look washing over her face as she says to me, "Well, that's fucking interesting."

My teeth clench so hard that my jaw aches. *Unbelievable.* "Nessa—"

"So, you do nothing?"

"I spend a lot of time with my dad," Scarlet tells them, everyone's eyes now on her. "I'll go back to uni one day."

"Sure." Nessa Anne gives her a quick, tight smile, and I know Scarlet doesn't know how to take her.

She politely smiles back.

"How is your dad, Scarlet?" my mum asks, sounding genuinely interested. It's probably the most real she's been all day.

"He's okay, doing well. Thank you."

"Good. It's been years since I saw him last. He was great friends with Douglas."

I close my eyes at the mention of my dad's name, the word only inflicting more agony on already open wounds.

Sensing Scarlet's gaze on me, I open my eyes and peer down at her, not hiding the awe from my face when she effortlessly chases away the bad shit in my head.

I nod, confirming her thoughts about who Douglas is.

"Are you and Lance a couple?" Chloe asks, likely watching us.

I reluctantly look at her, feeling the last of my patience fraying.

"Gosh," Scarlet says, her cheeks flaming as she takes a sip of her water. Her eyes flick around the table. "Umm…"

I don't want her here.

"We're friends, Chloe," I answer for her. "Scarlet is a really good friend."

"He even has time for friends now," Nessa Anne mutters, raising a dark brow as she shovels in more food. Ben nudges her in the arm, shaking his head at her to cut it out.

Ben works for Ellis and Frey. He's the head of tech and one of the smartest men I've ever met. The fact he ever wound up with someone like my sister is a mystery to me. The last I heard, they were done, and he didn't want anything to do with her.

I try to keep my voice level, removing any trace of the emotion bubbling up inside of me. "I have time for you too, Nessa Anne. Are you really going to sit there and pretend I haven't tried?"

"You think you've tried?" Chloe questions.

"Hmm." Nessa Anne chuckles knowingly. "How much has Lance told you about us, Scarlet?"

My nostrils flare at her tone, and I know I'm about two seconds away from snapping.

"A little," Scarlet says, her hand slipping into mine under the table and lacing our fingers. She squeezes tight. "I'd have loved to have had sisters. You're lucky to have one another."

No one replies to her, not that there is a lot to say, but the blunt way everyone's gone silent makes my blood boil.

I *have* tried. I've tried for years to be what they need. What my mum needs. But it's never been enough, and I don't think it ever will be.

I'm not enough for them.

The dog begins scratching at the door, and I stiffen.

Scarlet's thumb dusts mine desperately, and it's almost enough to pull me back. Almost. "If you can get those documents, Mum… I need to get Scarlet home."

"Lance, we—"

"I'm about done with this bullshit." Nessa Anne's utensils clang to her plate, cutting Scarlet off. "Your *documents* aren't signed, but you already knew that. I don't know why you even came over. You know mum is desperate and will do anything to get you to feel sorry for her."

"Nessa Anne," Chloe hisses.

I watch my mother's face redden.

"Am I wrong? No." She shakes her head at me as if I'm a piece of shit on the bottom of her shoe and not her flesh and blood. "He waltzes in here expecting us to play happy family and act like he's not trying to monopolise our lives, all while looking down his nose at us. I'm sick of it."

"Enough," Ben warns, his eyes pinned on Nessa Anne.

"You say you have time for us, Lance, and yet the only

time you show your face is when there are pound signs flashing at the start or end of the conversation. You don't care about us. You don't give a shit. You're just bitter and twisted over something you know you'd have been a part of if you hadn't been swanning off at university for all those years." She stands from the table and walks from the room, the front door slamming a second later.

Blind rage simmers on the surface of my control, a heaviness on my chest the only thing keeping it at bay.

A heaviness and *her*.

Both of Scarlet's hands now fiercely grasp my hand under the table, blindly grazing the cuticle on my thumb.

I sit and stare at my half-eaten plate of food, wondering why I thought coming here, or worse, bringing her here, was a good idea.

My mother breaks the silence. The silence and *me*. "Go home, Lance. Dinner's ruined, and I don't need Nessa Anne going off in one of her strops."

Scarlet's whole body flinches at my mother's words, her head snapping toward the woman at the head of the table as if ready to go to war.

I look down at her, embarrassed beyond words. "Let's go."

Scarlet

Lance leads me out of the house with calculated steps, his head down and angled from view. I follow him in disbelief, processing the words thrown across the dining table.

His mum told him to go home.

He didn't even say goodbye.

My family, no matter how dysfunctional, is the one thing that means more to me than anything else. Even when Mase is being a complete ass, I know he loves me. From what I've seen, family means just as much to Lance—maybe more than I even know.

And I know, can visibly see, that the words his sister voiced have struck a chord somewhere deep inside of him.

He knocked on his own front door.

Lance silently helps me into the car, his face hard. "Lance," I say, hoping he'll look at me and I'll find something other than the broken man he was at the table staring back at me.

He might wear a suit of armour Monday to Friday, but I saw the cracks in it today whether or not he wanted me to.

"I need to give these copies to my mum. Bear with me. I'll be two seconds."

I nod, watching as he reaches into the footwell for the envelope that was on the passenger seat when I first got into the car.

The documents.

I watch as he takes them into the house, then sit back and blow out a harsh breath.

He wasn't exaggerating when he told me about them. His sisters seem so angry at him and the way his mum just dismissed him like that.

I look down when Lance's phone pings, realising he left it in the car the whole time we were inside. I pick it up, spotting the missed call from Mason from before, a new missed call from Charlie, and then a text from Elliot.

Elliot: Happy Birthday, Sullivan

My brows meet as I read the message over and over, realisation sinking in.

It's… it's Lance's birthday?

My hand trembles as I process the last hour. The way they spoke to him. I shake my head as tears gather in my eyes. They sit as heavy as my heart feels before falling one by one.

Why wouldn't he tell me? Why wouldn't they… How could they just sit there…

The driver's side door opens, and I jump, not expecting him back so soon. I swipe at my face before I peer up at him, hoping my tears haven't stained my cheeks. They must, though, because Lance takes one look at me and his face drops. "Hey, what is it?" He slides in and pulls me closer. "I'm sorry. Shit, I'm sorry, they're a lot, and I shouldn't have brought you here."

I snivel and shake my head, trying in vain to cut it out. "No. No. It's not that."

God. I haven't cried like this in a long time.

"What is it then?" he questions, confused.

He wipes at my tears but more flow. I pick up his phone and hand it to him, letting him read the text. "Lance, it's your birthday."

He stills in the seat, his mask coming down almost immediately.

I grit my teeth, hoping the ache it sends along my jaw distracts me from the one in my chest. "Why didn't you say something?"

He blinks over and over, staring at me as his nostrils flare. He shifts his gaze to the house.

I can't imagine the disappointment he must feel.

"Did they…" I clear my throat and reach for him, smoothing my hand up the back of his neck. "Did your mum get you a card?" His head tilts toward me again, leaning into my touch. Then his teeth come out to pull his bottom lip between his teeth, and he shakes his head.

His pain bleeds out of him in waves, as if it's been searching for a home its whole life.

"Let me drown in you."

I let out a harsh breath, my tears flowing as I smooth my thumb over his jaw. "I'm so sorry."

"Don't cry, sunshine. You'll break me completely." He pulls my head to his chest, his hands smoothing over my back and neck. "Don't cry."

God. I hate them. I hate them for making him feel sad.

It's his birthday.

I look up, knowing my face is probably a mess of tears and makeup. I lean up and dust my lips to his anyway before giving him a slow, sweet kiss. My hands hold his face as I pull away, my eyes searching for a thread of happiness in him. Anything I can use to patch him back up. "Happy birthday, Lance."

He smiles at me, and it's so genuine, so wide, it makes my tears flow a little more.

"Can I take you to my place for a bit?" he asks, voice throaty and rough. "It's not far."

I pull down the visor and laugh through my tears, nodding at him as I start wiping the mascara from my face. "I'm sorry about this."

"Don't be sorry. You're perfect."

I sniffle, forcing down the ache in my chest as we drive away from the gated home.

I don't know what the man at my side ever did to end up with a family like the one at number sixteen, but I know deep down in my gut that Lance Sullivan deserves so much more.

EIGHTEEN

Scarlet

The drive to Lance's building is made in silence. And despite the miles we put between us and his childhood home, I feel his every thought drive him deeper and deeper into his head.

I wish I could take it all away. Wish I could spoil him and make him feel how I felt on my birthday, but I don't know how I can. There's a right thing to say and do, but it's not me he needs to hear it from.

He takes my hand as we cross the parking garage, still not looking at me. He doesn't say anything until we're inside his penthouse, and he pulls me protectively into his chest.

A sigh leaves him as he looks down his nose at me. "I'm sorry."

I shake my head vehemently. "You don't need to be."

His hands rub up the length of my arms, holding me gently at the shoulders. "Do you want a drink or anything to eat?" He gives me a half smile. "You didn't get to finish your food before."

I shake my head, my thoughts lost to him and the emotion in his eyes. He's trying to hide it, his hands working in an up-and-down motion on my arms as if to distract me. The small smile. It's all to throw me off.

I quickly scan the sunken lounge, open-plan kitchen and curved staircase. All decorated in dark greys, blacks, and wood.

It's a man cave.

"This place is amazing."

"Do you want the tour?" he asks, letting me slip out of his hold.

I catch his hand and pull him with me, his gaze shadowed by his frown as he watches me walk backward.

"Can you show me where your room is?"

He tilts his head, a spark igniting somewhere within him as he shifts on his feet. "I didn't bring you here for sex."

"I know you didn't. It's not…."

A smile spreads across his face, and my shoulders relax a little. I didn't realise how badly I needed to see him happy.

"Third room at the top of the stairs."

I turn and pull him with me, his hands snaking possessively over my summer dress the second he's close enough.

He may not have brought me here for sex, but I'm willing to give this man anything he wants if it means he smiles for me again.

We make it to his room, and I push on the door, groaning as his mouth works up my neck and across my jaw. The smell of him hits me like a freight train the second I step inside. In front of me, behind me, wrapped all around me. My stomach coils tight.

I spot the door on the other side of the room and smile before heading for it, knowing what I want to do.

"Where are you going, sunshine?"

Casting a glance over my shoulder, I find Lance leaning against his bedroom doorframe, his arms crossed as he watches me in fascination.

I give him a coy look and peer into the room, finding exactly what I was looking for. The bathroom suite is huge, with a large tub positioned in the middle of the room. "You have twenty minutes for me to fill this bath, and then you're mine for the night. Get naked," I tell him, slipping into the bathroom.

I pull off my bag, dumping it between the double vanity sinks. As I turn, my eyes are drawn up, and I gasp, finding the entire ceiling panelled with glass. The sun rages down, warming the space and setting a golden hue over the large white tiles. I can't imagine how it would look at night, the perfect view of the stars.

With a smile on my face, I step toward the bath and reach for the taps. But I'm stopped short when Lance's body wraps around my back, his hands sliding around and up my thighs.

"Lance—"

His fingers tease my underwear as he dusts them up my hips, pulling my summer dress to my waist. "I'm not waiting twenty minutes, Scarlet." I feel his head shake against mine as he rocks into my ass. "I need to be inside of you now."

"You said—"

"I know what I said."

I turn, smiling up at him. "Don't ruin this for me." His head dips, soft lips taking mine as his body looms big and heavy over my small frame. "Please," I beg.

Trying to deny this man seems impossible.

He groans in response, pulling back. "I'm painfully hard right now."

"And the quicker you let me go, the quicker I can do something about it."

He readjusts himself in his jeans but doesn't step back.

I turn, letting my dress fall back down my thighs as I reach for the taps. I run the water until it comes through hot, then bend and secure the plug.

After a few seconds, I feel his hand working its way under my dress again. He cups my pussy, and I close my eyes. "Lance."

"You're too clean for a bath."

I laugh and put my head back, the promise of his fingers easing back and forth over my underwear quickly, making me wet with need. "You're insatiable."

"You told me that already today. I hope that quick wit isn't running out." I can hear the smile in his voice and chase it.

He lifts my dress again, exposing my ass.

"I can't think of a better word right now," I tell him, my back bowing as his fingers slip beneath my panties.

"Greedy." Two thick fingers slowly ease into me. "I'm *greedy* for you, Scarlet."

He's ruining my plan to take care of him, and I'm letting it happen. Five minutes in the house with him, and I'm bent over the bath getting fingered.

I pull away and whimper as his fingers leave me. "You're

messing everything up." I turn, finding him topless with his jeans half-undone. "And you're supposed to be naked."

"I thought about that, but if I took it out, it was going inside of you, and I wasn't sure if you were ready for me. I was being a gentleman by checking."

I try not to smile. "We're not having sex right now," I say, defiant.

"We are."

"Lance."

He slowly slides his jeans down his legs, kicking them off. I swallow as I take him in all over again, my willpower telling me to shut the hell up. He steps forward and slides my dress straps off my shoulders.

"I wanted to take care of you."

My dress falls to the floor, leaving me standing in my thong.

He slides his thumbs into the front of my underwear and around to my hips, pulling them down while still looking at my face.

"Let me look after you," I whisper, desperate to smother him in affection before we resort to sex.

My panties pool at my feet.

I swallow as he steps closer, sliding my hair off my shoulders with the backs of his hands. The head of his cock slides through my pussy, and I shiver as I coat him in my excitement.

His body bends slightly, trembling as he brings his mouth in line with my ear. So gentle. "You're fucking perfect, you know that?" He lifts one of my legs around his waist. "I don't possess the patience it would take to have these hands on my body and not have you wrapped around my cock, Scarlet. You'll let me fuck you, and then you can do whatever it is you have planned, okay?"

He shifts his hips, lifting me slightly so he can sink into my pussy.

He feels too good to deny, and I give in within an instant, hoping it's what he needs. What he really needs.

I wrap my arms around his broad shoulders and lift my other leg, climbing his tall frame.

He groans as he slides even deeper into me.

"Fuck."

"My dad bought me a dog for my tenth birthday."

I close my eyes as the rasp in his voice flits through me. His arms wrap tighter around me, and I relax further into his chest.

We're lying in the steaming hot bath, our bodies spent as they bathe in a tangle.

I'm not sure I've ever felt as content as I do in this moment.

"I'd been begging for months, and they kept saying no. It was the only thing I ever asked them for. Dad was working nonstop at the time, and the girls were all so different… I was growing up, and we weren't what we once were when we were young. It wasn't until I got in trouble at school that Dad eventually caved and got me Ted. I was so fucking excited. I walked him every day. Would stay out on the playing fields for hours until Dad got home. He'd sleep in my bed and follow me everywhere around the house. Dad knew it was a distraction for me and what I needed. I thought everything would be different after that."

My brows furrow and I open my eyes. “It wasn’t?”

“I came home from school about a month after I got him, and he was gone. Mum said he went for Molly and that he was dangerous.”

“What? He was a puppy still?”

“Yeah,” he says with a bitter laugh. “She told me last week she was getting Bear, and I snapped.”

I can tell he wants to say more, but he’s gone quiet on me. I tilt my head and look up at him, sorrow in my eyes. “I’m sorry.”

His jaw works beneath his short beard. “Ted was a lab.”

“What?” I snap. “Why would she do that?” I ask, sitting up.

What the hell is her problem?

Lance pulls me back to him, kissing the top of my head and tucking me tight to his chest. “I’m not surprised by it, Scarlet. She’s been like that for years. I just never wanted to see it before.”

I take a deep breath in and let it out again.

Lance’s mouth dusts my ear. “You’re angry?”

“Yes, I’m angry. The way they treated you today and then what you’ve just told me.” They’re fucking assholes. “I don’t like it, Lance. At all. I think I hate them right now.”

“Forget about them. I shouldn’t have brought up Ted.”

I shake my head, pulling his arms tighter around me again. “I want to know….” *Everything*, I nearly say, but I don’t. I let the words die off, hoping he doesn’t notice.

His lips settle against my temple, and my eyes close, wondering how in such a short space of time, someone can become like a second skin. He’s wrapped himself around me like one of my favourite jumpers, silently promising to protect us from the elements.

"Lance?" I eventually murmur, my eyes tired and heavy.

"Hmm," he replies.

"Why did you shut down on me yesterday morning?"

I feel his mouth curve against my temple. "Because, like right now, Scarlet,"—he laces our fingers, binding them together—"I know I'm going to have a hard time stopping when it comes to you."

I twist my neck up and stare into his darkened eyes, with what feels like minutes passing before either one of us makes a move.

Lance lifts a finger and lazily traces my lips, his voice softer than I've ever heard it. "I keep asking myself why I'd want to stop at all."

"I don't want you to stop," I whisper, shaking my head. "Don't stop."

His stare is unforgiving, heavy, desperate—yet lost. I'd give anything to see inside his head.

"And if I fall in love with you?"

His words should pull me back with a grounding halt, but they don't have that effect at all. My heart only quickens, pounding. "Then make sure you take me with you."

Lance

There's only one reason I'm dead on my feet in the middle of my meeting this morning, and her name is Scarlet Lowell.

After we spent the late afternoon and early evening

solely in my bed, she made me promise to show her around the penthouse next time, and we headed back to the estate so she could check on Anthony.

It was an easy promise to make while she was on her knees, worshipping my cock.

A smile slants my mouth. "All right, see what you can figure out based on what you have there. I'll give Lowell and Montgomery a ring this afternoon and let them know what's going on." I nod at Ben and turn back toward the files on my desk.

After seeing Ben last night, I decided to call him in and have him pull together all the information we have so far so that we can figure out what's going on with the missing money. I've worked here for over ten years and haven't had anything like this happen.

I'm on top of my shit when it comes to any money moving around the accounts.

"Hold off on telling the top dogs, Lance. I'll figure it out."

"Those top dogs are my best friends." I raise a stern brow at Ben, telling him without words what I need to. "What's going on with you and my sister? I thought the two of you were long done."

"I saw her out a couple of months back. I thought you knew. She didn't say anything?"

I give him a second look, this one saying, *are you fucking stupid?*

"Right." He goes back to his computer. "She's a hard one to ignore."

I know how that feels.

I'm currently driving two hours a day so that I can lose hours of sleep getting my dick wet for a girl.

"She's a good girl."

I cringe, realising he's still talking about my sister.

"What about an ex of Mason or Elliot's," he asks, happily moving the conversation back to work.

"Unlikely. None of them would know how to steal from them."

"They might know someone who does."

I scrub my hands over my face. Fuck.

I don't need this right now.

They don't need this right now.

"I mean, this isn't someone who doesn't know what they're doing. They flew under the radar long enough without you noticing."

Pricks.

"Might just be a misunderstanding, of course," Ben adds.

They've been processing the payments as an expense, making it look like an onsite portaloo company. Which made sense until the payments got a little high. The fuckers filed fake invoices monthly to trip me up, looking legit, but when I couldn't find a single name on the bank account, I knew something was up.

"It's not a misunderstanding."

I think back on all the women Elliot and Mase have dated but draw blanks. I sigh. It's more likely to be someone within the company or a business rival. "Look into Hemmings and his son Cooper. They're shady as shit."

Ben nods.

"What about Mason's current fling? You didn't think

much of the woman when he first started seeing her a couple of months ago. Could she be paying someone?"

Nina doesn't have any money. She's got debt, if anything, for that studio she rents. "She has motive."

His eyes lift. "You think she'd do it?"

I shake my head, at a loss. Fuck no.

My phone rings in my pocket, and I walk to my desk, pulling it out to find Scarlet's name flashing on my screen.

"You miss me already?" I hear cars in the distance and frown. "Where are you?"

"I'm meeting the girls for lunch while Dad goes to his appointment. And yes, maybe a little."

"Does that mean you'll be in my bed tonight?"

"No."

"Baby Lowell—"

"You'll be in mine."

I smile, turning toward the floor-to-ceiling windows so that Ben can't see. I don't need my staff thinking I'm going soft. "I'll see what I can do."

"I'm sure you will."

"Don't be a cocky little shit."

"I'm not," she exclaims. "I'm being realistic. You can't get enough, Sullivan. Admit it."

I shake my head when she laughs to herself.

"I'm about to go inside and meet the girls. This was just a call to say hi."

I'm not sure anyone's ever called me up just to say hi. And I'm not sure my cheeks have ever hurt this much from smiling. "Hi, Scarlet."

She chuckles, and it does something to me way down in my gut. "I'll see you later—"

"Hey," I mutter, stopping her before she hangs up. "Let me know how your dad gets on today, okay? Let me know if you need anything."

She goes quiet for a second, and I have to check if she's already gone.

"I will," she says, her voice softer now.

I nod, staring out at the skyline. "All right, I *might* see you tonight."

She sniggers. "Goodbye, Lance."

I hang up and smile like a dickhead at my phone.

"What's her name?" I frown, turning around to face him. Ben tips his chin at me. "Mason's girlfriend?"

My face drops, reality sinking back in.

It's not Nina. I'm certain of that.

But I can't leave any stone unturned.

My lips thin, a shitty, gut feeling gnawing. "Anderson. Nina Anderson."

NINETEEN

Scarlet

Find yourself a man who drives over an hour from work every day just to eat dinner and climb into bed with you. Lance has stayed over every day since I passed out in the pharmacy, and I won't lie, having him here feels nice.

I've never had company outside of my dad, and Lance has effortlessly slotted himself into my routine as if he was never absent from it.

It helps that my dad loves him. I often find them in the front room or kitchen, talking business or sports. The *fun* stuff.

I smile as I hear the sound of Lance's car roaring in the distance and shut the diary on my lap closed, slipping it into my bag and making my way down the steps. After Lance's birthday, I did something sneaky. A little risky. Stupid—maybe, considering my brother has no idea I've been sleeping with Lance this summer and would likely kill Lance if he found out.

I had Lance's dad's bike collected from where it was stored in Elliot's garage and sent it to a team all the way up in Scotland that specialises in rebuilding Harleys.

I stand in front of the garage doors and watch as he swings his car in and around the circular drive.

He hops out of the car, looking like sin in his grey pin-striped suit and heads straight for me, lifting me up with one arm and spinning me around. I wrap my arms around his neck and lock my legs at his back.

"Hi," I say, peering down at him.

He looks up at me with a smile that seems to find his lips quicker lately. "It's been a day, Baby Lowell. Fix me."

I smile back at him, running my hand through his thick, dark hair. "What was so bad about it?"

We stare in a trance. Easy and safe. With no idea of anything that's going on around us. "You were too far away."

I pull him closer, ready to kiss him. "So needy, Sullivan."

He squeezes my ass as I plant a quick peck on his mouth.

"You call that a kiss?" he complains.

I wiggle free and drop to my feet. "I have something to show you."

He tips his chin. "What's that?"

My steps are slow as I walk backward toward the garage. I'm nervous. What if he didn't want it fixed? What if he wanted to fix it himself?

"Scarlet, you've gone pale."

I swallow and smile, shaking the feeling off. "I'm nervous."

He frowns, his interest piqued enough that he takes a step closer. "Why would you be nervous?"

My fingers wrap around the handle of the garage door, and I pull it up.

My heart's pounding so hard.

His eyes move past me, and then I watch as his features freeze, his body going visibly tense.

"I—umm… I—"

"Is that?" His voice comes out a choked whisper I barely catch. He walks into the garage, his eyes glued to the bike.

"It's your dad's."

He straightens, shaking his head in disbelief as he rounds the bike. "Did you do this?"

I nod, my stomach churning. "Mason and Elliot don't know. I found out from Charlie where the bike was, and he said Elliot would never notice if it was missing. I should have asked you, but I wanted it to be a surprise."

He laces his hands behind his head, eyes glossy as he looks over at me. "Scar… I don't know what to say."

I blink back the tears that threaten, my body jittery as I rein in my emotions. "You don't have to say anything."

He crouches down and runs his hand over the metal. "It looks perfect. Like it did."

I clear my throat. "I made sure they knew what they were doing. The guys who fixed it, they're the best in the country."

His head shifts toward me, and I give him a wary smile. "You don't have to keep it—"

He rises to his full height, moving for me. He has me in his arms before I can finish my sentence, his body mashed to mine in a fierce embrace. He walks me to the bike and sets me sideways on the seat.

"Lance—" I try.

He cups my face, bringing his body close. Too close. I swear I can feel him trembling. And seeing the emotion in his eyes, I didn't expect it. Or if I did, I thought he'd try to hide it from me.

"You fixed my dad's bike," he says in awe.

Don't cry, Scarlet. I nod, catching hold of his forearms. "Yeah."

His mouth drops to mine, demanding a kiss that's full of everything he doesn't want or can't say.

"Lance." I pull back. "You like it? You're happy?"

He shakes his head, his voice a heavy rasp. "Happy doesn't come close. It's completely the wrong word."

"But you're not mad?"

"Scar, I'm in awe." His thumb traces my cheekbone, and then he drops his forehead to mine. "The memories I have of being on this bike with him… You never cease to amaze me, sunshine."

My smile's instant.

His green eyes dance with a light so bright I wish I could bottle it and use it as night-lights. I knew it would mean something to him, could feel the way his heart beat out of rhythm whenever we talked about his dad, but the happiness in his stare… it hurts my heart how wholesome and perfect this moment feels—that it ever had to happen at all.

"It starts?" he whispers as if he doesn't believe it's real.

My eyes widen. I place my hand on his chest, putting distance between us. "Of course." I jump down and let him get a closer look while I fetch the leathers and helmet I purchased from Ned at the shop. "Here."

He turns and gazes down at them, and then his throat bobs. "Did you get a second pair?"

"No," I tell him, knowing I should have. I didn't want to take this moment away from him. It's his memory to have. "But the guy in the shop threw this in with the price." I walk to the bag of things I'd purchased and pull out the second helmet.

He grins and tosses me the leathers. "Put those on."

Adrenaline ignites in my veins as Lance throws his leg over the bike and pulls his helmet on. He readjusts himself in his suit, constricted, but the way his eyes bunch up, I know he doesn't care. He's still smiling.

I stand unmoving as Lance twists the key and the engine comes to life. He shakes his head, just listening.

When he looks across at me, standing with the leathers clutched in my hands, I swear I see a tear sneak free of his eye. "Give me a couple of minutes," he shouts.

I nod my head, my heart in my throat, as he takes off out of the garage and rides off down the lane. My feet take me to the gravel, watching him as long as I can before he disappears. And I know in this moment that I made the right decision. The uncertainty was worth it to see the look on his face.

"It sounds good."

I turn and find my dad on the terrace, looking down at me.

I'm still buzzed and manage a grin. "It's incredible."

"You did well to get it finished so quickly, sweetheart. I'm proud of you."

"Thank you, Dad."

"Are you going out?" he asks, nodding at the leathers.

"I think so."

"Well, be careful." He gives me a wink and then looks up, the sound of the engine roaring as it appears at the end of the lane stealing both of our attention.

Lance pulls up a couple of feet away and locks his eyes on me. "Get dressed, sunshine." His eyes go to my dad on the terrace as I slide off my black boots and pull on the leathers. "You want a ride, old man?"

My dad chuckles, leaning against the granite stone. "I'm just fine watching from up here."

I pull on the helmet, and Lance leans toward me, knocking my hands away and doing up the strap. He pulls it tight to my chin then checks it again.

"Am I good to go?"

He cocks his head for me to get on.

I grab my bag off the bottom step and practically jump onto the back, hugging his waist and pulling my feet up onto the foot pegs.

"I'm scared."

"Don't be scared," Lance shouts.

I wrap my arms around him. "It's a good scared."

"You ready, sunshine?"

"Where are you taking me?"

He sets off out of the drive, waving to my dad before picking up speed and flying down the lane.

I grip him tighter.

"Somewhere no one can hear you scream."

. . .

Lance had no idea where he was going when we left Lowerwick, and I ended up sending him down the back roads at Rosestone, knowing Frey and Glen wouldn't even know we were there.

There's an old cabin on the far side of the lake which is in dire need of renovation, but after Elliot, Mason, and I claimed it as our own as kids, Frey and Glen decided to let us have it for ourselves. It's also where Elliot and Mason would go to sneak girls over.

"Read me one more," I plead.

Lance smiles and takes the diary, placing it on the blanketed floor in front of him. I take a deep breath in and close my eyes, steeling myself as the last of the evening sun streams in through the open doors.

Lance starts to read aloud.

"I found out that I'm pregnant today. I knew before the doctor told us. I'd secretly known it for weeks.

It was Freya who noticed first, her excitement driving me to prove her wrong with a test I'd purchased from the pharmacy. Seeing those two lines appear shocked me, but that shock very quickly turned into something else. Pregnant—again. Mason is going to have a sibling, someone to share this beautiful life his daddy has worked so hard for.

I wouldn't tell anyone this, but I think it's going to be a girl. I've thought about it every day since I found out I'm going to be blessed with another child. And although we're surrounded by men on the estate, Freya and I can't stop calling the baby in my belly "her."

I can't stop imagining it. I'll be on my way to the nursery, drinking tea in the orangery at Rosestone, or lying out on the meadow with Anthony, and my mind will drift.

Pigtail plaits. Dungarees tucked into wellies. Dresses and skirts.

I want to paint her nails before the school disco. I want to dance in the kitchen on a Saturday morning with her while her brother and dad get mucky out on the grounds with a rugby ball. I want to hold her hand through heartbreak—show her, teach her and myself, that it's how it's supposed to be. I want a little girl I can hold on to for a lifetime. A friend—a mother-daughter bond I never had…" Lance trails off, not reading on.

A tear leaks down my temple, my smile fractured as I stare up at the ceiling. I feel Lance shift, moving to mirror my body. He lifts me, easing my head to lie in the crevice of his arm. And then he just holds me for the longest time, my mind reeling over all the entries I've had him read. "My dad and I put those up," I say after a while.

"The glow-in-the-dark stickers?"

"Yep. Mason and Elliot started sleeping out here in the summer, and I used to tell them I'd stay with them wherever they planned a sleepover. They had to call Dad every time to come and get me."

Lance chuckles, deep and throaty. "It's pretty fucking creepy out here. I'm surprised Mason and Elliot managed it."

"It was their favourite place to be for a while." I smile, reminiscing. My head drops to the side, knowing I need to chase away the heaviness in my chest. "I loved seeing you on the bike earlier. I think I win for the best birthday present this year."

He lifts a hand and swipes my hair from my face as if silently checking I'm okay.

"You definitely win." He pulls me closer to his firm chest, and I smooth my hand over his skin. "Thank you will never be enough."

"Well, if you make me feel the way you did when we

first pulled up here every day for like a month, that will be thanks enough."

"Are you sure, Baby Lowell? You kept moaning at me. I remember vividly, at one point, you said you couldn't take any more of me."

A full smile transforms my face. "And yet you continued and proved me wrong."

He chuckles and gently kisses my forehead, his hand spreading wide over my stomach. "I like working you to your full potential. You take it too well."

I smile like the angel I am, chuckling.

I want to tell him how grateful I am. How crazy it is to me that with such little effort, he can drag me back from the edge, making me smile as if there's not something missing and broken inside of me.

"These evenings aren't long enough," he mutters, watching through the double doors as the sun sets over the lake. "You've made me hate sunsets." He pinches my nipple, and I take it as a cue to get up, not wanting to start something we can't finish.

"The sun doesn't stop you, sex fiend," I tell him, giggling as I sit up and reach for my summer dress. "You've made sundown something I'm not afraid of." I shrug as I stand, looking down at him lying back with his hand behind his head. "Could be worse."

"Say that again," he murmurs.

"What?"

"That you're not afraid."

"I'm not afraid… not when I'm with you."

A small smile creeps across his lips. "Come here."

"No. We need to get back. If we start again now, we won't stop."

"Now, Scarlet."

He pins me with a glare I can't ignore. I step over the blankets and toward him. When I'm close enough, he grabs my leg and reaches to lift me, setting me on his lap.

"I need to speak to your brother."

I freeze. He wants to tell Mase.

What does that mean?

That he's serious?

I swallow the dryness in my throat and try to find some words.

"We can't keep sneaking around. A few weeks is long enough for him not to know, and we both know that's bullshit."

It is bullshit. Especially with everything that happened last year. The gala. The fact I fucked up a massive business deal and still get butterflies whenever Lance looks at me.

"He doesn't need to know about anything else."

"I don't know, Lance."

"It's not going to make a difference to us. He isn't going to do shit."

"But it labels this." I look between us, my knees hugging his ribs. "It makes it feel like it's something."

"It is something, Scarlet."

I lift my eyes to his, my body running hot. "This wasn't meant to happen."

"I know." He reaches up and pushes a lock of hair behind my ear. "But I don't think either of us can stop."

I shake my head, agreeing with him.

He swallows, nodding. "He's fighting with Nina. An ex

turned up and caused havoc, but she's gone now. I'll speak to him next week once things have calmed down."

"What?" They're fighting? "Are they okay now?"

"Nina's staying at Lucy and Megan's for a while. Mase didn't handle the situation well, and with her studio being sold, I think Nina needed some space."

Something aches in my chest. Nina lost her studio last week. The owner decided to sell with absolutely no notice. The idea that they're fighting makes me sad.

Nina and Mason seem so in love. The type of couple you look at and know they're just supposed to be.

"I'll call her tomorrow, have her come out to the estate. She's not been working, but she seemed okay on the phone when I spoke to her in the week."

His lips flatten to a thin line, and he only gives me another stiff nod.

"What is it?"

He thinks about it, telling me whatever it is on the tip of his tongue, but then he shakes his head. "Nothing. I'm just getting used to having someone else in our group. And with Nina comes Megan and Lucy. It's a different dynamic."

I watch him, my eyes tight as I try to figure him out. "You seem to have more tolerance for Lucy and Megan. You're still not sure on Nina?"

"I see them more, I guess. Nina's always with Mase, and he doesn't tend to let her out of his sight. I don't want to see your brother get screwed over again, and I don't think he even tries to protect himself from it."

He doesn't trust her.

"Again?"

I can tell he's tripped up when he sighs. "That ex," he

eventually tells me. "She once blackmailed him. That's about all I can tell you. Mason would kill me."

Do I know anything about my brother?

"Nina isn't going to screw Mason over," I tell him, almost defensively.

"I hope not."

I wonder how much of Lance's trust issues come from his mum and sisters. They took everything to Lance's name and destroyed it. And only tonight did he get a little part of that back.

I smooth my palms down his chest. "Thank you."

He frowns. "What for?"

"Looking out for my brother. I love that you care…." I shrug, wishing I could be so close to Mase. I'll take knowing that he has people who care enough to protect him instead. "And for sharing this experience with me tonight. It suits you, you know."

"The bike?"

"Uh-huh." I lean down and kiss him, his hands sliding up my back. "I was a puddle all the way over here."

He smiles against my lips. "Your pussy's never been wetter than when you slid across my lap."

My cheeks blush despite the fact I've already lived it. "It was the engine. It did things."

"I'll add it to our list of foreplay."

"You have a list?"

"A mental list."

I grin. "What's on it?"

"Elevators, purple vibrators, large bodies of water—"

"Irish accents?"

He snickers and tickles my ribs. I laugh and fall to his side, but he's straight on me.

"No! We have to go back. My dad."

"He's fine."

His head dips, the straps of my dress sliding from my shoulders so he can expose my breasts.

"Lance."

His mouth dusts over the heavy, aching mounds, his teeth teasing around one nipple. "Yes, darling."

My lips part. "Don't stop."

I'm feeling like a snake. My plan was to have Nina come out to the estate today so that I could take her mind off the studio and Mase, but she hasn't replied to my texts. I know I need to call her, but I can't stop thinking about the fact I know what's going on when she hasn't told me. And until she does tell me, I'm not saying anything. It's on Lance if he wants to tell Mason what's going on. I'm not outing myself.

"Hey, Scar," Nina sings down the phone.

I've got this.

Invite her over and pretend you have no idea about what's going on.

"Hey girl, what are you up to? I feel like we should be unemployed losers together these days."

I wince.

Jesus Christ, Scarlet. She just lost her studio.

Nina chuckles, and I relax a little. "Speak for yourself. Did you get the forms from the university yet?"

"Yes, I have, actually." A lie. The application forms Nina gave me on my birthday weren't the right ones, so she's spent the last few weeks telling me to go and get the right ones. "But I won't be starting until next September. I want to be here for Dad." I appreciate what Nina's doing, but I'm not ready to leave Dad. He needs me right now. Telling her I have the forms is a little white lie and it will pacify her for now.

"I know, sorry. I won't bring it up again—not unless you want to talk about it. I'm just about to go to the gym."

How do I get her out of that? Exercise is her thing. "Ugh, boring. I'm trying to strip wallpaper. I was looking for a willing accomplice…"

"I don't think I'd be much help, Scar. I told you I'm horrific at DIY."

"It's stripping wallpaper, you'll do great. I'll cook tea after to say thanks."

"I don't even—"

"Leaving now to pick you up! Are you at Mason's?"

I already know you're not.

"No." She laughs. "I am staying at the girls' apartment."

"What? Why?"

Maybe I should let go of medicine and explore my acting career instead.

"I'll send you the address."

I smile as she hangs up.

Perfect.

Now I've just got to act surprised when she gives me all the details.

TWENTY

Scarlet

I've not stopped talking from the minute Nina got in the car to the minute we finished up in the pink room—it's currently green, but it will be pink soon.

Nina's been a trooper, but she wasn't lying when she said her DIY skills are terrible. When I caught her trying to peel wallpaper with a kitchen knife, I took the makeshift weapon away and found her the scraper instead.

It was fairly easy to convince her to come out to the estate for the day. Did I have to pretend I had no idea what was going on with her and Mase until she told me herself? Yes. But until Lance speaks to Mason about us, I can't tell Nina what's going on. It doesn't feel right.

It was late when we eventually sat down for dinner. Dad convinced me to set up the table outside, wanting to enjoy the last of the late evening sun. He seemed to have a spring in his step today, and I can't help but think it's because Nina's here.

"I need to call a taxi."

I close the double doors to the terrace and see Nina digging in her purse for her phone. We've polished off a bottle of wine between the two of us, but I can tell it's gone straight to her head.

A pang of disappointment settles in my gut at the thought of her leaving. "Just stay. I can drop you home in the morning."

She smiles, dipping her head. "No, Mase would lose his head if he knew I was here."

I wave her off, heading into the kitchen. "Screw him. How would he even know?"

Nina's a friend of mine now. My brother can go suck it if he doesn't like it.

"I should go home." She rolls her lips, and I know she wants to stay.

"Nina, you're more than welcome here." My dad's voice floats in from the hallway, and I turn to find him walking through the kitchen door. He'd gone to bed a while ago, leaving us outside as the temperature dropped.

"It's nice to have the company around here with him sleeping the day away." I flick my head over my shoulder at him. "Besides, who's going to help me finish this?" I hold up the bottle of red wine.

She rolls her eyes, but I can see how easy it was for her to cave. She's loved being here today. "Okay."

I smile wide, grabbing the bottle opener from the drawer.

Today has been exactly what I needed, and I didn't even know it. Lance called me once, making me dip outside to take the call while Nina stayed up in the bedroom—which was the right thing to do, considering I was blushing hard within thirty seconds of being on the phone.

He was desperate to come over tonight, and I wanted him to. I *still* want him to. I told him I'd let him know when Nina left, but having a female in the house, and that female being Nina, who's so refreshingly normal and fun to be around, I feel like a night off might be exactly what we need.

"You okay, Dad?" I ask, eyeing where he's standing on the threshold to the kitchen.

"I just came down to take my pills." He gives Nina a sheepish smile, crossing to the medicine cabinet.

I get the feeling he feels a little humiliated at having to admit that. It's only ever me who sees this vulnerable side to him.

"The idea of not having to taxi myself back into the city is a weight off tonight, thank you both," Nina tells us as if to shift the attention.

I give her a grateful smile. "You're welcome here anytime."

Dad takes his pills and then rounds the kitchen island, pulling me in for a cuddle. I sigh as his warmth wraps around me. "It's been a pleasure having you for the evening, Nina. I hope you and Mason can figure this out. And I hope he can bring you out here himself sometime soon. You're truly a breath of fresh air for us all."

I swallow the lump in my throat and hold him a little tighter.

God, I hope Mason comes home soon.

For Dad's sake.

And he's right. Everything's been different since Nina

showed up. Mason's present for the first time in years, and I have friends. Actual real-life friends instead of the fictional ones from stories I tend to cling to.

"Good night, girls."

"Good night, Dad." I smile into his shirt. "I love you."

Once Dad is long gone to bed and we're nearing the tail end of another bottle of wine, I send a text to Lance letting him know Nina is staying over and that I will see him tomorrow night.

He texts back almost immediately.

Nina doesn't seem to notice as my eyes flick down, her attention lost to the chocolate pudding she found in the pantry that we're now cooking.

Asshole CFO: I like her even less now

I chuckle to myself and slide my phone into the back pocket of my jeans.

"Tell me more about this Joey guy?" I bump her out of the way with my hip and bin the instructions she's reading. "He's the one who photographed you in the studio, right?"

She leans back against the kitchen counter. "Yep. That's him. And honestly, there's no great tale. Just your brother being an overprotective fool for the most part."

"Have you known him long?"

"No. I barely even know him now. Enough I'd call him a friend but other than meeting for coffee once and running into each other on nights out, that's it."

"You've never had any kind of... relations?" I ask, popping a brow.

"Never."

"But he's asked you out?"

Curiosity mars her brow. "A few times. Did Mase tell you that?"

"No, the girls. They mentioned him on my birthday that night at the penthouse, and I remembered the name when you mentioned him earlier."

She nods. "Joey's a nice enough guy, but he's not my type."

"Of course, it's dramatic, entitled assholes you like, isn't it?"

Her mouth drops, and she bites back the laugh that threatens. "No comment."

I smirk, pulling open the oven door as I side-eye her. "I love the bastard, really."

She smiles. "He is a total drama queen, though."

I laugh, shutting the oven door and reaching for my glass of wine. "The worst."

I'm almost always a morning person, but this morning my head is pounding, and my body feels like it's failing me. When I eventually climbed into bed last night, it was past midnight, and I stupidly checked my phone, something I seem to do a lot more recently, and found another text from Lance.

And like every other night this week, he didn't let me sleep until my toes were curling and his name was falling from my lips.

If I'm being honest with myself, the reason I so desperately wanted Nina to stay over wasn't just because she's becoming such a close friend. I missed having Lance here last night, missed having him unpack his day and listen to me ramble on about God knows what. Missed the routine we've so easily fallen into night after night. And that realisation was enough to make me question everything. Because maybe I can do this with him.

To have a life outside of the estate.

"Meet me somewhere after you've dropped Nina off."

"No. You're supposed to be at work." I smile through my windscreen, watching as the clouds darken over the estate. I'm waiting for Nina to say goodbye to my dad so that I can drop her back into the city, and what was supposed to be a quick good morning text has turned into a negotiation with Lance Sullivan.

"I'm at work. I'll be done with my meeting by eleven, and then you can meet me at my place."

"Lance, I said no. I'm trying to avoid you if you haven't noticed."

"Yeah? How's that going for you?"

"Dandy. Now go do some work. I'll see you tonight."

"Text me when you leave Lucy and Megan's. I'll have lunch at home, and we can—"

"Goodbye, Lance."

"Make sure you're ready for me, sunshine."

I shake my head, cheeks warming from the way his voice rasps through the phone. "You're relentless."

"That's a good girl. It's nice to hear you finally listening to me."

"I never said yes."

"But you liked it when I told you to be ready for me, didn't you?"

I glance out through the garage doors, checking for Nina.

Goddam him.

"Are you already ready for me?" he purrs.

"Not even a little bit."

I can tell he's smiling before he even speaks. "Little white lies won't hurt me, Baby Lowell."

"I'm hanging up."

"Let me—"

I hang up, my eyes closing as I try to cool off.

He's so fucking intense.

I love it.

I smile to myself as my phone chimes.

Asshole CFO: Let me get my fill. I need to taste you, Scarlet

Asshole CFO: I need to be inside of you

Scarlet: Tonight

I could easily let him consume me right now, but I know I need to be careful with my heart. No matter how good it feels to be in his grasp.

Asshole CFO: Now

Asshole CFO: Fast and hard

Asshole CFO: I want to be buried so deep inside of you it fucking hurts

"Sorry, Scar. I didn't mean to keep you waiting."

I fumble my phone and drop it as Nina yanks open the door and slides into the car. She reaches for my phone, and I snatch it away.

"Thanks!" I say quickly with an over-the-top smile.

I lock the screen and toss it in the centre console of my Audi.

Nina leans against the door, her eyes closing. "I feel terrible today, and I have to go and look at a potential studio with Maggie."

"Maggie is Lucy's mum, right?"

"Yep."

"You'll be fine. Are you going to speak to Mason?"

She opens her eyes and sighs. "I tried last night, but I was tipsy, and we both ended up being dicks about the photos Joey took of me dancing. We're toxic with a capital *T*, but I'm ruined for any other man. Like, nothing comes after your brother."

"I beg to differ," I tell her with a smirk. "But maybe you just need some time."

"A lifetime."

I smile and head toward the main road, noticing my petrol light blinking at me to get some fuel. "Be patient with him. Mase will get there."

And I mean it. With the way Mason has been these past few weeks, I can see him finding his own happiness again eventually.

Nina twists her neck, a smile full of warmth tugging at her lips. "I know. And then I'll send him your way."

. . .

The roads are quiet as we head into the city, and I manage to drop Nina off before midday. I'm climbing back into the Audi with all intentions of going straight home when my phone chimes.

I ignore it, sliding into the driver's seat.

It pings again.

"Man is testing my patience today."

Asshole CFO: I have food

I pull the phone closer to get a better look at the take-away bag hanging from his finger.

It's from Poppies Sandwich Shop.

Of course, I'm starving.

Asshole CFO: Please, Baby Lowell

Say no.

You still need to have some boundaries.

If Dad gets his transplant, he'll need me even more than he already does, and if I'm tied up in Lance, it will be harder than just letting go of my career.

Scarlet: I need fuel, and I don't have my bank card. I can't drive to yours when I'll barely make it home

Asshole CFO: Come here, and I'll drop you home

I feel like my reasoning is slipping away from me day by day.

My phone rings in my hand, and as if it's the universe's way of screwing with me, my dad's name lights up the screen.

I pull on my seat belt and connect the call to my car.

"Hey, Dad."

"Scarlet, sorry. I just wondered how soon you'll be home?"

"Soon, Dad. I've just left the girls' apartment. I might nip to the Montwell and get some cash from Mase. Or I could pop in to see Charles. I need fuel, but I left my bank card at home. The light's flashing at me, and I'm crapping it that I won't make it back. I'm disgustingly hungover today." All the more reason to call Lance and let him give me a lift. He went to Poppies and got my favourite sandwich. "Anyway, it could be worse."

Dad chuckles under his breath, but it comes out short. It kicks me in the gut, reminding me how poorly he is at the moment.

When he doesn't give his usual "it could be better" I tell him, "I'll be home soon, Dad."

"Go and see Mason, sweetheart. He'll look after you. Don't rush back, okay?"

"I will! See you in a bit."

I hang up and reply to Lance.

> Scarlet: I told Dad I'd be home for lunch. Tonight, I promise.

As I start the engine, I peer down, seeing an image come through of a wrapped sandwich with "Anthony" written across the paper.

Asshole CFO: And I got you raclette & ham

I sit and smile at my phone, a chuckle forcing its way out.

"Don't rush back."

I pull out of the girls' apartment and drive toward Lance's penthouse, not being able to wipe the smile off my face the entire journey.

"What's the password?"

"Let me in, Sullivan."

"Wrong. It's *let me suck your cock, master.*"

The elevator eventually starts to whirl as it carries me to the top floor. I can feel his eyes on me, and I consider flipping him the bird, but I know reception will also have access to the cameras.

I can tell he's in a mood, and it's dangerous. Happy Lance is a rabbit hole I shouldn't fall down often. It has the ability to suck me in further than I already am. Like sneaky midday hookups in the middle of a working week.

The doors slide open, and my lip instantly twitches.

He's nowhere to be seen.

"If you jump out and scare me, I'll kill you." I walk further into the room, shaking my head.

When I realise he isn't in the kitchen or lounge, I bypass the gym and head toward what he said was his office. I never had a tour on my last visit, and it makes sense that he might be in there, considering it's the middle of the day and he should be at work.

I push open the door and find him behind his desk, hard face glued to his computer.

"Why are you hiding from me?"

He flicks his eyes up but drops them to his screen again quickly. This time a smile paints his face. "I knew you'd find me."

"I'm here for the sandwich. Don't think I came here for anything more."

"Okay, sunshine. Give me five minutes to fix this minor inconvenience, and I'll fuck you across my desk."

"Always so crass." I tut, walking into the room with my arms crossed as I look around.

His home office is bigger than most, and I take my time as I round the small sofa, running my hand over the dark leather. "This is very… you."

"Easy to wipe clean, too," he says with a smirk, not looking up from his computer.

"The fact you sound like you're speaking from experience is gross."

"It seems like it would be easy to wipe clean, Scarlet," he corrects. "Forgive my mind for running away from me whenever you're in the room."

"Better, Mr Sullivan." I turn and face him, smiling, when I find him now watching my every move. "What?"

He swallows before he cocks his head, telling me to come to him.

I do, a knot forming in my stomach when his gaze trails me around the room. He rolls back his chair to make room for me, directing me onto the edge of his desk when I'm close enough.

"Hi," I say, my stomach bottoming out from our sheer closeness.

It's been a day.

One night away from him.

Does he feel this too?

With a hint of a smile on his full lips, Lance rises to his feet and leans in to kiss me. Long and slow, his palms cupping my face.

And within a second, the air around us shifts. My chin lifts under his hold, desperately praying he doesn't stop.

It's too tender.

Too gentle.

He's never kissed me like this before.

I'm a little breathless when he eventually pulls back, and he pops a brow as if he wasn't expecting the kiss either. He clears his throat. "I missed you."

I chuckle, my cheeks flaming without warning. "I missed you, too."

He shakes his head and matches my smile, his eyes not leaving me. "Can I do something?"

"What?" I ask.

He has a look on his face I can't decipher. As if he's just learnt something new. "Can I take a picture of you?"

I recoil. "No. Why would you want to take a picture of me?"

"If you let me take it, you'll see."

I contemplate it, hating the idea of being under scrutiny, but the way his eyes are so focused on me, the way he just kissed me, I don't want to deny him.

I nod, and he reaches for his phone.

And it's the most awkward moment of my life.

"This is horrible."

"Just smile at me."

I smile, and he laughs.

"Lance!"

"All right, don't smile. Just sit there and look at me like you were before."

I do, and it's awful. "This is terrible."

"Shh…" The flat of his hand slides up my calf and smooths over my thigh. "Relax for me."

"Okay, that helps a little." I grin.

"It does, huh?" His fingers reach high under my dress, higher, and then his thumb dusts up the front of my thong.

I swallow and nod, my pussy aching for more.

"Helps a lot, actually," I whisper, arching my back.

I forget about the pictures he's taking as he loses the gentle touch and applies the pressure I'm desperate for. My legs spread a little wider on instinct, enticing a feral sound from deep in Lance's chest.

He watches me closely as he tucks his finger into the seam of my underwear and pulls the scrap of material to the side.

I can't take my eyes off him.

It all feels too much.

Not enough.

"You're so wet, Scarlet. You lied to me."

"I—"

His fingers spread me, his middle finger circling my entrance before he sinks inside. I hiss, rocking my hips and silently asking for more.

"I've thought about this and this only all night and day." His phone clatters to the desk, and I look at it with wide eyes, wondering what kind of photos he might've just taken. "You're perfect, Sca—"

We both look down as his phone rings on the desktop.

Mason's name lights up the screen.

"Oh my god." I close my eyes.

"Shh, I need to take this."

"What!" I panic as he reaches for his phone with his free hand, but he quickly connects the call and puts it on loud-speaker.

"Lowell, what is it?" He gives me a smirk and adds another finger.

I grab his wrist to still his movements, my body shuddering with a mixture of pleasure and panic as I shake my head no.

"Where are you? I'm in your office, and even your assistant doesn't know."

"I'm at home. Just taking care of some things." He bats my hand away and curls his fingers, making my eyes roll back. "The file you're looking for is on my desk."

"Lance!" I mouth.

He flashes me his perfect teeth, and then he dips his head, his tongue flattening over my clit before his soft lips wrap around the small bundle of nerves in a sucking kiss.

I moan.

I'm going to hell.

Lance groans under his breath, quieter than my own. And as if to shut me up, he slips his fingers from where I want them most and lifts them to my lips.

"Since when did you start buying purple fucking files?"

Lance drags his fingers over my lips, coating them in my excitement. I should be mortified by how wet I am right now. He pushes down on my chin, and I open my mouth, sucking on his long fingers when he slips them past my lips.

"It's a new favourite of mine," he says, smiling. "And if I were being fussy, I'd tell you they're lavender."

His eyes flare when I flatten my tongue, lapping up the saltiness coating his skin.

With his fingers sucked clean, he eases them out.

"Right, whatever. I've got it. Pull your finger out, Sullivan, and get your ass back in here."

"Pulling my finger out as we speak, boss man."

"Stupid fucking—"

Mason hangs up, and I breathe a sigh of relief, ready to kill the man between my legs.

His smile is smug—playful. "If you could feel how hard I am, you wouldn't be mad at me."

"My brother, Lance," I scold.

"You did great."

"No, you say you did great when you meet the family, not whilst you finger fuck your best friend's little sister on your desk while you tell him where to find your purple pigging files!"

"They're lavender, sunshine." He reaches out and slips a lock of hair behind my ear, completely unruffled as he leans over me. "And you did great."

I don't know what to do with myself. I'm so turned on, and him telling me how great I've just done is only getting me more worked up.

"Can I do something?" he rasps out, all throaty.

My eyes go wide. "Absolutely not," I proclaim.

I'm not falling for that again.

Lance stands to his full height, throwing his head back as

he laughs. It's the best sound in the whole world, and no one can tell me otherwise.

"You're such an asshole," I say, pushing his chest.

He catches my hand and tangles our fingers, stepping back into me. I straighten my back as he brings his lips to mine. "I'm sorry." His thumb traces the cuticle on my thumb.

"No, you're not."

He smiles, placing my hand over his chest as he hovers closer. His heart's pounding. "That'll do."

And then he's kissing me, lips coaxing me into submission.

I'm lifted from the desk and carried through the house, my legs slung around his waist.

Once in his room, he lays me on the bed and peels my dress from my body, not wasting another second. He pulls his tie loose enough to slip free and then unbuttons three buttons on his shirt before pulling it from over his head. I watch him, obsessed.

I'm obsessed with him.

"You're ruining everything, Sullivan," I murmur.

He doesn't smile as he unbuckles his belt and pops the button, and he makes quick work of sliding his boxer briefs down his legs.

And then he stands in all his naked glory in front of me.

"You're ruining me," I repeat, barely a whisper.

He kneels on the bed, gently parting my legs as he settles between them, putting us nose to nose. "I know."

"It's the middle of the day. You should be working. I should be at home."

He looks between us, lining his length up before slowly

sinking home. His body shudders above me as he's sheathed in me. "I know."

He kisses me, circling his hips deep and making me moan. His green eyes find mine, and my mouth parts. "When I showered this morning, I washed you all away. You weren't there to coat my cock in your scent. Your lips didn't dance across my neck and whisper in my ear that you didn't want me to leave. You weren't there, Scar, and I've felt fucking sideways ever since."

"Lance—" I groan, shifting my hips up and making our pelvises brush.

"And now you lie there and look up at me with those eyes." He sniggers and drops his head, thrusting forward once. "Telling me I'm *ruining* you."

I grab his strong arms, my toes curling as he finds a steady rhythm.

Deep, hard strokes.

"Sunshine, I might be ruining you, but you've already rubbed out my entire existence and left me twice the man you found. I'm fucked, Baby Lowell." He lifts my lips in a smooth kiss, pulling away quickly. "For you."

I wrap my arms around him and pull his body flush with mine, lifting my knees to accommodate his weight as he shifts over me again and again. It puts him deeper.

Too deep.

TWENTY-ONE

Scarlet

"You're a persuasive man, Lance Sullivan."

"Determined. I know what I want."

I smile as he stands at the end of the bed and buttons up his shirt. There are a million reasons why I should be getting my ass off this mattress right now but watching Lance dress for the office has to be one of the hottest things I've ever witnessed.

"You need to lose that look from your face immediately."

I bite my lip innocently, eyes trained on his fingers that straighten the knot in his tie. "What look?"

He drops his hands and looks at me before striding around the bed and whipping the covers off me.

I'm naked and exposed and smiling like a fool. "You don't like the look?"

"I don't like the fact I have to go back to work. I need you dressed and downstairs in the next ten minutes if I'm going to drop you home."

"If you can lend me some money, I'll get fuel and drive myself home." I reach up and run my pointer finger over his lips. "You don't have to drive me all the way out."

He bites the pad of my finger, his body rocking into mine as it cradles me on the mattress. "I want to drive you all the way out."

"You have a job to get back to. I don't want to mess with that."

I can feel him harden through his slacks, and my body heats. I'm not sure how much more I can take of him.

He kisses my neck. "I think I might miss you already."

I bite my lip, staring at the ceiling. I don't want to leave. "You have pictures of me now. Will they not be enough to keep you going through the day?"

He pulls back, nuzzling his nose across my cheek. "They haven't been enough for the past year, so I doubt it."

My brows pinch. "The past year?"

Lance rises from the bed and pulls his phone from his pocket. I sit and look up at him, unsure of what he's doing exactly.

When he flips the phone, my stomach bottoms out. "The gala?" I take the phone and stare down at the photo of the two of us in Mason's foyer the night of the Hamilton Gala. I'm standing next to him, his hand lost somewhere on my back and the way he looks down at me…

"I thought you deleted them."

"I did." I look up at him, my heart pounding. "From your brother's phone. After I sent them to myself."

He kept them?

I look utterly flustered. I'm looking at the camera, but my face is void of happiness.

"There's more."

I look back up, and he nods down at the phone.

I scroll to the left and find another picture. My body stills. "Charlie saw this."

"I know."

In the picture, Lance's body is leant into mine, his lips at my ear and instead of my body recoiling, I stand, mouth parted, eyes heavy and glued to him. We're electric, the energy between us unmistakable in the frozen moment.

I drop my gaze to the blue-filled heart on the menu bar, and everything gets a little real.

I keep scrolling, finding three more from that night, but then more follow. Images of me on the balcony on my birthday, sitting around the firepit. My back as I walk through the meadow. Me sleeping. Me with my dad.

I look up and tilt my head.

His cheeks redden. "I feel a little exposed."

My lip tips up, but I can't give him much more than that. I'm still stuck on this album full of photos. He favourited them.

"This is crazy."

"Bad crazy?"

I shake my head.

He leans over me again, taking the phone from me and placing it on the mattress so he has my full attention. "I want you to be mine, Scar. For real."

I can't help my smile, and I don't fight it. I can't. He's so unexpectedly adorable, and in this moment, nothing, not one thing, could make me believe this man isn't perfect.

I brush my lips to his, nodding as I breathe him in—let the excitement of being *his* settle inside of me. "I want to tell Mase—"

He sighs as my gaze drifts to my dress discarded on the floor, my phone lodged in the deep pocket and lit up through the thin material.

"Crap." I smile up at him.

Lance nuzzles my throat, kissing my jaw and then my lips before he lets me up. I quickly pick up the dress and pull out my phone.

Freya's name flashes on the screen.

I frown and connect the call. "Frey?"

"Scarlet… darling."

The hairs on the nape of my neck stand on end with the way she says my name, sending a shiver through my entire body.

"Hey," I say, my smile faltering.

"Darling, are you able to come home?"

Within an instant, my chest turns to stone. Cold. So so cold.

I shake my head, my hand clenching the dress. "Why?"

She pauses, and I swear the ground shifts beneath my feet. "The doctor's here. Are you close?"

"You're at the house?"

"Yes…" Her breath catches, sounding shaky. "Yes, I'm at the house… Scarlet…"

Cold. I feel so cold. From the very depths of me, it's as if it's burning me from the inside out.

"Why are you doing this to me, Frey?"

"Darling, please… I'm sorry."

No.

No.

I frown as tears fill my eyes.

"Scarlet—" Lance steps into me, his hands trying to hold me, but I can't. I can't stand the touch of his hands when my body is in agony.

No.

"I'm coming. I'm coming right now."

I pull my dress over my head and rush from the room and down the stairs.

"I'm coming, Frey."

"Okay, darling."

"I'm coming."

"Don't rush back."

"I'm coming right now."

I hear her stifle her sob and lose my footing on the stairs, sending me down three steps to the tiled floor with a slap.

"Go and see Mason, sweetheart. He'll look after you."

I feel nothing as I pull myself up and carry on to the door.

"Scarlet!"

I frown at the sound of Lance's voice. The fear. The unknown.

He's erratic.

Irrelevant.

I need my shoes.

My body whirls. "My shoes, I need my shoes." I whip past him and into his office, searching for my boots. "Where are they?"

"Here. Scarlet, please, look at me!"

I take them from his hands and pull them on as my mind reels.

"Scarlet, sorry. I just wondered how soon you'll be home?"

No.

I run for the elevator. Yell for Lance to make it move. Beg him desperately to make it go quicker.

When it eventually reaches his parking garage, he grabs my arm, a devastated look on his face. "Scar…"

I look up at him, shaking my head. "I shouldn't have come here."

He flinches, coming to a halt as if I've slapped him.

"I never should have been here with you."

I shake my arm free, leaving him frozen in place as I run for my car.

I start the engine, not looking back as I drive out of the garage and onto the street.

It doesn't take long for Lance to appear in my rearview mirror, and he follows me the entire way, weaving behind my car as I take every back road I know home.

And when my car judders to a stop a mile from the estate, petrol tank empty, I scream through the tears that fall. I fight him, kick him as he tries to take me from my car and put me into his.

I yell at him.

I yell the most horrid things at the man who only wants to help.

At the man I fucked while my dad died.

Alone.

Darkness has never been my friend, and yet as I stand in the doorway of my childhood home and hear my brother's roar shatter the last of the light in my heart, I welcome the promise of it.

My feet carry me to the front room, and for some stupid reason, I expect him to be in his chair, that maybe it was peaceful. Gentle.

Life isn't gentle with us, though.

My dad is lying on the carpet, his chest exposed with wires and pads stuck to him. Mason kneels at his side. There are people dotted around the room, but I can barely make them out. I can barely even breathe.

I'm not sure I even want to.

"Don't rush back."

"Scarlet, darling."

My fixated stare pans to Freya, her face distraught.

Mason stands when he hears my name, and the panic I feel deep in my veins isn't fair. The fear—I hate him for it.

His face is so pale. Lips thin.

My nostrils flare as I stare back at him, tears leaking down my face.

I break apart when he pulls me into his chest and holds me, but he shatters me completely, confirming my fears when he lets me go and walks from the room.

A sob escapes, but I catch it, pulling my shoulders back. I wipe my face and move to my dad's side, my eyes full, making him a blur. I blink the tears away, bending to smooth his hair from his forehead. My head meets his chest. The coldness against my skin makes my body cave in. "I'm so sorry. I'm so so sorry, Dad."

I lie with him for what feels like only minutes, but when a hand settles on my shoulder and they tell me they need me to move, I realise I can't feel my legs, and it's

Elliot's arms that slip around me and lift me from off the floor.

Lance

"Let me drive you." I reach for her again as she slams her hand on her steering wheel. She doesn't meet my eyes, and as I pull her into me, she flails in my hold.

"Get off of me!"

"Scar—"

"This is all your fault!"

I step back, despair tearing through my chest.

Her cheeks are mottled from her tears, eyes red-rimmed and full. "You talked me into coming over. You wouldn't stop. Pushing and pushing."

"I didn't know. If I did, I never would have—"

"I knew!" Her voice breaks up the words, breaking me. "I knew that he needed me, and I wasn't there! I failed him when he needed me the most, and you let me."

"No. Scarlet, no. This isn't your fault."

She starts to sob, her body folding. "Then whose is it?"

I rush to her, but she pushes me back. "I can't. Please, don't touch me." Her eyes eventually meet mine. "I'm sorry. I'm sorry. We never should've done this. I knew."

She backs away and climbs into my car, staring with a broken gaze out of the windscreen as her shoulders shake with each sob that leaves her.

I climb into the car and make the mile drive to the estate, my heart sinking when we pull up to the house and find the circular drive full of abandoned cars.

Her eyes flick up to mine. "You don't need to be here."

I stare at her from the kitchen doorway, her pain like a steel weight in my gut. Nothing I say or do right now can fix it.

Nothing.

What she's feeling right now never fully goes away.

A gentle hand flattens on my back. "Excuse me."

I turn and look down at Nina's solemn face. "Nina," I murmur.

She dips her head and brushes past me. Everyone's eyes fall on her as she enters the kitchen.

"Where's Mase?" Elliot asks.

She surveys the room, and I can tell she's trying to keep it together, her brown eyes swimming as she shakes her head.

He left.

Fuck.

"He hates it here. I don't blame him," Scarlet whispers from where she sits.

"He fucking left?" Elliot snaps, matching my internal rage.

I'm hanging on by a thread, desperate to take Scarlet in my arms like I want to. Is it selfish for me to want what she doesn't at a time like this? To need comfort from her when her world is falling apart.

A bitter jealousy stirs awake inside me as Nina steps around the kitchen island and wraps her arms around Scarlet's shoulders.

"What can I do?" she asks.

Scarlet grasps Nina's hand, squeezing it. "Nothing. Mase is going to need you."

I watch the anguish paint Nina's face, the unknown, what's to come. "I know," she murmurs sadly.

Mason won't handle this well, and we all know it.

My sole focus is on Scar, though.

How will she handle this?

"Don't touch me."

"We never should have done this."

I pushed her.

Constantly, to get what I wanted when she told me she couldn't.

"What if I want more?"

"Lance—"

"What if I need another date?"

The way she smiled at me—the way she gave me so much more.

"I guess the men in my life haven't always been the most reliable. I know it might seem unfair, but right now, while Dad is so sick and what's to come when he eventually gets his transplant, I can't commit to something more. Even a date."

"What if I said I won't let you down? What if I swear it? One date. If I lose interest, I'll be honest with you. I'll fuck off and leave you alone. But I won't disappear before you give me a chance."

I let her down, and I promised her I wouldn't.

"I knew that he needed me, and I wasn't there! I failed him when he needed me the most, and you let me."

"Scarlet, honey." I step to the side as Freya Montgomery eases into the kitchen, her short grey bob as pristine as ever. "Glen and I think it would be best that you come home with us this evening, or we can come here for a couple of weeks. We don't want you alone."

I should be with her.

Nobody else.

Me.

I wait for her eyes to find mine, wait for her to tell them she doesn't need them.

"Yeah, that's probably a good idea."

A shudder runs through my body, my chest working as my heart thumps.

She's shutting me out.

She can't.

I swallow the words working themselves free, needing them to come out right.

"I'm going to get things straight at the office," Charlie announces, nodding at Elliot. And then he shifts his eyes to me.

Leave.

I watch him kiss Scarlet's forehead. Watch her lean into him. "Call me if you need me, okay?"

She smiles at him, and my heart sinks.

"I'll come with you," I strangle out, clearing my throat.

Her eyes meet mine for the first time in over an hour, and I'm barely able to give her a nod before I turn and walk out of the house.

Everything inside of me roars, the feeling sickeningly familiar.

I'm not needed here.

I climb into my car and leave, knowing Charlie's on my tail. He follows me as I head down the back roads, pulling up beside me when I stop at the abandoned Audi.

I get out of the car and scrub my face with my hands, my throat thick with unuttered words.

"I shouldn't have left." I turn and look at my friend, throwing my hands out to my sides. "But how could I stay?"

"You couldn't." He dips his head. "I knew you were going to say something you'd regret."

I snigger and walk away.

She's in pain, and I'm not there.

She doesn't want me to be there.

My fist impales the rear window of my McLaren before Charlie can stop me.

"Sullivan—"

"No." I hold up my hand to stop him, untamed emotion making my voice shake. "No."

"Mate!"

"This wasn't temporary or some stupid summer fling!" I point toward her car, my eyes wild. "She wanted this too. She wanted this. I might have pushed her, but she came willingly every time, pushing me right back. I listened to her. To all of it. I know it's what she wanted."

I drop my eyes to my hand as blood slithers down my fingers. I shake it out, sighing as I lean across the bonnet of her car and drop my head to the metal.

"I thought I was giving her what she needed, but I fucked it all up instead."

"You haven't done anything wrong, Sullivan." His hand clasps me on the back of the neck and grips me firmly.

"She wasn't here when she should have been. She's going to live with that for the rest of her life." I twist my neck to look up at him. "And so will I."

Charlie blows out a harsh breath, and I see it's hit him just as hard as it has everyone else.

It's fucked. All of it.

"Go do what you need to do, Aldridge. I'll get fuel and take Scar's car back to the estate."

He nods. "Get that wrapped up in something. They'll have bandages up at the fuel station."

I flex my hand. The worst of the damage is halfway up my middle finger, the skin mangled. "Yeah."

Charlie leaves, and I walk to my car, observing the mess I've made of the rear window.

"Stupid dumb fuck."

I clear what I can of the shattered glass from the seats, then set off to the nearest fuel station.

TWENTY-TWO

Scarlet

I don't hear him coming until he's standing on the threshold of the kitchen, his tall frame seemingly stuck there in the entrance.

Dragging my eyes away from the tea I have cupped in my hands, I look across at him. "You can come in. Freya just popped home to get some things."

He nods as he steps into the room, stopping at the edge of the counter. "I brought your car back. There's a jerry can in the garage… in case you need it again." He places the keys to the Audi softly on the kitchen island, and I frown, catching the bandage wrapped around his hand.

I shift my gaze up and find his eyes boring into me. "I'm so sorry, Scarlet."

I manage a small smile, but it hurts. Everything hurts so bad. "Yeah."

All I want is to go to him. To stand in his arms. Just his presence is killing me. So close but out of reach.

I need him.

Lance made himself matter, and now I don't want to say goodbye.

"What I said before." I stare at my tea, barely able to look at him. "I didn't mean it, and I shouldn't have said what I did—"

"It was true."

"Not all of it." I shake my head and swallow. "It came from a place of pain, and I'm so sorry. If I hurt you—"

"Scar, just stop," he snaps. "You don't have to do this."

My face screws up, but I force down the tears. "It would be so easy to fall in love with you right now, Lance."

His face turns hard, the shock of my words a slap to the face which I don't want or mean but can't take back.

"You shocked me. Was more than I expected in so many ways that mattered to me. And I want you for so many reasons. I want…" I pause, more tears welling in my eyes that only make me angrier at myself. Angry at him, even, and I can't let that happen. Not Lance. "Dad's gone, just like that. And Mason can barely look at me. I can't do this with you now, no matter how much I want you… because I do want you, Lance." I peer up at him. "But I won't sit here and pretend it's what I need because it isn't. I need time. Time for so many things. I know it like I knew it when we first met. This wasn't a mistake, but it's nothing like what we thought it would be, and now there are consequences."

Like not being here, the one time I should've been.

"You're making this a goodbye, and I don't want to leave you."

"I don't think I want you to leave me either. But doing this now isn't right."

He moves for me with purpose, walking to the kitchen island. As his hands spread across either side of my face, I close my eyes, an unbearable ache spreading like wildfire throughout my entire body. "Let me help you, Scarlet."

My shoulders sag as I give in to the emotions building within me, and I shake my head. A tear slides down my cheek. "But it isn't right. I need to make it right."

He grasps my face harder, tightening his hold. Desperate. "You're blaming yourself."

I stare through him, the pain in my chest unlike anything I've ever experienced. "I know." I cry. "And I'll blame you too if you stay."

He inches back, his eyes searching my face. "What am I supposed to do?"

"Give me time." I turn my head into his bandaged hand and kiss the exposed skin at the base of his thumb. "It won't be forever."

He shakes his head, stepping closer. "You're lying."

My eyes swim with tears as I stare up at him. "I don't want it to be a lie."

"You want me to leave?"

My head tilts. "You should leave. There's a difference."

"Let me stay, just tonight," he begs.

I frown at the panic in his voice. And then it hits me. The realisation. I didn't think about him. Didn't consider how he would feel—I was only thinking about myself. I smooth my hand over his cheek, giving him the warmest smile I can find within myself. "Oh, Lance. You're going to be fine."

"I don't care about me." He pulls my hand away from his face, holding me closer. "Stop doing that."

"Lance—"

"Scar, baby, please." His forehead touches mine, eyes scrunched tight. His tongue slashes out, wetting his lips as he finds his thoughts. "Don't do this—"

I block him out and speak over him. "You didn't let me down. Not once."

"Scar—"

"Thank you for being everything you promised you would be."

"No."

"I'm going to go upstairs, and I want you to leave. Don't be mad. Don't drive out of here angry. I had nothing in my heart when you walked in here, but it's beating so damn hard for you standing here now."

His eyes peel open and lock on mine.

"It's got to mean something," I whisper through my tears. I close the distance, brushing my lips across his until he catches them in a full kiss. I push into him, taking everything. The feel of him, the smell, his mouth, the way his hands wrap around me, I take it all.

When we eventually pull away, my lips are sore. Lance's eyes are heavy, maybe a little defeated, and it sends a pang of sadness through my chest.

"I'm sorry." And I mean it from the bottom of my broken heart.

He smooths his hand across the back of my neck, not letting me go as his lips brush my temple, lingering as he rasps, "It's okay."

It takes everything inside of me to pull out of his reach and walk out of the kitchen, and with every step I take, the worse I feel.

I turn and start up the staircase, needing to be as far away from him as possible.

"Scar," he says, halting me. I turn halfway up the steps, waiting. "I won't give up."

I sink to the step, watching as he leaves… listening as the gentle roar of his engine coasts down the lane.

As I sit on the step with tears rolling over my cheeks, I wonder how he got both cars back here. Had he walked to his car and come back?

I sit for a while in the same spot, the silence something I'm used to in the house, and yet it feels so different now.

After a while, I make my way down the few steps I'd climbed, knowing everyone will be back soon. I'm surprised they left me on my own at all.

But maybe it's what I need.

I walk into the front room, finding it cleared of the mess that was left behind by the paramedics and doctors.

It feels empty.

Cold and surreal.

My feet carry me to my dad's armchair, and I stand staring at it. "Why didn't you tell me on the phone? I could have been here."

My chin wobbles, and I know I'm close to losing it completely. I turn to leave, considering a walk on the meadow, but something under the armchair catches my gaze. I move for it, wondering if it's a piece of discarded packaging left behind.

My breath hitches and I drop to my knees as I pick up the paper.

On the carpet, lying discarded as if it fell with him, is a handwritten note. I recognise my dad's penmanship immediately, despite the clear struggle he had when writing it.

It couldn't have been any better.

It couldn't have been any better.

A sob escapes me.

"Why, Dad." I weep. "Why?" I bend forward, my head brushing on the carpet as my body is racked with my cries. "I can't do this without you. I don't want to." I claw at the rug. "I can't."

"Scarlet." Elliot appears at my side, his knee locked at my side as he tries to pick me up.

"No," I howl. "No. No. No."

"Scar, please."

"I should have been here."

His arms band around me. "Come here."

"I wasn't here, Ell. All those years, and I wasn't here."

"Shhh. It's okay." He drops to the floor with me, giving in as he holds me in his arms while I sob.

"I wasn't here."

He rocks me. "It's okay."

"I wasn't here."

TWENTY-THREE

Scarlet

Three weeks later

September has always been a favourite month of mine. The way life on the estate prepares for the autumn sun, the view over the meadow growing even more beautiful.

My dad was buried two weeks ago, and every day I come out here and look at the mound of soil, wondering if I'll ever look at it and feel a shred of peace. I never felt the way I feel now about my mother because I simply never knew her. I felt something. The absence and unknown. But nothing like I feel when I stare down at this pile of dirt.

They say it's better to have loved and lost than never to have loved at all, and I'm truly so fucking lost right now.

"Good morning, Scarlet."

I turn and smile softly at Frey trudging through the grass.

"Morning."

"We're packed up." She wraps an arm around my back and clasps my left arm, holding me close as she looks down at the graves. "You sure you're ready for us to leave?"

"Yeah." I gaze at her, thankful to have her and Glen in my life. They've been here for a couple of weeks, and I have to admit, I don't know where I'd be without them. "I need to find a new normal now."

"I know." She rubs my arm, standing silently at my side for a while. "We're so proud of you."

I turn and hug her, hoping she knows I mean what I say. "I'd still be in bed, completely broken, if you hadn't been here."

I pull back and smile, letting her know I'm okay.

"You're stronger than you think, darling."

She's right. I am.

If the past three weeks have taught me anything, it's that I am strong. Being strong has felt like the only thing I can do. It's not a cure. It doesn't take away the pain. But moving, eating, breathing—or giving a forced smile for the people who love me—it's a mask that I've clung onto every day as I walked the floorboards of the house that took away so much from me.

"I'm going to be fine, Frey. I promise."

She nods with a strained smile, tears filling her eyes. "I took a call just now inside, on the house phone." She steadies her features. "It was the university. The course coordinator."

My heart jolts, thumping.

"You're going back?"

"I—I just thought I'd put in the forms." Guilt eats at me. What must she think of me? "I filled them out months ago, lied about sending them in to Nina and last week, it just felt like something to take my mind off everything."

"Scarlet." Frey smiles, her eyes shining. "My goodness, girl. You have no idea how incredible you are." She shakes her head, looking at me as she holds me at arm's length. "You, my sweet girl… you have to do this. I don't know anyone who can pull themselves up like you can. To watch you hurt as you have and then be standing at the stove come breakfast each day, and now this—university. Tell us what you need to make it happen. Anything. We're behind you one hundred per cent, every step of the way."

"Thank you, Frey," I tell her, feeling overcome with relief. "Thank you for being here." I hug her tighter.

"No…" she soothes. "No, you don't need to thank me. You make it easy to fulfil the promises I made her. I'm just sorry I ever had to make them."

Lance

Lance:

Nothing. Not a damn word seems adequate enough to send to her.

I've tried calling, but she doesn't answer, and it shouldn't surprise me. She told me she needed time. Apparently, I'm not a patient man. I've given her over three weeks, and it feels like fucking forever.

She's had Freya and Glen with her at the house, but I know from Elliot that they left a couple of days ago to go back to Rosestone, leaving her alone.

I've not had a wink of sleep since.

Mase: You free?

Lance: Can be

Mase: Aldridge is on his way over

I tilt my head back and sigh, giving the tension in my neck a brief respite. Losing his dad should be the worst of Mason's problems, but it's not. Everything's a mess. Unravelling before us without any control over it.

Pocketing my phone, I leave my office and cross to Ben's. I set him up on my floor last week after more money was moved between accounts. We need him to figure out who's responsible and soon. I don't like keeping it from Mason and Elliot, but they both have enough to deal with.

I rap my knuckles against Ben's office door. "I'm heading out. You wanted me?"

He rolls his chair backward into my line of sight. "Yeah. I was looking through everything I found on Nina Anderson, and some payments to her mother dating back years popped up. They stopped and started again for a while, and I'm thinking she might have run out of money?"

I frown. "I told you to drop it with Nina."

He clenches his jaw, shrugging. "All right. If you're sure."

I stand and watch him, knowing he's spent hours working on this and that it's messing with his head that he can't figure it out. "Just keep looking. There has to be something somewhere that points to who it is."

There's another person that should be looked into.

Someone who showed up weeks ago and turned Mason's world upside down.

I owe it to him to figure this out.

"Look into Cara Langer. Don't ask questions."

I leave the office and head for the elevators, riding up to the seventy-eighth floor.

Do I think Cara is capable of stealing from Mason… yes. She's done it before, blackmailing him to fit her agenda. But if she was smart, she wouldn't dare fuck with us again.

She paid the price the first time.

It's gone seven when I pull up to Lowerwick Estate, the need to speak to Scarlet too strong to put it off another day. A text wouldn't be enough. I need to know she's okay. Need to see it for myself and hear her voice.

I push open my car door and step onto the gravel, taking in the calm that settles around me. There's not a single light on in the house, and I frown as I jog up the steps to the front door.

I swallow and knock, trying to figure out what I need to say.

What does she need to hear?

When she doesn't answer, I take a step back and crane my neck up at the many windows, wondering if maybe she heard me pull up and is watching me, choosing to ignore me. The house is partially covered in ivy, wrapping around the windows and creating a shield.

I pull my bottom lip between my teeth and knock once more, waiting for a couple of seconds before I open the door.

There's a small lamp switched on in the hallway, but the landing lights are off. I look around the staircase and into the kitchen, seeing it's as dark as the rest of the house.

"Scarlet," I call out.

When my voice only echoes off the walls, I take the stairs. The light switches are located off to the side of each wing, and I wonder why she'd leave them off when she knows she'll have to walk to or from her room in the dark.

I flick the switch and head toward her bedroom.

My shoulders drop when I find it empty.

I stand in the doorway, my eyes heavy on her made bed. Thoughts of us together in here, pissing around in the tangled sheets, in the bathroom, and out on the grounds, flood through my mind.

Where are you, Scar?

My eyes catch on her bedside table and her phone lying on top. I cross the room and pick it up, finding it dead.

I snigger and shake my head.

Does she ever charge it?

Knowing she's likely home, I open up the double doors leading to her stone balcony. It takes me all of five seconds for my eyes to seek her out.

I plant my hands on the cold granite, watching as she manoeuvres a small caddy and trailer down the boundary of the meadow, her body bouncing as she moves across the bumpy ground. Her lavender hair is pulled up into a ponytail, and she's wearing a pair of jeans and a black T-shirt that makes my fully dressed frame shiver.

She stops and jumps down, reaching for something in the back of the trailer. I squint, trying to see what.

"Is that a fucking shovel?"

I watch as she starts digging into the ground. Over and over. Once she's done, she goes back to the trailer and heaves up a small tree in her arms.

My jaw slackens, and then my eyes quickly run back along the boundary of the meadow. A pained frown draws my brows close when I see the row of planted trees running the length of the field.

My heart aches in my chest.

"This one," she tells me, leaning down and holding her mum's diary out to me. "It's one of my favourites. Skip to the part she says she feels sick. Or further down when she talks about Dad taking a knee."

I take the book and rest it on her legs, giving her a lazy smile as the sun breaks through another cloud and dances across her flawless skin.

I look down at the page and read the entry aloud.

"I feel sick today. I don't like to admit it, but Anthony seemed to know the second I woke up that I wasn't okay. We walked the grounds together as a family, and I could barely hold Scarlet in my arms without feeling like I was going to collapse. Anthony had to take her from me, and for the first time since I was diagnosed, I felt like I could feel death on my tail.

I sat in the middle of the meadow and cried in front of my children. Something I always promised myself I would never do.

Anthony took a knee beside me eventually. I knew he was struggling. But he lifted my chin and told me it was okay.

And then he made me laugh through those tears when he told me he was going to plant twenty-four trees around the meadow. He has the most elaborate of ideas. He said... One for every year of your life, Ellis, so that I can look out across here for years to come and be reminded of the happiness I've felt during every single one of them.

I'm crying all over again just thinking about it."

I stand and watch her for a while in awe, the ache in my chest never easing in the slightest.

She eventually finishes on the tree and jumps back into the caddy, turning it around and driving back to the gate where she loads up another two.

I smile and walk into her room, closing the balcony doors behind me.

I plug her phone into the charger and then head to the kitchen.

Once I'm done, I make the walk across the first field toward the meadow gate. Scarlet's on her hands and knees halfway up the field, and I make quick work of pulling my sweater over my head, placing it in the bed of the wheelbarrow along with the cheese toastie and lemon water I've made her. I wedge the note between them.

Your love for life and everything in it knocks me on my ass every single day. Soon, sunshine x

It takes everything inside of me to turn around and walk away from her, but I do it.

And it's not until hours later, when I'm climbing into my bed, still on a head trip over leaving her out there alone *again*, that I know it was the right thing to do.

Scarlet: Thank you, Lance x

Scarlet

One month later

"Oh." I spin on the spot and smile, taking in Lucy's face. "Umm, I guess with the right accessories, it might work."

"Luce, it's awful," Megan says, looking at her friend as if she's gone mad.

I look down at the full-length dress and chuckle. "I agree it's doing nothing."

Lucy places her hand on her chest and reaches for the next bag. "Thank the lord. I thought you were vibing, and I didn't want to upset you."

"Your face told me exactly what you thought," I tell her, catching the package when she tosses it to me.

We're in her sitting room, delivery bags littered everywhere as we try to find me a holiday wardrobe.

When my brother called me and told me he wanted us to go away to our family lodge, I instantly said no. I guess for years it seemed impossible to go away with such little planning, and I'm still not quite used to not having anything to stop me.

Unless you class Lance Sullivan as an obstacle.

I've not seen or heard from him since he came to the estate a month ago.

"I liked this one in the picture, and I think it will be perfect for the evenings," Lucy tells me.

I rip open the cellophane and hold up the black knitted dress. It's long and strapless.

"I love this one, too," I say, stepping back into the bathroom to change. I leave the door open so that I can still hear them.

"Have either of you spoken to Nina?" I ask the girls.

"No way," Megan mutters. "I'm terrible with secrets."

"She still has no idea," Lucy tells us. "I spoke to her this morning."

I smile as I unclasp my bra. "Her and Mase are good?"

"So good it scares me."

We all chuckle, and I step into the dress. Mason asked us not to tell Nina we are going away. They've been a mess this past month. Nina even moved back to the girls' apartment for a while after she found out my stupid-ass brother was the one who had her studio sold. They say blood's thicker than water, but I didn't expect Mason to ever make that statement literal. "I think it's nice that she doesn't know about it. He said she won't come if he asks her, and with everything that's happened with her studio, it seems like the break she needs."

"Hmm, I still don't get the situation with Erin. Anyone got the tea on it yet?" Megan asks.

"Nope," I tell her, rearranging my boobs in the dress.

The details surrounding Nina's studio and Erin—the woman who owned it—have been kept tight lipped between the guys and Nina.

I hear Megan gasp. "Oh my god, Luce, you know!"

My back straightens, and I look around the door.

"Oh god." Lucy covers her face.

"Tell us!" Megan begs as I step back into the room.

"Elliot will kill me."

"We won't tell anyone. Nina was cagey as fuck. Who's Erin?"

Lucy rolls her lips. "She's a woman from Mason's past. She's horrible."

"So Mason knew her before Nina?" Megan questions, the shock evident in her voice.

When Nina told us that Mason was the one who sold her studio, she swore she couldn't tell us why but said Erin, the woman who owns the studio, wasn't who she said she was. She made it out like it was better if we didn't know.

"It's so fucked up, girls. Cara Langer is her actual name, not Erin. She met Mason at Melders over a year ago and ended up back at his apartment for the night."

"Holy fuck."

"It's so much worse than them once hooking up. So, Lance showed up at Mason's the night they met, needing to speak to Mase. It was late, early hours even, and Mason thought the girl was sleeping when he slipped out of bed and went to speak with him. Elliot wouldn't tell me what exactly, but whatever the two of them were discussing, Erin—or Cara overheard." Lucy looks at us both dead in the eye, and a chill snakes down my spine. "Cara started making these crazy demands on the spot, blackmailing Mason. Apparently, he panicked and gave her what she wanted."

The woman who blackmailed Mason. This is the woman Lance told me about.

"Mason was a mess. He'd fucked up letting her overhear what they were talking about, and now this woman was on a complete power trip. Knowing there had to be something to get the upper hand on her, Lance had Scott look into her. He found some really bad shit—like Erin wasn't the first person Cara impersonated."

"Fucking scammy bitch," Megan fumes.

"And that's when Lance turned the tables. They threatened to expose her to the men she'd blackmailed previously, sold every property she owned here in the city, and sent her to live in Australia. Which is why she was in a mad rush to find a tenant for the studio and leased it so cheaply to Nina when they first met. She knew time wasn't on her side. She used Erin's name on the studio, so it wasn't traceable to her, and then she left."

"What in the fuck."

"So why did Mason sell it?" I ask, my mind whirling at all the information.

"When he found out Cara was the real owner of the studio, he thought she was playing games with him. He had no idea it was complete fate that Nina ended up renting the studio. But whatever it was that Mason and Lance were discussing that night, Cara overheard it. He didn't want that linked to Nina in any way. He thought having his girlfriend rent the building that the woman *he* now blackmailed owned was too risky. He had her sell it."

Megan stares at the carpet as silence falls over us.

"It was something really bad, wasn't it?" I mutter, looking up at Lucy. "Whatever Cara overheard… it was really bad."

"Bad enough Elliot wouldn't tell me," she confirms.

When Lance told me there was a woman from Mason's past that had blackmailed him, my stomach twisted up at the thought of it, but this. Lance knew all of this and never told me. He knew Mason sold the studio. He knew everything.

No wonder he doesn't trust Nina. His mum and sisters and now this.

"We forget about this," I say. "The best thing we can do

is pretend this conversation never happened. For everyone's sake."

"Agreed." Lucy nods.

"Agreed," Megan adds.

I swallow and smooth my hand down the dress. "I like this one. I'm adding it to my yes pile." I turn around and show them the back.

"Yep, it's perfect," Megan says, standing. "Anyone for a whiskey?"

TWENTY-FOUR

Lance

Scarlet's coming to Bora Bora. That's about all I could focus on throughout the majority of my day. I've not seen or spoken to her since the day I found her planting trees in the meadow.

Not even a text.

And every day was spent with the hope and belief that she knew I was here when she was ready. The fact she hasn't needed me yet or wanted to reach out hurts more than I'd ever admit.

I remove my passport from the safe in my office and tuck it into my carry-on bag, then head for my desk so that I can sign off for the next week.

I'm just about done sending a message to Harry when an email pops up from Ben. He's not been in the office all week, and I was starting to think he'd given up.

My eyes scan over the attached bank note, a transaction

which I quickly recognise from the payments in question. This one looks the same as the documents I gave to Ben months ago.

I pull out my phone and call him.

"Lance, you got my email."

"What am I looking at exactly?"

"Could be nothing but check out the letters at the end of the account number. I checked every single payment and the history of all of them. This one bounced back and was the only one with NA at the end."

NA.

I look at the account number and the initials at the end.

"I'm about an hour from gaining access to all of Nina Anderson's bank accounts. Closed and current. Anything hidden, I'll find it."

"No." I close my eyes, pinching the bridge of my nose. The shit Mason has been through this year—this month. And then the way Nina has been there for him through it all. There's no fucking way, and even if there was, and it is Nina, maybe turning the other cheek is the only right thing to do. At least for now. "Drop it with Nina. Close the account, so they can't take anymore—can you do that? If you can find out who exactly sent the payments, tell me. I'll pay you for the extra work you've put into this, and you can go back to your floor." I sigh, deleting the email. "I appreciate the time you've put into this, Ben."

"Lance, it's her. It's right there in black and white."

I frown at his tone. "Is it, though? Nina wouldn't have the first clue how to do this. It's taken you months to figure it out, and you're the smartest bloke I know when it comes to this stuff. This isn't some random person, and you know it. Make sure it ends here and close the accounts."

He doesn't answer me for the longest time, and I get the feeling he's pissed off, which I understand, considering he's spent months working on this for me to tell him to drop it now.

"I'll see you when I get back from my leave."

"Yeah," he sniggers, seemingly shaking it off. "Yeah, all right, Lance. Have a good one, yeah?"

I hang up and scrub my hands over my face, hating the way my gut tells me I'm an idiot for ignoring what Ben's just told me.

I'm about to spend a week with Nina on holiday. If I can get her alone, I'll ask her myself.

There's a knock at my door. "Cheer up, mate." I look up to find Charlie on the threshold. "You ready to go?"

I shut down my computer and stand, unbuttoning my vest and then my shirt so that I can change. "I was ready last week. It's been the month from hell."

He checks his watch and then strides around the room to sit on my sofa. "There're not a lot of things I agree with you on, Sullivan, but even I can agree with that. How do you feel about seeing Scarlet?"

I shrug, sliding on a pair of jeans and a black T-shirt.

"She's doing great, in case you were wondering. Looking more like herself again."

The idea she wasn't herself, even for a second, is enough to make my jaw go stiff. I pull on my trainers. "Good."

I have no idea how it's going to go with her this week. Whether she will even want to talk to me. The fact she's coming is enough. And it means she won't be cooped up in the house all on her own.

When I eventually lift my head, I find Charlie twisted in the seat, looking at me with a smile.

Charles Aldridge isn't much of a smiler.

"What?"

"You surprised me, that's all." He looks like the guy I knew at uni. A little lighter. He probably needs this break as much as the rest of us after everything that unfolded. "Do yourself a favour and talk to her this week."

I reach for my suit and place it in my bag, cocking my head toward the door. "Let's go."

He takes his time to stand, a stupid smile on his face that he wears all the way out into the foyer.

Scarlet

A racing heart or heart palpitations can be caused by conditions such as dehydration, low blood pressure, blood sugar levels, and anaemia. I know this because I read it in my textbook just last week.

Highlighted the motherfucker for good measure.

I feel betrayed. Body and mind. Because Lance Sullivan is the only condition and cause for the state my heart is in right now.

I didn't allow myself the time to think about how this would go. Didn't get nervous or overthink spending a week with him and our friends. I buried myself in my assignments, making sure I was caught up and then some so that I could come away guilt-free and confident I was ready for uni.

Standing here now with my suitcase handle clutched in my hand, watching as he and Charlie climb from their taxi, I feel stupid for not giving him the headspace sooner.

"Why's your ass fidgeting?" Elliot asks, looking down at me.

"It's not," I defend too quickly.

My brother turns to us, frowning. "You okay, Scar?"

Charlie and Lance draw near, and I wonder if maybe Elliot can hear my heart thumping. I swear my chest is jolting with each beat.

I nod. "I'm fine. Just a little nervous."

"Nervous?" Mason questions louder than I'd like, and right as the guys reach us. "You don't get nervous. Especially not flying."

I roll my lips and look quickly between everyone, my eyes only skimming Lance's face.

Charlie's smiling, which is so unlike him and weird.

This is mortifying. I look at my brother and frown. "I'm surprised you even know what makes me nervous."

His face drops slightly, and I feel like a complete dick for making it a "him" problem when it's not.

"Where are the girls?" Charlie asks.

"On their way," Mason tells him. "Luce had a cock-up with her hair."

I cringe, feeling terrible.

Lucy called me this afternoon and asked me which box brand I use on my hair. I didn't ask too many questions, knowing Nina was there and listening in with no idea I was coming away with them. She called me back a couple of hours later in tears.

"She cut it?" Elliot asks Mase.

"No, she dyed it." I chuckle.

Lost in thought, I accidentally look at Lance and then abruptly throw my gaze at the ground.

Subtle, Scarlet.

"Are you okay?" Mason asks, concerned.

"I'm fine." I grab my suitcase and start toward our private lounge, needing to create some distance.

"Hey, wait," Elliot calls after me, catching up. "What colour?"

I look up at him and smile. He grins back, sliding his arm around my neck. "It's good to see you smile, Scar. Let's go get rum drunk in paradise."

Lucy's hair is pinker in person than it was on FaceTime. "I like it," I tell her as she pulls the cap on her head further down.

"Can we get a drink? I need a drink."

I nod and follow her to the bar, throwing a smile at Nina and my brother as we pass. The two of them seem more in love than ever.

Lance is behind the small counter, presumably playing host to Megan, who's standing chatting with him.

Our eyes lock as I step up beside her. "Hi," I say, knowing I can't ignore him forever.

"Baby Lowell," he mutters back.

My stomach clenches at the name. The memories that come with it.

"Make me a cocktail, Lance." Lucy leans over the counter, looking up at his tall frame with a defeated look on her face. "Pretty please."

He tips his chin, dragging his gaze away from me. "One. Then I'm going to my seat to sleep with no distractions."

"Spoilsport," Megan chimes. "I want a virgin something. I'll be sideways by the time we land if I'm not careful. I already ploughed through the prosecco Lucy picked up for us on the way here."

Lance shakes his head and picks up some bottles. "Luce?"

"Cosmo, please."

He starts to unscrew a bottle top. His eyes flick back to me. "And for Scarlet?"

The way he says my name sets off an explosion of fireworks in my gut. Thank God I didn't take my makeup off already; it's putting in a shift for my cheeks right now. "Umm… uh… Aperol spritz?"

"Oh, can I get a splash of prosecco in mine!"

I chuckle. "It's not a virgin if you add prosecco, Megs."

"No, it's not a virgin if you add cock, and there's no cock and balls going into it. We're all good."

"Jesus," Lance mutters, pouring Lucy's Cosmo. I wait for his smile, his lip slightly turning up at the corner, but it's as far as it goes.

I'd give anything for that smile. Just to know that he's okay.

To know that I didn't hurt him as bad as I think I did.

"Megan's trying to hold on to her virgin cocktail like Nina is her ass card on a Tuesday." Luce sips her full drink as Megan snorts out a laugh.

I shake the thoughts from my head and chuckle with them.

"Ass card?" Lance frowns, confused. "Like…"

"Like cock and balls in the ass on a Tuesday, Lance," Megan confirms. "I don't recommend it."

She looks at me, her eyes saying sorry before her mouth can. "Sometimes I wonder what you must think of me, Scarlet. Nina's terrified we're corrupting your innocence."

Lance sniggers and my body flushes with heat.

Our eyes meet as he adds the soda to the drinks, and then he lifts them onto the counter. Megan reaches for hers, moaning and telling the whole plane how good it is before insisting Luce try it.

My eyes are still stuck on Lance, though, following him as he steps around the bar and heads for his seat at the back of the plane, where he stays for the entirety of the flight.

We decided to all stay in one lodge while we're on the island. The Montgomerys' lodge is a little further down the coastal path, and although it would make sense to split the group and take a room each, we decided we could rearrange the beds to make it work.

Megan, Lucy and I are sharing the main bedroom. Nina and Mase have a room to themselves, and then Lance, Elliot and Charlie have their own rooms.

"Scarlet, how is this your life?" I follow Megan out onto the balcony with a gentle smile on my face, loving how the warm sea breeze rolls over the cliff tops and whips through my hair.

"We don't come out here much anymore. Mase uses it with the guys yearly. I haven't been in a while."

"You used to come with your parents?"

"We came together once, but I don't remember it. I was a tiny baby, and my mum was sick. We came here a lot with Frey and Glen growing up."

"It's beautiful," Lucy tells me, stepping up beside me and peering over the railing. The firepit is directly below our room to the right of the pool.

"It's good to be back. You girls are going to love it here."

"What time did Mase say we were meeting for dinner?" Megan asks.

"Eight." I smile.

"Can we go for a swim in the pool?"

"You don't need to ask, Megs. Anything you want to do, just do it."

"Yes, let's hydrate at the pool. Then we can go again tonight!" I smile at Lucy's enthusiasm as she disappears back into our room and starts to unzip her suitcase. "Scar, you have that black bikini you need to get your ass in. Nobody should look good in it, and it fits you like it was made for you."

We use the en suite to change and then make our way downstairs, where we find the guys lying out on the sofas. Elliot is in nothing but a pair of black shorts and a cap that he's using to cover his face as he sleeps. Lance and Charlie are still fully dressed and chatting, oblivious to our presence at their backs as they look at something on Charlie's laptop.

Lucy puts her finger to her mouth and tiptoes to the side table. She picks up the jug of icy water and then pads around to stand behind Elliot.

"Tip that water on me, princess, and I'll have you off the cliff top." He gasps as the first drip splashes over his wide chest. "Luce!"

"Oops." She empties the jug, quickly dropping it down when he bolts up from the sofa and clears the back of it. They run through the kitchen and out the folded doors to the terrace.

There's a huge splash a moment later.

"They need to have sex or something. The sexual tension is killing me."

Charlie and Lance both turn at the sound of Megan's voice, but she's already turned and disappeared to the kitchen, leaving me standing like a lemon.

"You guys better not be working right now," I say, unsure what to do with their stares locked so intensely on me.

Charlie swallows, clearing his throat when Lance's eyes only linger on my body. "I'm done for the week. In fact…" He stands, shutting the laptop. "I should go shower and change before dinner."

He gives Lance a slap on the back as he leaves, and it seems to shake him out of whatever trance he is stuck in. He scrubs at his face and shifts his attention away from me again.

I know I should speak to him.

I *need* to speak to him.

I'm just terrified of what he might say.

"Lance." I round the sofa and sit beside him, bringing my legs up and under me so I can face him. "Can I speak to you?"

He smooths his hand from his face, back through his hair, and then turns his head toward me.

And the heaviness, the pure, unfiltered need in that one look, makes my mouth go dry, my heart thudding uncontrolled.

"Are you okay?" I ask, resisting the urge to reach for him, knowing how badly he craves physical touch. My physical touch.

His eyes roam every inch of me, bouncing from my eyes, nose, hair, then lips. My breasts and neck even. Taking everything in.

And as if it pains him to look at me, a frown creases his brow when he eventually speaks. "Are you?"

I drop my gaze, toying with the loose thread on the pillow between us. No. Not even a little bit. But instead, I say, "I'm fine." Because I made a choice to not make it his concern, and burdening him with it now isn't fair.

I look up, finding his stare burning through me—through my lie.

He sighs, and I wonder if he'll call me out, pull me to him, and tell me he's missed me like I've missed him.

He doesn't do any of those things, though.

And it's not until he stands from the sofa and simply says, "Good," and leaves the room that I see just how much I hurt him.

Lance

Come to Bora Bora, they said.

It will be fun, they said.

I even managed to convince myself that it was a good idea. To be able to see Scarlet and confirm that she's all right. That she's doing as well as Charlie said she is.

She looks beyond fucking well.

We're seated on the terrace at the dinner table, everyone relaxed and loose after one too many drinks. The lanterns and candlelight alone illuminate the small section of the cliff top we're sitting upon, radiating a golden hue over Scarlet's sun-kissed skin. My eyes have barely drifted from her all evening, and when they have, it only takes that laugh to fall from her lips, and my head turns straight back.

I rib Mason, telling him he's whipped with Nina, but I'm not sure I've ever been so enamoured by a woman in my life.

And while she might look perfectly fine, might tell me she's perfectly fine, I know that she's a million miles from the word.

"Guys, I want to make a toast tonight." I watch as she stands, lifting her glass and waiting for everyone to settle down. She's been drinking cocktails with the girls all night, and I can tell she's struggled to keep up. She's smiley and rosy-cheeked. Perfect, but maybe a little drunk too. "I want to toast us being here together. It's been years since we've been out here, Mase, and I honestly never expected to feel as content as I do standing here now." She looks around the table and smiles. "I think I can speak for everyone when I say it's been a hard couple of months." Her voice cracks, and so does my chest, catching us both off guard. "But the crazy thing is, at least to me, is that I can stand here confidently with old and new friends and say that anything I've lost has been returned tenfold." I wait for her eyes to meet mine, but they don't. "You girls don't give my feet a chance to fully land most days, and it keeps me exactly where I need to be." Nina reaches out and takes her hand. "I'm blessed— beyond measure to have you all. And—I…" She frowns, her emotions creeping up on her fast. Too fast. "And I want to toast… to you—us… for that." She swallows as she lifts her glass higher, forcing a smile. "To us."

"To us!" Everyone follows, standing to clink glasses, the girls cheering.

I watch as she sits back down in her chair, her stare heavy as everyone else carries on around her. I watch it consume her second by second. Dragging her all the way down.

When she stands and slips quietly from the table, I follow, making sure to use the sliding doors that connect to the bedroom instead of the one she went through. I walk down the hall and catch her on the threshold, my arms wrapping around her body as she ploughs into my chest.

She gasps, looking up at me. "Lance." She blinks, swallowing hard before forcing that same haunted smile she wore at the table onto her face.

"Your smile is my undoing, sunshine, possibly my favourite thing in the entire world, but you don't have to be brave in front of me."

Her chin wobbles, eyes shining as she shakes her head. Lost. She looks so fucking lost it steals my ability to breathe. "I forget… so easily it makes me sick to my stomach. And then I remember he's gone, and it's like being back in that moment all over again."

"I know," I say, barely a whisper.

"I'm broken."

I pull her into my chest, my hands weaving in her hair. "You're not broken, Scar."

It took everything inside of me to walk away from her sitting on that sofa this afternoon.

To not reach out and touch her.

Inhale her.

Her eyes lift, wide and lost, as tears coat her cheeks. I lean in and gently smear a tear away with my nose, my lips dusting as they follow. She pushes up onto her tiptoes, turning her face toward my mouth as I move, searching as I ease back and catch the tears on the other side.

It's been so long.

I've missed her so fucking much.

"Lance." Her body presses into mine, so familiar, so fucking *her*.

My parted lips drag down her cheek, too far gone and flirting with the corner of her mouth.

"Scar—"

She dips her head, sealing her lips over mine as she slides her palms up the back of my neck. I shudder.

It's desperate. A messy clash of tongues and teeth. Everything I need and want and miss.

I frown, breaking the kiss. "Scar." Our foreheads touch, breaths ragged.

She pulls away, her eyes heavy as she smooths her hand down the side of my face and neck. Her touch: my undoing. "I want you," she says breathlessly.

My jaw clenches, and I step back, fighting it. "But will you want me tomorrow?"

Her face drops, sadness washing out the slight rose tint staining her cheeks from our kiss.

I look down at her, wanting nothing more than to take her in my arms, take her to my room, wrap her in every bit of happiness she ever gave me and tell her everything is going to be okay. "You were upset at the table. I'm not going to fuck this up completely by taking you like this. Before we have a chance to talk."

Her face screws up in pain, and she drops her head. "You weren't the one who fucked this up, Lance."

"Not true."

"It's the only truth I know. You didn't deserve to be cut off the way you were." She stares at my chest. "I'm sorry for that."

I push her hair off her face, stepping into her again as I cup her cheeks, lifting her head back up. "Enough. Don't do that."

Not knowing my own limits and losing a battle against myself, I smooth my hand gently from her jaw down her neck, then over her chest before roaming back up to weave my fingers through her lavender hair. She melts into the touch, and my body only craves more. I lean in, an ache dancing all the way to my fingertips as I bury my face in her neck, inhaling. *Fuck.* My lips search, hungry and desperate until I find her racing pulse. I dust over it twice before caressing the skin with a light kiss.

Scarlet whimpers, making my cock stir in my shorts.

A door clicks open somewhere down the hallway, and I pull back in a rush, eyes wide. Scarlet doesn't so much as flinch, her stare locked on me.

"Jesus Christ," I rasp, scrubbing at my face.

"You should find yourself a nice girl, Lance. Someone less twisted up inside. Someone who wouldn't hurt you…

like I did," she whispers the words with a sad smile, meaning every one of them.

I shake my head, barely able to look at her as her eyes shine. I swallow the lump in my throat, hating that I've just denied her but knowing she isn't ready. "She wouldn't be you."

She tilts her head, a tear sliding down her cheek. "Exactly."

TWENTY-FIVE

Scarlet

"I feel disgusting."

Nina chuckles as she hands me a bottle of water and lies down next to me on the lounger. The two of us decided against going with the others down to the shops on the island. Or I decided against going, and Nina felt sorry for me and my hungover ass and said she'd stay with me.

I was drunk last night, probably the drunkest I've been since university and yet I haven't been able to shake every word that left my mouth while I stood practically begging Lance to kiss me.

"I'm in heaven," Nina says, and I can sense the smile on her face without the need to open my eyes. "I didn't realise how badly I needed to be away from city life."

"I think we all needed the break," I murmur, letting my body sink further into the lounger.

I don't think I've ever seen my brother as relaxed as he has been the past two days. He's slowly becoming the person

I knew when we were young, and although a part of me wishes he'd found his way back on his own, for other reasons, I can't help but love Nina for making him so happy. She's got to be a saint to put up with his shit. But then I've heard enough stories to know that Nina can be her own breed of stubborn at times. I guess both of them have been shaped by the lives they've been handed.

I look across at Nina and purse my lips. Her dark-chocolate hair hangs in soft waves over her shoulder, partially covering her arm. She has her eyes closed, a smile curling her glossed lips as if she's happy and content just to lie quietly in the sun. I've not known her long, a matter of months, but it was Nina who brought my brother back to me. And it was Nina who stood at my side as I picked out a coffin for Dad's burial. I never thought Mason falling in love would be a benefit to my life. And yet I have the girls now. Genuine, incredible friends who I know would drop anything to be there for me.

"I can feel your eyes on me, weirdo."

I chuckle and wait. She lifts her hand to shield her eyes as her head tilts to the side. "I'm just thinking about how nice it is to have friends. I sometimes wonder how long I would've hidden away at the estate if Mason had never met you."

Her smile is warm, gentle. "You'd have gone back to uni eventually, Scar. And you're an easy person to love. Friendships would've come easy." She looks out over the cliff's edge, rearranging her legs on the lounger. "But I get it. For years—even now, on the bad days—I find myself thinking about what life would have been like if Lucy and her mum never took me under their wings. Like, where would I have ended up? Would I be like she was?"

Her mum, she means.

"Have you spoken to her recently?"

Nina shakes her head, her face a little harsher than it was moments ago. "No. Not for a few weeks, and I don't want to. I used to help her out from time to time, but I think for the first time in a long time, I don't feel like I need her. She's an addict, which is hard because I tend to feed her addiction while chasing my own."

"What do you mean?"

"She calls, I give her money, she buys her drugs, and then I wait, desperate for the next call to land." She swallows, her gaze permanently lost to the horizon. "I think when I was little, I craved affection from her so badly I'd end up doing anything to get it. It made for a really unhealthy relationship. Like this one client of hers used to come back time and time again, and I hated him. I hated him so much. But when he was done with her, leaving her money on the kitchen counter, I wouldn't want him to go. She was only happy when she had money in her back pocket." She turns to look at me, her face softening. "I didn't realise how fucked up that was until it was too late."

I think back to my birthday and how Nina chose to pay for her own treatments. "I'm sorry, Nina."

She waves me off along with her threatening tears. "Don't be. You've met Lucy. And her parents, Maggie and John, are the most incredible people on earth. If there's any good left inside of me, they're the reason for it."

"There's plenty of good," I tell her, smiling as my throat goes tight.

"This shit is like therapy," she says, sitting up a little straighter. "Anything you want to get off your chest," she adds, laughing as she swipes at her under eyes.

Lance.

He's something I should get off my chest. But something keeps me from telling Nina about all the ways Lance Sullivan has brought me back to life—or did… before I lost Dad.

"I started reading the diaries," I tell her instead.

She turns in her seat, placing her feet between the two loungers. "You did?"

I nod, wondering how much of the stories my mother left for me I want to share.

When Mason told me he wasn't ready to go through Dad's things with me, it was Nina who showed up at the house to help me. We spent the day rummaging through the boxes Dad had stashed away in the cupboards and loft space, finding an array of items that made my heart break all over again.

Videos I barely remember being filmed which I now watch at least once a week. His clothes—jumpers I'll never wash that smell exactly like him. We donated anything that didn't have sentimental value, and the rest I kept.

The most surprising thing we found, though, was my mother's diaries, the original ones that my dad told me were ruined. They weren't as damaged as he'd said, but they did contain words I'm not sure Mason and I will ever be ready to read.

She wrote to us personally. When she was sick… as she was dying. She told me about Dad, about her parents and her life and what she and Frey might have done that day.

I'd been given the reprinted copies when I was twelve, and although they gave me insight, nothing could have prepared me to read the aching truth that was Ellis Lowell's short life.

"I've not read all the entries," I tell Nina. "I read the first few and then the last, curiosity getting the better of me." I give her a guilty look. "I'm about halfway through them now."

"Are you… are you glad you found them?"

I nod before I can even consider her question. "Yes. I think Dad wanted me to find them."

"I agree," she whispers, grasping my hand in hers. "He probably just never knew the right time to give them to you."

She's right. I know that Dad would never have kept them from Mase and me. I think he was being careful as to when to give them to us.

I look at Nina and smile wide. "She would have loved you, you know. She'd be proud of Mase and would've been besotted with you."

As her dimples pop, she leans closer and squeezes my hand in hers. "Maybe."

"Thank you, Nina. For everything. Bringing Mase closer again and helping me this past month. You're a true friend."

She straightens in her lounger, not letting go of my hand as she closes her eyes and soaks up the sun. "You're welcome, Scar."

Scarlet

I'm not sure how a week flew by quite as quickly as it did, but today we have to go home, and I dread it a little inside.

It's been a week of healing.

I spoke to Mason and spent time with him and the girls —memories made as a group that will last a lifetime.

I wish I could look at Lance and know what burns between us, but I don't anymore, even after an entire week with him.

His gaze wasn't careful, as if he didn't care who saw, and yet it never lingered for as long as I wanted it to. He hasn't touched me once.

And the only time he's spoken to me has been to ask me if I'm okay. Sometimes he didn't even speak the words. He'd just throw me a look I couldn't ignore, and I'd nod, knowing.

I didn't think I'd be so relaxed with him here, but if anything, I've felt safer than ever. Looked after, with cheese and ham toasties that were left on the kitchen counter after my morning walks and then the twinkling of fairy lights, which I found wrapped around my wooden bedpost on the second night.

I give the man nothing for two months, and he still finds a way to steal my heart.

I just don't know if I'm ready for him to keep it.

Lance

She isn't ready.

If she was, I wouldn't have hesitated. I wouldn't have

kept my distance. I'd have taken what I wanted and never let her shake me off again.

The only way this is going to go is her coming back to me. I'm not going to chase her for it. I kept to my word for over a month without caving, and even then, I made it clear my head was still in it from a distance.

"Where's Nina?" Elliot asks, pulling me from my trance.

I shrug.

"She's finishing up packing. I'll go get her," Lucy tells him, placing down her drink and sliding from the counter.

"Are you packed?" Elliot frowns, looking around for her case.

"Almost." She smiles.

"Let's go. Now."

Lucy sighs as Elliot turns her around and walks her down the corridor.

"I'll go," Scarlet says, leaving Charlie and me in the kitchen.

He looks at me and cocks his head.

I roll my eyes and catch up with her.

"Scar."

She turns and smiles as she continues to walk down the hall and up the stairs. I fall into step beside her.

"Are you looking forward to going home?" I ask, not really sure why I'm making small talk with the love of my life.

"I guess. For some reasons, yes and other reasons, no."

I nod. "You start your degree soon; they're letting you start late if you can catch up." I thumb over my shoulder. "I overheard you speaking to Charles."

"Yep. I caught up."

"Of course you did." I smile.

Her lips twist, an accusing smile. "You didn't doubt me?"

"Never."

She chuckles, and I decide to shoot my shot.

As we reach the top step, I stop her with a hand on her hip, twisting her so our bodies are flush and I'm staring down at her.

It's the most I've allowed since we ran into each other in the hall, and I can't hide the way my body sinks into hers even if I try. She feels too good.

Too much like mine.

But she isn't.

"Do you know how long it takes me to get to Lowerwick from my place?"

She shakes her head, her eyes locked on me.

"Too long." I smile. "And I ground my car on the cattle grid every fucking time, but Scar, and I mean this with my entire fucking being." I lift her chin and brush my lips against hers. "If you need me, you call me. Day or night."

Her chest works, and I sense her panic as I pull back an inch. Her heart's pounding.

"Hopelessly fucking wild," I mutter, giving her a small grin as I step away. Her eyes dart around my face, so unsure they almost stop me in my tracks.

Almost.

Instead, I turn and walk down the landing, rounding the corner to where Nina and Mason's room is tucked away.

I hear Nina's voice floating from the room as I push open the door.

"Sure, Mum, I'll just wire across a couple of grand from Mason's account. He won't even notice."

I stand frozen in the doorway. Watch as she hangs up and tosses the phone on the bed, just staring at it.

She scrubs at her face and turns, sighing before dropping her hands and catching me.

I speak on autopilot, unsure how to process what I've just heard or what it means. "We leave in half an hour. Lowell is looking for you."

Her shoulders drop, and I see the sadness lurking in her eyes. Or is it guilt? She's been quiet, moping around for days, saying she feels ill.

"Yeah, I'll be down in a minute."

I back out of the room, passing Scarlet as she heads toward the room. I don't even look at her.

I can't.

Mason doesn't deserve this.

It's going to fucking break him.

I sit with my head in my hands as Ben walks into my office. It's been the longest Friday in the history of Fridays.

"Got it."

I sigh and take the folder from his hand, opening it up and scanning the first document.

Nina's name is on the first bank statement, and it's all the confirmation I need before I send it flying across the room.

"I'm sorry, mate."

"Yeah, me fucking too," I seethe, sinking down into my

chair. I tip my head back. "How do I tell him she did this? He wants to marry her."

"I don't think there's an easy way to tell him. But I'd rather it came from a friend than anyone else."

"I just want her gone," I mutter, the frustration and anger inside of me threatening to erupt. "He's good right now," I snap. "After all the shit, he's good."

"He'll get past it, Lance… eventually."

I lift my head and frown at him. "You reckon? Cause I never did."

For the last ten years, I've lived with the fact that four women who should love me unconditionally only ever wanted me for the money I make. The money my dad made.

They screwed me hard, and it messed me up worse than anything else I've ever lived through.

He swallows and nods. "Sorry."

Nina hates Mason's money. She's pushed him away every time he's tried to buy her a thing. Was it her way of covering her tracks?

"Who made the payments? It wasn't her."

"I can find out. It will be easier now we know it was her."

I nod, running my tongue across my teeth.

He's so fucking in love with her.

"What if I don't tell him? What if I get rid of her another way, make it about something else instead of his money?"

"You don't think he'll leave her?" Ben asks, understanding my train of thought.

"I don't know."

I don't know shit.

"Could you make her leave him? You've got that stag tomorrow night. You could plan something, something that will see her off."

My nostrils flare as heat burns in my chest.

If she left him, he wouldn't ever know it wasn't real for her. He wouldn't know that she used him.

I'd give my right arm not to know how utterly disposable I was to my family. To go back to before I knew what they'd done.

Anything for a better reason than the truth.

My eyes meet Ben's, and I give him a nod.

TWENTY-SIX

Scarlet

If someone had told me this time last year that I'd be going to the shops to buy a pregnancy test for my brother's girlfriend right now, I'd have laughed in their face.

"All right, girls, in and out this time."

I smile as Lucy makes hurried strides ahead of Megan and me as we approach the pharmacy. We tried the closest shop to Nina and Mason's place, but when Lucy reached the front of the checkout line and spotted one of her mum's friends on the tills, she panicked and stuffed the test in the magazine section.

"Just let me pay for it this time," Megan tells her, rolling her eyes at me. "Such a damn drama queen."

"I'm sorry, but I do not need my mum asking questions. Because if it's not mine, she'd want to know whose."

"She's not allowed to say anything, Luce," I reassure her.

"Yeah, I know." She shakes her head. "I just panicked."

Lucy and I stand at the entrance as Megan goes in search of the tests. "How's Nina today? She hasn't been answering my calls."

"She isn't answering any of our calls. I think she's worried one of us will say something to Mason when she's so sure she isn't actually pregnant."

"Do you think she is?"

She side-eyes me, then shrugs. "I don't know. She's careful and takes her pill religiously. I think she's just scared right now. And it doesn't help that her mum has been hounding her again for money. It goes against everything that she is to say no. She's all over the place."

I frown. We arrived home from Bora Bora three days ago, and I only spoke to Nina a few days before that on the terrace. Had her mum called since? "I didn't think she'd called in a while."

"She hasn't. But Sarah Anderson is a complete dick. A nasty woman who only cares about herself."

"All right, let's go make the little whorebag pee."

"Megs," Lucy warns, eyes wide. "Don't go upsetting her tonight. She's a donkey on the edge."

"I know. I know." We follow Megan out of the shop and bundle into my car before heading back toward Mason's building.

The guys are out at Elliot's neighbour's stag do tonight, which gives us girls plenty of time to do the test without my brother being his usual overprotective self over Nina.

I've been on edge for days, my thoughts occupied not only by Nina and her potential pregnancy but by Lance and the fact I might run into him at my brother's tonight. Or that maybe he might just be thinking about me too.

Because every night, I lie in my dimly lit room and think only of him.

"Is anyone else nervous as hell?" Lucy mutters, turning to look at Megan in the back.

I tighten my grip on the steering wheel. "I think it will work out regardless. Nina and Mase are both good people. It might be terrible timing, but I have no doubt that they'll figure it out."

"If anything, it's probably exactly what your brother needs," Megan says.

I nod. "I think so, too. It would be the making of him."

"And Nina would boss it. She's one of them who just gets on with it," Lucy tells us.

"Exactly." I nod, swallowing as I look between them, my stomach coiled tight.

Silence falls over the car, all of us likely feeling the same way.

"It's going to be fine, guys," Lucy eventually says.

I'm not sure who she's trying to convince.

Lance

My whiskey tastes like shit, a bitter betrayal coating my tongue every time I even cast a look at Mason.

The idea of this night seemed simple two hours ago. Save my friend from another woman who's happy to do him over, all to save herself. What from? I'm not sure I care at this point. Not after Cara, my mum, and my sisters. Women who take and destroy. So selfish they don't see they could have everything they wanted if they only loved what was in front of them.

I can almost believe Nina really does love Mason. That maybe she needs the money for reasons other than greed, but again, I've watched my best friend give her the world over the last four months, and he'd give her the rest of it too. If she'd only asked for it.

That feeling of betrayal when you find out the people who should love you can hurt you… he isn't going to know what that feeling is—she is.

And then she'll be gone.

Mason was there for me when I had nothing left. It's my turn to be there for him.

"You've had enough tonight, Sullivan. Time to head home, buddy." Elliot leans down and takes my glass, his own eyes glazed.

"I'm fine," I tell him, standing. I stagger, knocking into the table. The few discarded drinks go tumbling.

"Sure you are. Come on."

My right arm is lifted and placed over his shoulder, aiding me toward the entrance of the club.

"Montgomery, I've got it." Mason appears on my left, jerking his chin at Elliot as if to ask him what's wrong with me.

I stand to my full height and shrug him off me. "I said I'm fine, Lowell."

His brows furrow, and then he nods. "I'm heading back, too. I'll call Vin."

I don't wait around for him, pushing out onto the street and letting the cold whip me across the face with a slap. The roads are busy, the cars passing with a constant stream, the motion making me feel sick.

Let him go home.

He's finally happy.

I wait. I wait for Mase to come back out, but he doesn't. And when the churning in my gut doesn't ebb away, only getting more twisted, I stumble to the alleyway and vomit.

My hands scrub over my face when I'm done, harshly wiping away the wetness around my eyes and cheeks.

What the fuck are you doing?

"Mr Sullivan, I've flagged down a taxi. Do you need anything?" I twist to look over my shoulder, finding one of the club owners standing at my back.

I shake my head. "I'm fine." I stagger toward the waiting taxi and slide inside. Everything hurts. My head, my chest, my gut.

"St. John's Wood," I tell the driver.

I dig out my phone and pull up my messages but get caught off guard by the missed call from Scarlet.

I sit forward in the seat, my head spinning. It's the first time she's called me since her dad died.

My fingers move on their own accord, like a sequence they've learnt from repetition. I stare down at the picture of us at the Hamilton Gala.

God, I miss her so fucking much.

And now she is calling me. While I'm blind drunk and stinking of vomit.

I snigger. I wasn't there for her when she needed me, when her dad fucking died from years of being a drunk. And I can't be there for her now.

My shoulders slump, my head hanging low as I stare at the image.

I swipe up and pull up a new message to Ben.

Lance: Change of plan. Call it off

It's not until hours later, my phone waking me as it rings and rings, that I sit up in my bed and see the multiple missed calls lining my screen. I squint at the light, trying to read the names.

I have missed calls from everyone but Mase.

And one text.

Ben: Too late

TWENTY-SEVEN

Scarlet

One year later

My dad told me my mother's diaries were breaking apart at the seams, and he wasn't lying. They're just as big of a mess as life is right now.

But amongst the ripped, faded pages are entries that never made it to my copies. The ones my dad had reprinted were void of some of my mother's hardest days. Days when she so clearly knew her fate and decided to write to Mason and me personally. It's been a year since we found them stuffed in boxes at the bottom of my dad's wardrobe, and I've been lost inside them ever since.

Scarlet,

There's a guilt that seems to weigh heavy when-

ever I write these letters to you. Mason's contain memories—moments he'll hopefully never forget. And yet you, my sweet baby, might never even know my voice.

I try to picture it sometimes. How you might be. Like now, my eyes watch as you sleep spread out on your blanket, the wind fussing you every so often as it rolls through the meadow. And all I can wonder is how old you will be when you eventually get to read this. Until you can read these letters and know me. I tell you out loud. I tell you every word I desperately want you to remember. But you won't. I thought I had a good imagination until I tried to picture you as a grown woman.

So instead, let me tell you what I do know.

You're going to be strong, Scarlet. Likely stronger than the people around you if what I know is true. It's in the small things. The way your eyes watch me. The way you seem to wake in the moments I find despair in the middle of the darkest nights, never crying or in need as I embrace you. It's like you know, and you're there solely to comfort me.

You're going to save the people around you, and then you'll save yourself too.

I just know it.

And in the moments you feel like you can't save them, or you feel like you've failed, know that you've done it once already, and you can do it again. Because even as I sit here feeling like I've failed my family by *getting sick, having to write these silly letters, I only have to snap my gaze an inch to the left, and I smile.*

And that's because of you.

My heart is yours,

Mum.

I'd call it my favourite of the entries, but it reduces me to tears each and every time I read it. They got longer as they went on, this being one of the first she wrote. It was as if she was afraid of what to say at first, as if maybe she didn't know what to say at times. Eventually, I became a friend to her, a sounding board for ideas that went unanswered and a reader of some of her most treasured stories.

I skip ahead to her last entry.

Scarlet,

This book has plenty of empty pages left, but I'm scared I'm not going to be able to fill them. Your dad, as I thought, is in complete denial, trying to carry on as if everything is normal when in reality, I can't close my eyes at night without the terror of never waking up again consuming me. But it's terror for them: your dad and Mason, not me or you.

I feel ready. Not in the way that I can leave and be okay with it, but in the way that my body feels tired and it needs the peace that leaving this world promises.

And as for you, Scarlet... (I'm smiling wide just at the thought). I've held you in my arms every day for the last twelve months, and I don't know how you do it, but out of everyone I have to say goodbye to, our goodbye doesn't scare me. You have here everything I needed you to know about life, and yet you're going to be whoever you want to be regardless of it. You're fierce. Wild and free. Scarlet, I'm not afraid because this won't impact you like it'll impact them, and when it does impact them, I know with the love and guidance you have around you, you'll make me the proudest mother in the world.

Your Auntie Frey has been around a lot more recently, actually, and I know that she knows. She's going to watch you grow for me. She'll be the mum you deserve, and I can promise you she'll never steer you wrong. Listen to her, Scarlet, she's wiser than I've ever been, and as you now know, she's saved my ass on more than one occasion.

The doctors are on their way out to the estate as I write this, and I'm supposed to be resting before they arrive. They'll poke me and prod me and tell me the same thing I was told only days ago. I'd rather make the most of these quiet moments instead. Whilst the fretting stops, and I can be just me. It gives me a chance to talk to you some more.

I remember when I used to feel guilty for not knowing what to say to you. Turns out I had a lifetime of stories I could give you—I hope you've enjoyed them. I hope you can find things in them that bring you the parts of me you need. A part of me hopes you'll never need them, but I don't believe someone can be as special as you are, Scarlet, and not live through some adversity.

You've seen all of my struggles through these pages, maybe lived through the pain they've brought me at times, and if that's a burden, I'm sorry. I never planned on giving you so much, but there isn't a page of this book I'd take back. I'm glad you know. I feel like you do know now. Me.

Today, you're just my sweet baby. There's a whole life for you waiting to be lived, and I won't ever know those days.

But don't you dare for a minute think that I'm sad, Scarlet Lowell. The thought of the life you and your brother will live is the only excitement I can feel or find anymore. Nothing else comes close.

Live that life.

And, my baby girl, whoever you are when you read this, know that you saved me a thousand times over.

If I lived another day, it was because of you.

My heart is yours,

Mum

Based on the dates, my mother lived for another three days after she wrote that last letter. The rest of the diary is blank pages, and on the days following my dad's death, his funeral and every day since, I know I could have filled them three times over.

For the first time in my life, I feel a little something more than I knew was possible for my mum. The pictures that have always been around our home, along with her words, make her someone I feel like I know. But it's even more personal than that. She gave me the most vulnerable side of herself. When she couldn't speak to Dad because he'd worry or felt like a burden putting it on Freya, she came to me. I wish I had them sooner, but maybe my dad was saving them. I've never lived through pain or suffering like what my mum described until this last year, and it's not like the diaries were hidden from me. My dad knew I'd find them eventually.

Mason has the ones dedicated to him now, but even in her letters to me, she told me he wouldn't read them.

How did she know?

I was a baby.

Mason was four years old. And yet she saw right through him.

And she's right. He probably won't read them.

I flick over the paper to the first blank page and roll my lips as I contemplate what exactly I should say. My mum took months to get into the swing of speaking from her mind without thought, somehow always saying exactly what she needed to by the end of it.

I want to try.

Mum,

It never used to be hard to say your name out loud. Then I was given your diaries at age twelve and fell in love with your life. The life you had with Dad—before us, the life you had with Mason—after. Your name got a little harder to say out loud after that.

I've spoken to you for years out in your garden, not truly knowing who you are, and it's only now that I have all of your letters that I feel like I might have lost something I probably desperately needed in life.

Mum, I started this letter with your name because I need you now.

Mason has a child. Ellis (named after you) was born in October, and although he's the light in all of our lives, nothing has been okay for a long time.

Nina and Mason aren't together. They co-parent Ellis with the help of all of us and haven't spoken to one another since the days following the birth.

Mason messed up so badly.

I believe him when he says he never did anything wrong—that the pictures Nina received of him with the woman were staged, but the situation, the way he gave up on her so easily when she told him to go, it makes my blood boil to this day.

He's as stubborn as Dad ever was.

I started my degree this year, and it's been really hard. I try to keep my head above water, but if I let myself be alone with my books for too long, I tend to feel myself sinking. My friends would never allow that to happen, though. The girls have been my lifelines after Ellis. They call me almost every day, and Nina brings Ellis out to the estate to stay at least once a month. Mason still hasn't been out here since Dad died, but I've given up on trying anymore.

Freya is and always will be a rock grounding me to earth. You were right about that. She's held my hand through the last year, making sure I'm eating and sleeping and not missing classes.

The estate is thriving, but you know that. Dad always said the grass got a little greener when you left us. I feel you both around me here. It's weird when I write that thought down, but the comfort I feel isn't something that's meant for words.

There's someone else that I'd love to tell you about. To rid him from my head once and for all. I've never told anyone about him. He tends to play on my mind a lot when I stop and allow myself to think too hard.

It's been nearly a whole year since I've seen Lance Sullivan.

I think I fell in love with him a little bit last summer. Not full-blown love, but it wasn't nothing, at least not for me. I don't know what it was for him, but I can't seem to forget him.

The only thing is, one day, he was telling me he'd be here when I needed him, and the next, he was gone.

I think I was mad at him for a while, but now I just feel sad.

Charlie says he's fine.

That he's just busy.

I can't help but wonder if he's telling me the truth. I guess I cared about the man more than I ever realised.

And I pushed him away.

Anyway, I read your letters today because I felt a little lost and I decided that I was going to start writing in this thing. To fill it the rest of the way.

Although things aren't okay right now, I think they will be. You've shown me they can be.

Soon,

Scarlet.

TWENTY-EIGHT

Lance

Two weeks later

"Wait. Nina let you in the house?" I stare at Mason in surprise as he finishes the last of his reps.

He places the barbell down. "Don't get too excited. It was awkward as fuck."

Good. This is good. "It's a start," I tell him, nodding.

"Too right, it's a start." Elliot claps Mason on the back, his chest heaving. "You're both too stubborn for your own good sometimes. We all needed this."

Elliot isn't wrong. After Nina gave birth to Ellis, she didn't want to see Mason, and without even discussing it, we became the bridge between the two of them. It's easy when the kid has us wrapped around his little finger.

If Nina and Mason can stick being in the same room as one another, it'll take the weight off everyone. Especially Lucy and Elliot. They seem to do the most out of us all.

For months things have seemed to level out. I've even started to let go of what happened last year. What I did. I've watched Nina raise Mason's son. Watched her become important to my friends—to me. And through every second of it, I tried to tell myself that she was the one in the wrong. What I did was beyond fucked up. That's on me. But she took that money. She's never admitted what she did, and neither have I.

I don't really know what sort of person that makes me.

Nina isn't a bad person, though, and if there's one thing I'm sure of, it's that I made a mistake. I'd give anything to take it back, but I can't.

"I agree that we need this." And I mean it. It feels good, the idea they might figure it out.

I rarely allow myself to think about Scarlet Lowell for long, but I can't help standing here now and wondering if Nina and Mason working their way back to one another might bring Scarlet back to me.

That maybe if they're okay, it's okay for us to be okay too.

Again, I don't know what sort of person that makes me.

Charlie nods, scrubbing a towel through his hair. "You'll come out the other side of this, Lowell. Give it time."

If only time could heal all wounds.

It can't.

It won't.

Not when it comes to her.

She deserves the world.

Mason shakes his head and sniggers. "You make out like we're getting back together. Which isn't what I want."

No one bothers to respond to his bullshit.

I push down my wandering thoughts, not needing to torture myself thinking about Scarlet.

He lifts the barbell again, his muscles rippling. "She walks away whenever shit gets hard. And she didn't give me a chance to figure out what was going on when I begged her to stay. With or without those pictures, she would have walked eventually. I'm *done*."

I shouldn't let his words ease my guilt, but they do.

Logan, the owner of the gym, crosses to where we're working out and tips his chin at us. "Gents." His eyes move to Mason. "Lowell, the room above this place, we're still keeping it for Nina? I have some equipment coming in today and could do with using it for storage."

Charlie looks away.

Elliot grins.

And I stand, hands on hips, trying to slow my throbbing heart. Still, after all this time… one lost thought to her, and I'm fucked.

"Leave it the fuck alone, Morgan," Mason grunts, doing another rep.

Logan nods, already accustomed to Mason's colourful mouth, and walks away.

"Remind me never to go into business with you, asshole," Elliot mutters.

Mason says nothing.

"Anyway," Elliot goes on. "I'm *done* here." He walks across the room and steps onto the treadmill, turning it on.

"So *done*," Charlie chuckles, picking up the ropes he was working on and starting again.

Mason drops the barbell, the weights clipping the floor with a jolt, pulling the attention from the people around the gym. He puts his hands on his hips and stares at me, his body wound tight.

I tip my chin, stepping back. "Whatever you say, mate."

His gaze pinches despite the fact I wasn't trying to piss him off. "Fuck the lot of you."

Yeah, he's not done.

And neither am I.

Scarlet

Mum,

I went out last night. What was supposed to be food with the girls at Nina's apartment turned into an impromptu girls' night out. We danced for hours. It's the first time Nina's been out since she had Ellis, and I think it was the easing back in she needed. She's amazed me these past few weeks, letting Mason come to the house to put Ellis to bed so that he settles better. I was there when they saw each other again for the first time. It was electric, like nothing I'd ever seen before.

They make me mad at how perfect they are for each other. They just haven't worked it out yet.

They will.

We all will.

I think we'll be able to place Dad's headstone soon. They think the earth's settled enough, which is *great, I guess. It seems final—a headstone with words on it. Dates set in stone.*

I had more flowers sent to me at the hospital from the doctor. The married one. He's so hot it disgusts me, and if I was to listen to Megan, I'd be in a lot of trouble already. I'm happily ignoring him, but I kept the flowers because they made me smile.

The house is so quiet sometimes. I think about calling Frey some nights, but then I know she'll worry all the time. It's easier to pretend on those few nights than risk an overbearing Freya. LOL - that means laughing out loud.

I thought about throwing an event in your honour. A charity ball here on the grounds at Lowerwick. A marquee with lanterns lighting up the meadow, food—tons of it, and an auction. I've seen the pictures of you and Dad. I want that fairy tale you made for yourselves.

I'll think on it.

Soon,

Scarlet

Lance

The knock at my door should be enough to rouse my attention from the boring-as-shit figures I'm working on.

It doesn't.

"Lance, I have Charles Aldridge for you."

I flick my chin up.

Harry disappears, and within a few seconds, I hear the sigh of my best friend from the doors of my office.

I move my eyes to where he stands.

"You coming up?"

I nod once, shutting down my computer, then stand and button my jacket. We walk toward the elevators in silence.

"You seem rattled, Sullivan. Anything I should be aware of?"

I shake my head, staring at my reflection in the steel wall of the elevator.

We're having lunch in Mason's office today. Like always. Only today will be the first time I meet Jasmine, his new receptionist.

I'd call it karma, but I haven't been able to shake the feeling something isn't adding up.

Just as everything is working out, Nina and Mase are finally getting somewhere, and then Vinny finds *her*.

Jasmine is the woman Mason was photographed with last year.

She's also Nina's half sister.

It's been weeks since I found out the two were linked, that Jasmine, the woman who was paid—by me—to pose in pictures with my best friend, was related to the woman I was trying to fuck over.

"I've just got a lot on."

I never even knew Jasmine's name when everything was set up. She should never have happened, and Ben paid the price for it with his job.

Mason spent a year trying to find the woman. Desperate

to clear his name while I stood back and said nothing. And then, when he did find her, he found out she was just as much a victim as he was, and he decided to help her.

And now she's here, working for him so that she can get back on her feet.

Nina's fucking sister.

I can't shake it. Haven't been able to since she showed up. The feeling that it's all wrong, that I got it all wrong.

There are coincidences, and then there's straight-up fuckery.

"Have you spoken to Scarlet recently?" Charlie asks, halting my thoughts as his words tear through my gut.

I flare my nostrils and twist my head to level with him. "Why?"

He stares right back, his face hard. "This mood you have going on. She's got one too. Up and down all the time."

"She's not okay?"

"It's Scar. She's fine." He tuts and runs a hand through his hair. "You've not slept with anyone in a year, Sullivan. You're happy one minute and then straight up fucking icy the next. I'm not an idiot—"

"I've not spoken to Scarlet since the night Nina gave birth."

"What?" Confusion screws up his face.

"When did you last see her?" It's the most I've asked about her in months. Only allowing myself to take the titbits I could from Mason or Lucy and Megan's conversations.

It's been too easy to avoid her when she's so far away at the estate, and yet living with avoiding her has slowly fucking killed me.

"Last night."

I nod, biting down on the inside of my lip until it bleeds.

"She's lonely. Wouldn't tell me that, but I can see it. She's working every hour she can get her hands on and spending time with Ellis and the girls around that."

I don't need to hear this. "It's been a year. If she's sad, it's not because of me."

Charlie sniggers, following me out of the elevator when the doors open.

My legs seem to become weaker the further away I walk, my chest burning. I could have spent the past year with Scarlet. I wanted to. But did I deserve to fall back into her whilst her brother lost everything at my hands?

No.

My guilt would never allow it.

Some days I can forget—even convince myself that it wasn't my fault.

Today isn't one of those days.

"I have something I need to chase up. Tell the others I'll catch up with them on the weekend."

"Sullivan." Charlie grabs my bicep as I turn to head back to the elevators.

My head's a mess.

Such a fucking mess.

"You can talk to me. Anything…"

I nod, pulling my arm free as I leave.

No, I can't.

I don't like to rely on gut feelings. I like facts and happen to be able to obtain those facts easily.

It's why I'm at home on a Friday night with files spread out on my bed.

The invoices.

Nina's name on bank statements.

Money. So much money taken.

It should validate everything.

My gut tells me it doesn't.

Jasmine showing up has stirred up a shitstorm. Old wounds for Nina and Mason opened up. Painful memories for them both. And yet it might just be the thing that brings them back together.

At first, that wasn't what I wanted, but I didn't know Nina then. I never gave her a chance.

Would the truth fix this mess? Fucking maybe. But if I tell Mason the truth about what I did, he'll know what Nina did too, and I can't help but feel like she's already paid enough.

I pick up the original bank statements, the ones I found myself—nameless.

Then the ones Ben found—the ones initialled NA.

Then the ones he brought to me that day when I already knew it was her—Nina's name on the account.

I pinch the bridge of my nose. I need to speak to Ben and find out how and where he found Jasmine that night.

Lance: Are you with my sister?

Ben: What do you want, Sullivan?

I was raging when I fired Ben. He did what I asked him to do, but at the time, I couldn't stand to hear someone tell me I'd done the right thing. I blame Ben just as much as I blame myself and Nina for this mess.

Lance: Are you at the house?

Ben: Yes

I collect the files and pull on a T-shirt.

I take my bike, not wanting to waste time in traffic on a Friday night in the city.

Pulling into the gates of my childhood home never gets any easier, and I don't allow myself time to take it in as I climb off my bike and pull the file from my bag.

I knock on the front door and wait.

My mother answers after a minute, her face transforming when she sees me. "Lance—"

It shouldn't be so hard to look at her. "I'm here to see Ben."

Her shoulders drop, her throat bobbing. "Oh." She nods, opening the door wider and letting me in.

"Thank you."

"I've not seen you in months," she tells me as my eyes dance along the stripped-back walls.

"I've been busy. You're redecorating?" I ask.

"Trying to."

I watch her, her tired eyes shining. She's wearing her work clothes, a sweatshirt with the local supermarket logo covering the pocket.

I hurt her pride, making her get a job.

She probably hates me even more than she ever did because of it. It's why I haven't bothered to come here, sending the money for rent and bills and not giving them a minute more of my time.

"Ben's in the office," she tells me.

I frown. "Dad's—" I cut myself off, gritting my teeth and shaking my head. "Dad's office?"

She stares at me, her eyes widening at my reaction.

I turn and head down the hall.

Ben's sat at the large wooden desk in the centre of the room, my father's pictures now replaced by stark white walls.

"Lance," he greets, not looking up at me.

I shake off my emotions, striding to the desk and dropping the file. "Jasmine Lockwood." His eyes meet mine, bored. "Where did you find her?"

His lip tips up, and he pushes away the file with a finger. "Really, mate? You can't even say hello now?"

"I don't have time for pleasantries, and you can wipe that smug smile off your face before I knock it clean off. What do you know about this?"

He shakes his head, sitting back in his chair.

"Hello, big brother. I thought I heard your voice." I turn, catching Nessa Anne on the threshold, her togetherness making my brows furrow momentarily.

Her hair is freshly washed, down and curled, skin clear—flawless even. Clothes pristine. The opposite of my mother in every way.

"*Nessa Anne*," I mutter.

"Did someone die?" she asks, falling back onto the Chesterfield sofa that's been pushed back against the wall. "I presume you came for a reason."

"I need to speak with Ben in private—"

"She can stay," he tells me, waving me off.

I watch as Nessa Anne stands and rounds the desk, smiling smugly as she settles on Ben's lap.

"Your brother wants to know how I found Jasmine Lockwood."

"You told her?" I ask incredulously. "What the fuck is wrong with you?"

"Watch your tone with me, Sullivan. Unlike you, I happen to trust your sister."

My nostrils flare. "You're a fucking idiot."

Nessa Anne laughs. "Maybe. Or maybe you should be thanking Ben for making her impossible to find. Have you thought about that?"

"They found her."

I watch them flinch. The both of them. Ben recovers first, tipping his chin. "How?"

I shake my head, lifting the file. "I don't know. And to be honest, I don't give a fuck. I want to know where you found her, who you paid—because it wasn't her who received the money."

"Her boyfriend," Ben tells me simply. "He's a dealer. Happily put Jasmine to work."

"There's more to it than that. I know there is. Jasmine—"

"I'd be guilt-ridden too, Lance." Nessa Anne cuts me off, looking down at her nails as if they're more important than the conversation. "But coming here demanding answers after nearly a whole year is a push even for you. Do you think it's fair after the way you treated Ben? You fucked up. If Mason found Nina's sister, that's your problem, not ours. Deal with it."

"What did you just say?"

She rolls her eyes, sighing as she looks up at me. "What part are you struggling with?"

"Nessa Anne—"

"You said Nina's sister," I say, cutting Ben short. "But how do you know that?"

She slowly rights her tilted head, her mouth slackening as the colour drains from her face.

"I found out after—after everything went down," Ben assures me, his eyes not meeting mine as he sits up in the faded leather chair. "You laid me off, and I was pissed enough not to tell you."

I stare at the both of them.

Ben—the smartest man I know. It's why I asked him to help me.

And Nessa Anne—my fucking flesh and blood.

"I'm a fucking idiot, aren't I?"

Silence.

I drop my burning, unhinged stare to the file, flicking it open and lifting the first document.

The account numbers.

NA.

I look up at Nessa Anne, my hand shaking. "They're fake."

"Lance—"

"You're sick," I say in disbelief. I swallow the bile rising in my throat, my next breath harder than my last. "You're fucking sick in the head, the both of you… I knew… I knew Nina would never. Fuck, I knew it, and you…." I stare at Ben. "You talked me into it. You spent months working on it. Months telling me you found nothing, and all the time, it was *you*."

"I'd be careful what accusations you throw around if I were you, Lance."

"Why? Why Nina? Why would you do that?"

They remain mute.

"Tell me why!"

Ben sits forward too slowly, his face a mask.

I flip the desk, smashing it into the granite stone floor. "Fucking answer me. Now!" I roar.

"Because!" Ben thunders back at me, face red with fury. "Because she was too easy!" He pulls at the roots of his hair in anger. "Jesus Christ, you wouldn't let it go. I tried to make you drop it for weeks before you pulled me upstairs. And when I saw her name—the initials that matched Nessa Anne's so perfectly, the distrust you had for her, it made her easy! You made it easy!"

Nessa Anne swallows so hard I see it in my peripheral.

One beat of silence falls between us, and then I slam my fist into his face, cracking the bones in his cheek.

"Lance!"

I round my dad's now broken desk, dropping down on top of him.

I can't stop.

Years and years of pain unleashing.

"Mum!" Nessa Anne screams. "Mum!"

Ben swings his fists in an attempt to halt me, but nothing works. I'm unhinged. Thoughts of Nina, Mason, and Ellis. Thoughts of Scarlet....

Fuck no.

What I've done. It only fuels me. Blow after blow.

I ease off the moment I feel my mother's touch. Her arms wrap around me, my sister not daring to touch me.

I fall back to the ground, my chest heaving.

"What is going on?" my mum demands.

I'm in shock, my hands bloody and numb, eyes unfocused.

I stand, my knees shaking.

"Lance needs to leave," Nessa Anne rushes out, bending to help Ben sit up. "Now. Go!"

I take a step backward, staggering. "I hate you," I tell them, my eyes blurring with tears as my stare darts to my mum. "I hate you all."

Her own eyes fill as I turn to leave.

And I won't ever come back.

"Sullivan," Ben mutters, spitting out the blood filling his mouth. "I know about Marcus."

My back stiffens. My whole body coming to a stop as I think back to that night all those years ago.

"You think I wouldn't cover myself? You had it hidden well, but then you gave me time to look for everything I needed. Jasmine included. Turns out you and your friends have skeletons far darker than any of mine. I'd think about that before you walk out that door."

I don't turn, don't give him the satisfaction of seeing my face.

"I think we're clear," he tells me.

TWENTY-NINE

Scarlet

Two weeks later

Mum,

I spent the entire day with Ellis today. Nina was job hunting, and Mason had a meeting he couldn't miss. I was supposed to have him for an hour, but when Mason called to let me know he was done for the day, I told him to leave us alone for a while longer.

We went to that ice cream shop in the city that Dad loved. Ellis ended up in a sticky mess, but we had a great time.

I think Nina and Mason are having actual

conversations now too. They seem to be managing the new routine without killing one another, at least.

I've not lost all hope on them.

Vinny's driving me today. I left it too late putting fuel in my car, and it broke down on the bridge at Dunford. You'd think I'd learn. I told Vinny I was writing to you and felt so stupid the second the words left my mouth. Vinny being Vin, told me to say hi.

Dad really lucked out when he picked him.

This one's going to be short, we're nearly at the Montwell, and I better get Ellis awake and looking alert before Mason notices the danger nap I've just allowed him to have.

Wish me luck!

Soon,

Scarlet & Ellis

I close my mum's diary and sigh, looking across at Ellis, who's fast asleep beside me.

"All done, love?"

I look up at Vinny and smile. "For now. I should wake him up."

"You *should…*"

I chuckle and shake my head. "You're not so subtly putting ideas into my head, Vinny."

"I've seen the monster after being woken up, that's all."

We park in the underground parking. Vinny grabs Ellis's changing bag and pushchair out of the car while I wake him up. I let him snuggle into my chest, his fists clenching my bra strap at the sight of his pushchair.

My eyes scan the car park, spotting Elliot's and Lance's cars. The sight of the McLaren makes my heart somersault in my chest, and I look away.

"Are you okay carrying him, Scarlet?"

"I'm fine," I tell Vinny over my shoulder, walking ahead and into the warmth of the building. It's much quieter entering from this level, and I appreciate being able to bypass the main reception.

Vinny leans in and uses a key to call the elevator down.

It whirls, drawing Ellis's head up. "What's that noise, Ellis?"

He points to the steel doors, and I smile. "Clever boy."

The doors slide open, and I take a step. Just one. Because my second is halted. Thrown off-kilter by the man standing in the waiting elevator.

"Lance." Vinny steps by me and into the space. "You heading home for the day?"

"Uh, yeah. I was in early this morning." His eyes briefly leave me, just long enough to clock Vinny before they boomerang straight back. "Hey," he says with a frown.

"Hi." I smile because why not?

And because it's Lance.

The man I shared so much with.

His face remains passive, as if he doesn't know what to do. He even reaches up and rubs at the back of his neck, looking at Vinny again and then at me.

"You're dropping Ellis back to Mason?"

"Yep. Nina's job hunting today, so…."

He nods. "Right, I knew that."

I watch him, taking in the dark circles around his eyes, the messy wave in his hair, and the wrinkles in his suit jacket that I didn't notice at first glance. I've been angry at this man for the best part of a year, thinking he'd simply grown tired of me. That he had moved on. And yet looking at him now, all I see is a broken version of the man I once knew.

"I better head out."

I twist as he goes, my eyes following his back as his feet eat up the floor.

He's… different. And I stand frozen in place, wondering if that's it. If that's all he'll say after all this time.

After a whole year.

I blink, tears burning in the backs of my eyes.

Did it really mean nothing to him?

"Actually, Sullivan," Vinny calls after him. I look up at Vinny, waiting, but he doesn't speak, doesn't even return my stare. And I know he knows I'm looking at him. "I need to get Ellis and Mason home as well as this one." He nods down at me, and my stare widens. "I don't suppose you can help at all?"

I swallow and look back at Lance, his jaw clenched, his face as hard as I've ever seen it.

"No, I can get a taxi," I say, shaking my head vehemently. "I already said it's not a problem, Vin."

"I can drive you home, Scarlet."

I close my eyes, my throat going tight. I face him, gauging his reaction. If I'm going to be stuck in the car with him for over an hour, I can't have him looking at me as if he hates me.

"Perfect," Vinny says. "I'll take Ellis up from here. Unless you want to see your brother quickly?"

"I can wait," Lance agrees.

I look between the two of them, then at Ellis.

What do I do?

He bounces in my arms, seemingly wide awake now and desperate to get to Lance.

I smile and follow his gaze, but Lance looks away from him.

He's mad at the kid too?

"You can take him up, Vin." I give Ellis a kiss and pass him to Vinny, smoothing out his hair and whispering, "Be good for your daddy, Ellis. I love you."

Vinny unlocks the Audi so that I can retrieve my things, then I wave goodbye and walk to where Lance is waiting at his car.

The air seems to grow thicker the closer I get to him, my steps a little cautious. I wish I had waited and got a taxi home. It would have been a whole lot less awkward.

I've seen pictures of Lance from the last year. Dinners he's attended with the company that I found on the internet and then pictures Charlie, Elliot and Mason have posted on social media. Even photos that he's posted. It's like a smoke screen was pulled up in front of him, though, because the man in the photos isn't the man in front of me now.

"Why are you looking at me like that?"

I frown at his tone as it pulls me from my thoughts. He's not mad. In fact, it barely even passes as a question with the way he mutters it. "Sorry, I… I guess I haven't seen you in a while."

He nods, eyes dropping down the length of me before he meets my eyes again and cocks his head toward the car.

"Come on," he says softly as if he's been waiting forever and a day for me.

I get in and wait for him to round the driver's side, allowing myself a moment to immerse myself in him.

My eyes flutter closed as I inhale.

I've missed that smell. The way it reminds me of long nights and lazy mornings. Being held in his arms and feeling safe. So unafraid.

Lance climbs in and closes the door, taking a second to adjust himself in his seat. His almost black, dark-grey suit is fitted to perfection. He's so insanely man, it wrecks me.

Makes me a little bit stupid in the head, even.

"Where's your car?" he asks.

Of course that's what he wants to know. I side-eye him, rearranging my mum's diary on my lap. "On the bridge at Durford."

I feel his frown, his focus solely on me.

I meet his stare. "I forgot to put fuel in it," I say sheepishly.

His face seems to falter, a slight tic in his cheek. "You're terrible, you know that?"

I smile and twist my head, hiding it as I look out of the window. If he isn't going to give me his fully, then I'm not going to give him mine either.

He pulls out onto the road, his body relaxing in the seat as we join the traffic. It's busy on the streets, the roads gearing up for rush hour.

I speak before I can think much about it, hoping to cut the tension that's coiled tightly between us. "I think putting fuel in my car is my least favourite thing to do on earth. I'll do anything to avoid the task."

"You don't have to explain yourself to me, Scarlet."

I roll my lips and look at him, wishing he'd say my name again. It's been too long.

"Charlie said you started at the hospital. You're back at university full time."

I blow out a long breath, going with the conversation, no matter how awkward it feels. "I did. I knew it was time, and it's honestly been amazing. I love it there."

He gives me a half smile. It's small, but it's there… as if he still cares.

"I know I'm going to have a hard time stopping when it comes to you… I keep asking myself why I'd want to stop at all."

"I don't want you to stop… don't stop."

"And if I fall in love with you?"

"Then make sure you take me with you."

"You never called me back that night, Lance," I say without thought.

He must catch something in my tone because his head twists, his relaxed form growing tense.

He looks utterly exhausted, with dark circles heavy under his once-intense green eyes. I wonder what stole the light from them and pray it wasn't me.

I carry on, knowing I need to get it off my chest regardless of whether he wants to hear it. "I felt like it was all my fault. You were there for me when my dad died, and I told you I didn't want you. I pushed you away. I felt like it was my own fault when you were done with me after Bora Bora, but the things you said to me last summer—"

"You didn't do anything wrong," he cuts in, shaking his head. "I should've spoken to you after… after everything that happened. I should never have just ignored you."

I frown. "Why did you?"

He blows out a harsh breath. "I had some things… with my sisters and your brother's business." He pauses as if he doesn't want to tell me any more than that. "It messed with me for a bit." He stares through his windscreen, frowning, and I can feel him fighting with himself to not look at me. Something tells me whatever kept him from me is still keeping him from me now. "I'm sorry, Scarlet. You deserved so much fucking more than that."

A lump forms in my throat, unexpected and not welcome. I've rarely cried since my dad died. But sitting here and listening, feeling every word out of his mouth—that he means them, it hurts. "We're good at this, you know." I blink rapidly to rid the emotion gathering in my eyes. "Going a whole-ass year without seeing one another." I smile, trying my hardest to lighten the mood, but now all I can think about is the first time he danced with me at the Hamilton Gala. "You seem to pop back up every single time."

He huffs a laugh, pulling forward when the light switches to green. I wonder if he's thinking about that night too. Or any of the ones that followed. "Were you hoping to get rid of me for good this time?"

"No… but I wasn't prepared to see you today."

He finally looks at me, his green eyes homing in on me. "Me neither." He tips his chin at my lap before clearing his throat and forcing his stare back to the road. "What's that?"

I raise my brows and dig my fingers into the hard edges of the diary. "It's my mother's diaries. Her original ones."

He does a double take at them. "I thought they were ruined?"

"They were. Dad kept them, and I found them after he… I found new entries, ones she wrote for me and Mase over the years. They've been incredible to read."

"Shit. That's amazing, Scar."

"Yeah," I say absentmindedly, my eyes not leaving him. I decide to give him a little more, if not just to hear the light in his voice again. I'm pretty sure it could see me all the way home. "I started writing in them. I write to her."

"What do you write?"

"Everything. Anything I do. Feelings. Fears. My good and bad days—mostly after a shift at the hospital. I tell her everything."

All the things I used to tell you.

I wonder how many of those nights he remembers. The hours we spent in the meadow, the lake, and in my bed. How much does he really remember of it? Because I can't seem to forget.

"I miss all of those things, you know." His voice echoes into my thoughts like soft thunder in the distance, setting my heart racing when he adds, "*Everything.*"

I still in the seat, barely managing a swallow as his hand grips the steering wheel painfully tight. "I—uh—"

"You don't have to say anything." I go to open my mouth, but he carries on. "I wouldn't let it mean anything, no matter how much I want it to."

I frown at him, not understanding why he'd say that.

He gently shakes his head, clenching his jaw. "Please. Don't say anything, Scarlet," he mutters, sounding pained.

I sit in silence for the remainder of the drive home, not daring to even look at the man by my side. He's a solid wall. Nothing like I remember.

When we pull up to Lowerwick, I don't wait for him to open my door, getting it myself. I meet him at the bottom of the steps, looking up at him.

And it's the tortured look on his face that tells me to invite him in. Extend the olive branch. "You're welcome to come inside."

Say yes.

Please say yes.

Come inside.

Don't leave me here alone.

He shakes his head no, pushing his hands deep into his pockets.

My throat burns, and I advert my eyes to his chest. "Thank you… for driving me home." Saving myself the pain of looking at him for another second, I take the steps to the front door and slip inside, kicking off my shoes and heading straight for the kitchen.

I need to make dinner and then study before my lecture on Monday.

My hands shake as I reach into the fridge and take out the fresh tomatoes. I carry them to the kitchen counter and grab a knife, staring down at them.

"I'm sorry, Scarlet. You deserved so much fucking more than that."

My eyes mist.

"I miss all of those things, you know. Everything."

"Bastard," I mutter, chopping into the tomato.

Lance

I'm a fucking asshole.

I sit in my car, staring at the iron gates that lead to her mum's garden, knowing I've just hurt her. Hating that I even have the ability to do so.

She's supposed to hate me.

It would be easy that way. Not that it would stop me from wanting her, or needing that smile, or the way she sparks me to life simply with a look.

I push open my car door and take the steps two at a time, gently easing open the front door and stepping into the house.

I can hear her chopping something in the kitchen, and follow it, coming to a stop when I see her with her back to me at the kitchen island. Her arm works fast as she slices the veg on the wooden block.

She pauses momentarily when she senses my presence, the knife slapping the wood as it comes to a stop.

I step up behind her, but she continues again as if telling me she won't make a move to acknowledge me.

I guess I deserve that.

My body brushes hers, and I frown at the feeling. Steadfast, I reach around and run my hand over hers, covering the knife.

She eventually lets me take it from her, dropping it onto the chopping board. My other hand lifts to move her hair from her shoulder, brushing it away.

She sucks in a sharp breath as my lips meet her neck.

I take it as a green light to move a little closer, slipping my arm around her waist.

My body ripples at her back, at the feel of her, the sweet scent of her perfume. I drag my lips over her skin, nuzzling the side of her face as my eyes drift closed.

There are no words.

And it's not enough.

She's the only thing that makes me feel anything anymore.

"Don't think I'm not proud of you," I whisper, trailing my nose up the length of her throat. "Because I am… I'm so fucking proud of you, Scarlet."

She whimpers, and I screw my face up as pain slashes my chest.

I turn her, wrapping my arms around her neck, pulling her into me.

Eventually she hugs me, her hands running up my back and holding me just as tight.

"Lance?" she whispers, her voice wary.

I keep her in my arms, breathing her in. I didn't realise how badly I needed her.

This.

I forgot the sheer fucking magnitude of this woman's soul. The way it bleeds into me without question and makes me feel alive.

Reluctantly, I inch back, holding her face in my hands. I smooth away her hair to look at her, a rueful smile teasing my mouth before I lose it again. She stares up at me, brown eyes big and wide.

She looks as lost as I feel.

I drop my lips to her forehead, lingering them there for a beat, not ready to let her go. "You are life, personified."

Scarlet stands with her arms bereft as I pull away from her, turning and walking out of the door.

Scarlet

Mum,

I lied before. I did fall in love with him.

And I think he needs me.

I'm not done saving myself yet, but I really think he needs me.

Soon,

Scarlet.

THIRTY

Lance

"It's my birthday, Lowell. Of course you're fucking coming." Elliot falls heavy onto Mason's office sofa, his hands running over the front of his suit.

"You think it's a good idea both me and—"

"Nina being there." I smile on the inside as Elliot tuts. He's on one today. "I heard the same shit from her. You're fully grown adults—regardless of the size of your dick. We're going out. All of us."

Mason rolls his eyes, looking back at his screen.

"I'll be there, Montgomery," Charlie reassures him.

"Thank you, Charles… Sullivan?" he asks me.

"Wouldn't miss it." I sigh, agreeing, despite the fact I can think of a million reasons not to go.

Elliot pops his brows at Mason, waiting.

"I'm happy for you, mate. You've got Mr Fucking Smiley"—he points at me—"and the guy who can't have sex unless he pays for it."

"Fuck," I mutter, chuckling under my breath.

Mason's mouth curls up in a grin, his eyes falling to Charlie, who's shaking his head with a smirk on his face.

"On a serious note, it's good to see you here, Sullivan. You've been a miserable prick for weeks," he tells me, nodding his head.

"Yeah, whatever. Asshole."

Turning up seemed like the least I could do, all things considered. I paid the last of what my sister stole from Mason's company back last week, and I'm pretty sure it's the only reason I can stand here now and look at him in the eye.

"Come to mine before. We can toast to another year of fuckery," Elliot tells us.

"What about the girls?" Charlie asks.

I wonder if Scarlet will join them, but I don't ask the question out loud.

I've not seen her in weeks.

The day after I gave her a lift home and held her in her kitchen, she sent lunch to my office. I don't know how she knew that I hadn't eaten. I should have texted her or something. Gone out to the estate and begged her on my knees to let me worship the ground she walks on. But I didn't. I knew I needed to fix the things I broke first. Pay back the money my sister stole.

And then yesterday, she had twenty-four red roses delivered to my office.

Soon. She'd written on the card. Soon.

Elliot shakes his head. "The girls are getting ready with Luce—she has that date before."

"Montgomery will be rabid by the time she shows up,"

Mason taunts. "Watch him pretend to be interested in anyone but her for the night."

A smile curls my lips as I come back to the now.

"I'm sorry," Elliot retorts, "but have you forgotten that the mother of your firstborn son wants you fucking dead?"

Mason chuckles. "Bit dramatic, mate."

"Fuck you," Elliot mutters, the nerve well and truly struck.

"I'll be there." Mason stands, walking around the sofa and ruffling up Elliot's hair. "Of course, I'll fucking be there. Is my sister coming?"

"She is," Charlie tells him.

"Even better. It'll be good to get the gang back together."

Maybe. Fucking maybe.

One thing is for sure. There's only so long I can ignore Scarlet Lowell.

Scarlet

Nina, Megan and I clamber into the back of the Audi together, Lucy having already been picked up by her date. It's Elliot's birthday, and we're all out to celebrate. The first time in over a year that we've all been together in one room. I know that Nina's been freaking out over that fact all week.

I'm pretty sure the vodka she consumed before we left the apartment is helping with the nerves now, though.

"Cockblock the shit out of me tonight, girls. You see me beelining for him, and you slap me. Hard across the face. Okay?"

I laugh as Megan salutes her friend. "We've got your back."

"Thank you."

"We can just dance," I suggest, adjusting my strapless black midi dress. "My brother won't bother you on the dance floor."

"He likely won't bother with me at all. It's me that's the problem." She sighs, catching Vinny's stare in the rearview mirror. He's grown close to Nina this past year. It's obvious he's always had a soft spot for his boss's ex-girlfriend, but since she had Ellis, they've levelled up. I sometimes wonder whose side Vinny would take if he had to pick. "He looks at me, and it's like a siren goes off in my brain that I have to follow."

Nina still loves Mason. I'm not sure she's admitted it to herself yet, but to everyone else, the people who love her, it's obvious.

"He's like a penguin," Megan says, refilling Nina's glass despite the car making it difficult. The drink sloshes over the sides.

"Who is?" Nina frowns.

Megan smiles up at her. "Mase." She throws her head back a couple of times and lets out a bizarre squawk. Then says, "Nina." She hunches back over and pretends to waddle on the spot, mimicking them both.

We laugh together. Even Vinny.

"Not tonight. Tonight, I'm going to turn around and run the other way."

"Remember when we first met Elliot and Charlie, and Joey was pestering you constantly for a date?"

"God, yes. Poor Joey," Nina cringes.

"Well, that's what we need. We need you locked up tight like you were for him."

"I can do that."

Megan cringes.

"What?" Nina frowns, sipping her drink.

"Thinking about it, Joey's a terrible example… I mean, you've still got him lingering around."

"He's my friend," Nina defends.

"Who definitely wants you."

Megan isn't wrong. Joey seems to spend a lot of time with Nina on the days she doesn't have Ellis. She does spend a lot of time with us girls, but when we're working, she doesn't have anyone else. I kind of hoped they'd see less of each other now that Nina's working again. It definitely rubs Mason up the wrong way that Joey gets to spend so much time with her.

Not that he'd admit to that.

"Are we really doing this now?" Nina sags in the seat.

"No, we are not." Megan nods, grasping her friend's hand. Apology enough.

I smile at my two friends and raise my glass. "To us, girls. And Luce. And breaking stupid penguins' hearts."

"We'll never have a normal toast, will we?" Nina chuckles.

I clink my glass with theirs and lean into them when Nina's arm wraps around my shoulders. "I hope not."

I can pretend I haven't thought about Lance and him being here tonight, but that would be a big fat lie. I've thought about it plenty. I'm thinking about it right now—as the music pelts me beat after beat, carrying me with purpose into the club.

Envy sets my shoulders square as I follow the girls, knowing Nina's handling the prospect of this night better than I am. I concentrate on their weaving silhouettes instead of the knot in my stomach. I haven't had as much to drink as Nina, the idea of drowning my nerves in alcohol not appealing to me like it might usually. I want to be sound of mind when I see him. Or as sound of mind as I can be when in the presence of the man.

"There they are." Megan points.

The knot grows tighter, and I watch as Nina stumbles. Megan slides a hand around her waist, pulling her close. "Vodka's working." She gives me a knowing grin and walks with Nina to the table.

I follow behind, happily letting them go on ahead. It gives me time to gauge the rest of the group.

To gauge Lance.

I've not seen or heard from him since the encounter in my kitchen weeks ago when he held me as if it was all he needed. As if it was something he'd needed more than air. A hug.

He told me he'd disappeared on me because of his sisters and work—a shoddy excuse. But one that I don't doubt after seeing him. His eyes looked so heavy that day in my kitchen. Tired and void of their usual intensity. He looked a little broken, and when he hugged me, I couldn't help but want to put him back together.

I only feel stupid for it now.

I swallow and step out of the shadows of the people around me once Nina's done saying hello. Lance is the first to greet her, and then he moves to Megan, kissing her cheek… and then he turns to me.

I force a smile, big and bright. Nervous as shit. "Hey."

He smiles back. "Scarlet."

A shiver snakes down my spine as he rasps my name. My eyes rake him. Even in the crowd, his presence has the ability to disarm me. To make that knot in my stomach snap into a million butterflies.

He leans in to kiss my cheek, and I close my eyes briefly as I melt into his hold. I place a gentle hand on his shoulder to keep myself upright, my fingers flexing into the rigid muscle beneath his black shirt. It's the same story. Me and him, a year later, dancing around one another as if we're mere strangers.

Imagine the shock our friends—Mase—would have if they knew the truth.

I step back and turn to greet Elliot, needing to pull away before questions are asked.

Because what would be the answers?

"Why do I feel like it's been a million years?" I hold on to Elliot tight, welcoming his warm embrace as he spins me around.

"You could come and see me, you know," I tell him, chuckling as he sets me down.

"You're a doctor now. You don't have time for me." He smirks at me, giving me a wink.

"Not a doctor." I shake my head. "And happy birthday."

"Thanks, Scar."

He moves to let Charlie hug me. The familiar face smiles and he pulls me into his chest, his lips settling on the crown of my head. "Not a doctor," he whispers. "But you will be."

I smile. "Hello, Charles."

"You okay?"

Pulling back, I look up at him and nod.

He acknowledges it with a small nod of his own. "Good."

The woman Charlie Aldridge falls in love with will be the luckiest woman in the world. I'm not sure I've ever met a man like him. The way he can be so gentle and kind, terrifyingly smart to the point he gives off that lethal calm he wears like sin. Beautiful. Because he simply is. No matter how much I see him like a big brother, I can still appreciate how insanely gorgeous he is. He's checked on me week after week. Texts I've missed—forgotten after shifts or classes… or those days I forget I even have a phone and don't charge it. He still sends the texts, usually waiting a couple of days before he makes the trip out to the estate. I love the man, scars and all.

"Scarlet." I turn at the sound of my brother's voice, and his lips graze my cheek a second later. I love him, too. So much. But I can already feel his energy shifting. I know it's because of Nina. That even being in the same room as her makes him something else entirely. It's not necessarily a bad thing, but for the likes of his friends and me… we don't get a look in when Nina's in the room.

"Hey, big brother," I tell him, easing out of the embrace.

He clears his throat, standing off to the side and waiting for Nina to be done greeting Elliot so that he can.

I watch him, the way his hands run through his hair, his jaw tight.

Nina turns to him, a small smile pulling at her lips.

I frown. *Should I slap her?*

I look across at Megan, and she shakes her head, a smile stretching her face as if she knew where my mind had gone.

"Hey, Mase."

I wait for my brother to move, but he takes his sweet-ass time, just staring at the poor girl as if he's stuck somewhere between awe and stupid. Slowly, he leans in, dragging his lips up to her ear. We all turn away in unison as he starts to whisper in her ear.

Someone's getting slapped tonight.

"I need a drink." Nina turns toward us, clearly ruffled. "Ell, what do you want to drink?"

She walks off to the bar, not even waiting to get Elliot's order.

She's panicking, but before Megan or I can follow, Mason is hot on her heels.

"Do we?" I ask Megan.

"He beelined for her so…."

"Don't get involved, girls," Elliot tells us. "Not worth it."

Charlie sits back in the wingback chair, his eyes already slightly glazed. "He's right. It's Elliot's birthday. Enjoy your night. Let them do the thing they do."

Megan and I look at one another, our uncertainty mirrored.

"Let's give them five minutes. See if they can manage a conversation."

Megan nods, agreeing as she takes my arm and pulls me down onto the sofa.

"You ladies are late," Elliot complains, but my attention shamelessly gravitates to Lance, who's already looking at me.

His eyes blaze across my skin like a lost ember starved in

the firelight, desperately searching for a place to settle on me.

The green in his eyes seems to only grow brighter the further they travel. Until they lock with my own.

I tilt my head, wondering how he can be so blatant in front of our friends. In front of me when just weeks ago he was—

"I miss all of those things, you know… Everything."

I'd sent flowers to his office this week and heard nothing back. Not that I expected anything… but I wanted something. A call… or maybe a message telling me what giant idiots we both were last year and that he still wants me.

God, I'm pathetic.

"How are you, Lance?" I snap, instantly wondering what depths of my audacity I've pulled it from.

His head tilts, gauging my changed mood. "I'm good."

"Just good?"

"Miserable. He's been miserable." Elliot chuckles, knocking back the last of his whiskey.

"Still?" I question.

I feel Megan blanch at my side. Maybe my questions are coming off a little left field, considering Lance and I rarely have anything to say to one another.

"I said I'm good," he reaffirms, his eyes pinching into thin slits as he watches me.

And it's only now that I allow myself to fully see him, with no distractions like when I walked in here. Too afraid to give him a second glance in case I saw it—felt it. That pull, like a rope bound between us. The same pull I had in the elevator that first day. At the gala. On the lake. In my bedroom. The list… it's endless.

And there's no way he doesn't feel it, too.

His eyes will always give him away.

Only it's not just that feeling consuming me now. No, I feel a little pissed off. Because not only did the man make me feel a pull stronger than anything I've ever experienced, but he cut the rope I'd been clinging to so fast I fell hard on my ass.

"Girls, can we dance?" Nina pulls my attention away from him, her stare wide and telling as she looks at us across the table.

"We're dancing." I stand with Megan and walk with the two girls toward the dance floor.

My brother whisked Nina away from the dance floor over an hour ago. Megan and I didn't have the heart to stop them, deciding we'll deal with the wrath of Nina tomorrow. The two of us are climbing down from the platform we're dancing on, sweaty and in desperate need of a drink, when Lance approaches us. He reaches out and hands Megan a glass first and then me.

"I need to pee," Megan tells me, handing me the full drink as she slips away. "Thank you, Lance."

He shakes his head after her, then twists back to me.

"Thanks," I tell him, sipping the vodka and cranberry mixer.

He just watches me as if he can't take his eyes off me. "You're welcome."

I don't drop his stare, holding it. I sent the motherfucker flowers; he can make the first move.

I didn't plan on drinking much tonight, but when we

arrived and I saw Lance, felt the bitterness growing in my gut, I decided letting loose was exactly what I needed.

"You're mad at me."

I'm mad at both of us. "No… I'm disappointed."

He lifts a hand to his chest as if I've shot him. And the bastard smiles. "Scar—"

"You think it's funny?" I accuse, but I crave it. That old easiness between us that he promises with a curl of his lip. "It's not."

"I know it's not." He looks down at me, getting serious despite the spark in his eyes. "But I can't go back and change the asshole things I do. Can I?"

My eyes narrow on him. "You're in a mood."

"It's not a bad one," he defends.

"I know…" Shit. "I like it." It reminds me of the Lance I had last summer. The one I… "Are you drunk?"

He smiles, stepping closer as someone passes my back. He crowds me, placing a hand on my waist. Everything shifts. Just like that. "Maybe a little."

I'd give anything to know what he's thinking.

"Not enough to make bad decisions," he adds.

"What kind of bad decisions?"

He looks down his nose at me, wetting his bottom lip after a beat and making me think he won't answer. "Not kissing you."

I huff out a nervous laugh and step out of his reach. "You think I'd let you kiss me?"

"*Scarlet.*"

"Don't do that," I warn, but it's a playful chide.

He holds his hands up, childlike and so unlike Lance. "What?"

God, I've missed this man so damn much. "The way you say my name. You know."

"I didn't say your name like anything."

"Narcissist," I accuse, finally letting out a laugh. "I'm adding it to the list."

He grins, taking a step into me again. Doesn't even look around us as he lifts his hand and fingers a loose strand of my hair. "Mine." The word echoes back and forth between our pounding chests. "Aren't you, Scarlet?" His head dips and my skin ignites as his breath tickles the shell of my ear, lips a gentle caress. "Every time I look at you, I feel it. That primal need to claim you. To say what we both already know. It's fucking killing me. And, sunshine, I am sorry. For disappointing you." He eases back, and I swallow thickly. *Mine*. "I'll add it to the list."

I stand in shock as he steps away, walking backward into the crowd of people.

What the actual fuck just happened?

What happened to me being in control?

To being mad?

I lost it within a second.

One touch.

"Mine."

My heart won't stop, the beating jarring. I tuck the strand of hair he touched behind my ear, looking around me.

And then I smile.

THIRTY-ONE

Scarlet

Lucy turned up whilst Megan and I were dancing, the actual reason Mason came to pull Nina from the dance floor. He was worried after Lucy arrived and seemed upset.

The fact she showed up so early into the night after her date makes me wonder what might've happened.

"I need to go home." My head drops heavily on Charlie's shoulder.

"No, Scar, don't leave yet!" Megan whines, placing the tray of shots down on the table.

We failed terribly as friends tonight.

Mason seemed to haul Nina out of here when no one was looking. The only person who could've seen was Lucy, and she was apparently too busy with Elliot.

All four of them have left already, leaving Charlie, Megan, Lance and me.

"I'm ruined. I need sleep." I smile as I look up at Megan. "Let me leave."

"Fine!"

"I'll share a taxi, Scarlet. Are you going back to the estate?" Lance asks.

I nod, not daring to attempt words. My eyes are locked on him.

He drags his attention away to Charlie. "Aldridge, you coming?"

"I think I'm with Megan on this one. I'm not entirely done for the night."

"Yes, Charles!" Megan grins.

He gives her a look. "You can't come where I'm going. Sorry, Megs."

Megan loses her excitement, her shoulders dropping. "Why not? You know I'm down for anything."

Lance and Charlie seem to share a look, and then Lance smirks. "It's members only," Charlie explains.

"Last I checked"—we all turn to Lance—"you could take a guest a month with you to the Nightingale."

Charlie rolls his lips, and I know I should dig him out of the hole Lance has shoved him into.

"Come on, Megs. Come home with me!"

"Fine." She hands out the shots, and we knock them back. "I need to get my jacket."

"I'll give Vin a ring," Lance says, walking toward the exit of the club.

I stare after him, wondering if he'll come back to mine. I want him to. I shouldn't, but I do.

"Something caught your eye, Miss Lowell?"

I look down at Charlie, giving him the evil eye. "Shut it, Aldridge."

He grins, nodding as he laughs. "He's a different man tonight, you know."

My heart seems to wake with his words. He is? "So." I shrug.

"So," he drawls out. "What did you say to him?"

I shake my head. "I didn't say anything."

He watches me, analysing me like he would one of his clients. "Nothing?"

"Nothing much. I ran into him a few weeks ago at the Montwell. He gave me a lift home."

He seems to do the math in his head. "Well, that makes a lot of sense."

"What does?"

"Vin's busy. Will be an hour." I blush as Lance appears at my side as if I've been caught doing something I shouldn't be.

"I'll just get a taxi back," I tell him.

His eyes settle on me. Unsure but desperate. As if he wants to say something but won't.

"I'm going to regret this," Charlie mutters with a sigh, turning away from us. He stands and buttons his jacket.

As Megan reaches the table, Charlie throws out his hand to her. "Let's go."

Her eyes widen. "I'm coming with?"

"I have rules."

She beams at him, sliding her hand into his. "So do I."

"Bloody hell." Charlie lets out a long breath, but I can see the slight smile pulling at the corners of his mouth.

They pass us to leave, Megan throwing her free arm around my neck to hug me goodbye. "You okay with Lance? I know he's an oddball and barely interacts with us."

I hide my smile and nod. "I'm good, Megs."

Charlie mutters something to Lance, and then they're gone. Lance and I left alone in the club.

"What did he say to you?" I eventually ask.

"That I owe him one."

I bite my lip and twist my head to look up at him.

I've never known Charlie to be so candid in front of me, especially not in front of the girls. He's a private person, and for good reason. It would've taken a lot for him to invite Megan with him tonight, and it makes my heart happy to think he trusts her—and me, enough to do it so blatantly.

"When was the last time you checked the Nightingale's policies, Mr Sullivan?"

His cheek tics, and then he drags his teeth over his bottom lip. "Too fucking long ago."

I smile. "Are we waiting on Vin?"

"No. Will you come to mine?"

"I'd prefer you didn't ask me."

"Why?"

"Because I should say no."

"Why?"

Because you're an asshole.

He smiles.

I shake my head, knowing I'm an idiot for it, knowing I'm going to go home with him. I'm pretty sure neither of us could stop this, even if we wanted to.

"You're coming home with me tonight," he tells me, voice as smooth as silk.

I say nothing.

Lance

I wake before Scarlet. My eyes are glued to her as I lie in the quiet of my home, painfully taking her in.

It's been too long since I've had her this close. Too long since I've heard her laugh and felt her hands on my body—roaming my skin. We didn't have sex last night. I wouldn't let myself have that part of her.

But we kissed. Kissed so damn much my lips are in tatters. We lay together for hours while she told me about her job, the estate, and her mum. I only listened, committing it all to memory.

And now, lying here next to her in the cold light of day, I only feel hate. Hate for myself. For allowing her to want me. Allowing her to wrap around me like only she knows how, smothering the bad parts I never want her to find.

She does it every time.

Over and over, no matter how long it's been.

No matter what I've done.

Last night proved how weak I am. How easily I can forget what I did to Nina and Mason and act out of pure selfish need. She was mad at me, and I couldn't stand it. Wouldn't let it be.

"You're awake, but I don't smell coffee." She peeps open one eye, chasing away my thoughts. "What gives, Sullivan?"

"You sleep like the dead."

She smiles into the pillow, not bothering to move her body as her arm slips from the sheets. The back of her hand brushes tenderly down my chest. "Good morning," she whispers.

I can't help myself. I lean in and dust my lips over hers. "Good morning, Scarlet."

She rolls her lips as I settle back on the pillow as if it'll savour the touch. I lightly catch hold of her hand on my chest, savouring her.

The silence settles around us, comfortable yet loud. And I know she's thinking about last night. The way we were. The way she kissed me as if nothing had happened. As if time hadn't passed and we hadn't been through all we had.

"I'm sorry," I tell her, the elevator whirling as we're carried to my floor.

I can't stop kissing her.

Touching her.

Holding her.

"I'm so so sorry, Scar."

Her hands are in my hair, on my neck, her legs slung tightly around my hips as she clings to me. Desperate. And I'm desperate for her. Needing her to keep chasing away the feelings I don't want to feel. The feelings I haven't felt since she arrived at the club tonight. The feelings that will fight to drown me the moment she's gone.

"Stop apologising." She pulls back an inch to look at me, her eyes searching my face. "Forget about what we've done. I don't care about any of it tonight. I just want you, Lance."

My jaw locks, and I reach up, sliding a hand into her hair. I should stop. Wanting her this much is dangerous. "I don't think I can do this again if I don't get to keep you at the end of it. I can't walk away from you again."

Her smile drops, recognition of the stripped words tumbling from my mouth.

"You have me, Lance," she whispers the promise. "You always have me."

Panic. I feel it like a weight within me, ready to pull me all the way down. "No matter what?" I ask, closing my eyes as I say it. Because I can't take those words back, and it makes me a complete fucking bastard to ask it of her.

Her hand slides up my neck, forcing my head down to hers. She frowns back at me, sobering completely. My body grows rigid as I wait for the next words out of her mouth.

"Yes." She swallows, cheeks reddening. "There's not been a day, not one, that I've not thought about you. That I've not come home and broke a little inside because you're not there to listen. To hold me." Her eyes shine, her words getting tighter. "I missed you, Lance. I missed you so much." She drops her forehead to mine, nodding. "No matter what."

I shudder, pulling her impossibly closer to me as I wrap my arms around her.

"What happened to you, Lance?"

I don't look at her.

I can't bear to look at her.

Everything's righting itself. Yet I'm torn between seeing Mason and Nina work their way home. Together. And the void of time that they lost apart.

At my hands.

No matter what my sister and Ben did, I was the one who did *this*. It was on me that night, and it's still on me now.

To tell the truth and lose everything.

The people I call family.

All over again.

"I fell in love with you." My head drops to the pillow, my frown deep as I inhale her. All that she is. "I'm so fucking sorry for that."

Scarlet

Mum,

It's been weeks since I last wrote, and I guess it's because I needed some time to gather my thoughts. They've been as scattered as ever. Kicked up and tossed around like the fallen leaves in the meadow.

I'm currently on my lunch break, but it's four o'clock in the afternoon, and I'm long past hungry. I have something to tell you anyway... the reason for my wayward thoughts.

Lance told me he loved me.

It was weeks ago now, and although I wish I had a story to tell you of what happened next, one like yours, I don't. We've seen each other once since. It was in passing, and there were no stolen kisses, barely even a glance with Mason there.

He'd been the man I remembered at Elliot's birthday. The pain still lurked there, but everything about him was the Lance I knew. The Lance I told you I loved. And then we went back to his, and he said all the right things, apologised over and over, and wouldn't touch me because we'd been drinking.

He told me he loved me the next morning and then apologised for that too, like his love was a bad thing.

If ever there was any doubt that men are complex creatures, let Lance Sullivan be written into the history books. The man puts me in a spin.

I'll see him again soon. He's coming to the estate with the guys to help finalise plans for the memorial ball. I'm excited. Excited to have something outside of the hospital and something that will honour you and Dad. The girls have been helping me. Nina's been a godsend when I've needed her.

We've not told Mason about the ball. Nina's still waiting to tell him, and she's desperate to get it over with. I really don't want him to be asked yet. One: I don't think he'll even show up. And two, I don't want to give him the chance to disappoint me. Better to leave it to the week of. Blindside him and hope for the best.

I wish you were here. Or were able to tell me what to do. I know you'd make the ball perfect.

I miss Dad. He always knew what to say to make everything make sense.

Soon,

Scarlet.

Lance

It takes me all day to get my shit together and make my way

up to the seventy-ninth floor of the Montwell. The majority of staff have already left for the day, but I know that Mason will still be here, cooped up in his office to avoid going home to the silence. He only started working late after Nina left him last year, and unless he has Ellis for the night or over the weekend, he'll spend as little time in his home as possible.

It only adds to the bullshit ache in my chest.

I probably don't deserve to feel it. Not when I caused everyone else something so much worse.

Guilt drives me, and I lift my hand and knock before stepping into Mason's office.

He has his head down when I enter, his hands raking through his hair as he clings to the roots. "What is it, Sullivan?" he questions, a sigh leaving him.

"I need to talk to you…." I take an unsteady breath in. "It's about Jasmine… and that night."

"Not now."

"Mase—"

He lifts his head, ready to cut me off. I frown when I see his face, the red-rimmed eyes that stare back at me. His nostrils flare as he takes me in. "You look like shit."

I slant my head, shrugging. "You don't look so great yourself."

He sniggers and sits back in his chair, staring up at the ceiling.

I likely do look like shit. I've not slept in days—weeks, even. Not with knowing what my sister did. What I did. And after spending the night of Elliot's birthday with Scarlet, hearing her tell me about her year, her mum, her healing—I knew, even as I selfishly pulled her closer, I knew I couldn't do it to her.

The truth would come out eventually. Because the truth *always* comes out.

I walk to the small bar and pour two glasses of whiskey, placing one on the desk in front of Mase. "Wanna talk about it?" I ask, wondering what might've caused the raw emotion still lingering in his eyes.

He rights himself in the leather seat, shaking his head as he stares at the tumbler I just placed down.

I should tell him now. Get it over and done with.

My hand shakes as I lift the crystal to my mouth and take a sip. If Mason notices, he doesn't say.

"My sister—my fucking baby sister, Lance." I feel the blood drain from my face, my entire body stiffening. Does he know? How could he? Unless she told him… "She called me weeks ago. Told me my dad's headstone was ready to be placed, that the ground was settled enough. You know what I did?"

I shake my head, swallowing the dryness in my throat as my body relaxes.

"Nothing." His eyes glimmer and I see it, the pain, the guilt, the ache. "I did nothing." He stares across his office toward the floor-to-ceiling windows. I sit wide-eyed, staring at him. One of my best friends. My family. "How did we end up here? I mean, I know life throws curveballs, but *fuck*."

I take another sip and then clear my throat. "You're not a bad person, Mason."

"Maybe," he retorts, bringing his attention back to me. "But I'm not a good one either." He shakes his head. "The things I put Nina through since meeting her. And the brother I've never been to Scar. Or the son I stopped being long before Dad—" He controls his emotions with a heavy exhale. "The damage isn't something I can ever change. It's forever."

"We all make mistakes," I tell him. "Nina's coming back to you. You guys will figure this out… and Scarlet loves you." I swallow hard, forcing down the lump forming. "Your sister loves you, Mase."

He sniggers and I fight the urge to reach over the desk and shake him.

"She does," I snap.

"I know." He frowns at me, finally taking a sip of his drink. "I think it's what pisses me off the most." His eyes move over the papers on his desk. "I can't help but sit here now and think back on all the things I should have done differently, what I should have been for you all."

I flinch, rebuking, "You owe *me* nothing."

"No? You didn't stand with me through the shit with Cara? Cover my ass when Marcus was killed? I dragged you, Elliot, and Charlie through all of my mess. All of it." He peers down at the golden liquid in his glass. "You're a solid friend, Sullivan."

"No, I'm not," I grit out.

Not even close.

Mason knocks back the rest of the whiskey and places his tumbler down before picking up the thick piece of paper on his desk, scanning it. "I guess sometimes the guilt gets too much, and it's impossible to let go of."

"That's because we're not supposed to let it go." I pull back, desperately searching her face. "We learn to accept that people make shitty decisions, Lance, and that they're not ours."

"What if it's not something you can just accept and drop? What if it's family?"

She shifts her attention to the other side of the dance floor toward her brother. "Then we carry as much as our hands can hold. And we don't feel guilty about anything that spills over."

God, she's so fucking beyond me.

"What is that?" I finally ask, lifting my chin at the paper in Mason's hands.

He stares at it, the pain in his eyes making my heart beat a little faster. "The deed to the house," he says softly. "It's hers now."

Rage boils inside of me, and I barely contain it, my teeth cracking as my jaw locks into place. He's not going home. He's never going back there. She'll be alone, and Mason knows it.

And it kills me inside.

"I want to be better. I know I have to be." He drops the deed and looks down at where I sit on the other side of his desk. "For Scar, Nina, Ellis—everyone. But I can't do it all. Not all at once, at least."

He's trying. I can see he is. I *know* he is. But it doesn't make it any easier to let go of the fact his actions, signing over the deed, will hurt Scarlet. It's Scarlet who will suffer the most. She's the one who ends up alone in all this.

And if I tell Mason the truth, she loses me too.

"You know, your sister once told me that when you're carrying all that you can in your hands, you can't allow yourself to feel guilty about anything that spills over."

His jaw turns to stone. "When did she tell you that?"

I stand, buttoning my jacket. "A long time ago."

I've always known Mason cares, no matter what he's

done. He might've pissed me off at times, might even be pissing me off right now with his actions, but he'd never intentionally hurt Scarlet. He *can't* go home. Not with the memories he's harbouring inside of him.

He's broken, just like the rest of us.

"Is Charlie holding it for you?" I pick up the deed on his desk, clearing it away, so he doesn't have to rip himself to shreds staring at it.

Mason nods in answer.

"I'll take it," I tell him.

"Where are you going?" he asks as I step back, heading for the door, my hands full and spilling in waves at my feet.

A tidal wave of mistakes to wade through.

"I'm going home."

Scarlet

It's late when I roll down the lane at Lowerwick. It's a Saturday night, and I've just worked my last shift of the week and won't return for eight days. I still have assignments that need to be handed in for uni, but I decided to request the week off so that I could handle the preparations for next Saturday. I'm exhausted to the bone. The planning's been a welcomed distraction at times, but the work that's gone into the one night has completely worn me out.

Nina's tried to slow me down. Elliot and Charlie too. But they're busy themselves, and I know that if I don't get the jobs done, it won't happen.

I'm easing closer to the house, my head resting back against the seat, when I spot Lance's black bike parked at the bottom of the steps. I sit forward, my heart kicking up a beat as I near.

I sit and wonder if he's let himself in. I don't lock the house. We never have. The lane's so narrow that there's not many who'd attempted it at the risk of meeting another car, and it's a dead end to anyone who doesn't know what's down here.

But Lance isn't in the house. I realise it as I climb from my car and spot the gate to my mum's garden half-open.

The grass is long and ready to be cut, but I want to wait to make sure it is freshly manicured for the ball.

Lance is standing off to the side of the graves, his head lifting when I enter the garden. He doesn't move, maybe gauging my reaction to him being here, but I don't give it enough thought. I walk to where he's standing and stand shoulder to shoulder with him.

"You had the headstone placed."

"Months ago, now."

I see him nod out of the corner of my eye. "I've not been out here in a long time."

"No," I agree. The last time he was here he saw me plant the trees and then left me the note. "It's quieter without you."

He smiles and pockets his hands. "You sure that's not his fault?" He nods his head toward Dad's grave. "I can't get all the blame."

"Oh, it's definitely his fault, too," I agree, looking at the dark-black granite with my father's name carved into it. "But you were just as… present."

I smile tenderly up at him, remembering.

"Have you eaten, Scar?"

I shake my head. I've been looking forward to climbing into my bed all day. Food wasn't even on the agenda.

"Why don't you go inside and get showered? I'll get us something."

"Us."

"Can I eat with you?"

I blink in surprise. *An olive branch.* "I guess that would be okay." Without another word, I turn and walk toward the house. Not looking behind me once.

But I feel his eyes on me with every step I take.

Lance

The closest takeaway is an Indian restaurant twenty minutes away. I manage the trip in half an hour on the bike, but when I eventually get back to the house, discarding the bag on the kitchen counter, I stand at the entrance of the house and try to listen for a single sound to tell me where Scarlet might be.

I wait for ten minutes, the tapping of my foot under my bouncing knee the only sound in the silence. But that's all I have in me before I give up and take the stairs, looking for her.

I push on her bedroom door and pause. She's curled up asleep at the bottom of her bed, still wearing her work clothes as the shower runs in the bathroom.

My shoulders drop as I let the heaviness leave me.

I came here unable to stop myself. I'd waited weeks, too damn long, while she's been here alone. I haven't slept properly since the night of Elliot's birthday. It was the first time

I'd slept for more than an hour in months. It's like it was a tease. Having her back in my bed.

She's been working and planning for the memorial ball she's hosting here on the estate. Charlie said she's overdoing it, that he's worried she'll crash before she can make it to next Saturday.

And I'm just about done with being *told* how she is.

Constantly wondering if she's looking after herself and coping.

I want to know.

I want to dictate it even.

Not to control her, but to be here.

To help her.

It makes me selfish to want her again. To come back here and buy her dinner. To wake her up and slide back between her sheets. To love her.

But it doesn't feel like a choice.

Not when Mason has no desire to be here.

Maybe Scarlet needs me as much as I need her.

I'm gentle as I lift her, letting my lips meet her forehead as she settles in my hold. Her eyes blink open as I walk us into the bathroom.

"I fell asleep," she moans, her eyes heavy.

"It's fine." I lower her to her feet and push her faded lavender hair off her shoulders. "Let me."

It's not a question but a plea, and she indulges me, nodding. My fingers go to the hem of her tunic, lifting it from over her head. I slide off her trousers. She's wearing a plain black sports bra, and I peel it off, dropping it on top of the rest of the clothes before slipping her legs out of her underwear.

I pull off my jumper and lower my jeans, quickly kicking off my socks.

Her eyes remain heavy, but I don't miss how they rake me. It's not until we're in the shower and I've washed every inch of her that I allow my own eyes to roam her.

She's slimmer than she was. No less beautiful and not unhealthy, but she's lost the fullness she had at her hips, her face even.

Her breasts are still as full and perfect as ever. My hands seem to linger on them as I move the soap suds over her skin —I'm still a man.

Her body has gone lax in my arms, soft moans falling from her lips as I rub over them and then deep into the rest of her tight muscles.

"Sleep or food?" I whisper into her ear, appreciating how good she feels in my arms.

Her neck twists, deliberately bringing her lips to my jaw. "You." It's barely a whisper.

"That wasn't on the menu," I groan.

She links her hands over the top of mine and places them back on her abdomen, moving them up her body. "Don't stop."

"Scar."

"Please." She moans, grinding her ass into my growing cock. I've done all I can to keep it at bay while I wash her, the task near painful. "I've spent too many nights pretending it's you. Even when all I've needed is sleep and food. I've climbed into bed and thought of you. I need *you* now, nothing else."

A sound vibrates from my chest, my cock twitching at those words.

She doesn't stop rolling her hips, and when her legs widens on the shower floor, my cock naturally slides between her legs, grazing her pussy.

"Lance?"

My jaw clenches, hands flattening on the wall above us. It's been too long. "What?"

"You should've kicked my foot out yourself, and you should be inside of me already, telling me how greedy I am when I take every inch I know you'll give me. If you don't want to do this, it's okay. Just leave. But—"

I snigger and drop my head to lie between her shoulder blades. I've woken in cold sweats after dreaming about this woman. Twisted, fucked-up dreams where she finds out everything I am and hates me. Dreams where I fuck her so hard, I wake up in a fucking mess. Dreams where I tell her I love her, and she tells me she loves me back.

I lift her, and she gasps, my cock sliding home the second I have her turned and facing me. Her legs hang over my thighs, fingers entwined with mine above her head as I force her up the wall with a thrust so deep my breath catches.

"Lance," she mutters, barely forming the words.

"Fuck."

My lips dip for hers, taking her mouth in a desperate kiss. Her mouth slants over mine, eventually opening for me. I take her hands into one and lower the other to her ass, hauling her up and sinking deeper.

It's everything. This feeling.

"You… you. Are. Everything."

My tongue strokes through her mouth, across her lips.

She moans.

I don't hold back. I fuck her against the wall harder than

I've ever gone with anyone. Her body jolts with each thrust, legs stiff as her hands come down and her nails rake over my back. And when I feel it building in me, the release I've been so desperately craving, I let her have it. All of it. A guttural sound tears from my throat as I come inside of her.

THIRTY-TWO

Scarlet

The grounds are lit up like something out of a fairy tale. I'm not sure I've ever seen my home look so beautiful, and it's only deep, deep pride that I feel as I stand on the terrace overlooking the front of the house. The marquee is the centrepiece of the view, but the way lanterns spread a soft glow, guiding the pathways to and from the house, my parents' garden, the meadow. The gentle coaxing of the string quartet as it drifts effortlessly around the boundaries. It's truly something special.

I'll never forget this moment.

Seeing this.

People have been arriving for the past half hour, and I should be down there. I should be welcoming them. Thanking them.

I just needed a minute first.

"Scar, you really outdid yourself. It's perfect." Nina

stands at my side, her throat working as she beholds the vision before her.

I swallow the lump in my throat, knowing tonight will be too emotional to fully clear it. "You really think so?"

She tilts her head, smiling in answer.

"I did good, didn't I?" I grin back.

She seems to get lost in the view again, her eyes roaming every detail. I hired a team to help me set everything up, but Nina's been here every day, every spare second, making sure we'd be ready. I've been impossible at times, the pressure and stress of not pulling this night off making me a snappy, moody cow. She didn't let it deter her, though. She still turned up.

And then so did he.

Every night Lance showed up and carried on when I couldn't, crawling into bed and holding me in the early hours.

It's as if he never left.

"Have you heard from Mason?"

My throat seems to tighten further at Nina's question, and I clear it. Nina invited Mason on Wednesday night, and he, to our absolute shock, agreed to come. They seem so close to finding their way back to one another, and I can only wonder, selfishly, that maybe the only reason he'd come tonight is because of Nina, because of what that might mean for them. "No," I tell her, grasping the railing and leaning back, looking up at the clear sky. It rained all week, and at one point, I didn't even think we'd get the marquee up. "Not even a text," I eventually add.

Nina doesn't say anything, and I'm glad she doesn't. We've known each other for well over a year now. She knows

I don't want excuses made for my brother. If he wanted to reach out to me, he would. And if he wants to be here tonight, he will be.

It will not affect my night, regardless.

"There's Mummy." I turn at the sound of Lucy's voice, my face lighting up when I see Ellis in her arms. He's dressed in a black tux, his thick dark hair combed back. He looks absolutely adorable.

He looks exactly like Mason.

"There's a guy downstairs who says he has a fifty-kilo block of cheese."

My face drops.

No, he didn't.

"What?" Nina laughs. "Why so much? The pantry is full of everything we need.

"Oh my god." I rush past them, picking up my gown as I make my way through the bedroom.

I take the staircase as quickly as I can, my dress pulled up around my knees as I round the door to the kitchen.

"You're moping."

"I'm not. I'm fine."

He wraps his arms around me, pulling my back to his front as "Night Changes" starts to play from the speaker. He forces the dishcloth from my hands and spins me. "You are."

I turn in his arms and look up at him, finding a teasing smile on his lips. "I'm sorry I ate the last of your cheese. I'm going to make it up to you, Baby Lowell."

I narrow my gaze on him. "How?"

I bite my lip as it threatens to curl.

Vinny stands with his hands on his hips, baffled by the giant block of raclette sitting on the kitchen island.

Lance

She did so fucking good.

Pride washes over me in waves as I step foot inside the tent. *She'd kill me for calling it that.* I've been here every night. Long after everyone's left and she's barely able to stand on her feet. I've seen her to bed, making sure she's taken care of… and then I've carried on with anything she's not got to that day. It's different this time. More. As if that attentive unknown of getting to know someone is gone, and we've simply fallen back into a history book of our own.

I know how hot to run the bath.

I know that she hates pickles.

Loves cheese.

I know that on Sundays she'll spend an hour, rain or shine, in her mother's garden and that she doesn't want to be bothered.

That she likes lemon in her water but not ice.

Reads vicariously. And it's filth, pure filth.

That she can't stand the covers twisting around her feet at night, but if they expose even a toe, she'll know it.

And I know that she'll walk this floor tonight with a smile, the epitome of understated elegance, and yet somewhere deep in that unbelievably beautiful soul, she'll fracture.

She'll smile, but it won't be as easy as she makes this thing look.

I've seen what this night has done to her. Seen what it's

taken out of her. Seen how the pain blemishes her face at the mere mention of her brother's name.

I kept away from her for too long. It's not selfish to love Scarlet Lowell. Not when she deserves the world to fall at her feet for simply existing.

"Anyone see the girls?" Elliot asks, scanning the room.

We make our way to the bar, waiting, and it's not until a little while later that the girls find us. Nina first, gravitating to Mason's side as she carries Ellis. And then Megan, closely followed by *her*.

My *it girl*.

Her eyes seek me out, nervous despite that smile I knew would be there. Worn with delicate precision.

She's wearing a pale-lavender silk gown, the promise of the body beneath making my mouth water.

"Here she is." I watch as Elliot pulls her under his arm. "The brains and beauty of the family."

"I need a drink." Her eyes scan the room beyond, and then she briefly relaxes. "I feel like if I stop, I'm going to fall asleep at this point."

"Everything is perfect, Scarlet," Charlie admires, earning a broad smile as he leans in to kiss her cheek.

I pick up the drink I ordered and hand it to her. My fingers brush hers, a soft intake of breath whooshing past her lips.

I do nothing to hide my smile and give her an easy wink.

I don't need to tell her how incredible everything is, or that she looks fucking breathtaking—she does—or that my heart is currently going wild beneath my tux. She knows. Knows exactly what she does to me. And if she somehow doesn't, I'll spend the rest of my life making sure it's written in the fucking stars.

She turns to Mason, and I pick up my drink, allowing them the privacy of the intimate moment.

This ball matters too much to Scarlet.

I'll bide my time and be ready when the night comes, chasing away her shadows.

Scarlet held a charity auction tonight.

She told me she was going to auction off a date and that if I didn't bid on her, she'd be wounded. I told her she'd be doing no such thing, wrote her a cheque for a hundred grand, and told her to find someone else to do it.

That didn't go down all that well with Mason and Elliot.

Not when Lucy and Nina ended up as the dates.

Lucy's date went to Elliot, forcing him to show a hand I'm not sure he was ready to reveal, especially with Lucy's boyfriend in attendance tonight.

And Nina's date… That went—to my absolute dismay—to Cooper Hemmings.

The prick needs to die already.

Mason sat back during the entire spectacle, eyes trained on Nina and nothing else. When I started bidding, sensing the awkward quiet mist over the room from Cooper's idiocy, Mason lifted a hand and stopped me.

He let Cooper have the date.

And then he crossed the floor, lifted Nina into his arms and left the party.

The message was clear. Nina belonged to Mason. And to bid on her would only make her feel bought.

"Would either of you two gentlemen care to dance with me?" A flash of lavender catches my eye before she rounds on us, coming at us from behind.

I've barely had five minutes with her all night, and the sight of her makes my heart somersault in my chest.

Her flowing, long hair is down tonight, the relaxed wave soft against her flawless skin. She's wearing a gown that matches the colour of her hair, expensive silk that moulds to the very parts of her my hands, lips, and body had been devoted to last night.

"You don't hesitate, jackass," Charlie mutters, shaking his head as he holds out a hand to her. "I'd be honoured, Miss Lowell."

"Just the gentleman I was looking for, Mr Aldridge."

I set a steely gaze over them as they step onto the dance floor. Charlie bows, and I laugh to myself, annoyed I let my mind get caught up on thoughts of her when I could have the real thing.

They move effortlessly together, and I have to give credit to Freya for teaching Scarlet. She's never been to the functions she should have as a Lowell. Hasn't ever been a part of the company in the way she likely deserved to be. And yet Freya had made sure she knew, if needed, how to dance. How to smile that smile. Looking at her now, you wouldn't know she was on her hands and knees gutting the weeds around the house in the rain just yesterday. Or that she stayed up for the whole of Tuesday night to finish her assignment and then helped a classmate with hers, too, not crawling into bed until late the following afternoon.

She's incredible.

Selfless.

Smart.

Kind.

I wonder if everyone sees it, but as I gaze around the room, I don't see anyone as fascinated by her as I am.

I stride for them, my intentions clear as I step up to her side. Charlie smiles, easing back. "You lasted longer than I gave you credit."

Scarlet laughs.

"You bet on me?" I ask, waiting for him to move back completely.

"You make it too easy, Sullivan. You kids enjoy your night."

He kisses Scarlet's cheek and clasps me on the shoulder, making his way to the table we'd been seated at for dinner.

"That's a very pensive look you're wearing, Mr Sullivan. A penny for your thoughts?"

"I was just thinking about all the people in this room." I place my hand on her hip and bring her to my chest, making a mockery of space and time as I stare down at her. She has a slight shimmer on her eyelids, but the way her eyes glint up at me has my fingers lifting, clearing the loose lock of hair obstructing my view to behind her ear.

She swallows. "And?" she asks, smiling as I run away in my mind again.

"And…" I lace our fingers, trailing a strong hand up her exposed back, my lips lowering to her ear. "I decided they're fucking idiots if they don't see what's in front of their faces. What they choose to ignore."

"Which is?"

"You."

Our temples touch and I feel the heat as her cheek flames against mine. "Flattery will get you fucked, kind sir."

A deep laugh ripples from my chest. "I'm not trying to make you fuck me, sunshine." I step away, and her head dips back as I start to move us. She comes back to me on cue, the delicate swell of her breast rising and falling as her chest works, my lips skirting dangerously close in the room full of people. "I'm trying to make you fall in love with me."

I spin her, not brave enough to gauge the look on her face. A coward to the truth. The reminder isn't welcome. She goes into the spin willingly, letting me lead her around the dance floor for the remainder of the song.

Only when it finishes do I chance a glimpse down at her.

Her eyes soften almost immediately, her body sagging against me. Not a care in the world for the people around us. I hold her to me, strong. "Are you afraid of what I might say?"

I shake my head. "When you look at me like that? No."

Her smile widens, and it's more than enough.

But she doesn't say it back.

Scarlet

The night was better than anything I ever could have dreamt of. There wasn't a single person who didn't thank me or tell me what an incredible evening it's been, and I've already booked the caterers for next year.

The *annual* Antlis Memorial Ball.

"She'd be so proud of me," I muse, smiling as I roll into Lance's side.

The meadow is still lit up thanks to the lanterns. We're lying on top of Lance's tux jacket side by side, flattening a patch of wildflowers as we stare up at the stars.

I wasn't ready to go to bed or to be indoors. This night seemed too good to leave behind, and after everyone left, my ears still ringing from the band, I knew I needed the quiet sanctuary only the meadow could offer me.

"I don't doubt it for a second," Lance tells me, voice throaty. He turns his head and kisses my forehead. I lean into the kiss. "Everyone is proud of you, Scarlet. All of us."

"Even Mase came." And it was perfect. Ellis and Nina were here with him. A family. "They're going to get back together again. The way Mason was with them tonight."

"I hope so." He swallows, his head twisting back to the starlit sky. "If anyone deserves happiness, it's them."

I watch him, his eyes still harbouring slight shadows. This week has been hard on him. He works out, works, and then drives all the way to the estate and helps me, repeating the process after a minimal amount of sleep. But I'm not stupid, and I know that the man I ran into last month was hurting. I think he's still hurting now, but I haven't and won't say that out loud. "We all deserve happiness, Lance," I murmur, leaning in to settle on his chest. His arm wraps around my waist, pulling me impossibly closer.

"Maybe." He sighs.

"Have you seen your mum or sisters recently?" I ask.

Lance loves family. And although my brother and the guys are the closest thing he has to that, having his mum and sisters be what he needs, what he's always wanted, is something I'm not sure he'll ever let go of.

"Not really. I'm only in contact with Mum, and it's to

pay the rent and the bills. The conversation doesn't stretch past that."

"What if we go to the house? Try going together again, or maybe your mum could come here. Have dinner with us, and then we can see if the girls want to join too, eventually."

I feel his heart quicken, the only tell that this conversation means anything to him. "I don't think that would change a thing. But thank you."

I smooth my hand across his chest, trying to ease the tension building there. "Well, the offer is open for as long as you keep putting up with me."

"You'll get rid of my sorry ass long before I'll be done with you, Lowell." He links our fingers, and I stare at them as he dusts his thumb down and then around my cuticle.

"You were such a hard-ass that day we met in the lift. I hated you a little bit."

He sniggers. "I was. Although I'm pretty sure you fancied me."

"You told me I looked like a hippy."

"Fuck, I did." He chuckles.

"But you also held my hand. I didn't know it was you at the time, but the way it made me feel was… safe, maybe." I drop my hand and fiddle with his shirt button absentmindedly. "It was the first time I'd been in complete darkness and not felt alone."

There's silence for a couple of seconds, and then he rolls us, lying on his side, his body shadowing mine. "You want to know a secret, Baby Lowell?"

I tilt my neck back, locking eyes with him. "What?"

"I was a little bit obsessed with you from the minute you walked into that elevator with your eyes closed. You were unexpected. A welcome distraction, and fuck if you didn't distract me."

"Imagine I took a different elevator. Imagine what would've happened if the Irish man had sent me away from you."

His large palm covers my stomach, smoothing up and over my left breast, fingers splaying. "Mason would've invited you to the gala, and I would've run into you there." He gives me a look that says, *Final. No doubt about it.*

"I wouldn't have phoned him. If you hadn't been there, I would've just gone home. He rarely answered the phone for me back then, and I knew better than to disappoint myself even trying."

Lance squeezes my desperately heavy breast, my nipples pebbling. "Scarlet Lowell, will you stop trying to tear out our pages, please? You'll maim me."

"Yeah, well, you maimed me with that hippy comment." I fight my smile, pulling away from him when he laughs. I stand, watching him lying on his back. "Did you ever get rid of the gifts I got you from Nells?"

He tucks his hands behind his head and smiles up at me. "They're in my bedroom drawer at home. Why?"

"I'm just curious." I kick his shoe. "You really couldn't fit yourself inside the penis extender, huh?"

"What do you think?" he challenges, cocksure. A look he's earned after the multiple orgasms he's given me.

"I think we should go back to Nells and get you a bigger size."

"Bigger?"

"I want more."

He tilts his head, a dangerous glint in his eye. I crave it. The promise in it. "More?"

I nod, and he stands, taking his jacket with him as he moves.

"Home. Now."

"You're staying?" I ask with a sarcastic frown, walking backward. He's stayed over every night this week. He even hung a few of his favourite suits in my wardrobe and filled one of my drawers with casual clothes.

He reaches for me, lifting me into his arms and spinning me in circles. "Whether you like it or not."

I throw my head back and laugh as we spin, the fresh night air carrying me away to the place I love most. "Like it," I tell him. I smile when he laughs with me, spinning us faster as I throw my hands out, trusting that he'll catch me. "I like it!"

"What did you do with the cheese?" Lance asks as he goes to the cupboard and pulls out two champagne flutes. We went down to the wine cellar when we came inside. I wanted to toast, just with him, to the night we'd celebrated.

"It's in the pantry." I chuckle. "You'll be helping me cut it down into chunks tomorrow and storing it. Idiot."

He tuts. "Not even a thank-you."

I slide up onto the kitchen counter and wait for him to pass me, grabbing his shirt and pulling him close. He works his way into the space between my legs.

"I can think of a hundred ways to say thank you to you."

"A hundred? Hmm, that could take us all night."

"It's three a.m.," I mumble as he kisses my lips, staying

close and making it hard to focus on him properly. "We'll never manage it."

His strong hands curve up and over my thighs, making my stomach coil tight. My eyes watch his hands, big and heavy, where they lie.

It's seductive. Dominant. Just the right amount of pressure to make my clit throb against the lace of my underwear.

"The way you come alive under my touch makes my dick ache, sunshine."

Biting my lip, I lift his right arm and remove his cuff link. Then I pop the buttons at his wrist and slowly roll back the sleeve, exposing his tanned skin. My fingers dust down the perfect smattering of hair coating his forearm, my thumb trailing a thick vein on the underside.

I move to start on the other sleeve, and he swallows, shifting from one foot to the other.

He seems to be just as turned on as I am. The bulge in his trousers, flush with my centre as he leans his torso back a little, leaving me room to enjoy my task.

I remove the cuff link and pop the buttons, ready to go through the same process, but as I roll back the sleeve of his shirt, I find the hair on his arm shaved.

"Did you know that a *meadow of quivering aspens* is the meaning of the name Waverley?"

"What?" I smile, looking up at him when his fingers reach to adjust the fallen strap of my dress.

"I was looking up ideas for my tattoo session this afternoon, thought of you, and then found out it's the exact meaning of the name."

"Are you going to tell me you're getting some random

chick's name tattooed on you now because *we* once had sex on the dock?" I grin, loving that he puts so much thought into these things. "I might get jealous, you know."

He shrugs, watching his hand as he continues to toy with my dress strap. *He's nervous?* "I liked that only you and I know what it really means."

My body tenses. "Liked?" I look down at the shaved hair and then back up at him. "Tell me you didn't get the name Waverley tattooed on your body."

When he only shifts his eyes to mine, searching, I flip over the material at his wrist twice to find the fresh ink etched into his skin. My heart stops.

Vines. Pale-lavender-coloured vines dance across his skin, wrapping around his forearm like barbed wire before disappearing under his shirt. I keep going, rolling the material with shaking hands.

I push it up, forcing the material until it refuses to go any further past his elbow. In a rush, I fumble the buttons on his dress shirt before pulling it off his broad shoulders and away from his body. "Lance…"

At the end of the vine on his inner left bicep, Waverley is inked into his skin.

"A meadow of quivering aspens. You, that first time on the lake."

"Oh my god." I shake my head, bewildered, as I stare along the vines again. It's fresh, and I don't dare touch the broken skin. "Oh my god… I—I love it. It's…" I look up and find him watching me with an intense fascination. His eyes dart around my face, then drop to the hand that holds his wrist. "You're wild, Lance Sullivan. Completely and utterly wild."

His chin lifts in knowing. "You love me wild."

He takes my face and gently coaxes my lips into a kiss. My arms lock around his neck, deepening it as his hands lift me from the counter so that he can ease my dress to my waist. He works open his trousers before pulling himself out.

I'm slid to the edge of the counter, my underwear discarded, and then he's cock in hand, trailing the thick head through my wetness.

I moan into his mouth, and he pulls back with a groan, biting my lip.

Satisfied I'm ready for him, he lines himself up and slowly sinks into me until I've taken every inch of him.

He stills and eases back, hooking his fingers into my silk dress straps and letting them slink down my arms, freeing my breasts to his hungry gaze.

"I do," I pant. "I do, you know."

"You do what?" He smiles down at me as his lips take mine in a tender kiss, thumb brushing my sensitive nipple.

I pull back and swallow. "Love you," I say. "I've known it for a long time now." I shrug, not knowing what else to do as my cheeks heat at my spoken words. "I just didn't feel safe saying it when you could disappear on me again so easily."

There's a moment of silence, panic rising in my chest when I swear Lance's face pales.

"Say that again."

I take a steadying breath. "I love you, Lance."

His chest expands on a shaky inhale, and then his mouth crashes to mine. He cups my face, slowing the kiss as he leans impossibly closer, still hard inside of me, his torso bare and trousers only unzipped and opened enough to free his cock.

I feel his body rippling under my palms, and his own hands roam me, spanning across my exposed back and up to my neck as he simply kisses me as if it's the first and last time.

An ache forms in my lower abdomen, the feeling of being so full of him making my insides clench. I whimper, rolling my hips to gain some friction.

But Lance isn't ready, and the second my hips lift, a deep groan reverberates from his chest.

"Scar."

"Yes," I pant, catching my breath. "Please, Lance."

His hungry mouth falls to my neck, and my pulse quickens. Still, Lance doesn't move, his hips firm at my pelvis.

And I'm desperate for it, for that slow drag of his hips before the harsh thrust deep back inside. I need it. Need him to give it to me.

As his lips work down my throat, his hips shift, but it's not enough, not when he fights against the movement.

I lower myself back onto one elbow, my other hand smoothing through his hair and down the centre of his muscled back. He palms my full heavy breast, splayed fingers grazing my taut nipple as he squeezes.

"Scarlet, tell me you love me," he rasps.

His mouth covers my nipple, tongue flattening first, followed by the harsh suction of his soft lips. My back arches, hips rolling as I moan.

He chuckles—a breathy laugh that tickles the damp spot left from his mouth.

As he eases off me, I see the heaviness in his eyes. The need and want. Untamed.

"I love you," I whisper, the air crackling between us.

He stares down at me, a slight shake of his head. "You know, the last person to tell me they loved me was my dad. I was fifteen." My heart splinters as I see what it means to him. See just how badly he needed those words. "I never thought it could feel like this. Never knew it even existed."

I reach for him, my lips barely brushing his when his hips roll, putting him so deep my body rears back, my mouth dropping open. He pulls back, then thrusts so hard, so deep, I grunt.

"Again."

I ripple around him, my body heating all over. "Lance—"

"Say it, Baby Lowell."

"I love you."

"Yes!"

On the next thrust of his hips, I meet him with my own. And the angle, impossible depth—the man, and this moment—it sets me off. I come around him, my limbs shaking uncontrolled as I give in to the demand my body makes.

Lance groans against my ear, kissing his way across my jaw as he holds me, letting me ride out the waves of my orgasm.

When he pulls out of me and drops his arms to hug my hips, I shake my head, knowing I can't take more.

He nods, his head dipping.

"Again."

His mouth covers my pussy, tongue swirling between his soft-as-sin lips. I'm so sensitive my hips buck, and I try to roll away. Try to pull him closer. Try to rub myself to orgasm on his face. The feeling almost too much to crave. But I do. I crave the next sweep of his tongue despite the overwhelming feeling I'm about to crumble at his hands.

"I—" My toes curl, legs stiff. "Lance—" My body shatters as another orgasm roars through me. I rock against the feel of his mouth, the wisps of his beard, the heat of his tongue. "I love… you."

He moves up my body, his hands promising devotion as he trails them over my hips, waist, breasts, and into my hair.

He looks at me and gives a slow smile, mouth glistening with my pleasure. He looks high with his eyes barely parting and features so relaxed.

"Tell me," he begs.

"I love you."

His kiss comes hard, messy, demanding. I match his hold on my hair, pulling at the roots of his hair. He steps forward, and with little help, he sinks into me. He pauses the kiss, body trembling, our mouths still flush. "I don't just love you, Scarlet." A kiss. "I live and breathe *you*." He swallows, leaning back a half inch. "I am nothing without you, Scar, but I feel like the best man on earth when I'm with you."

He frowns, pulling back as pain flashes across his face as if he's been slapped.

"Lance?" His haunted eyes come back to me, and I try for a smile. "Where'd you go?"

He winces, closing his eyes briefly before opening them again. And what I see in them should scare me.

The vulnerability.

The pure, untamed love should terrify me.

And yet, I've never been less afraid to fall.

"I hope it hurts," I tell him.

His face falters.

"If it's not life-altering—messy, crazed love, capable of tearing me apart—I don't want it." I lift my chin, brushing my lips to his. "I hope it leaves me in ruins because, Lance, your love's worth hurting for."

He buries his face in my neck as he thrusts forward, his body shuddering. "I'm sorry," he bites out, his knee lifting to the counter. I gasp as his other follows, his body stretching over mine as he lifts onto the kitchen island.

On his knees, he looks down at me, my dress bunched at my waist from our haste. "It's beyond words." He places a hand around my back and angles my body as he whispers again, "It's beyond words."

And as he slides inside of me, sinking into the deepest parts of me, I shatter completely.

THIRTY-THREE

Lance

I have to tell them.

I don't want to. Not at the risk of hurting so many people that I care about. But I can't lie to them either. Not anymore. Mason deserves to know what I did, and Scarlet deserves a choice.

And if she does choose to leave me, then I'll beg on my knees for her to stay.

Being with her makes everything I did last year tolerable.

Her smile makes me believe I was acting based on what Ben told me, and I wasn't to know. Her laugh tells me I only love Mason like a brother and would never intentionally hurt him. Her words… fuck, her words make me believe that even after what I did, no matter how bad, that I still deserve her love.

And yet I lie here now in the silence as I have for the last month, with the truth lingering like a shadow that's weighing me down. I rarely sleep anymore, and if I do, it's from pure exhaustion. It's eating me alive, and deep down, I know that the only thing stopping me from telling them is my own selfish needs.

Because I don't want to lose them too.

Her.

But seeing Nina and Mase here this weekend, watching them fumble over themselves as they come back together, as they fall in love again… it makes me sick to my fucking stomach that it was all because of me.

I did that.

Me.

I can't claim to want to protect them and then keep the truth from them at the same time.

I can't keep this from them.

I love you, Lance.

A tear streaks my temple as I roll to my side and kiss Scarlet's forehead. I pause, breathing her in.

"My sunshine, when all I can see is the moon and stars."

My knee bounces as the lock on the elevator clicks from the floors below, a deep whirling sounds a moment later. I swallow the bile that rises in my throat. I have everything with me. The photos Ben had printed and the money trail to Jasmine. I knew I couldn't tell them about Ben and Nessa Anne's involvement and risk the truth coming out about Marcus. Ben made it impossible. But even if I could tell him, why would I? It was me who gave Ben the nod. It was me who stood in a club with Mason as his friend and let him walk into a trap I'd set.

I disgust myself.

"Lance?"

I lift my head from my hands, my heart pounding when I see Nina standing at the entry.

"Nina. Where's Mase?"

"At the estate." Her eyes move to the folder and USB stick on the coffee table. She frowns. "What are you doing here?"

He didn't come back with her. Fuck. "I came to see Mase."

She nods, eyes flicking back to the file. "What's that?"

I steeple my hands in front of my mouth as I rock on my bouncing knees. I can't even look at her. It's time.

"I fucked up."

"Lance—"

"I watched it happen with Cara, and I thought you were going to do it too. I-I—"

"Lance," she snaps, cutting off the mess of words tumbling from my mouth. She comes to sit next to me on the sofa, and I finally look across at her. "Stop." Her eyes are locked on the file, unblinking. *She knows.* "You set him up, didn't you… It was you."

Acid burns in my throat, and I force it down as I fight to explain myself. "You'd been together a couple of months. I didn't think he was so deep, and if I knew you were pregnant, Nina."

Fuck, this isn't how I planned it to go.

She turns to look at me, and my eyes blaze over her pale face. "Lance—"

"I'm so sorry, Nina," I rush on. "I couldn't keep it from you and Mase anymore, it's not right. I can't live with it."

And it's true. I can't.

Lies—so many lies twisted between us all.

They don't deserve any of this.

Nina shakes her head at me in disbelief. "Did you plan it beforehand? Did you plan it before Bora Bora?"

No. God, no. And if I'd only trusted my gut. I knew she would never do it. I knew, and I still let Ben make me believe she could. "I was off my face that night. It's no excuse, but Lowell was fucking all over the place for months. Everything came out about Marcus and Cara, and I felt like everything I spent the year burying was being dug up."

The half-truth.

The only parts I can tell her.

"So after? You planned it after the holiday?"

I grit my teeth. I fucking hate myself. "It was after you spoke to your mum on the phone at the lodge. You told her you'd send her money, and I read it all wrong. I read you so wrong, Nina. I'm so sorry."

A tear rolls down her cheek, and I fight the urge to comfort her.

I want her to lash out. To hit me or scream at me. Anything but this.

"You're in love with Scarlet," she says in a daze, lip trembling. "What will she say? What will she do, Lance?"

My chest feels like it's breaking in two. I've pushed her so far out of my mind. It was the only way I could ever walk in here. I drop my head to my hands, running my fingers through my scalp and pulling at the roots. "She told you about us?"

"No." She sniffs. "It's painfully obvious, though. It has been since Anthony passed away. I knew she wasn't alone."

Fuck… fuck. "Does Mason know?"

"No. But it wouldn't have been long. He heard you last night in the kitchen."

I scrub at my face.

I can feel myself breaking. Feel the lump in my throat getting thicker and thicker. "I'm so sorry. I'm so so sorry." My eyes blur, and I swipe at the corners, reaching forward. "I have it all here, every copy of everything that was sent to me. I'll stay away from you, from Scarlet too. I won't be around."

"He's your best friend."

"I know."

"She won't forgive you."

My jaw cracks as I clench it. I don't bother to hide the tears that fall. Nina doesn't deserve to see my pain. She has enough of her own to deal with, and I'm the root of it. But when it comes to *her*, I can't fake it. I *can't* hide it. "I know."

And I do know it.

Mason means the world to Scarlet. They're the very thing I dream of for myself. I won't blame her if she walks away from me because if I had someone—a family who loved me as fiercely as they love each other—I'd burn the world down for them.

Nina's hands run through her hair before she sighs and stands. She reaches for the USB and file. "Go home, Lance."

"I can't," I mutter. "It has to come from me."

I wouldn't let Nina take Mason's wrath for me.

She shakes her head, not looking at me. "No. Go home, Lance."

"Nina—"

"GO HOME, LANCE!" she screams, tears filling her eyes. "You've caused so much unnecessary pain. You've kept me from my family." My nostrils flare as she cries. "But telling Mason that you did this won't lessen it. It won't change anything, and it will break him. The boys too." She hesitates, looking into my eyes so fiercely I can't look away. "I want my family back now. I want to stop hurting him. I want to see him happy. I need to see him happy."

My face screws up as I try to comprehend what she's saying. "You want to keep it from him?"

"Not just him." She tilts her head. "Mason would never forgive you, and that would hurt both of you enough, but Scarlet wouldn't forgive you either."

I shake my head, not wanting to think about her. Because losing her would be like losing my purpose. I'm not Lance without Scar. "Nina, I don't deserve her."

"Maybe not, but Scar's the only person who gets to decide that. Telling them won't change this, Lance. It only brings it all back, for us all."

I swallow, looking down at her. "I don't know what to do."

"Go home," she tells me, her voice resolute. "You've made a lot of mistakes… we all have." Her eyes pin me. "But don't let her be one of them."

I stand in utter disbelief, tears streaming down my cheeks. I step into her, praying she lets me hug her. This woman who, for all her faults, loves the people around her enough to carry their pain. Just to protect them. To protect me. I got her so wrong.

I leave the files.

I leave it all behind me.

Or at least I try to.

Scarlet

"Mr Sullivan… where are you? If this is what you felt when I abandoned you in bed when we first met, then I'm so very sorry, and you can come home now. Point proven."

"I'm not abandoning you, Scar."

"Then where are you? The bed was cold when I woke up. And who are these people you've sent in? They're doing everything and won't let me help. One of the men even told me it was a health and safety risk to have me help carry the chairs back to the house and would breach their contract if I did." It has Lance's name written all over it.

"Mason was asked to attend a meeting down in Cornwall tomorrow. I made a last-minute decision to go instead. He needs the time with Nina, and I needed to clear my head for a bit. I left my car in your garage. I'll move it when I'm back."

I lie across my bed, still in my towel and smile. "When will you be back?"

"Wednesday. And those men are there for a reason. Humour me, please."

Three whole days. "Why didn't you take me with you? Imagine the fun we could have had."

He chuckles, the sound making my eyes close as it soothes me. "As fucking good as that sounds, Baby Lowell. I needed this. Just a bit of time."

I worry my lip between my teeth. "Okay." I swallow. "It's not… It's not because I told you I love you, is it?"

“What?” I can hear the pain in his voice. “What… No! Fuck, Scarlet, you have no idea.”

I relax again, trusting his words.

“You’re… you’re everything I….” He sighs, and I picture him scrubbing his hands through his hair. “Give me until Wednesday. Please. I don’t want to have this conversation with you over the phone. You deserve more than that.”

I run my fingers over my lips, wishing he could be home right now. “You took the bike?”

“Yeah.”

I smile, tears unexpectedly filling my eyes. He really does need this. “Okay, then. Wednesday.” I pause. “Ride safe. And call me, yeah? I love you.”

He lets out a heavy sigh, like the weight of the world leaves him in an instant. “I love you, too.”

My jaw is on the floor, and I know I need to pick it up and recover fast. I met the girls at The Elm for breakfast this morning, and Nina arrived in a complete whirlwind.

Yesterday morning after the ball, she went to check in on her friend Joey after his brother passed away unexpectedly last week. When she arrived, she found him in a bad way and decided to stay and help him, but then he tried to kiss her.

“Does Mason know?” Megan gasps.

“Mason knows. That’s why I went to his yesterday.” She looks at me and then drops her eyes. But I catch the sadness in them. “I knew I had to tell him.”

“Are you okay?” Lucy asks.

She shrugs. “Yes and no. Mason was amazing, and I

couldn't ask for the situation to be better with him right now."

I frown, sensing there's more to it.

"Oh, I love this." Lucy grins. "I feel proud of you both already. Tell me more."

Nina swallows. "I'm not going to see Joey for a while."

Lucy nods. "I actually think that's a good idea. He's been at the centre of some of your arguments with Mason these last couple of months."

Joey became closer to Nina after she and Mason broke up. And although we know that Nina made it clear it was just a friendship, we also warned her multiple times that we thought Joey wanted more from her.

"I know. And it was my choice, but I worry so much about him, girls."

"Because of his brother?" Lucy asks.

She nods. "He isn't right. It scares me to think he's in that apartment on his own at the best of times, but now that this has happened, it scares me. I found him in the bath on Sunday. He was asleep, and I had to wake him. He's always been Joey, you know. I've never seen how his illness affects him when it's bad, but he isn't acting himself, and I don't know if that's because of his brother or because he isn't taking his medication."

I zone out a little as I think about Joey and what he's likely feeling. I know from Nina that he lost his mum in a house fire when he and his brother were young. And now he's lost his brother too.

"He'll be okay, babe," Lucy tells her, placing a hand on Nina's.

Nina nods, swiping at the corner of her eye. "I hope so."

"I know this is hurting you, Nina," Megan says, a soft look relaxing her face. "But I think this will be a good thing. You and Mason made big steps this past month. You have a chance to get your family back here."

"I know."

"And maybe it will mean Joey makes new friendships. He seems stuck on you," Megan adds.

Nina stares at the table, still nodding. "I think Joey cares. Maybe too much at times, but he isn't a bad person."

I can only imagine what Joey must be going through. But the girls are right. Nina needs to focus on Mason and Ellis right now. Her family has to be her priority.

"So you and Mason are okay?" I ask.

"Yes, but he wants to take things slow." She gives a small smile, the first since she sat down. "We're going to date."

"Slow?" Megan laughs. "Mate, you can't fuck him yesterday then be like… Oh, we're taking it slow today."

We all chuckle in agreement with her.

Nina waves her off. "You know what I mean. I already know he won't last five minutes. We're just not going as fast as last time."

I sit forward, keeping my voice lower than Megan's. "Definitely… like condoms this time, right?"

The girls laugh with me as Nina plucks out a salt packet and takes aim at me.

It feels good to have these girls around me, especially after the weekend we've just shared.

I don't feel ready to tell them about Lance. It's a long-ass story for a cuppa coffee. But today isn't the day I feel like explaining it.

"Nina, if you want me to, I can check in on Joey?" I

offer, knowing it's a small thing that would put her mind at ease. "Maybe send over some bereavement leaflets or something? Just to check in, so you don't have to stress."

"You'd do that?" she asks.

"Of course! I get what it's like to lose someone you love. Maybe it will be good coming from me?"

"If you could, that would be amazing, Scarlet. Thank you."

Silence settles around the table for all of thirty seconds before Megan turns to Lucy and says, "You going to give us the tea on Elliot?"

THIRTY-FOUR

Scarlet

I'm in the kitchen, my hands deep in the sink when I hear the roaring of the engine. My head lifts with the sound, and I abandon the dishes, rushing for the front door.

He's already parked and jogging up the steps when I push through it.

"You're home."

He looks up and smiles so big and wide, my stomach bottoms out. "I'm home." He doesn't stop, and neither do I, walking straight to me and picking me up.

I wrap my arms around his neck, letting him hold me for a second before I lean back and take his lips in a searing kiss.

He said he'd be back on Wednesday, but it's been a week.

A week too long.

"You missed me, sunshine?" he asks, squinting up at me.

I pinch two fingers together. "Maybe a little."

He chuckles, letting me down to my feet, but he doesn't let me go. "Yeah, me too."

"You went to see him?"

"It felt like the least I could do. Nina and Mason are finally sorting through their shit, and Joey instantly throws a spanner in the works."

I made the trip out to see Joey after I finished work today. When he eventually opened the door, I gave him the forms I'd picked up from the hospital and spoke to him for as long as he'd tolerate me before brushing me off. "He seems like a really nice guy. He's obviously not sleeping, and I told Nina to see if someone he knows can go over and offer more support. I'd go inside, but it seems like a lot right now and pushy when he doesn't know me."

Lance smooths a hand over the top of my thigh in soft circles, his eyes still scanning the pages of the book he has spread across my legs. "You've done what you said you would. And you're busy with uni and work. The fact you made an effort at all is enough."

I nod, watching him.

He found my stash of raunchy romance books yesterday when I took him on a tour of the lower level of the house. I rarely come down here because it's only lit up by the windows on the back of the house. It houses the wine cellar, library—which we're hidden out in now, and gym. The wine cellar is the only room I've ever really found use of.

It's dark as shit down here.

For years I've wanted to move the library to the main

living level, but I have a million other rooms to redecorate first.

"I have a secret to tell you. But you can't tell anyone else."

He lifts his eyes this time, his interest piqued.

"Mason is going to ask Nina to move back in."

He stares at me for a second, and then his lip curls. "I know."

"You know?" I snap. "Were you not going to tell me?"

"I know what you girls are like. You can't keep anything to yourselves."

"You weren't going to tell me?" I say, shocked.

Asshole!

"Mason told you anyway." He turns the page. "What does it matter?"

"It matters. I'll remember this."

"Hmm."

I smile as he quietens again.

"A book about a woman fake dating a rugby player?"

"Yep, but there's a twist. And there's this one scene where they get to the hotel, and there's only one bed," I add, smiling as if it will help sell it to him.

"Who comes up with this shit?"

"I like to call them literary queens. The givers of the world, doing the lord's work."

"You sure it's not just a cult of horny women thirsting over fictional men?"

"That cult of horny women thirsting over fictional men taught me how to do that thing you like with my tongue, Mr Sullivan." I pull the book from the shelf and thump it against his chest. "Read it. Maybe you could learn a thing or two."

He started the book this morning and hasn't put it down since.

"Where are you at?" I ask.

He shakes his head and looks up. "She's in a group call with her friends. Is this how you girls talk when you meet up?" He peers back down, reciting the words. "I did it. I fucked him. He's big, girls. So fucking big that he had to finger me again just to stretch me out a little more. And when we eventually did it... Christ. I've never been so full."

I try to stifle my laugh as his gaze comes back up. "Like, I'm sorry what? Who's having these conversations?"

"You'd be surprised."

"No wonder you wanted to go and get a bigger cock extender from Nells. I thought I was doing okay for size until I read this."

I throw my head back, laughing, and then I hear the book close and a light thud. His body moves over me, and I widen my legs to accommodate him as he settles over me. I cup his face. "I promise your penis is perfectly adequate for me."

"Jeez, thanks, sunshine."

I can't help but chuckle.

"Adequate." He huffs. "Don't go giving up the day job to pen any raunchy novels of your own."

"I won't," I promise, still smiling as I pull his face closer. He's hard in his jeans, and I can feel the outline of him against my thigh. "But if I did, I would write that your cock fills me up so good it makes my pussy wet just from the thought of it."

"Oh yeah?"

"Uh-huh. Or that when you do sink inside of me, you

fill me up so good I end up feeling you there the next day. That I crave having you inside of me, even in the moments I shouldn't. In my pussy. My mouth. Between my tits."

A deep groan leaves him, and he grinds himself into me. "I've always wanted to fuck your tits."

He kisses my neck once before leaning back and lifting my dress over my head, discarding it. Then he works his way up my body, knees at my ribs, smirking down at me as he reaches around to unhook my bra.

I have a class today at eleven o'clock, and after sneakily slipping away and out of Lance's bed, I made the decision to stop by and see Joey again.

We've never spent much time at Lance's place, but this week I've been prepping for my first set of exams and asked if we could spend our nights closer to the city. Lance reeled off all the reasons it made sense, mostly the extra time he gets to spend in bed with me.

But it was Lance who asked when we'd be going back to the estate this morning, his love for my home making my heart swell.

"I'm happy for them. It's good," Joey tells me.

I smile over at him, watching as he works at his small round dining table. I've been over to see Joey twice since the first time I told Nina I would. He invited me inside last week, and I couldn't say no. He's a genuinely lovely guy. He's just going through some stuff right now.

"It is good. Them living together is huge for Ellis. It's his life that would've been impacted the most if they didn't sort things out."

Joey doesn't answer me, his focus elsewhere.

"Did you catch any of those sessions you signed up for?"

He nods, flicking back a strand of his dark hair from his face. "The first. I have another on Friday."

My brows rise in surprise. I really didn't think he'd go. I thought he only agreed to shut me up.

"You didn't think I'd go, did you?"

"I—" My phone rings in my pocket, and I pull it out, finding Lance's name lighting up the screen. My eyes go back to Joey's, and he nods as if to say take it. "Lance?"

"You left me."

I smile, dipping my head. "You were taking too long."

He tsks. "I was waiting for you to join me. And then I come out to find that note." I held out for twenty minutes for Lance to reappear from his shower this morning. When he didn't, I left him a note telling him all the things I'd do to him when I got home tonight.

"Well, you'll have to wait, won't you?"

"Mean, mean woman. Where are you, Baby Lowell?"

"I'm at Joey's. First class is at eleven."

He pauses. "You okay?"

Lance told me he wasn't happy with me visiting Joey alone, but I promised him I felt safe here. Even Mason would agree that Joey is a good bloke, no matter how much he hates him.

"I'm fine."

"Can you text me when you get to class?"

I smile. "Yes."

"Good girl."

"Goodbye, Lance." I hang up and hope that my cheeks aren't as flushed as they feel. "Sorry about that."

"Your boyfriend?"

"You could call him that." Lance and I aren't officially a couple, but to call us anything else would be a lie. "Nobody knows I'm seeing him, so if you see any of my people." I make a signal to keep his mouth shut, and he sniggers.

"Got it."

"It's not a big secret or anything. It's just so much has happened over the last year and a half, with my dad and Ellis and all the crazy in between. I like that I have him to myself. No expectations or questions from anyone else. I think he feels the same."

I watch Joey watch me as if he's truly taking in my words. "I like that. It sounds nice."

I smile. "It is nice. We have something that feels special. Different—maybe."

"Do you think you'll tell your friends eventually?"

"I'm pretty sure it will come up," I say, chuckling. "Lance isn't the most discreet. They've just been so caught up in their own lives that none of them has noticed us."

He gives me a warmish smile—or at least a semblance of one. I take it for a win. "I better hit the road before I make myself late."

He straightens from his spot at the table, tapping his pen on the top of his other hand. "You don't have to keep popping in here, you know. I get that you're busy."

"I know I don't have to. But you make a good cuppa, and now you can be my listening ear when Lance is playing up." I grin as I walk backward to the door. "Make sure to text if you need anything, Joey. We can chat any time about anything."

He tips his chin, smiling. "Sure."

It was definitely a warmish smile.

Lance

Scarlet, you're it for me. Be with me?

Sunshine, I think you're the smartest, most funny, wild girl on earth. Will you be my girlfriend?

Scarlet, I love you. Will you be my girlfriend?

Why does everything I come up with sound like cheesy schoolboy confessions?

Girlfriend. She's already more than my fucking girlfriend. That's why it sounds so dumb.

But I can't go all out and ask her to marry me. Not yet. She'd freak out. Mason would likely keel over.

I need to talk to him about us after tomorrow night.

"Still nothing from Nina's mum?" Charlie asks Mason from the other side of the studio, pulling me from my thoughts. Mason just shakes his head.

He's been planning his *asking Nina to come home* for weeks, roping us all in to get the studio he bought for her last year ready.

Scarlet's convinced Nina doesn't have a clue, and I'll admit, even I'm excited to see her reaction to the whole spectacle Mason has planned.

"She's probably drinking herself into a ditch somewhere," he muses, dropping the paintbrush to the tray and looking around the room.

"You did your best, mate. Don't let it hang over your head," I tell him. Mason reached out to Nina's mum around the same time Jasmine showed up. He'd taken Jasmine under his wing in the hopes that one day she'd be someone to Nina—the family she's always wanted. And I guess reaching out to her mum, helping her get clean and sending her to a facility in the city was all in the hopes they could reconcile any relationship between them all. Masons never properly met the woman, but she's the only living grandmother of his son, and I know how important it is to him to make Nina happy.

"You think this is going to dry in time for tomorrow?"

The studio above the gym is nearly done. After being told he couldn't have the grand piano moved to the top floor of the building, we presumed Mason would let go of the idea. Instead, he had three windows removed and hired a crane to lift it in.

"It will be ready," he tells me, sighing as he runs his hands through his hair. "Whether or not she will be is a whole other story."

Scarlet doesn't notice me as the hospital doors drag open, spitting her out into the frigid night air. She's got her head down, looking at something on her phone, her hand aimlessly reaching for her bag strap twisted on her shoulder.

I smile as I watch her.

I tried to think of all the ways this night could go. How I could make it mean something without it being cringy as fuck.

Truth is, sometimes you have to be that guy, standing outside her work with flowers and chocolates.

She steps to the edge of the drop-off bays, ready to cross the road. Her head lifts, scanning left, then right. She seeks me out immediately, not even doing a double take. Surprise cramps her features before she smiles.

My eyes track her as she crosses the road, making her way to me. When she's close enough, I right myself from my perch on my bike and pull her into my arms.

"What are you doing here?" she murmurs into my jacket.

"Am I not allowed to be here?"

"Yes…" She looks down at the brand-new leathers and helmet slung over the back of the bike. "But what are you doing here?" she chuckles.

"Can I take you somewhere?"

"Is it somewhere nice? I smell grim."

I hold her close, inhaling the smell of her shampoo. "You smell perfect to me."

"You're lying, don't be disgusting." She steps out of my hold and flicks her head behind her. "My car."

"We can come back and get it in the morning. We have Mason and Nina's thing tomorrow anyway."

"What?" She frowns as if she's not a millionaire with a sprawling estate and holiday home in the South Pacific. "It'll cost me a fortune to leave it here over—"

"Scar." I huff out a nervous laugh, shaking my head at her as I cut her off. "Will you shut up and do as you're told? Just tonight?"

Her eyes go wide, knowing. "Are you going to ask me to be your girlfriend?"

I roll my eyes, turning my back to her. "No."

"You are." She rounds me, taking the flowers from my hand and bringing them to her nose. "You've got that nervous look. And you never pick me up. You want me to be your *girlfriend*."

"I don't."

"We'll see."

I grip her neck, pulling her flush to my body so that I can kiss her. When I eventually drag my lips from hers, everything calms. "We will."

She purses her lips, looking up at me with a lazy stare. I dust my thumb under her lip. "You had a good day, sunshine?"

Her shoulders drop as she sighs, sinking further into my chest. "Yeah. But it just got a million times better."

Scarlet

I'd know these roads with my eyes closed. I squeeze Lance tighter, wondering why he'd ride out to the hospital only to bring me right back home.

He pulls to a stop and waits for me to climb off his bike, then he stands and removes my helmet, followed by his own.

"I'm trying to figure out if this was just foreplay, and you wanted me wet from the engine."

He throws his head back, laughing.

I grin, laughing with him. "I don't get it. Why couldn't I drive home?"

"Your car isn't even at the hospital."

I frown. "Yes, it is."

"It isn't." He looks past me, tipping his chin at the garage.

I follow his gaze, then step backward, confused. "I don't get it."

"You're not supposed to get it." He turns me fully, setting me in motion. "Go."

I roll my lips and walk to the garage, the knot in my stomach pulling impossibly tight. "I really hate surprises, Lance. Dad bought me books every birthday for over twenty years solely so I could avoid the anxiety of it."

His lip curls. "You could call this the same thing."

What is he up to?

I reach for the handle and hesitate for only a second before pulling the door up.

My jaw drops.

Sitting in my garage is a brand-new Mercedes-Benz. It's huge. Like a fucking bus. "What did you do?"

"It's fully electric. And you have a charging point here in the garage." His hands slide around my waist, pulling me into his warmth. "No more running out of fuel or overthinking trips to the petrol station."

I see the heavy-looking cable attached to the place the fuel would normally go.

My head tilts, looking up at him. I smile so wide it hurts. "No more getting fuel?"

He shakes his head no at me, his face a mask of something I can't place. It makes my throat grow tight. "Go have a look," he tells me.

I bound from his arms and rush to the driver's side, pulling open the sleek door. "I love the black!" I get a look at the leather interior. "Lance."

He gives me a huge smile.

"I love it." I climb inside and grab the wheel, inhaling that new car smell. "Can we take it out for a spin?"

"It's your car, Baby Lowell. You can do what you want."

"Get in!"

Lance removes the charging cable and climbs in. Excitement bubbles up inside of me as I bounce in the seat. "I've never had a brand-new car. I always went for used because you lose so much money just driving anything new off the forecourt."

He chuckles. "Your dad told you that, didn't he?"

I nod my head, my eyes glued to him as it all sinks in. What he's done. Why he did it. "Thank you, Lance. I don't know why you'd do this for me, but thank you." I lean across the centre console and kiss him long and hard.

Lance

I linger as she pulls back, holding out the keys to her. "I did it because I love you."

The sun slowly dips on the meadow's hilltop, creating a glare that streams in through the garage doors. Just like I knew it would.

"Lance?"

I pause on the threshold of the kitchen, walking back a couple of steps until I'm outside the sitting room. Anthony is sat up in his armchair, his face unnaturally pale.

"Anthony, are you okay?"

"Yes, I have something here, could you…"

I walk into the room and take the envelope he holds out to me. My eyes scan the words on the front. The last will and testament of

Anthony Lowell. I swallow the tightness in my throat as I stare down at the envelope.

"Are you able to pass it along to Charlie? I trust he'll make sure it ends up in the right hands."

I clear my throat. "Yes. Of course."

He nods, and I turn, not knowing what to say, what to do, how I go back upstairs and climb into the bed with Scarlet after holding this in my hands.

"Lance." I turn again, frowning. He watches me for a moment. And for what—I have no idea. I've spent weeks in his home, with Scar, with him. He nods as if he's made up his mind. "You'll do just fine for my daughter. If ever you need my blessing, know that you have it."

My heart sinks in my chest. "I—I—Umm." What the... "Thank you. I... I don't know what to say."

"You don't have to say anything, but let me say thank you. You pulled her out of this place with ease. I didn't think I'd see the day, but I knew it would eventually come. I'm glad I got to see it. So, thank you."

"Jesus shit. The sun," Scarlet snaps, holding up her hand to shield her eyes.

I smile and drag my bottom lip into my mouth, biting down.

We roll forward a couple of inches, approaching the edge of the gravel when she reaches for her sun visor. As she snaps it into place, the box drops into her lap.

The car rocks to a halt as she brakes.

"What's this?" she asks, staring at it.

"Open it."

She picks it up and then looks at me. "No."

"Why?"

"Because," she rushes out, eyes wide and telling.

"It might be earrings," I offer.

"Is it?"

I shake my head, my heart wild. "No." I lean over and take the box from her hands. "But you don't have to look so scared. It's not that ring—well, kinda—"

"Lance," she warns.

I twist in the seat, flipping the box between my fingers. "You can't just be my girlfriend, Scar. I don't want to scare you off or rush into anything. But I refuse to sit here and make a mockery of what you truly mean to me. So, this isn't a ring to say anything other than I *don't* want you to be my girlfriend."

She tilts her head, her smile soft and growing. "You don't want me to be your girlfriend?"

I roll my lips as a smile threatens. "Not even a little bit." I swallow and open the box, my hand steady. "Will you be my it girl instead, just until we're ready to make it something a little more official?"

She looks down at the ring, covering her mouth with her hands. "Oh my god."

"I love you, Scarlet—more than what's healthy. And I swear it…." I wait for her wide eyes to meet mine, needing her to know I mean every word. "I'm not going to disappear on you."

She nods, and her tears fall. And then she's reaching for me, holding the sides of my face as she kisses me. "I love you, too," she whispers against my lips.

I beam at her and pick up her right hand, throwing her a soft wink as I slide the ring on her finger. "All right then, sunshine. It's settled."

THIRTY-FIVE

Scarlet

"After all these months, you're finally going home." I grin over at Nina as I pick up an empty moving box, the excitement from yesterday and last night still coursing through me. "How does it feel?"

She smiles at me from the other side of the kitchen island. "Exciting."

Nina will be moving back to the penthouse today, and I was the only one up early enough to come with her to pack. I got the sense she didn't want to wait around after Mason's grand charade last night. I was surprised at how perfect he'd made everything for Nina. I never knew he had it in him.

For the first time in a long time, everything feels exactly as it should be.

Mason's happy.

Nina's going home.

Lance is… too much and not enough.

I look down at my right hand, the pale-purple oval-cut diamond ring glaring up at me. I haven't been able to stop staring at it since he gave it to me.

"I knew you'd get here. I just didn't think it would be yet. I'm so happy for you guys."

"Thank you, Scar." Nina smiles over at me. "And thank you for helping me today. Hopefully the girls will show their faces this afternoon."

I laugh with her because we both know there's no way. We celebrated hard for Nina and Mason last night, some of us more so than others.

"Megan was blind drunk." I chuckle. "I don't expect to see her at all."

"True." Nina laughs, taping up another box and placing it on the floor. "How's everything going at the hospital? Are you still enjoying it?"

I sigh, an easy feeling settling in my stomach. "Yeah, it's great, actually. I have big plans for the future, which I never considered possible when I started."

"Like what?" Nina asks with a frown.

"Well, I've been thinking about going into paediatrics."

"With kids? That's amazing, Scar!"

"I need to choose a speciality, and I love children. I do worry it will be tough sometimes, but I think I could handle it."

"You could! I know so. You're stronger than you think."

I shrug, excitement stirring again. "We'll see! What about you? Do you think you'll start up less—"

The rapping of knuckles against the door cuts me off. "Just a sec!" Nina shouts, placing down the curtains she'd been rolling up and walking to the door.

I hope the guys wake up soon. There's so much to move, and I don't want to disappoint Nina by telling her we won't get it all moved in one go. Mason told her he'd get a moving company in to help, but Nina and I both agreed we could do it between us all.

"Joey, hi."

I snap my head up and smile.

"Hey. How are you?" he mutters, heading for the lounge. "I brought you these." He places a box on the coffee table and then picks it up again. "Do you want them? I presumed you did. You don't have to."

I frown, watching him in confusion.

"Is it…"

"Your photos," he finishes for Nina. "Scarlet told me you were back with Mason."

Nina nods, smiling. "Yeah. Yeah, I am."

It's been weeks since Nina's seen Joey, and the last time they did see each other, he'd tried to kiss her.

He seems a little off today.

"Did you catch that session yesterday, Joey?" I ask, giving Nina a small shrug when she looks at me.

"No." He frowns, rubbing at his neck. "I didn't sleep, and then I slept through it."

"Ahh. I see." I step further into the lounge. "How are you feeling?"

"Fine. Why?" He tips his chin at me. His gaze narrowed, and then he looks back to Nina.

"I'm just asking, Joey. I haven't been over in a couple days, that's all."

He flicks his eyes between us, then picks up the box of photos. "What was that?"

Nina looks at me, frowning, then back at Joey. "What was what?"

"What did you say?" he asks Nina, placing down the box again.

"I didn't say anything, Joey."

He relaxes his brow, and then his eyes drift to me and seem to soften even more.

I give him a warm smile.

"Thank you for bringing these over, Joey. I really appreciate it," Nina tells him, wringing her hands.

"Of course." Joey nods. "You haven't been over."

"No," Nina mutters, swallowing thickly. "I'm taking some time. I came and told you that already."

He seems to stand in a trance, just watching her. "Joey, are you okay?" Nina eventually asks, her voice full of worry.

"You asked me that already." He continues to stare at her.

Nina steps forward. "Sorry, Joey, I think—"

The door clicks shut in the entry, and we all turn to look toward the sound.

I tilt my head when I see the woman standing at the entrance.

"Well, haven't you done well for yourself."

"*Mum*?" Nina mutters in disbelief. She shakes her head before her features settle as if remembering. "You got my letter?"

My own brows lift in surprise, watching the bizarre exchange. Nina looks nothing like her mum. There are similarities, but nothing like Nina described.

"I got your letter, but there wasn't my money," she slurs the words, and my heart sinks.

A feeling of deep sorrow for Nina, my friend, seems to chase away our earlier happiness.

Her mum's drunk.

"What do you mean your money, Mum? You haven't asked for money in months."

Nina's mum sniggers. "Because you cut me off!" she yells, gripping her bag with trembling fingers. "Is this him?!" She sneers at Joey, and my heart all but stops when I realise she thinks Joey is my brother.

I watch her take a step further into the lounge, and something inside of me, a deep protectiveness I can't explain, has me stepping with her.

Nina's voice barely shakes me out of my own head. "By him, I presume you mean Mason. And no, this is Joey—my friend. And Scarlet, Mason's sister."

A snigger. "Don't get smart with me!" I frown as she fumbles with the strap on her bag, her grip white-knuckled. She's livid. Her anger like a tidal wave in the room, getting higher and higher.

Her eyes snap from Joey to me, then back to Nina. "Where is he?"

Mason.

She's looking for Mason.

"Are you serious right now?!" Nina fumes. "How dare you come into my home and speak to me like this!"

Her mother flinches, or at least it seems like a flinch, her hand dipping into her bag before she pulls it out again.

I still as she lifts her arm to where I'm standing.

Everything stills… but my racing heart.

I've never seen a gun in person. My dad wouldn't allow them on the estate, always saying they were too dangerous to have stored with kids around. He always did everything he could to protect me. Mason too.

Who's going to protect me now?

"Mum?" Nina's voice is barely a whisper, and something that feels like pure dread fills my gut.

I don't move, but my eyes blur as traitorous tears fill them.

"Mum, please calm down," Nina says, voice shaking. "I will get you money, okay?"

Her head snaps to her daughter, and my chest instantly starts to work. I can't… I don't think I can breathe.

"I want my money, all of it. What he promised."

"Okay, I will get all of it." I hear Nina pause like she doesn't… like she doesn't know what her mum's talking about. "What did he promise?"

"A new life. A fresh start. A lot of money, and then he took it all away," she spits.

Nina shakes her head at a loss. "Mason? Mason promised you that?"

I blink back the tears.

What have you done, Mase?

"Yes! I went to rehab. I did the time, and then when I came for my money, he told me no."

"You went to rehab?" My heart breaks at Nina's tone, the hopelessness in it.

"Yes!" She shakes her head, like Nina not getting it makes her angrier. Her arm jolts and she adjusts her hold.

I see Nina tense.

She puts her hands up as if to stop her. "I'm going to go and get my phone, okay, and then I will call Mason. Mum, please put the gun down." Her voice is soothing now, child-like, but her mother's face only reddens.

"Get me the money!"

A tear falls down Nina's cheek, and I fight the urge to go to her. How fast could I make it to her if I had to? If this woman turned the gun on Nina. Mason couldn't lose her again. Ellis couldn't lose his mummy.

Nina's eyes drift to me, her face devastated. *I'm so sorry,* she mouths.

I'd make it to her. No matter what.

I nod, letting her know it's okay.

She looks back at her mum but mutters over her shoulder, "Joey. Go to my bag at the kitchen island and get my phone, okay?" She gives her mum a look, nodding at her as if it will make her understand. "I'm going to call Mason and get him to send me your money, Mum."

Joey doesn't move. He's staring at me, at the gun, desperate. Terrified. He's terrified. I shake my head no, telling him with my eyes that it's okay. *I'm okay.*

"Joey," Nina repeats, looking between us.

He doesn't move, stuck in a trance as he stares at me. "Joe!" Nina snaps, but it's a plea. A desperate plea for help. "Go to the kitchen and get my phone so that I can call Mason."

Joey's head twists at the grit in Nina's tone. The pain. The fear.

"*Please.*"

She won't leave me here with her. That's why she's asking Joey. She thinks her mum might hurt me.

"Okay." Joey nods.

Nina breathes a sigh of relief as he walks around the sofa and toward the kitchen.

Nina turns back to her mum, and I break a little inside as she frowns at her daughter in disgust. "Mum, please put the gun down. I'll get the money. You're scaring us all."

"He should have just done as I asked," she sneers, staggering as she steps back.

"He was going to give you money to go to rehab?" Nina asks again, casting a lost glance at me.

"You knew!" she spews. "He said it was for *you*! So that I could be there *for you*! Poor, poor, Nina. Always needing to be babied. You couldn't ever go a day fending for yourself. Now look! What are you going to do now? You couldn't do it yourself, could you? You had to weed out a hotshot billionaire to fund your dreams. Then you got yourself knocked up. Stupid girl."

"You don't know me," Nina mutters, chin wobbling.

"Oh, but I do. You think you're any different from me?"

I stare at the gun, at the one thing that would take me away from this world. I think of my dad. My mum. Her words. All the words she ever gave me, and yet I feel utterly hopeless standing here now.

"Mum, please put that away," I hear Nina begging, the panic in her voice only confirming the feeling inside of me.

The energy in the room.

It's changed.

My head snaps to the side when I see Joey inching closer out of the corner of my eye, the blade of a kitchen knife poised in his grasp.

I release a panicked breath, fighting for my next.

"I want my money!"

"Nina," I whisper, my blood frozen in my veins.

Joey moves fast, Nina too, but she's barely able to catch her mum's arm before Joey reaches them both.

"Joey, no!" I snap.

They collide, the sound of the gun firing making my eyes pinch tight as I twist, shielding my body.

I hear the thud and turn. "No!" I scream. *Nina.* "God, no! Please, no!" I fall to my knees at her side, panic rising in my throat, making it impossible to breathe.

No.

No.

She shot her.

Nina.

No.

What do I do?

What… what do I do?

Everything quiets as I zone out, forcing the sounds, Joey, her mum, everything away.

She's struggling for breath.

She can't breathe.

Roll her.

The second I have her facing me, I scan her body.

There.

I bear down on her stomach, my hands covering her side where the blood's seeping through her tank.

"Scar," she croaks.

It didn't go straight through.

Stop the bleeding.

I pull my thin cardigan off one-handed, peeling back Nina's tank and forcing it into the wound.

There's so much blood.

I close my eyes.

Shock.

She could go into shock from the blood loss.

I need to keep her awake.

"Keep her warm."

"Remove any tight clothing."

"Scarlet," she begs.

Her chest is heaving.

She can't breathe.

Cover her body.

Keep her warm.

"Mum," Nina mutters.

You're going to be strong, Scarlet. Likely stronger than the people around you if what I know is true.

A stray tear falls from my eye, landing on Nina's bloodied hand that covers mine.

"You always did mess everything up." I hear the gun hit the wall, the bullets scattering across the ground. The door rebounds off the wall, and then with only Joey's panic filling the apartment, Nina's entire body relaxes.

No. Please. Please.

She can't.

I can feel her eyes on me, begging me to look at her, but I can't. I can barely stop this bleeding and… I can't look at her.

You're going to save the people around you, and then you'll save yourself too.

I just know it.

And in the moments you feel like you can't save them, or you feel like you've failed, know that you've done it once already, and you can do it again.

Nina's hand falls limp atop mine, her lungs taking a half breath before they settle completely.

I don't hesitate as I rise on my knees and start chest compressions.

THIRTY-SIX

Lance

"What did the message say?" Mason repeats.

"It was vague, Mase. But I know something isn't right. Scarlet's been going to see Joey because Nina wasn't. She didn't answer when I called."

"What did the message say?!" Mason asks again, and I know I have to tell him something.

> Scarlet: Come now he s he has a gun and wants money

> Scarlet: It's Joey. Nina needs u

My hands tighten on the steering wheel, my heart pounding.

If anything happens to her…

"It wasn't from Scarlet. It was Joey. It didn't make sense, but he said he had a gun."

"Why the fuck is Joey texting you from Scarlet's phone?"

He pulls at his hair. "Why aren't they answering their fucking phones?"

"Call Vinny," I tell him.

Mason is out of the car before I fully come to a stop. I follow him up the steps to the fourth floor and push past him when he stops outside the door, a distressed cry echoing from inside the apartment, wrapping around my throat and threatening to strangle me.

I just need to see her.

To know that she's okay.

I just need— "What the fuck."

"No." I turn at Mason's broken cry.

My knees sway as his face pales, his stare fixed on Nina's lifeless body. And *her*. Scarlet. Leant over Nina as she gives her CPR.

"No," Mason mutters disbelievingly as he stumbles toward them.

I take a step to follow him, but my foot knocks into something hard, and I look down, finding a gun on the ground.

"Fuck." I pick it up, my hands shaking.

What the fuck happened?

That crying.

That wailing.

It's not Scarlet.

I scan the room, my eyes searching. And then I see him, shaking and spluttering, a bloodied kitchen knife grasped in his hands like a blanket.

Joey.

"What the fuck did you do?" My wide eyes blaze over him as realisation sets in. "What the fuck have you done?" I roar, my body vibrating with rage and fear.

"I–I–I–They…" His body trembles, maybe just as much as my own.

I look away, catching Mason at Nina's side, Scarlet still working furiously as her brother begs her.

"Scar."

She doesn't flinch.

"Scarlet."

Nothing.

"Tell me she's going to be okay."

Her eyes close tight.

"Scar!"

How is this happening?

How?

Mason leans into Nina, taking her limp hand in his as he strokes her hair away from her face.

Paramedics rush the room a moment later, rushing for Nina. I stand in disbelief and watch as Scarlet checks out.

"We can take it from here," they tell her, but she doesn't stop. Her lips are moving, but nothing's coming out.

Mason grabs her, wrapping his arms around her waist and pulling her away.

"Sc-car-let."

My eyes dart to Joey, nostrils flaring as terror erupts inside of me.

No.

"I–I–"

Not Scar.

Not her.

"Stay fucking still," I warn, lifting the gun without hesitation.

"Put the gun down!" I hear the paramedics scream at me.

"Nina. Oh god, N-Nina. I-I'm so sorry."

I grit my teeth, readjusting my hands on the gun. "Stop."

"Sc-ar-l-let. I-I didn't mean to, I—" He steps toward Scarlet, and I don't hesitate.

I can't hesitate.

If I hesitate, I lose her.

His eyes meet mine and blaze, and then it hits him… right in the chest, and he falls.

Relief crashes into me like a wave. Chilling and cold. Stone cold to my bones, numbing me.

"Let me drown in you."

"No!" I hear Scarlet screaming, the terror in her voice so far from anything I'd ever want her to know.

"Put the gun down."

I drop it, staring at the ground as my entire body starts to tremble.

I've lost count of the number of times I've driven the road to Lowerwick Estate over the last two years. My sole focus almost always lost to thoughts of her and the night or weekend we'd spend together when I arrived.

But all I can think about now as I sit in the passenger seat of Charlie's car, driving that same road, is that maybe hoping for a lifetime with her was asking a little too much.

Exceptional circumstance.

That's what this is.

What was granted by a judge, thanks to the man at my side, to allow me a chance to say goodbye.

"The lights are out," Charlie mutters, staring up through the windscreen at the house, oblivious to the pain lacing my chest and throat. "I should have called her. Warned her we were coming."

I keep my head on the rest, staring straight ahead.

I killed a man.

Watched Scarlet lose him right in front of my eyes as she fought with everything she had to save him.

After a few minutes of silence, Charlie sighs. "You'll regret it if you don't do this." I feel his eyes on me. "Get out of the car, Sullivan."

I look at him, barely concealing my emotions, begging him to just drive us away.

"Think about *her*," he snaps.

I look toward the meadow, my jaw tight as I frown.

"Think about the weeks, months, and years that she's about to face and then get the fuck out of the car and say goodbye. You don't get to let her down, and I sure as shit won't sit here and let you."

I pull open the door and climb out, hating that the first thing I smell is the wildflowers. Hating that I might forget it.

"You've got half an hour."

I shut the door with a thud and make my way across the drive, heading toward the first field.

I know exactly where I'll find her.

It's the same place I fell in love with her.

My feet trudge through the fallen flowers, a path formed from her own footsteps.

Scarlet's sat on the hill, her back to the house. The sun. Her parents.

Me.

I stop when I'm a few feet away, staring at her. Not knowing how I'm supposed to say goodbye. Not wanting to.

"Why does it feel like every time I have you in my grasp, you slip right through my fingers, Lance?" I inhale sharply, setting my face to stone before she can turn her head. When she does, my world stops. "I didn't think you'd come."

Her eyes are red-rimmed, the skin around them puffy and raw.

I wish I'd never met her.

I'd do anything to go back and undo everything we ever were.

All I've done. The hurt and suffering.

Anything to take that look off her face.

I take a step forward, and she quickly stands, her face getting more and more distorted the closer I get. I close my eyes as she hurtles into my arms, knocking me back a step. I daringly breathe her in. Allowing myself to feel her one last time.

"Lance," she whispers, her voice breaking as she cries. I peel open my eyes, dropping my forehead to hers. "I don't want you to go."

I ground my teeth, my nostrils flaring. "I'm so fucking sorry, Scarlet."

"Please, don't leave me."

"Baby," I beg. Because listening to her beg *me* might just finish me.

"You said—" She sniffs, her sobs making her body jolt.

"You said you wouldn't leave me. Wouldn't disappear on me. You promised."

"I have to, Scar…." I swallow hard, but a tear falls down my face. And I finally give in to them, letting them fall with us. "I have to."

"I don't want you to—I don't want to be alone."

I shake my head, lips brushing hers as her fingers knot in my shirt. She holds me so fucking tight. "I'm so sorry."

"You can't leave me," she weeps.

I stagger back, and she steps with me, my hands wrapping around her.

I'd rather die.

I'd rather die than put her through this.

I grasp her face, wiping away the tears from her cheeks. I hold her just as fiercely as she does me. "When the sun sets, and you start to forget me, remember every moment you fell in love with me in this meadow. Please, baby." The lump in my throat threatens to give completely, but I force back the burn as I lean in and gently kiss her lips. "Remember me. Because I will never forget you," I whisper.

Her face screws up in pain. "I could never… I could never forget you, Lance."

I shake my head, eyes a blur of unshed tears. "Don't be afraid."

She lets out a sob, sagging against my body. I take her weight, sinking to the wildflowers with her in my arms.

"You're going to be okay, Scar. You're going to wake up and carry on tomorrow. Carry on loving all the little things that everyone else takes for granted. The very things I love about you. You're going to keep studying and become a doctor, you're going to be amazing, and I'm so proud of everything you are and will be." I take a breath and steady my voice as I tell her, "No matter what it takes, no matter what you have to do, you do it, okay? You keep dreaming your dreams even when the sun's gone down. You don't be afraid, and you don't give in to the darkness. You're going to be amazing, Scar. And I promise it's going to be okay."

I keep her in my arms for longer than I should as she cries.

Longer than Charlie told me I had.

Slowly her sadness seeps into me, taking root as her body tires. And when she eventually goes limp in my arms, I lift her, carrying her the rest of the way home. One last time.

I lay her on the bed in her dimly lit room, not able to say or do anything else before I turn and leave.

I climb into the car and stare through the windscreen at the meadow, her mother's garden, the house… the house where she once again lies alone.

After a while, Charlie circles the drive and coasts down the lane. I let the tears brimming my eyes fall. "I've sorted everything, Sullivan…." He clears his throat, his voice thick with emotion. "We'll look after her."

I could never forget you, Lance.

But she will. I'll make sure of it.

To be continued…

THE GRAND RUIN CONTINUES IN...

The Grand Rise

You can pre-order on Amazon now!

ALSO BY JC HAWKE

Grand Lies

(Mason & Nina's story)

Grand Love

(Mason & Nina's story)

The Grand Pact

(Elliot & Lucy's story)

AFTERWORD

Thank you so much for reading!
If you enjoyed The Grand Ruin, please consider leaving a review on Amazon.
Reviews are so important to authors!

Want to be notified about future book releases of mine?
Sign up to my Newsletter via my website
www.jchawkeauthor.com

Come join my Facebook reader group for a first look at sneak peeks and teasers. This is a PRIVATE group and only people in the group can see posts and comments!
Hawkes Hangout - JC Hawke's Reader Group

ACKNOWLEDGMENTS

Chalks and my girls, thank you. Thank you for being the most understanding, supportive, loving team I could ask for. I wouldn't be able to do this without the three of you.

Jessica Grace, I love you lady. A reader told me she'd be gutted if I ever left this series incomplete. I told her I'd have to be dead for that to happen and that if I do die… 1. you'd be so mad at me because you'd have to come to my funeral, haha. 2. you'd finish the series for me. Morbid, I know. But if that doesn't show my love for you, then I'm all out of ideas.

Jodie, I'd be a mess without you, and I'm so happy to have you with me at Ivy Rose Pub! You and your lists will one day make me an organised person (maybe… I'm trying okay). You're wonderful, and I appreciate the shit out of you.

Katie and Billie, thank you for not only your friendship but also your knowledge and drive. You're incredible, and I adore you both.

My beta team…. Why you put up with me is wild. I throw you these words, and you drop everything to devour them. You help shape my stories to be the best they can be, and without you, they'd be a lot less whole than they are. Thank you, Rach, Jo, Lindsay, Amy S, Amy F and Gem.

My *Butt Slut Society*: Thank you for motivating and

cheering me on! You girls are the absolute best, and I couldn't ask for a better team.

To all the members in Hawkes Hangout and the Cygnet Inkers, thank you for supporting me. I adore you all.

Murphy, Ellie, Rosa & Britt, thank you for being patient with me and for making everything shine.

And to my reader

You're the most special of them all (Shh, don't tell the others ^). You put trust in me and this story with no clue if it's going to be any good. So, for picking this book up, or maybe all of them, thank you. You're making my dreams come true!

Until next time,

Stay Wonderful

xo

ABOUT THE AUTHOR

JC Hawke is an author of contemporary romance. She lives in the South-West of the United Kingdom with her husband, two curly haired daughters, and beagle woofer.

Made in the USA
Columbia, SC
12 December 2024

49130283R00312